A DARK REDEMPTION

Stav Sherez

A DARK
REDEMPTION

Europa
editions

Europa Editions
214 West 29th Street
New York, N.Y. 10001
www.europaeditions.com
info@europaeditions.com

Library of Congress Cataloging in Publication Data is available
ISBN 978-1-60945-117-2

Sherez, Stav
A Dark Redemption

Book design by Emanuele Ragnisco
www.mekkanografici.com

Cover photo © Peter Zelei/iStock

Prepress by Grafica Punto Print – Rome

Printed in the USA

For Jane

CONTENTS

A DARK
REDEMPTION

BACK THEN . . .

They came more often now, the headaches. Raging storms within his skull, crippling pain, flashes of light. There was nothing to do but shut his eyes and lie back, let the pain and visions take over.

Memories and flashbacks trailed the headaches. Jack would close his eyes and see blue sky, green jungle, red road. He would try to watch the trees outside his window divesting themselves of leaves, the slow spinning fall of September, but instead he saw the leaves of the jungle, leaves so big you could sit inside them and be wholly encased, leaves which vibrated and twitched and reacted to your presence as if sentient beings.

They'd arrived in the middle of a heat wave. David buckled as he exited the plane, feet planted on the stairway, the sun leaching all colour and breath from his face. He stood there and took in the burned yellow country in front of him then turned back into the plane as if the pilot had made a mistake, but Jack was right there, taking his arm, leading him back out into the light, whispering in his ear *We're here*.

They deplaned onto the gleaming cracked tarmac, the customs hall five hundred feet away, shimmering like a mirage in the heat. The other passengers rushed past them, pushing, elbows out, as if there were a prize for the first to get to the hall.

They walked as slowly as they could, savouring the air, the unfamiliar sky—those first moments when you land in a new country and feel a sudden quickening, a snapcharge rattling through your bones.

Their friends were in India, Peru, Vietnam. They were sitting on beaches, cocktails in hand, watching the surf break against the sand, waiting for the night, the drugs, the screaming music and torrential sex.

'Everybody goes there,' Jack had protested after David suggested a trip down the Ganges. 'We'll be on a boat in the middle of nowhere and we'll bump into everyone we know.'

It had been the afternoon of their graduation. They still wore the robes and mortars, still wore the smiles they'd flashed for the cameras, degrees in hand, or parents held close, each trying to outgrin the other. Now the parents were gone, the degrees stuffed into a desk somewhere, the beer and cigarettes flowing.

'Jack's right,' Ben replied, sipping a pint, his fingers playing with an unlit cigarette. Unlike Jack and David, Ben had worn a proper suit underneath the gown and now seemed out of place and out of age in this noisy student pub. 'We might as well stay here as go to India.'

'Just because everyone goes there doesn't mean it's a bad idea.' David slumped back into the booth, his hair draped like a shawl around his shoulders, the button-down shirt and drainpipe jeans a strange contrast with those long black locks.

'Doesn't mean it's a good one either,' Ben replied as he spread out a map of the world in front of them.

Jack moved the glasses away so they could have more room. 'Uganda.' He pointed to a bright orange square halfway up the map. 'Cheap, safe, guaranteed sun, and no chance of bumping into anyone we know.'

They stared at it as if ensnared, the mass of multicoloured land that delineated the African continent, the regimented lines of borders, the names of countries they hadn't even known existed until they saw them printed on the map.

That was all the decision there was to it. David, as usual, acquiesced. That they would be together was more important than where they went. They all knew this would be the last time. Summer was approaching fast and then would come autumn and jobs and careers and the beginning of something, the end of something else.

They went through customs without a hitch. They caught a cab and threaded through sunburned fields, the driver speaking English so fast and fractured he sounded like a man drowning. They nodded their heads, mustered an appropriate *yeah* every now and then, but their faces were turned away, staring through the grimy windows, watching the plains of East Africa roll by, a landscape of tall grasses and spindly trees, skeletal cattle and dark beckoning mountains punctuating the distant horizon.

Jack rubbed his head and stared out into the London night remembering the tumult of sense and smell and noise as they entered Kampala. His headache began to recede as he let the memories flicker and spin. He remembered David exiting the taxi, bending down and vomiting in the street, his skin pallid as a corpse. Jack had crossed over to a stall, kids instantly surrounding him, their little hands waving and clutching cheap plastic objects he couldn't make sense of, old boxes of matches and photocopied pictures of Michael Jackson. He bought three warm Cokes and came back to find Ben handing out crumpled banknotes to the bright-eyed and smiling children.

They sat on their backpacks and drank the Coke, warm and sickly sweet, and it was the best Coke they'd ever tasted.

The kids delighted them even though they could see beyond the smiles and welcomes to the grinding poverty which underlay their lives. There were always more kids, more hands outstretched; what they asked for was so little in English money that it seemed mean to deny them, but then you found all your time being taken by handing out money and you forgot to look up at the buildings, the sky, the trees, the surly young men lounging on every street corner.

They all went through it once: tears, jags of self-pity, wanting desperately to go home—even Ben, who'd travelled almost everywhere by the time he'd got to university. 'Just good ol' culture shock,' Jack quipped after Ben had come back from the hostel toilet having found it overflowing, an army of cockroaches big as baby shoes swarming over the bowl. When they lay down on their pillows that evening they could smell other men's nights, puke and booze and blood.

'I think we should pick up the car and get out of here,' Jack suggested on the third day.

They paid twice what they'd agreed back home but it was still cheap—they still thought in English money—and though the car, an old white Honda Civic, looked like it would fall apart at the first kick of the engine, it managed to glide effortlessly through the cracked and teeming streets of the capital.

They took the Masaka-Kampala Road west out of the city. In less than ten minutes the concrete gave way to flat pastureland, dry and cracked, small villages everywhere, circular patterns of daub-and-wattle huts just visible on the side of the highway. The road was empty apart from army vehicles blazing down the fast lane, young soldiers bumping along in the beds of open-backed trucks, their eyes lazily drifting to the three white boys and then back to their cigarettes.

They made a detour down to the shores of Lake Victoria and ate fruit and crackers as the sun flashed along the calm surface of the water and Ben explained the history and naming of the lake, the great foolish Victorians with their hats and pomp and retinue of carriers and servants.

Jack suggested they head for Murchison Falls national park, the name a siren song to him, its grandiloquence and archaic quality like something out of a Sherlock Holmes novel.

'We could just stay in Masaka and check out the Ruwenzoris.' Ben was consulting their second-hand guide book. 'What's so special about Murchison Falls?'

'I love the way it sounds,' Jack replied, seduced as always by the poetry of place names, the worlds conjured up by phonetic accident.

'That's why you want to go there?' David had the gift of always sounding flabbergasted, surprised at the world in all its variance, an antidote to their measured and unearned cynicism.

The waters of Lake Victoria glowed like polished glass. 'Forget the guide book,' Jack replied, staring out towards the dark shadowed rim of the horizon, 'let's just start driving.'

Ben and David exchanged a glance that reflected years of growing up together, sharing hidden jokes, conspiring against parents—and agreed, but Ben kept the guide book safely in his bag just in case.

They backtracked and took the highway north, watching the land change. The fields and crops and empty plains gave way to more rugged terrain; mountains loomed out of the sky and disappeared; the road deteriorated until it was only a narrow lane. The heat became worse, not just sun striking the roof of the car, but a deeper denser heat, a humidity they'd never experienced before, a rottenness in the air that crept into your bones and brain, making your eyes water and the breath die in your throat.

Sweet potato and maize fields stretched out either side of them, dry and willowy in the early-evening heat haze. Termite mounds stood ten feet tall, skyscrapers among the cornstalks and grasses, like totem poles from another race, the tenements of a forgotten people.

The town of Masindi appeared out of nowhere. One minute they were driving the dirt road, yellow fields bordering them on both sides, and the next they were on a dusty corrugated street with white single-storey buildings, women carrying baskets on their heads, kids and more kids, the whole African movie-trailer cliché right before their eyes.

They stopped for beer and food at a tiny stall still bearing the name of the Asian proprietor who'd established it before being expelled by Idi Amin in '72. The old man, the new owner, served them warm Niles, the slogan 'The true reward of progress' making David chuckle as he swigged the sweet beer.

They watched cars go by leaving trails of dust in the air. Far-off volcanoes shimmered on the horizon like things unsubstantial and contingent. Children came and held their palms out, smiled, laughed and danced on the spot as Ben handed them money.

They sat in the rear of the cafe washing the dust and heat from their bodies, glad for the stillness after eight hours of bad road. Murchison wasn't far, another few hours' drive north; they'd stay in Masindi for the night, it was decided, and head there tomorrow.

'I still can't believe it.' David was sitting under a palm tree, peeling the label off a bottle of Nile. 'Being here, I mean.'

'Remember how much we talked about it?' Ben leant forward, spilling ash over the table. It had been their only topic of discussion these last few months, cramming for exams, finishing their dissertations, the horizon of the holiday the one bright thing to look forward to, the question of where to go burning in their minds.

David finished off his beer. 'The three of us here, together.' He paused so they could all savour this. A shadow briefly crossed his face. He stared at the thin tapering road. 'Who knows where we'll be this time next year.'

'I think Jack's got a pretty good idea,' Ben smiled, his teeth shining white in the sun.

Jack looked off into the distance, the volcanoes smoky and out of focus like cheap back-projections in a pre-war movie. 'I wish I did,' he replied, thinking back to the day, three weeks ago, when he'd broken the news. At first, he'd wanted to keep it secret, alternately proud and a little ashamed of his good luck, the way you always are with close friends. But they'd got drunk one evening, another in a long line of housemates' birthday parties, and he told them about the deal: three albums, a decent amount of money, a cool London-based record label.

'I wish it felt real. I wish it felt like something I could celebrate, but I keep thinking I'll come back and find a letter apologising for the mistake they've made.' Jack focused on the table, the empty green bottles like soldiers standing silent sentry.

Ben clapped him on the back, gave him one of those Ben smiles they all knew, the smile that had got them girls, entry to parties, whatever they'd desired. 'Nonsense. Too late for that, it's coming out next month.'

'September,' Jack corrected him, his legs shivering despite the humidity. Only a couple of months to go until the album was in the shops, on the radio. It felt too surreal, too weird, to accept as fact. It had been only a dream for so long that its reality seemed conjured from nothing but wish and desire. He'd made the album, just like he'd made the ones which preceded it, in his room on a four-track. He'd laid down the guitars, vocals and drum machine himself. He'd sent it out like he'd sent the countless tapes before, but this time the record company had got back to him; a man with a silly accent raving and ranting about how Jack was going to be the next big thing. He'd travelled down to London, signed the deal in a Soho restaurant and was back in Manchester in time to finish his exams.

'To *Top of the Pops*!' David held his bottle up, Jack and Ben crashed theirs against it, the clink and scrape amplified in the still air.

'Yeah, as if . . .' Jack finished off his beer. He got up and went to get the next round. He thought about his songs on the radio, tentacles reaching out of the speakers and into the ears of listeners—and then he shut the thought down, knowing the dangers that lurked in daydreams. It was just a small release on a tiny label, nothing to get excited about, the first rung of many. Still, as he took the beers, the cool glass sweet against his palms, he couldn't help but feel that things were coming together for the first time, that his life was at last taking some kind of shape and that he was here doing exactly what he wanted to be doing with exactly the two people he wanted to be doing it with.

He noticed that something had changed when he came back out with the drinks. Ben and David were sitting silently, their eyes fixed on the opposite side of the road. He sat next to them, doled out the beers, was about to say something when Ben's expression stopped him, made him look across the street.

Two policemen were leaning over something. They were tall, young, dressed in dark blue. They held black sticks in their hands, like truncheons but longer and skinnier. Jack squinted, trying to focus through the heat haze, and noticed the heap of clothes lying on the ground between them. He watched as the heap moved, gradually revealing a face, eyes, hair. The soldiers swung in long deliberate arcs. The crunch of truncheon against bone echoed all the way across to where they sat, a thick heavy stuttering splitting the air. They watched silently as the policemen started kicking the man, passing around a bottle of clear liquid, wiping their mouths, then wiping the blood from their shoes on the crumpled man's clothes.

'No!' Ben grabbed David the moment he stood up, held him firmly by the arm. 'It's not our business.'

David swayed and shuddered in his grip. The soldiers had regained their momentum and were swinging on the man as if breaking rocks. Jack shook his head. 'Sit down before they notice us.'

David pulled away. 'They're going to kill him,' he said, his voice pinched. 'Of course it's our business.'

'David!' A thin line of sweat broke out on Ben's forehead and his voice caught in the sticky air.

Jack sat and watched the soldiers beat the man. His legs felt like they were on fire, as though the only thing that would make them better would be to get up, cross the road and stop this terrible thing, but he couldn't move. The heat and dread sealed him to the spot. With every blow he felt something inside him rip. He gripped the rough splintered edges of the chair until he felt a warm trickle of blood covering his fingers.

Suddenly the policemen stopped, noticing their audience for the first time. They turned towards the three white boys drinking at the bar and started clapping their hands as if they were the ones watching and not the other way round. Jack stood up.

'No!' Ben was almost shouting. 'What the fuck do you think will happen to us if we interfere?'

Jack looked at David, saw his own thoughts and fears wheeling through his friend's eyes, the space between them, the time it would take to cross the road. He sat down. 'Christ!' he ground his feet into the dirt below him, beetles cracking like eggshells under his heels.

David stood for a few seconds staring at the policemen, then shook his head and sat down too. They opened their beers and drank them without saying anything. The policemen eventually stopped and walked off. A woman came and knelt by the bleeding man, crying and shouting at the empty road. They finished their beers and headed upstairs to their rooms.

The next day they drove across dusty dirt roads, bumpy and bone-rattling, the tall weeds bordering them on both sides, trees rising out of the sea of grass like the masts of sinking ships. The land was flat, the mountains always shimmering on the horizon. Their heads raged with pain, last night's beer barrelling through their skulls. Trucks laden with people and clusters of jerry-cans passed them every hour or so, men and women strapped to the roofs like wayward luggage. The passengers waved and they waved weakly back, smiling though the locals weren't. Every now and then an army truck screamed by laden with scowling soldiers, whipping up dust and rocks, heading north. They passed small villages, all identical, a circle of mud huts by a stream and nothing more. They ate peanuts and crackers and cheese squeezed out of a tube like toothpaste. The sun sank somewhere in the west, blazing the mountains red like a caul stretched over the rim of the world.

The landscape began to close its arms around them. They found themselves climbing through high valleys and twisting ravines, the jungle almost imperceptible in its embrace until, all at once, they noticed it was there, right above and to all sides of them and they couldn't remember how the land had changed so quickly or when.

They passed a village of burning huts just before the light finally died, thick black plumes of smoke emerging like serpents from their roofs. An eerie stillness in the air. They drove a little faster and didn't say a word to one another.

Dark came suddenly, not like back home with its languorous twilight, but like a switch being flicked—one minute they could see the mountains and fields, the next only the tunnel ofwhite illuminated by the car's headlights as if they were carving out the road from the darkness itself.

They stopped at a place where the road widened and switched on the in-car light, spreading the map out across elbows and knees.

'We won't make it,' Jack said, looking at the multicoloured squiggles, the distance they still had to cover before reaching the park.

David sighed, turning his face away.

'What's up with you?' Jack snapped, the tension of the day making itself felt in his voice.

'I just wish you'd stop being so negative. Just for once.'

Jack stared out into the night. 'You want to try driving another six hours in this?' He felt bad as soon as he said it and saw the hurt look on David's face.

'What are our options?' Ben asked, diplomatic as ever, though Jack could sense a tremor of unease in his voice.

'We can camp here,' Jack replied, looking around at the dark bush, then back down at the map. He lit a cigarette and traced the small lines like capillaries branching out from the main road. 'Or there's what looks like a short cut.' He pointed to a thin ribbon of red that veered out towards the left. 'We passed the turn-off about fifteen minutes ago.'

Ben stared at the dark bush surrounding the car, the rustling of the grasses like old women whispering to each other, the scary smear of galaxies above. 'Fuck camping out here.'

They backtracked and found the turning. There were no signs marking which direction the road headed or even what its name was and they had to take it on faith and an old map that this was indeed the Jango road. They drove slowly over the dark surface of the land. The grasses hissed in the wind, a flickering chatter that made them roll up their windows.

'It sounds so human,' David said, his face pressed up against the glass.

Ben looked at him strangely, then turned back to the road and braked suddenly, the car's wheels spinning out from under him. Jack flew forward, arms crashing hard against the dash.

Ahead of them the road forked. There were no signs and each branch seemed of equal width, both disappearing into blackness at the edge of the headlights' domain.

'Shit,' Ben said, pulling out the map, spreading it on his knees, his hands shaking. 'There's no fork marked on the fucking map.'

'Africa,' David replied with a sigh. It had become their code word for anything that defied logic, that did the opposite of what it said it did.

Jack unbuckled his seat belt and got out of the car, the ground crunching and squirming under his feet like something living.

He walked up to the fork, trying to see whether one side was more used than the other, looking for tell-tale tyre tracks, but there was nothing to distinguish between them. Something flickered across his vision—an antelope? Gazelle?—and just as quickly disappeared, bounding up the left fork, its white hoofs illuminated by their headlights. He stared into the black distance where both roads disappeared then walked back to the car.

'There's nothing to tell them apart. We'll have to guess.'

David looked at him, his eyes sagging with sleep and frustration. 'You liked the way it sounded; shit, you choose.'

Jack stared at the place where the road divided, thinking: left or right? Trying to work out which direction they were facing, looking for a sign, a hunch, a spasm of intimation, but there were only the odds. Fifty-fifty.

The others were waiting for him to make the choice. The hours on the road were weighing on them and they just wanted to keep moving. He thought of the ghostly gazelle he saw, the small circle of hoofs flashing in the black night. 'We're taking the left,' he finally said, trying to sound authoritative.

'You sure?'

He turned to Ben, about to answer, then saw that Ben was joking and for a moment all the fear and nervousness was gone and they were three friends in a car again, hurtling towards the next adventure.

Ben turned the engine back on and shifted into first. The road felt crinkled and folded beneath them as if loathe to let them go. They swung onto the left fork and disappeared into the night.

They had driven for an hour on the fork when they saw the first flicker of the fires.

Ben slowed the car instinctively, the wild raging light making them blind to the darkness. When their eyes adjusted they saw the roadblock, the logs stretched across the dirt track, the blazing fires crackling wildly in the breeze, and then they saw the eyes of the soldiers glaring at them, guns drawn and pointed. Ben brought the car to a stop and they began to make out voices, barking orders, shouting *Get out!*, shouting *Mzungu!*, the soldiers' guns flickering in the firelight, the black barrels staring at them like the gouged-out eyes of some implacable god.

Part One

London, 2012

1

The coffee machine wasn't working. It burbled, hissed and spluttered to a stop. Jack Carrigan stared at it in disbelief. He'd bought it only three months ago and it was supposed to last a lifetime. He turned it on and off, jiggled and gently shook it, and when that didn't work he hit it twice with the side of his fist. The machine coughed, hummed, and then, miraculously, started pouring what looked like a passable cup of espresso.

The sound of the coffee slowly oozing through the steel and silver pipes always made him feel better. He began to notice the morning, the thin streamers of sunlight leaking through the gap in the curtains he'd never got round to fixing, the sound of cars being put through their morning shuffles, coughs of cold engine and shriek of gears, the doors of houses closing, the patter of tiny feet on the pavement, the clatter of human voices arising from the early-morning air.

The machine groaned once and stopped. He reached for the cup, the smell making his mouth tingle, and was just about to take his first sip when the phone rang.

He staggered over to the table, his fingers brushing lightly over Louise's photo, picked up the receiver and held his breath.

Carrigan walked through the park trying to shake off the previous night. He'd arrived back from the coast late, scraped the mud from David's grave off his shoes and fell heavily onto the sofa where he'd awoken crumpled and cramped this morning. It had been a last-minute decision; he'd be down there with Ben in a couple of weeks but something yesterday had called him, a pulse beating behind his blood.

He spent a few minutes staring at the trees, soaking in the heat, trying to ignore what lay waiting for him on the other side of the fence. Late September in Hyde Park was his favourite season, the grass still scorched by summer's sun, the trees heavy, the first leaves fluttering down to the waiting ground. He closed his eyes and Louise's face rose out of the dark, this park her favourite place, holding hands in snowstorms, watching kids playing by the pond, both of them thinking this life would last for ever.

Carrigan exited the park and walked on the road to avoid the clots of tourists emerging from Queensway station. He watched them huddling in tight packs, wearing the same clothes, staring up at the same things. He envied them their innocence, seeing London for the first time, a city with such history yet without personal ghosts. When you'd lived here all your life you stopped seeing the city and saw only the footsteps you'd carved through it, a palimpsest traced in alleyways and shop windows, bus stations and bends of the river.

He reached the building and looked around for Detective Superintendent Karlson, whose call had interrupted his morning coffee, but he was nowhere to be seen. He took out his phone and made sure he had the right address. Two PCs had been called to a flat in King's Court earlier. When they saw what they were dealing with they immediately called the Criminal Investigation Department.

Carrigan looked up at the towering facade and pressed the porter's buzzer. He knew the building well. They received a call every week about something, mainly waste-of-time stuff, noise complaints, funny smells, burglar alarms going off for no explicable reason in the middle of the night, but, like any building with over five hundred residents, it had its share of domestic abuse, suicide and small-time drug dealing. He tried the buzzer again. He could hear voices crackling faintly through the intercom, conversations in languages he didn't recognise, floating in and out of hearing, criss-crossing each other until they dissolved into static and white noise.

A woman with a pram was wrestling the door from inside. Carrigan held it open for her and, as she thanked him, slipped past into the marbled lobby, its cool mirrored surfaces and swirling carpets making him feel instantly dizzy. He knocked on the door to the porter's booth but there was no answer. He peered through the frosted glass, squinting his headache away, and saw the slumped shape of a man inside. This time he gave it his four-in-the-morning police knock.

When the door opened the stink hit him like a fist. Body odour, cigarettes and despair. The porter was a small withered man with three-day stubble and eyes that looked as if they never stopped crying. His face twitched intermittently, revealing dark gums and missing teeth as he struggled to pull himself back together. Jack knew exactly how he felt.

'Detective Inspector Carrigan.' He showed the man his warrant card but the porter only nodded, not looking at it or at him, and shuffled back into his room, collapsing onto a chair whose stuffing poked out like mad-professor hair.

The porter's cubicle looked as if it had once been a luggage locker. There were no windows, no room for anything but a table, a chair and four small TV monitors with a constantly running video feed of the building's entrance. The porter was breathing heavily, lost in the screen, watching the unpeopled doorway with such riveting poise it could have been the last minutes of a cup final he was witnessing.

Carrigan shuffled a few steps forward, bending his head to avoid the low ceiling. He took small, shallow gulps of the stale air. 'You keep spare keys to individual flats?'

The porter barely acknowledged him, a faint turn of the head, nothing more. He eventually looked up from the screen and scratched his stubble. 'Not no more. Used to be everyone left them with me, but things change.' He didn't elaborate how.

'Flat 87's the one directly above 67, right?'

The porter nodded. 'I thought you guys were in 67?'

'We are,' Carrigan replied tersely, wishing he'd had time to get breakfast. 'Do you have keys for flat 87 or not?'

The porter opened a drawer and pulled out an old ledger. He rapidly flicked through the pages. Sweat poured down his face as he squinted at the shaky handwriting. He ran one yellowed finger down a list of numbers, then stopped. 'Uh-huh. Flat 87. No spare.' He zoned out in front of the screen again. Carrigan craned his neck but there was only the image of the front door, fish-eyed, black and white, empty. He thanked the man, found out when his shift ended, and left the sweatbox of an office.

He saw the two constables nervously chatting outside the door to 67. The look in their eyes told him this wasn't just a prank, something they could all laugh about on their way back to the station. He nodded, walked past them and knocked on the door. He waited as a series of locks tumbled and unclenched until the door finally opened and an old woman stared at him as if she'd never seen a man before. It took him a few seconds to realise she was or had been a nun, the habit faded and worn, the crucifix dangling like a medallion from her thin wattled neck.

'I'm Detective Inspector Carrigan.' He showed her his warrant card. The old nun didn't acknowledge, just turned and walked back into her flat.

He was never surprised at how people lived and yet he was always surprised. Fifteen years on the job, how many flats, houses, mansions had he been into? How many lives marked out by the geography of walls? He told all his young constables that the key to a person was in how they lived their lives—study their surroundings, how they chose to arrange themselves in this world—you'll learn much more from that than from listening to them talk or staring deeply into their eyes.

He walked through the small hallway and into the living room. The furniture was mismatched, as if collected over time from disparate sources. Chipped and cracked paint everywhere. Pieces of drawers and light fittings missing, replaced if at all by masking tape. The carpet was worn and thin, showing through to the floorboards. Stains described maps across the floor like countries never visited, dark and sticky spots where tea or ketchup or custard had landed. The old nun coughed, hacking into her hand. She lit a cigarette, the smell instantly filling the room.

The mantelpiece and bookshelves held no books, only a staggering variety of porcelain dogs. Carrigan stepped closer and saw they were all West Highland terriers, produced in a variety of finishes and styles. A few looked almost real while others were the product of some kind of artistic myopia, resembling sheep or clouds more than they did dogs.

But it was the two pieces at the far end of the mantelpiece he couldn't keep his eyes off. It was these two that the old lady was silently pointing to with the end of her cigarette. These dogs weren't white like the rest. They were red. A crimson caul covered their bodies.

The old nun was gesturing at them, speechless, as if such a thing had no referent in language. Her eyes had receded deep into their sockets and when she pulled on the cigarette she looked like a Halloween skull. Carrigan inched forward. He looked at the dogs and then he looked up.

A patch of red, in the shape of a teardrop, was slowly spreading from one corner of the ceiling. The constables followed his gaze and, as they watched, a single red drop fell, exploding against the white mantelpiece like an exotic flower.

2

Carrigan walked up the stairs to the next landing, his heart sinking, his feet dragging behind him. He couldn't see where the hallway ended. The mangy carpet disappeared into a funnel of darkness a few flats down. It reminded him of those long nightmare corridors in *The Shining,* a film he wished he'd never seen; its images promiscuous and relentless long after the watching was over.

The hallway was lit from above by twitching fluorescents recessed under a metal grille that rained down the light in black spears against the walls and carpet. The air seemed packed tighter here than on the floor below, filled with heavy, textured smells, the various scents commingling and forming new alliances in the corridor. All around buzzed the noise and hum of lives lived behind closed doors. Muffled announcers on blaring TV sets, broken conversations, pounding drum and bass. The rotten reek of cooked cabbage and garlic. Arguments and shouting. A faint whiff of weed.

He heard the two constables come up behind him, their faces pale with what they'd seen and what they were about to see. He stopped in front of number 87 and knocked. Two old ladies wrapped in thick muslin that made them look mummified walked past, their eyes lingering on Carrigan, unspoken suspicion in every muscle twitch. He ignored them, knocked once more, then got to his knees.

There was no letter box, but he could see a half-inch gap between the front door and the hallway's filthy carpet. He pressed his face against the floor, feeling the sticky shag-pile grab at his beard, but he couldn't see any light coming from inside the flat. He moved, pressing his face closer, took a deep breath and immediately started coughing. He took one more to be sure, then got up, brushed the dirt off his clothes, and called it in.

He sent the constables back downstairs and waited for the scene of crime officers to arrive. He spent the time watching the flow of bodies in and out of flats, a constant shuffle of lives enacted in this dim and dank hallway. He knocked on adjacent doors. There was no answer from the flats either side of 87. He knocked on the flat directly opposite. The door opened and an unshaven man with a cigarette that seemed moulded to his lips looked at Carrigan and said, 'Huh?'

Carrigan showed him his warrant card, asked if he knew who lived opposite. The man wouldn't make eye contact with him. Somewhere inside the flat Carrigan heard a woman shouting in Greek, Romanian, he didn't know, the man's eyes narrowing as if each word were a splinter driven into his flesh. 'No police,' he said. 'I done nothing wrong.'

Carrigan wedged his foot in the door as the old man tried to close it. The old man looked up at him, a rabbity fear in his eyes. 'I'm not interested in you.' Carrigan pointed to the flat across the hall. 'I want to know who lives there.'

The man looked down at his slippers, torn grey things exposing yellowed and cracked toenails. He shook his head but the action seemed to be commenting on something bigger than Carrigan's question. 'I seen nothing and I don't want to see nothing.'

This time Carrigan let him shut the door. People in these blocks never heard or saw anything; he knew that from experience. It wasn't that they had anything to hide, not like trying to canvass witnesses in a hostile estate, but in the countries

they'd fled from a knock on the door could mean imprison-
ment, torture and often worse. How were they to know that
police all over the world weren't the same?

The SOCOs and DS Karlson arrived a few minutes later.
They suited up in the stairwell and gave Carrigan his oversuit,
latex gloves, and foot protectors. The starchy chemical smell
filled his nostrils as he unsnapped the gloves and slipped
them on.

'Any idea what's in there?' Karlson was filling the sign-in
sheets, smiling that thin begrudging smile of his. He'd never
liked Carrigan, couldn't understand why someone with a university degree would want to be a policeman. Didn't like the
fact that Carrigan hated sports, wouldn't drink the station's
Nescafé and rarely joined the others for after-work drinks
down the pub.

'We'll see when we break down the door, won't we?'

Carrigan moved back as the two constables took hold of the
ram. The door was old, had been painted over so many times
it cracked in two like a rotten fingernail. The stench hit them
immediately.

'Jesus Christ.' One of the constables, Carrigan always forgot his name, pedalled back so quickly he ran right into
Carrigan, his body warm and taut like a greyhound's.

Carrigan stepped past him, taking a deep breath. His nostrils filled with a metallic sweetness and he wished he was in the
corridor again with the garlic and cabbage, anything but this.

It was a studio flat. Small and self-contained. A narrow hallway, kitchen to the left and bathroom to the right. The bed-
room/living room stretched out in front of them. At the far end
a small window opened out onto a rectangle of sun and trees.
Carrigan focused on the leaves, golden brown already, as they
swayed and trembled on the branches. Then he looked back
towards the bed.

Her arms were tied to the ends of the headboard. Her arms

looked as if they'd been stretched beyond their capacity, the skin tight against the bone. Translucent plastic ties snagged her wrists to the brass. He could smell the dark heated mulch of blood, ammonia and sweat. He tried breathing through his mouth as he stepped closer.

He could hear the constables cursing behind him, Karlson taking deep swallows of air, the clutter and clump of the SOCOs setting up their equipment, but they all seemed as far away as the detonation of trance music that was coming from an upstairs flat.

He stared at the girl as flashbulbs popped and burst. Her body was sporadically revealed by the light then disappeared back into darkness.

Her nightdress had been cut down the middle so that it hung on either side of her torso like a pair of flimsy wings. The knife had gone deep into her chest, a dark red line running from navel to ribs. He stared at the wide canyon carved into her stomach, the dark brown shadows and glints of white poking from within. He felt last night's dream rise in his throat and he swallowed hard to keep it down, taking short breaths, keeping his feet evenly spaced. He saw Jennings, one of his young detective constables, catch a glimpse of the bed, then rush straight to the bathroom. Outside he could hear doors being slammed, the shuffle of feet and ongoing lives, but in here there was only the stillness of death.

He didn't want to look at her face so he looked at her legs. It was almost worse. Small puncture wounds ran like bird tracks criss-crossing her skin. He leant closer. Too small to have been made by a knife or blade, grouped in pairs. He moved back and saw that they continued up the torso and along the undersides of her arms. Small pointed punctures, black with blood, evenly spaced, the flesh around them mottled, torn and weeping. They looked like animal bites, he thought with a shudder.

'Christ, what the . . . ?' Karlson stared down at the open cavity of her chest, the perforation of her limbs, her cracked front tooth.

Carrigan said nothing, headed for the window, took a deep breath as he watched the laundry flutter in the courtyard. He could see people going about their daily chores oblivious and unconcerned. He turned back, finally ready to look at her face. He stood next to Karlson, smelling the man's sweat and fear, the reek covering his own. He tried not to look at her chest, the gaping hole, white shards of bone poking out like stalagmites, but the wound had its own terrible gravity. He heard Karlson curse under his breath and turn away.

Behind him, a scene-of-crime officer was setting up his video camera, his colleagues drawing out strange containers of powder and unguent, miraculous dispatches from the frontiers of science. One man was unpeeling a roll of sticky tape, the horrible screaming sound filling the room as he cut it into strips in preparation to 'tape' the body; a slow and painstaking job intended to capture any rogue hairs or fibres caught on the skin. The man looked up at Carrigan and shrugged. The SOCOs wanted them out, they had work to do, evidence to collect. They didn't even see the girl, she was only a surface from which information could be gathered, conclusions drawn.

Carrigan bent down again, ignoring them. He put his mouth to the dead girl's ear. They heard him whisper something to her but not what he said. They looked at each other uncomfortably. This was hard enough without the senior investigating officer talking to the dead, but Karlson and Jennings only shrugged; they'd learned to ignore the idiosyncrasies of their DI. Carrigan surveyed the girl's body once more then leant back in and froze.

'Karlson, over here,' he said in a dry, raspy voice. He stood over the body as the sergeant looked at the cavity in her chest.

'What?' Karlson said. 'I can't see anything.'

'Exactly,' Carrigan replied, pointing through the ribs at the empty space underneath. 'It's not there.'

Karlson stared at him, confused, then looked back down at the body.

'Her heart,' Carrigan said. 'It's gone.'

3

This was it. Her last day. She could feel it in the way people walked past avoiding eye contact. People she knew. It was like being made to wait outside the headmistress's office while everyone shuffled by, whispered to each other, glanced, giggled, and went on about their business while you sat suspended between your life as it was and whatever awaited you behind the door.

She stared at the posters on the wall opposite her, trying to stop thinking about what was coming. Couched behind glass they seemed like museum exhibits, not bulletins from the inner city. The slashed face of a teenager, the scar like a centipede crawling up his left cheek; below him locations where knives could be handed in. The eyes of a drink-driver watching the stretchered bodies of his victims being taken away from the smouldering wreck. The appeal for vigilance on the Tube.

It wasn't working. She couldn't stop looking at the door to the super's office. Waiting for it to crack open and unleash her fate. She stared down at her shoes, remembering she hadn't had time to polish them, thinking about last night, coming home after getting the super's request for this meeting, sitting down on the green cushion, opening a bottle and then what? She woke up fully clothed in her bed, half an hour to make the meeting. She didn't remember a thing. The bottle was almost empty and her shoes looked terrible. It was acceptable for a man to come in looking dishevelled but for a woman it could only count against you; the higher-ups hadn't yet managed to divorce the notion of sex from that of capability.

She watched the clock, the slow spin of seconds accruing into minutes and hours. She ran her fingers through her hair, trying to untangle last night's knots. She wondered if he'd finally decided to press charges. How happy her mother would be at this turn of events.

'Detective Constable Miller!'

She jerked up and saw Superintendent Branch leaning out of his office, entirely filling the space left by the door, looking exasperated. She must have zoned out. Christ!

Her smile was wasted; he'd already stepped back in by the time she realised he was calling her. She straightened her shirt and followed him in.

This was her second time in his office this year. The last meeting hadn't gone well. He'd had a stack of files on his table, all with her name on them. He had detailed witness statements and DI reports. He said he had photographs. She'd looked through the window at the empty space left by the recently demolished church and wondered who'd informed on her.

'You hit a superior officer,' Branch had said.

'He was out of line, sir. He would have killed the boy,' she'd countered breathlessly, unable to meet his eyes.

'You blew your cover. You could have both been killed.'

'I couldn't let him do that, sir, even if it meant blowing the operation.'

'Yes.' He sat back down, put one hand to his temple as if aware of a sudden pain there. 'I've read your report. You should have waited until you were both alone. He was your commanding officer, for God's sake.'

Then he'd told her about the demotion. Detective sergeant to detective constable. Five years of hard work reversed just like that. She'd kept quiet, knowing any argument on her part would only increase their fears, make them even more wary of her. So she shut her mouth, nodded, and took her punishment.

Now, sitting down in the same chair, staring at the same wall, she couldn't believe how stupid she'd been.

'Geneva.' Branch was leaning back, his massive bulk making the chair look like it was about to collapse. His North Riding accent crunched down hard on the vowels, stretching them so that her name no longer sounded as if it belonged to her. 'You don't mind if I call you Geneva, do you, Detective?'

She shuffled forward on the seat. It was too low, forcing her to arch her neck uncomfortably. She flashed back to being a girl again, sitting in class, the teachers looking down from their high perches demanding an answer they knew you didn't have, the rest of the girls just waiting to burst out laughing.

'It's my name.'

Branch smiled and pointed to her shoulders. She looked down and saw that her earphones were still slung across her jacket and looped around her neck. She snatched them off but they got caught and she flinched, feeling several strands rip. Her face was hot with blood as she shoved them into her pocket. 'Sorry, sir.'

Branch nodded, eyes partly closed as if assimilating some vital new piece of information. 'And how have things been since your reinstatement?'

She knew it was a question but also not a question. She wasn't sure what was expected of her. Humility? Gratitude? Resentment? 'It's a different pace. I'm getting used to it. I was a DS for two years. It's like going back to school.'

Branch smiled, leant forward in his chair so that she could smell the dark tang of stale cigar smoke on his breath. 'Very well put. I think we should all go back to school at some point. Good for the soul, you know. I spend a week every year out on the streets in uniform. Sometimes you climb so fast you forget what you leave behind.'

She nodded but wasn't sure what point he was making. Branch was notorious for his gnomic non sequiturs; it was a clever technique, never quite pinning anything down, letting the other person join the dots, and if they screwed up—well, obviously they'd misinterpreted him.

'A woman's body was discovered this morning in King's Court, Queensway.'

Why was he telling her this? Did he expect her to know the case, only a few hours old, the other side of the Westway from her normal patch? She half-nodded—let him interpret that— and scanned the table in front of her, the boxing gazettes and grey match programmes, the multitude of mobile phones lined up square and precise.

This wasn't what she'd expected. Waiting outside, she was certain this was going to be the beginning of the dismissal procedure. That he'd finally put in a formal complaint. She'd begun thinking of other jobs, what she would do, the naked horror of being flung back into the world.

One of the phones rang, breaking the silence, but Branch didn't even glance down at it. 'This is one of those cases that has the potential of turning into a major fucking headache.' He leant forward across the desk and a stray bit of tobacco caught onto his blazer cuff and hung there like an ornament. 'She was African. A student. You remember the murder of the two French students a couple of years ago? Young, good-looking foreign students being tortured to death in their London flats is the last thing we fucking need on the front page of the *Standard*. We've got to keep this small and close. No press releases, no blazing blue-light entrances. You understand?'

She didn't know where he was going with this, what it had to do with her, but at least he wasn't dipping into a file with her name scrawled in red on it, pulling out a form waiting only for her signature.

'It's DI Carrigan's case. You know him?'

'I've heard of him,' she replied neutrally.

Branch nodded, his eyes glistening behind his round-framed glasses. He put his fists together in a gesture almost akin to praying and she noticed the scuffed knuckles, bulbous and round like the skulls of midgets. 'Yes, I dare say most detectives working out of West London have. Something of an office legend, our Carrigan. Takes files home with him and studies them at night. Cases that aren't his. Thinks he'll work out what other men couldn't. You can see how that would not endear him to his peers,' Branch darkly confided, 'but if it was just that . . .' He pressed something on one of the phones and a red light started blinking. Geneva noticed that his fingers were scored with tiny white lines as if they'd been tied up. He leant forward, his shadow stretching across the table towards her. 'Frankly, Detective Miller, I'm worried about him being in charge of this case. I don't know how he got to the scene first, how he always manages to get to the scene first, but I would have been much happier if a DI with a little more discretion was in charge.'

Was he insinuating something? Geneva stared at Branch, trying to gauge the tenor of his comments, but either she was too hungover or she just wasn't good at reading faces. Instead, she flashed Branch her favourite smile. The smile she liked to give men in bars. It seemed to work; the super was momentarily flustered, resorting to shuffling papers and clearing his throat. 'This is all between you and me, not your DI, not your husband . . . understand?'

Her skin flushed hot and itchy at the mention of Oliver. Her heart double-timed as she finally understood she wasn't here to be fired.

'Carrigan's been getting sloppy. His cases have begun overlapping and his reports don't make any sense. He keeps photos of all the murder victims he's investigated at his house. At first we humoured him, what with what happened and all, but recently he's been getting worse, more secretive. He's never been one of us. Never wanted to. His main concern isn't going to be keeping this out of the press.'

'I thought our main concern was to catch the killer.' It tumbled out before she could shut her mouth. She bit the insides of her cheeks until it hurt.

'Yes, of course, but don't act so gauche, Detective. You know as well as I do that keeping this out of the public eye will greatly enhance our chances of catching whoever did this.' He looked up at the wall, lost in silent thought. Photos of boxers lined the perimeter of the room. Bloody and sweat-soaked, caught in a flash of action, their faces grimaced into scowls that made them look like dying dogs. Each of the photos had been signed and dedicated to Branch. 'I'm going to second you to Carrigan's team as DS,' he continued. 'I want you to work closely with him on this.'

She wasn't sure she'd understood correctly, or that she liked what he seemed to be saying. 'And report back to you, sir?'

Branch smiled, his eyes crinkling behind the glasses. 'Yes, exactly.' He picked up a stack of files and evened the edges. 'I'm glad you share my concerns.'

'You want me to spy on him?' She tried to keep the disappointment out of her voice.

Branch shook his head as if she'd misunderstood something incredibly basic. 'Don't be so melodramatic, Miller. All I want is your report every week. No different from the report you'd hand your DI.' He stopped shuffling papers and met her eyes. 'I'm offering you a chance to get back to detective sergeant. On probation, of course.'

She looked out of the window but the space created by the demolition of the church was now filled with a gleaming tower of mirrors. All she could see was their own building reflected in the shimmer. She turned away, focused on the still point of the super's table, breathing her nausea down. 'Can I take a day to think about it?'

Branch pursed his mouth, his lips smacking silently against each other. 'I assume at some point you'd like to resume your former position permanently. I've read your file; there's no reason you shouldn't go as high as you want.'

She took a deep breath. Her chest ached and her head throbbed. This was one of those moments—life before and life after—except this time it was in her hands, her choice. She wanted to say no, to stand up for what she believed in, but when she opened her mouth the opposite came out.

Branch frowned. 'I thought you'd be more pleased.'

'I don't like the idea of spying on my direct superior.'

'But you don't mind hitting them.' A small smile curved the edge of Branch's top lip.

'He was out of line, sir. He did things he shouldn't do.'

'Why do you think I chose you for this case, Detective?'

She walked out into the blazing September sun. Her eyes immediately squished inside their sockets, pulsing. She'd left her sunglasses at home. Alka-Seltzer too. She took the earphones out of her pockets and set about untangling them but her fingers were too clumsy and she ended up putting them in lopsided and looped. She scrolled through the iPod's playlist, couldn't make her mind up, put it on shuffle. A scratchy guitar twanged and wailed in her left ear as she jumped onto the bus.

She almost missed her stop. She spent the journey neck craned, trying to see through the condensation and breath-mist, but she only recognised the road after they'd passed it. She ran up to the bus driver, pleaded and cajoled until he let her out. She took a minute to find her bearings, the houses and streets all looking identical to her, then headed down the narrow tree-lined avenue towards her block of flats. She searched through her purse until she found the key that was more like some science-fiction gadget than any key she'd previously used, slid it into the lock and heard it click and tumble. At least locks still do that, she thought as she climbed the stairs to her flat.

Her flat. She needed to get used to saying that even though it was only a rental and she'd probably move when the contract was up. The house would be put on the market when the divorce went through and then she would use her share to buy somewhere else if the prices didn't go nuts in the interim. But that would take a while. And there had been no question of staying on at the house; they'd tried it for a couple of weeks, sleeping in separate rooms, but even that, seeing him every morning, hearing him every night, had been more than she could bear.

She sat down on one of the large green cushions her sister had given her when she'd moved in. She hadn't had a chance to buy an armchair or sofa yet, kept meaning to do it but was always busy. Just as she'd promised herself that this weekend she would unpack the boxes lying haphazard across the room like obstacles in a maze. All her life was contained in these boxes. Her clothes, photos, books, memories. She wasn't sure if she wanted to open them yet and besides they doubled as tables and TV stands and places to throw all her work junk.

In the fridge she found half a pint of milk. She sniffed it and it seemed all right; she couldn't remember when she'd bought it. There was still some vodka left from last night and enough Kahlua for a couple of drinks.

She sat on the couch savouring the rich smell rising from her glass, picked up the King's Court file, lit a cigarette, and was about to take her first sip when the landline rang.

'Yes?' She put the glass down on one of the boxes and looked around for an ashtray.

'I'm glad to hear you're alive.' Her mother's voice always sounded more accented over the phone, she could never understand why.

'I've been busy.' She looked down at her glass and cursed

herself for picking up. She'd bought an answering machine with a screening feature to avoid just such ill-timed interruptions. 'I just got in, Mum.'

'One phone call? That doesn't take much time, does it?'

Geneva bit down on her lip, flicked ash on the floor and took a sip of her drink, not really tasting it at all. 'I'm sorry, Mum,' she said, knowing this was the quickest way to end the conversation.

'What was so important, then?'

'I was seconded to a new investigation. A murder. You know how long I've been waiting for this.' She couldn't suppress the hope and excitement in her voice and it made her feel momentarily better, putting it into words like this.

She heard her mother exhale a long plume of breath on the other end of the line. 'Murder? This is what gets you excited? Blood and suffering and all these horrible things? How do you ever expect to be happy when you spend your days dealing with the worst things that are on offer?'

It was the conversation that skirted the edges of their relationship since she'd taken the job, first year out of university. It was the reason she'd bought the answering machine. 'I do it for the victims, Mum, you know that. You should be proud after what you went through. That someone wants justice.'

Her mother laughed, surprising her. 'You have too much of your father in you. I wish it wasn't so but it is. It made him disappointed all his life and it'll do the same to you.'

She slammed down the phone, pleased it was an old corded model and still allowed this now-antiquated gesture. She finished the rest of her drink, made another, and picked up the file Branch had handed her. She opened it up, flicked through the three scant photocopied pages, then took out the photos and stared at the ravaged body of the dead girl, feeling a strange quickening in her blood.

4

He was almost at the morgue when his phone rang. He checked the display—Superintendent Branch—knew it could only be bad news. He stood outside the grey brick building overlooking the murky waters of the Paddington canal and debated answering. Sharp drops of rain worked their way under his collar. He scanned the empty plaza, the fountain that didn't work, the shops yet to be leased, and put the phone back in his pocket. He didn't want to hear anything Branch had to say. The meeting this morning had been enough.

He'd been working on the initial file, going through the preliminary crime scene descriptions and photos, starting up an incident log, when Branch had called him in.

Branch had spent the first five minutes edging the papers and photos on his desk while Carrigan ran through what they had so far. DC Jennings had got an ID from the porter's tenant book. Personal items inside the flat confirmed it. The murdered girl's name was Grace Okello and she'd listed her occupation as 'student'. The constant rearranging and the concentration Branch gave it was making Carrigan irritable and jumpy. He resisted the urge to sweep everything off with a flick of his wrist.

'I'm seconding a DS to come in and help you.' Branch looked up from his organising, noted the expression on Carrigan's face and continued. 'You're short on bodies and I want this wrapped up before anyone even knows it happened.

You know as well as I do what kind of case this could turn out to be.'

'I've done well enough with the team I've got.' He hated the way his voice sounded when he talked to Branch, as if the super could bring out a younger version of Jack, a version he thought he'd left far behind. 'We're always understaffed. We're used to it.'

Branch picked up a brown file, met Carrigan's gaze. 'DS Miller will meet you at the morgue. Anything else, Detective Inspector?'

Standing outside the morgue, waiting for DS Miller, watching the rain slough off the scaffolding and puddle at his feet, Carrigan knew that Branch no longer trusted him. It wasn't the past that mattered, it wasn't even the last case or the one before that. No, it was something personal, something other cops, real cops, could always sense about him. A feeling of disengagement, not one of the boys, does things his own way—every cliché they could muster for someone from such a different background. Miller would be one of Branch's stooges, a watchful eye to hover over him.

He stared at the new buildings going up, the skeleton frames of scaffolding poles stretched across the horizon, the grey spurt of the Westway rising like some Greek god from the huddle of flat roofs and satellite dishes. He remembered when this part of Paddington was wasteland, empty lock-ups and all-night caffs for taxi drivers. Now gleaming massifs of glasswork rose at every horizon, blocking out the sun. He binned his coffee cup, was about to go in alone when he when saw a young woman heading towards him, white iPod earphones dangling from her ears. He waited for her to shove a map in his face and ask him how to get to . . .

'DI Carrigan?' The woman asked in an accent that could have come straight from a pre-war BBC radio play, all clipped vowels and Oxbridge nights. He stood there trying to make sense of this as she offered her hand, small and perfectly formed.

'DS Miller. Superintendent Branch told me you'd be waiting.' She was shouting, her voice rising above the background hum of rain and construction work. Carrigan pointed to his ears then to hers. She looked bemused, then realised, and pulled out the earphones. They hung loose over her shoulders like the straps of some invisible backpack.

'Sorry. I was in such a hurry . . . '

'It's okay,' he murmured, noticing how nervous she was, her hands and legs fidgeting the ground. 'You can wait outside, you don't have to see this.'

DS Miller's face scrunched up, making her nose wrinkle, and he realised she wasn't as young as he'd first thought. 'If I still had my 'phones on I'd think I didn't hear you right.' Her eyes met Carrigan's. They flashed blue, then muted.

'Okay,' he replied softly, 'though it's not going to be pretty.'

'They teach you that at the cop school of clichés?' But this time she was smiling.

Bentley, the pathologist, was expecting them. They followed her through the long white hallways and into a succession of smaller rooms. The older woman walked ahead of them, nodding to assistants, her speed belying her age. She looked as mummified and lifeless as the corpses she spent her days hunched over but they were finding it hard to keep up as she led them down a set of dark stairs, the smell of mouldy brickwork and old wood exploding in their nostrils, and into a dazzling basement, tiled white and lit with savage intensity by strips of fluorescents criss-crossing the ceiling.

'Which one?' Bentley said, as if she were a florist asking them to pick out a particular bouquet. The heat in the room was making Carrigan sweat, his nausea rising and ebbing in waves as the fluorescents winked and flashed like knowing eyes. All around them white-suited orderlies were laying bodies on tables, prepping skin, washing instruments. He could hear the crunch of saw on bone, the whispered notes of other pathologists, the gurgle of blood sluicing down drains.

He watched Miller closely. He had no idea what kind of police work she'd done before, whether she'd been handing out traffic tickets or investigating murders. She looked pale and sickly, a figure made somehow more insubstantial by the bright lights. There was also a faint smell of alcohol but he couldn't be sure if it was coming from her or from the embalming fluids and disinfectants that permeated the walls.

'Trust you to always pick the worst ones, Carrigan.' The pathologist's voice was a strained smoker's whisper. 'That's why I love you.' Her fingers were dark yellow at the tips with nicotine stains, the skin like old leather or parchment, and what was left of her hair had been fashioned into a wavy Thatcher hairdo which was wilting visibly in the heat. When she reached for the handle Carrigan tried to help her but was quickly shooed away. She pulled hard and the slab came rolling out, the wheels squeaking against the runners, the sound amplified by the tiled surroundings and the quiet which had descended on the two detectives.

As the pathologist lifted the sheet to reveal Grace Okello's features, Carrigan saw Miller flinch but, he noted, she didn't look away. He took his jacket off and wiped the sweat from his brow. 'It's like bloody Rangoon in here, Bentley.'

'Air-conditioning's broken. Went down this morning but the electricians haven't shown up yet.'

Carrigan nodded, the heat, noise and smell welling inside him.

'Been working on this one since early morning,' she continued, peering down at the body of Grace Okello. 'As I said, you always come up with the best ones. A lot of stuff to work on. Poor girl and all, but for us it's a bonus.'

'A bonus?' Miller asked, and Carrigan could hear the astonishment in her voice. She'd never dealt with a murder case, that much was obvious. He wondered why Branch had picked her.

The sheet had been washed so many times the edges had turned translucent and shiny, revealing the skin beneath as if it were tracing paper. The silver instrument tray gleamed back the fluorescents' insistent highlights. This was the part he always hated and yet it was also the best part. This was when the body started talking to you. When it was just you and them. He could have easily phoned the morgue, got all this without leaving his office, but it was his last chance to see Grace, the last chance to fix her in his mind. To remember why he was doing this.

The pathologist slowly pulled back the sheet, making sure both sides were even. Miller's sharp inhalation filled the room like the sound of a punctured tyre. She looked as if she were about to faint.

'I can do this if you want.' Carrigan tried to get the right tone in his voice, a mixture of compassion and authority, but Miller just glared at him, eyes blazing.

'She took a long while to die.' Bentley's voice sounded scratchy and distracted.

'Time of death?'

The pathologist squinted. 'Can't say for certain yet, the heaters were turned up high in the flat. But sometime Sunday night, definitely. If I had to guess I'd say between nine and midnight, but I need to do more tests.'

Carrigan shook his head and shrugged, he knew not to rely on the pathologist making everything simple and clear as they did on television. She could only give him facts and numbers. How these related to a person, a death, a time and place, that was up to him and his detectives to find out. This part of any murder investigation was like reading the map before you set out on the journey.

He saw Miller swallowing rapidly, her throat constricting and gulping as if she'd swallowed something too big for her. She looked so ghostly, Carrigan thought, more so even than the dead body. Her eyes were scrunched in concentration and her teeth were biting down on her lower lip, turning it white as a candle. He stared back down at Grace, the torn skin, the burst blood vessels in her eyes, the broken nails on her right hand, and when he looked back up the room began to spin.

It came out of his stomach with such force that he doubled over, vomiting all over the floor and Miller's overshoes. When he thought he was finished his stomach spasmed again, a hot burning pain in his throat as everything rushed out. His eyes lost focus and he gripped the side of a nearby table, the metal cooling his skin. He used his hand to wipe his mouth and beard. Miller and the pathologist were staring at him. Bentley looked as if she were about to laugh, as if it was the funniest thing she'd ever seen, but in Miller's eyes he saw something else even though her complexion looked as green and pallid as his felt.

Miller took a pack of hand wipes from her bag and handed him several. He felt her recoil in surprise as her fingers brushed the shiny scar tissue that ran up his arm from palm to elbow. He rubbed the wipes against his mouth, the rich sharp smell of lemon making him feel instantly better. She palmed him a small tube of mints.

'Thanks.' He balled up the wipes, dropped them in the sanitary bin and slid a mint into his mouth. A young African woman had come over and began mopping up the mess. She didn't acknowledge the pathologist nor the two detectives, just silently carried on cleaning. Carrigan was about to apologise but Miller already had her back to him and was staring at the body.

'Can you construct a sequence of injuries from what you have?'

Bentley looked at Miller and nodded, pointing to the dark mass of dreadlocks and pooled blood on the left side of the dead girl's face. 'She was hit with something relatively soft—a fist, I should think. Several times. There's intracranial bleeding, which means it happened while she was still alive. She was also raped.'

Carrigan leant forward, staring at the long gash running up the corpse's stomach, the bite marks and contusions, wondering why so much overkill.

'We found blue cloth fibres lodged between her teeth,' continued the pathologist. 'She was probably gagged during her ordeal. Cause of death, however, was this.'

Carrigan watched as she delicately lifted the skin on the left side of Grace's torso. He swallowed hard as it revealed a mess of fat and tissue, the ribs white and jutting out at strange angles. Bentley put one gloved finger on a rib and pointed underneath. 'He cut her open, slit her from navel to clavicle with a very sharp curved blade, then reached in and cut out her heart.'

'She was still alive when he did this?' asked Miller. She thought back to her mother's words last night, tried to get that voice out of her head.

'I'm afraid so,' said Bentley. 'For a while, at least.'

'He took the heart with him?' asked Carrigan.

'Yes, something of a romantic, our killer,' the pathologist drily replied, a weird twinkle in her eyes. 'Thirty years and I've never seen anything like this.'

Carrigan stepped back from the body, the dazzling lights exploding in his eyes. He could hear Miller saying something but he couldn't make out what it was. He looked up at the doctor, knew he had to ask, didn't want to . . . 'What about the bites?'

'I was wondering when you'd get to that.' She pointed out the small circular bite marks on Grace's arms, thighs and face. 'I counted sixty-nine separate bites, quite deep, most of them. And yes, before you ask, Detective,' and this time her smile was wide and genuine as if detailing some special talent of a favoured grandchild, 'the bites come from human teeth.'

Miller leant forward and examined the small punctured semi-circles wondering what kind of man got his pleasure from taking something beautiful and turning it into ruin.

'Not just ordinary human teeth,' the pathologist added, gesturing to one small bite mark along the inside of Grace's right thigh. 'Pointy teeth.'

'Like a vampire bite?'

The old woman laughed, startling them both. 'We all know there's no such things as vampires, Detective Carrigan. No, whoever did this has had his two front teeth filed to extremely sharp points,' she paused as if to contemplate this. 'Perhaps even expressly for this purpose.'

5

She watched him from every part of the room. Her eyes stared lifeless across the vacant desks and empty chairs. Her limbs were mute against the gloss of the blazing lights, her wounds the only story left to tell.

Carrigan adjusted one of the photos, stepped back, and surveyed his work.

Photos of Grace Okello were pinned to every available wallspace of the incident room. Images taken at the scene and ones with white backgrounds from the morgue. Images repeated and juxtaposed. Images overlapping. Close-ups and long shots. Eyelashes and ripped flesh. Bedposts and kitchen appliances. The room laid bare, duplicated and blown up, each element gaining significance in its isolation.

This was all his idea, the way he always did it from the very first murder he'd worked on back in '97, the little girl found behind the Tube depot, until now. Every case began with a body. But that body was soon forgotten amidst the pathways and tunnels lit up from clues and background work. Policemen became seduced by logic, discrepancy, coincidence. Two days into a murder investigation and they'd forgotten the victim, remembered only the MO, the errant boyfriend or estranged uncle. The photos made sure they wouldn't forget. They weren't here to make statistics. They weren't here to make a living. They were here to avenge the dead. This was his only certainty, the rock that had held him for so long to this strange and surprising career.

The team filed in slow and stooped looking like reluctant night-shift workers, their feet dragging behind them, trying to delay the moment for as long as possible. They all knew how he worked, what awaited them in this room. He watched them shuffle to the mismatched desks, temporary solutions salvaged from some bankrupt school. He was proud of them, these moments making him realise he could never do this alone and how they had forced him to accept this over the years.

Karlson sat at a table to his right, fingers trailing through his stubble as he watched Carrigan. Next to him sat DC Jennings, DC Singh, and some of the younger constables. DC Berman, their internet whiz, sat, as always, in the back, his face half on Carrigan, half glued to the computer screens in front of him.

While they organised themselves, found somewhere to look at that didn't have Grace staring back at them, Carrigan gazed out of the window but saw only a greenish mist. Outside the sun was sizzling low in the autumn sky, maybe one of the last days of pure sunshine before winter set in, but it didn't penetrate the green builders' mesh stretched taut and firm around the building's scaffolding like an oversized pair of tights.

Three months now they'd been covered in green. The station was undergoing major refurbishments and Carrigan's Murder Incident Team as well as most of CID had been moved to the new extension, promised that it would be the latest in office environments. Unfortunately, it was still in the process of completion and they had to make do with what they could scavenge and hope the builders would be finished soon. The mesh cast a greenish glow on everything. Their computer screens. The food they ate. Their skin.

He turned back to the room, saw them sitting, faces at strange angles, staring down at their notebooks. He pointed to the blown-up image of Grace Okello's face that he'd pinned to the whiteboard directly behind him. His mouth still tasted sour from this morning at the morgue, his suit smelling faintly of sweat and vomit. 'Most of you already know that Grace Okello was discovered dead in her flat at 87 King's Court on Queensway at 10.34 yesterday morning.' He looked down at his hands, trying to stifle the sensation in his throat, the pathologist's final revelation.

'Ms. Okello was brutally beaten then tied down to her bed. The perpetrator raped her several times, secreting O-positive semen. It seems he bit her as he was doing this.' He paused, watching the silent faces of his squad, the realisation in their eyes of what they were dealing with. 'When he was finished, he used a curved blade to open up her chest, then reached inside and extracted her heart. We can only presume he took it as a souvenir.'

Jennings and Berman were shaking their heads, trying to look anywhere but the walls. The photos had been bad enough but now they knew the sequence of events that had produced this abstract display of horror and atrocity it was much worse.

'The scene of crime officers are just finishing up in the flat now so we should get the preliminary results soon. The HOLMES team are coming in this afternoon. Berman, I want you to go through the CCTV footage from the building's entrance. The porter handed over the tapes from the last seven days; after that they record over the old ones.' He'd checked the camera on his way out. Trying to save money, the management of the building had installed only one CCTV camera at the front entrance. It recorded who came in and who went out, but gave no indication of whom they were visiting. 'I know it's a pain in the arse, I know we probably won't get anything from it, but we need to do it.'

Berman nodded, his fingers already tapping furiously at the keyboard.

'Jennings, run a list of the tenants against the PNC—also, talk to the porter. He was drunk, way beyond drunk actually, when I approached him. Find out if he's a lush or he only got blotto that night. Check him out too, most of these porters have form of one kind or another. Talk to the neighbours; they won't be very cooperative but push them—someone must have seen or heard something.'

'We tell them it's a murder enquiry?' Jennings asked hesitantly.

Carrigan shook his head. 'I know, this makes our life harder, but not a word as to why we're asking about Grace. The super was very adamant about that. The papers find out about this, we're all fucked.' Everyone laughed at Carrigan's rare lapse into profanity, the tension in the room dissipating for the briefest of increments. 'DS Miller and I will be looking at the victimology, trying to find out what we can about who Grace was, why anyone would want to do this to her.'

Karlson had his hand up. In the other, an unlit cigarette jumped like a child's toy. 'She was a pretty girl, isn't that enough?'

Carrigan rubbed his temples. 'We don't want to start making too many assumptions yet, John.' His words sounded false to him, he knew they all had their theories, and that often it was those primary assumptions, based on nothing more than a feeling, which opened up a trail of clues that would eventually lead to the killer. 'On the surface this does indeed look like a sex killing. He raped her brutally. The force of the injuries, the anger and personal nature of the attack, the fact he took a souvenir. What we have to ask ourselves is whether this is a one-off, perhaps someone known to Grace, or is this the first in a series? There were no marks of forced entry so we have to assume that either Grace knew this person or he got in under false pretences. The SOCOs found two half-drunk glasses of milk in the kitchen—hopefully we'll get the DNA results before the end of the next millennium. In the meantime check all the usual utility companies, see if they report anything strange, stolen uniforms, that sort of thing. I'll be looking at recent unsolveds to see if there's a similar signature.'

'Then you don't think this has anything to do with witch-craft?'

Carrigan stared hard at Karlson, not sure if he was taking the piss or not. As usual, the sergeant was immaculately dressed and groomed as if he'd just stepped out of a glossy men's magazine. 'Why do you say that?'

Karlson had been waiting for this, Carrigan could tell. 'The mutilations, the missing heart, the fact she's African—'

'This isn't witchcraft.'

The voice had come from somewhere at the back. Carrigan scanned the room until he spotted Miller, hunched down into her table, taking notes, a can of Coke obscuring her face. He hadn't even noticed her come in, impressed at how well she'd been able to conceal herself. 'Enlighten us, DS Miller.'

Karlson and one of the constables shared a joke, the kind of joke which has no words, only facial expressions and common prejudices. Geneva sat up in her chair, ignoring them, scanned her notes and took a sip of Coke, aware that everyone was watching her.

'First of all, there's almost no proven cases of African witch-craft in England. Not on this scale. Amulets, herbs and potions on sale in markets, yes. Murder, no. It's too far-fetched, too small a possibility. Also, this is too messy.'

'Too messy, DS Miller?' Carrigan tried to keep his voice neutral but it wasn't working; he could still remember his embarrassment in front of her at the morgue, his conversation with Branch that morning.

'Yes,' she answered. 'In African ritual murder the perpetra-tor kills so he can use body parts or blood for his magic. He wouldn't go for all this overkill. Certainly wouldn't have raped her, which I'm sure diminishes whatever power they think the body parts hold.'

Carrigan nodded to himself, having come to the same con-clusion. Witchcraft and ritual were a fool's last hand hold when everything else fell through. He knew that people mostly killed for petty reasons: to protect their position, to avenge an imagined slight, for money or for sex.

'What we should be concentrating on,' Miller continued, finding her voice now, 'is why he did the things he *didn't* have to do.'

'He didn't have to kill her at all.' Jennings tried to make a joke of it but no one laughed.

Miller sighed. 'True, but not very useful.' She checked to see if Carrigan was about to stop her but he seemed lost in thought, staring out of the window into the green sky. 'He raped her and killed her. If we accept that this is a sex killing then we have to ask why the overkill? Why not just rape her and strangle her? The things he didn't need to do but did—the bites, the physical assault, the missing heart—we have to ask why did he do those things specifically? What does it tell us about what kind of man this is? Did they have some symbolic value for him? Did something about Grace so enrage him that he felt he needed to kill her twice, three times?'

'Very well put,' Carrigan interrupted. 'It bothers me too. Why beat her, bite her and then extract her heart?' A hush descended over the gathered detectives. Outside the builders were laughing, joking, playing the radio. The music made Carrigan wince even though it was only a faint flutter of notes, barely audible. He thanked DS Miller, then pointed to the photos tacked up around the room. He waited until everyone had turned their heads and was staring at Grace Okello.

'We need to catch this guy immidiately. This is the sort of thing you don't do on impulse. This kind of slow and deliberate murder, the perpetrator's been building up to it. Rape. Assault. He'll probably have form. And even if this is his first time, he'll do it again. That's beyond doubt. This kind of thing doesn't happen in isolation. You don't rape, torture and kill a girl then go back to your wife and kids and ordinary life. There is no life after this but more of the same.' He stopped, acutely aware he was going off into a rant again. There'll be daily briefings here at 8.30 A.M. and 6.30 P.M. so that we can review where we are.' He turned to the whiteboard. 'Remember these photos. We can't bring Grace Okello back but maybe we can tell her we caught him. And maybe, if we're lucky, she'll be listening.'

6

He sat at his desk, an Everest of paperwork in front of him, the phone lying silent. He'd pushed his other files to the side, the growing mountain of unsolved cases, only the occasional phone call from a distraught relative to remind him they were still active. Each was accorded a separate coloured folder and as he placed them to the side he felt a spasm of guilt. He held the black file in his hands for a moment longer.

This one was different. This one wouldn't go away. No one else reckoned its contents amounted to a crime but Carrigan thought otherwise. He briefly flicked through the pages inside, the missing-person reports, the detectives' summaries, the relatives' statements. There were four photos, uncannily similar. Four teenage boys, three reported missing and one found dead. No one else thought there was a connection. The cases were spread too far apart, up and down and across the country, several years between them. Boys that age often disappeared for their own reasons. Many were never found because they didn't want to be. But these four, something about them, the way each boy looked like the others, black glasses, long brown hair, something in their gaze. He slipped the pages back inside and put the file to one side.

The drinks machine was at the other end of the building and he walked through empty corridors and the smell of fresh paint then into the old part of the station. Immediately he felt the buzz of the busy squad room, the constant ringing of phones and voices of his colleagues, ears pressed against mobiles, fingers busily tapping keyboards. He nodded and said hello, checked the daily incident logs to see if there was anything that related to his case, then walked past more incident rooms filled with other detectives pursuing killers, drug dealers and internet fraudsters. The walls around him were covered in photos of valorous heroes, injured or killed in the line of duty, and he walked past these sombrely as he always did, not wanting to see their faces and read the futures that would befall them in those eager poses. He waited for his drink to dispense and stared at the crime-stat sheets lining the walls, the rotas crossed out and replaced by illegible scrawls, the reminders of best-practice procedures.

He returned to the incident room and sat back down in his chair, turning on all the lights to offset the gauzy green mist, took a sip of his drink and began going through the stacks of paper amassed on his desk.

He'd faxed Grace's details, what little they knew, to all the London universities and colleges. The replies had come back quickly. Grace was enrolled at the School of Oriental and African Studies studying East African History, in the third year of a four-year course. He'd stared at the smudged fax and felt his heart beat a little faster. A coincidence, he told himself, that was all. He crushed the polystyrene cup in his hands and sent it flying towards the bin.

Jennings had secured a list of all the tenants in the block from the management company. He'd fed it through the computer, looking for hits, criminal records, complaints, the usual. Carrigan leafed through the printouts—he had an hour until he was supposed to meet Geneva outside the School of Oriental and African Studies to interview Grace's professor. He ran through the list floor by floor; small-time drug offences, a few fraud cases, benefit dodgers, noise complaints.

The names of the tenants were like a roll call at the UN; it seemed that every nationality was resident in King's Court, names that were too long for the forms, names with diacritics and letters not found on police-issue keyboards, names and more names. The case, he knew, would centre around Grace herself—who she was, what she did, her friends and acquaintances. He looked down at the page, the list of names, the floor below Grace's, then back up at the photos pinned to the walls of the incident room. Then he looked back down again. Read the words twice to make sure his eyes weren't deceiving him. He couldn't believe Jennings hadn't picked up on it, then realised it was his fault, he'd only told the DC to print out the results, not go through them.

It was there among the small-time crooks and weed pushers. It was there in black and white and in capitals. George Monroe. Flat 62. Three years for sexual assault and battery. Released from the Scrubs two years ago. Carrigan's fingers twitched. He stared down at the page, read *sexual assault*, wondering if Monroe had bumped into Grace in the lift or maybe downstairs in the lobby. Perhaps they said hello to each other, Monroe thinking there was more to it. If she knew him by sight she might have opened the door for him, invited him in for a glass of milk.

Carrigan felt a sharp electric flash spark through his fingers. He turned to the computer and typed in Monroe's name but the mainframe was down and he was left staring at an infuriating egg timer telling him the system would be back online soon. He punched the keyboard in frustration, the R and Y flying out from under his fist, texted Geneva that he couldn't make the interview, grabbed his coat and paged Jennings.

The rain had started as he left the building and was now coming down hard on the grey pavements of Queensway. Carrigan sipped his coffee, chewed on a Kit-Kat, and manoeuvred through the evening crowds. A shop that hadn't been there yesterday was already open for business, the city continually remaking itself. He walked past the souvenir stalls and kebab joints, the Russian supermarkets and money changers. Most of the signs made no concession to English—even the alphabets were unrecognisable, a wondrous riot of crazy squiggles that could have been advertising anything.

He surveyed the building's entrance from the other side of the road, scanning the faces, hoping to see something that didn't feel right, but there was only the rush and bustle of the crowd, too many people, too many eyes.

Jennings was waiting by the front entrance of King's Court. Carrigan saw that he had two cups of McDonald's coffee in his hand and squirmed. The steam covered the constable's schoolboy face, wilting the lick of hair that rested on his forehead like an upside-down question mark. Carrigan thanked him, said he'd already drunk too much, and tossed the cup into the nearest bin. Jennings didn't seem to notice and kept fidgeting with his mobile. He was young but one of the better constables assigned to him. Carrigan had seen a glint of something on the last case when Jennings had spent days going through useless computer records, a job no one else wanted, and then came back with the one piece of evidence that the jury would accept. Carrigan had learned not to judge the young DCs by their looks, his own advancing years making them seem that much more naive and callow.

'I'm sorry I didn't go through the list,' he apologised.

Carrigan waved him off as they entered the building. 'I didn't ask you to.'

'I know, sir. But I should have done it anyway.'

Carrigan nodded, kept walking, staring up at the CCTV camera, heading towards the porter's cubicle.

'You won't find him in there, sir.'

Carrigan stopped and turned towards Jennings.

'He's at the Rat and Firkin down the road. Next door to

McDonald's. I saw him going in there while I was getting this.' He lifted the coffee he was still holding. 'There'll be no point talking to him till he's sober.'

'We need to check his alibi,' Carrigan stated flatly.

'You think he was involved?'

He could never get over Jennings's naivety. He knew the young DC would have it ironed out of him if he stayed another couple of years, but he liked it, the sense of genuine surprise at the world and its turnings. It reminded him of an old friend but the memory was sour and filled his heart with pain. 'No, I don't, but we need to check anyway.'

Jennings was smiling now. 'Actually, I already did. When I saw him going in, I thought I'd have a word with the landlord. He was at the pub Sunday night too; apparently he's something of a fixture. I talked to the barman and three regulars, all alibied him for the whole night. Dead drunk, had to be helped home.'

Carrigan thought about this. 'Good work.' Jennings smiled. 'I want you to wait in Grace's flat for me,' Carrigan continued. 'The SOCOs are done but I'm not. We need to go through her things. I've got a call to make on the next floor down; I want you to start making an inventory.'

Jennings smile had frozen in place.

'What is it?' Carrigan asked.

Jennings shuffled his feet, hands deep in pockets. 'I'd rather not go in there again.'

Carrigan remembered the look on the young DC's face when they'd entered the flat and seen Grace's body, the way he'd immediately rushed to the toilet and contaminated the crime scene. 'She's gone,' he said. 'It's only her things there now.'

'Okay.' Jennings tried to smile. 'I'd just rather . . . '

'I know, so would I.'

The long corridors, drained of light, reminded Carrigan of

mental hospitals, Victorian sanatoriums, places of deep darkness demarcated by dimly lit hallways and locked doors. The stuttering lights added another level of gloom, the creaking and shuffling of floorboards, the buzzing of telephones and TV sets. He knocked once on George Monroe's door and waited.

Monroe was taller than Carrigan, over six foot four, and almost as wide. He flinched when he saw the detective, quickly regaining his composure. 'What is it this time, Officer?' His voice sounded both weary and petulant at the same time but his eyes told a different story.

Carrigan pulled out his warrant card but Monroe didn't even bother to look at it, just stepped back from the door. 'Don't suppose I have a choice in the matter?'

Carrigan followed him into a flat that was almost a replica of Grace's. When these blocks had been built there were only three apartments to a floor, five or six bedrooms to each. But in the last seventy years the flats had been cannibalised and cut up into ever smaller divisions—more money, less space. Leonardo said small rooms concentrated the mind, but he'd obviously never lived here.

The room contained a TV, a DVD player, a coffee table, a bed and an armchair. There was nothing else, no books, magazines or decorations. It smelled of burned toast, cigarettes, old beer and bad breath. The TV was blaring loud, the voices cracking and distorting against the tinny speakers, accents from another century, the warm swell of the English countryside, fields and farmhouses and country roads. Carrigan's left ear began buzzing. 'One of your favourites, *The Railway Children*?'

Monroe shrugged as he sank down into the deep armchair, the fabric almost encasing his body. 'A classic,' he replied, flicking the mute on the remote. 'So, what is it I'm supposed to have done this time, Constable?'

There was nowhere to sit but the bed. Carrigan stood by

the small glass coffee table, staring at the layers of stains and discolourations, trying to work out what the original hue would have been. 'It's Detective Inspector, and we're knocking on everyone's door, making enquiries.'

Monroe nodded and continued to stare at the silent screen, his left foot nervously tapping the floor. The children were in a house, enshadowed by eaves, talking conspiratorially, their faces in close-up.

'Where were you on Sunday night, Mr. Monroe?'

'What happened Sunday night?'

'Answer the question.' Carrigan hated interviewing ex-cons, they knew the tricks, knew how to goad the police, had spent all that time inside reading up about their rights.

'Something happened Sunday night and you found my name in the register which is why you're here hassling me.' Monroe was casually biting his nails, spitting half-moon shards of skin down onto the carpet. Carrigan looked down, the toes in his boots curling up involuntarily.

'If a newspaper arrives at your door,' he looked up but Monroe's eyes were glued to the screen, 'and the newspaper is in German and you know the man three doors down once served in the Wehrmacht, then it's reasonable to assume . . . '

'What the fuck are you talking about?'

'I'm explaining why I'm here. I'm answering your question.' He took out the photo, let it fall onto Monroe's lap. 'Do you recognise her?'

Monroe looked at Grace's photo for a long time, running his cracked fingers down the edges and nodding to himself. 'She's dead.'

Carrigan's mouth went dry. 'What did you say?'

Monroe met Carrigan's gaze for the first time. 'Why else are you showing me a photo like this? C'mon, she's either dead or missing, otherwise a detective inspector wouldn't be wasting his time.' He handed the photo back to Carrigan.

'You still haven't answered my first question.' They always thought they were cleverer than you but it was their need to show it off that was also their weakness.

'She lived here, right?' Monroe nodded to himself, his eyes glued to the silent screen, the pull of the locomotive disappearing into the vanishing point of a grey horizon. 'That's why you're asking. You found out I'd been inside and—'

Carrigan took two quick steps forward, leant down and whispered in Monroe's ear. 'Tell me what you know about this woman now.' He said it softly but his grip on Monroe's shoulder was firm and unrelenting. He could feel the man's muscles popping and flexing under his touch.

'No. Never seen her. Wouldn't even notice her if I did. Can I go back to my film now?'

Carrigan kept himself between the TV and Monroe. 'Where were you Sunday night?'

Monroe folded his hands in his lap. 'I was at church.'

'Church?' Carrigan replied.

Monroe crossed one leg over the other. 'Yes, church. What? You don't think people like me should be allowed into church? You don't think we deserve communion?' Monroe shuffled forward on the armchair. Carrigan caught sight of something glinting white under the cushion. 'Carrigan. That's Irish, right? Catholic?'

'I don't belong to any church.'

'Yes, I can see that in your eyes. You're lost and you don't even know it.' Monroe sat back, crossed his legs and bit at his left thumb.

'Anyone who can confirm that?' Carrigan tried to keep his voice low and steady.

'The priest, some of the regulars. It's St. Joseph's, over the road. You can check.'

Carrigan made a note though he knew exactly where it was. 'Can you please get up, Mr. Monroe?'

'Are you arresting me?'

'Stand the fuck up.'

Monroe got up reluctantly, his face white and stretched, as Carrigan bent down and lifted the seat cushion. His stomach yawned against the constraints of his trousers and he felt the blood drain from his head. Underneath the cushion was a square white photo album.

Monroe was staring anywhere but at the armchair. Carrigan could smell his fear now, the rank meaty scent coming off the man in waves. He felt every muscle in his own body tense and sizzle as he picked up the photo album.

'No . . . please,' Monroe mumbled, sitting back down as Carrigan opened the book and saw a six-year-old boy modelling a pair of swimming trunks, the image ripped out of a catalogue. His breath stuck in his throat and he could feel the pulse in his fingers as he turned the pages.

Photos of young athletes torn from newspapers. Olympic swimmers, glistening in dewy relief against blue swimming pools. More pages from catalogues, young blond boys playing board games, modelling T-shirts and underwear, each page ripped out and then carefully neatened up, pasted into the book with little translucent butterflies.

Carrigan cursed himself for running out half-cocked like this, knew he'd been slipping these last two years. His arms came down so quickly that even he was surprised. He picked up Monroe and slammed him against the wall. The photo book fell to the floor. Monroe's face crashed against a framed Elvis print and his body buckled in Carrigan's grip.

'When did you last see her?'

Monroe turned, his eyes misty and his lip split at the edges. 'She's not my type.' Blood poured down the side of his cheekbone. 'Get your facts right, Inspector.' He spat out some more blood. It landed on Carrigan's shoe. 'You show me this fucking picture, ask me when was the last time I saw her. You fuck-

ing pricks, you don't even do your homework, do you?'
Monroe's teeth glinted red. 'I don't like girls, Detective; never
have, never will. And I don't like anyone this old.'

Carrigan felt the pulsing of the blood in his fingers, the heat
of the flat, the whine in Monroe's voice. He buried his fists in
his pockets, felt them jumping inside. He stared at Monroe,
cursing himself. Monroe pointed at the TV, two boys running
together on a railway track, and emitted a high-pitched cackle.
'That's right—come to Daddy.'

Carrigan shoved him hard against the wall, feeling a shock
of electricity rip down his arm and through his chest. He saw
Grace falling to the floor, blood trickling down her cheeks. He
heard her scream. He let go of Monroe and exited the flat,
slamming the door behind him.

7

Geneva made her way through the press of bodies and up the stairs. Her stomach reeled and rolled, her palms clammy and hot. She stopped and took a deep breath of hazy London air, her vision going scrambly for a split second. She couldn't believe how nervous she was. Knew she was going to fuck it all up. She stared at the cool columns and smooth steps leading up to SOAS's main entrance, trying to focus on nothing, just the blankness in front of her, but it wasn't helping. Her first interview working a murder and she felt like a schoolgirl about to be reprimanded.

She'd been surprised when Carrigan had called an hour ago, told her to conduct the interview by herself. He'd sounded distracted and tense, she'd tried asking him what he was up to but he'd hung up before she'd even finished the sentence. It had been a while since she'd had a new DI and she'd forgotten how hard it was; how it would take weeks, months sometimes, before you clicked, understood every unsaid thing. She didn't know what to make of him yet—he didn't dress like a policeman, he didn't look like one. A depressed lecturer in medieval history perhaps, with his crumpled clothes and even more crumpled face, the hair that wouldn't sit still in the wind, and his ridiculous fake Barbour interlaced with biscuit crumbs. He wore a wedding ring but didn't look like a man who went home every night to a loving wife.

She took a swig of her Coke, binned it and entered the building. The hum of student life surrounded her, the frayed newsletters, wanted notes, mimeographed posters for bands with unpronounceable names and political pamphlets, their covers stark with 20-point headlines in black capitals, so sure of their messages it made her heart shrink a little.

A secretary guided her to a chair and paged Professor Cummings. His office was on the top floor of the building, encased by corridors and bookshelves. In front of her a large window opened out onto the square below and she watched the students gather, chat and slurp soft drinks in the late-afternoon sun, their faces filled with exhaustion and wonder. She thought back to Norwich, her time at the University of East Anglia, the shadow of her mother far away and the screaming riotous nights of music and laughter that engulfed her fresher year.

'If only we could . . .'

She turned from the grease-smeared window and looked up at the man addressing her. Mid-forties, prematurely grey but dressed in a Grateful Dead shirt and sporting a ponytail.

'Pardon?'

'Go back.' Professor Cummings smiled. 'Change the past, take the other turning, the one we never took. But we can't. Just as they . . .' he pointed out of the window, the nails on his hand long and curved like a guitar player's, '. . . just as they won't be able to go back to this day. You think they know this? Did we? Do you think it would make us enjoy each day more or less?'

The professor's office looked as though it had been caught in the maw of a hurricane. She stepped inside and her feet scraped and jostled against the loose papers, photocopies and pamphlets spotting the floor. More piles of paper and spiral-bound dissertations leant and quivered in corner stacks.

Cummings took his seat, apologised for the mess, but she could tell it was always like this. His T-shirt had blue clouds and yellow skulls against a purple background. His cargo pants were loose and hung asymmetrically, pens and who knows what else weighing down the side pockets. 'Bloody smoking laws,' he muttered as Geneva took out her voice recorder. 'Used to be I could smoke in my own office, didn't harm anyone. Now I have to go down ten floors and stand outside in the rain. You know how much valuable time I lose every day?' Cummings let out a deep sigh as if only now realising this wasn't another student sitting in front of him. 'No, of course, you don't want to know about that.' She watched as he shuffled on the seat, making himself comfortable, slouching one leg over the armrest. 'You said you wanted to see me in relation to Grace Okello, but you didn't say what she's done wrong, detective.'

Geneva took out her notebook, flipped through the pages. 'Why do you think she's done anything wrong?' she asked, looking directly into his eyes.

'I get a call from the police asking to speak about Grace, what else would I think?'

'I'm afraid Grace was killed on Sunday evening,' Geneva stated flatly.

Cummings dropped the pen he'd been kneading between his fingers the last few minutes. He stared at Geneva, waiting for a smile, relaxation of facial muscles, any indicator that this was some elaborate practical joke. 'She's dead?'

Geneva nodded, watching Cummings's eyes turn dark and hooded. He reached into the pocket of his cargo pants and extracted a pack of Gitanes. Without looking at Geneva he took one out, tapped the end on the table several times to let the tobacco settle and lit it with a lighter in the shape of a rhinoceros horn. 'Jesus,' he said, taking three deep drags in succession as if he were a dying man sucking oxygen. He coughed into his hand, his eyes turning red and watery.

'What happened?' he finally asked, the ash on his cigarette now longer than the unsmoked portion. Geneva stared at it, waiting for it to fall. She related the basic facts: Grace found dead in her flat. Said she couldn't go into details or theories, which was true, though she also wanted to see how much Cummings could fill in.

'You were Grace's dissertation supervisor?' She looked down at her notes though she knew the questions off by heart.

Cummings took another drag and cleared his throat. 'Yes. It was transferred to me when she proposed it. Anything East African gets parcelled out to me.' He looked past Geneva, to a point on the wall, a poster of a desert scene, camels trudging through a sea of sand. 'My accounts of Grace will inevitably be biased, so be forewarned.'

Geneva watched Cummings carefully as he told her about Grace Okello. When he began speaking, his face lost a couple of years and sleepless nights; something in his eyes lit up and she could tell that he'd be a favourite among students. He had a way of talking, imparting information, that wasn't condescending and yet guided you along so that when you came to the conclusion you thought you'd got there yourself.

'Grace was bright, articulate and funny, that was easy to see, but I don't think I really spoke to her alone until it came time for the students to hand in their dissertation proposals. You work here ten years as I've done, you see the same ideas and theories recycled every year, so when something new comes along it leaps out at you. Grace was that kind of student. International students tend to be far less trouble than English ones. They understand what a privilege it is for them to be here studying while their friends are facing hunger, war and unemployment back home. They don't use their three years as an opportunity to get drunk, stoned and laid every night.'

Geneva scribbled some notes in her pad though the digital recorder was preserving every utterance of the conversation. She sometimes found that her notes were wildly divergent from the recordings. One was for facts, the other for feelings, hunches, suppositions. She was also aware of the effect it had; how people got nervous when the person opposite them was writing things they couldn't see. 'You mentioned her dissertation. What was it about?'

Cummings leant back in the chair. 'She was interested in rebel groups. Revolutionaries. The thesis was a study of post-colonial African insurgencies and coups.'

'You said it struck you as original. What made it so?'

Cummings took a few seconds to think, rubbing his hands through what was left of his hair and nodding to himself. 'Most of these students, most young people, are enamoured by men with guns who come bearded and filthy out of the bush after years of fighting and take control of the country. I bet one in three students still have posters of Che Guevara on their walls.'

Geneva smiled, thinking of the Che poster her mum had in the kitchen, the letter the Argentine doctor had written to her mother before he set off on his fateful Bolivian journey.

'Well, Grace saw beyond that,' Cummings continued, more at ease now he was back in his area of expertise. 'She didn't think that Che and Mao were such heroes. She saw how African insurgencies, like all insurgencies, began with good intentions and ended in blood, torture and jail cells. How every rebel regime that came to power became the very thing they'd sworn to destroy. She was looking primarily at her homeland, Uganda, at Museveni who grabbed the presidency sixteen years ago after fighting as a bush guerrilla. She looked at Charles Taylor in Liberia and Laurent Nkunda in the Congo, Gaddafi, Mugabe and Mobutu. And she was very interested in Joseph Kony.'

'Joseph Kony?' Geneva was lost, history never her strong point, African history a total blur to her like Conrad's white map.

'The papers like to call him Africa's Most Wanted Man, though there's a new contender for that crown every day.

He's a northern Ugandan who began a rebel offensive in the mid-eighties against the government of Museveni. His soldiers are called the Lord's Resistance Army, LRA for short, and most of them are abducted children. He says he wants to bring the rule of the ten commandments to the region but in twenty years he's achieved just the opposite.

'What was so original in Grace's work was her take on these rebel movements. She saw them not as some glamorous Marxist emancipation but as men who were only interested in blood, money and power but who had learned to disguise their motivations in ideology and charisma. You see, Grace understood rebel movements not as political forces but as death cults.'

Geneva made illegible notes, acronyms and names skipping by her like station signs through a train window. She knew she'd need to get a handle on some of this material later and kicked herself for falling into the professor's soothing tones when she was supposed to be interrogating him. 'And how was her work going?'

'She was having problems these last few months,' Cummings admitted, looking down at the table. 'She kept coming to see me, tearing out her hair, wanting to give it all up.'

'What kind of problems?'

'She was a perfectionist. She kept criticising her own work, much more than I ever did. She wanted it to be perfect, to take account of everything. She thought that if she had all the facts about a given subject, the answer would be bound to reveal itself.'

Geneva nodded, thinking back to her own time at university and to how similar Grace's ideas were to hers concerning police work.

'But it doesn't work that way,' Cummings continued. 'We can never have all the facts. There's too much information and it's constantly changing. And even if in some way you could gather all the information, it wouldn't necessarily lead to an answer. I tried to explain to her that undergraduate work was about realising this. Finding the limitations of your methodology. It's more about unlearning than learning, but Grace had a hard time with this. To be honest, most of our international students do. They come to London expecting certainty and accuracy and we tell them it's impossible, a chimera.'

'Did Grace have any arguments? Any falling outs?' She remembered her own days at university, the heady shuffle of people, late-night discussions fuelled by booze and slogans, the shouting and placard waving. She watched as Cummings took a moment to think it over.

'Most students like to take a bite out of us former colonisers, the white man,' he replied without a hint of irony. 'Grace wanted to take modern African leaders, the modern African system, to task. She wasn't interested in colonialism or its after-effects.'

'Did that get her in trouble?'

'Occasionally. I remember one day at the refectory, I was sitting at a table with Grace and some of her friends. They were having a debate—no, it was an argument really. One of her fellow African students harangued her for going after black men. Said their job wasn't to attack their own but the white man. It got quite heated for a while until another friend calmed them down. But these are students, Miss Miller, they get heated over which brand of coffee the canteen uses, if there are too many black cleaners in the building. I'm not sure this has anything to do with what happened.'

'Everything has something to do with what happened, Professor, we just don't know it until we have all the details.'

Cummings shook his head mournfully. 'You sound just like Grace, Detective. I'm sure the two of you would have got along very well.'

Geneva ignored the comment, not sure whether it was intended as rebuke or compliment. 'Did she have a boyfriend?'

Cummings laughed. 'I have no idea. They don't tell us these things. She was a very pretty and highly intelligent girl. I would think she had one or maybe several, but you'd have to talk to her friends about that.'

Cummings riffled through his notes again but Geneva could see he wasn't really looking at them, his eyes clouded as if some debate were raging inside.

'But something changed, right? Something happened?' She was guessing but she saw him flinch, then shake his head.

'I don't know how relevant this is but you say you want to know all the details.' He took a deep breath as if making some kind of inner decision. 'The last couple of terms she'd been slipping a bit. Grades down, a few essays not handed in on time. It happens to a lot of students but I never thought it would happen to Grace.'

Geneva felt a blast of heat rushing through her. 'When was this?'

Cummings thought it over. 'When she came back from the Christmas break. There was something . . . something different about her.'

'Different how?'

'She seemed less communicative, more fervent, I don't know—maybe I'm just imagining it.'

It was probably nothing, a break-up with a boyfriend, the pressures of work. 'Did you ever meet her parents?'

'No. We rarely do. Even with domestic students. She hardly ever talked about Uganda or her childhood. Not to me, anyhow. She was a member of the East African Association but that's normal for students from her part of the world. Most of them stop going after a year, they start making friends because of shared interests and hobbies rather than history and genealogy.'

'Drugs?' Geneva stared at the professor.

'What, Grace? I very much doubt it. She didn't even drink. As I said, she was a serious student.'

'Until the start of this year.'

Cummings nodded. 'I can only tell you my impressions; I'm afraid they're probably not worth much at all to you, Detective.'

Geneva stood up and shoved the notebook back in her pocket. 'They've been of more use than you can imagine, Professor,' she said, watching Cummings stare at the files on his desk. He looked smaller, encased in his chair, buttressed by paper, and despondent too, as if now that the interview was over his last link to Grace had been severed and all that remained would be memories.

She was reaching for the door when he spoke.

'I've just had a thought . . . I don't know if this has anything to do with anything but Grace's friend, Cecilia . . .' He tapped another cigarette on the table, sighing almost silently. 'Well, we were supposed to have a meeting yesterday to discuss her dissertation but she never turned up.'

8

Grace Okello had not been a hoarder. For someone who'd spent two years in the same tiny flat, she had amassed very little.

Carrigan flicked through the inventory, lining up words and phrases with the objects they described. He glanced up at a poster advertising safaris in Uganda. A bitter taste filled his mouth as he stared at the family of lions in the bottom left-hand corner. He could almost taste the jungle, that deep wet sour stench that was always present. People saw jungles and thought they were places of life, an uncontrollable spurt of growth, but he'd been there and knew that jungles were only about death. Murder was an every minute occurrence. The ground was made of the rotten mulch of leaves and dead insects. The plants had sharp spikes and devious poisons. The animals spent all night either killing or hiding.

He got up and crossed the room, still a little out of breath from his confrontation with Monroe. His hand was throbbing, the flesh swelling around his wedding ring. The ring was too tight against his finger, sized for a younger man, but he liked the constant pressure, the close proximity of the metal which never allowed him to forget.

He stared at the bed, stripped of sheets and mattress, and thought about the nights Grace had slept on it, the lying-awake nights wondering about life, about boyfriends and grades and money. He turned to see Jennings staring at the wall. He followed the DC's eyes to a small circular pattern of dried blood.

The specialists would tell them angles, height, trajectories—but there was no mistaking the stain for anything else. Blood was always blood, but it was also so much more. Blood was evidence of a life interrupted. The heart sent it crashing through the veins and arteries and even when those were ripped or violated the heart continued sending fine sprays of blood everywhere, on the wall, clothes, weapons, as if it were the body's last utterance, a final attempt to point from the grave and avenge its own death.

'I keep looking at it,' Jennings mumbled. 'I can't stop.'

Carrigan put a hand on his shoulder, felt it buckle under him. How long had he left Jennings in the room by himself? 'I know,' he replied. 'It . . . it has a certain attraction. Go talk to the porter. I'll meet you back at the station.'

Jennings blushed and thanked Carrigan. He took one last long look at the circle of blood, as if hypnotised, and walked out of the flat.

When Carrigan was finished he let himself out, locked the door and replaced the crime-scene tape. Grace's possessions would be transferred to the incident room later tonight. He'd detail Miller to go through the reams of papers, the books and notes and graphs he'd found. It was pointless work but it needed to be done and there was something about his new DS that told him she would do a good job. The fact that it would also keep her out of his way was an added bonus.

He knocked on the door next to 87, waited until a Japanese man peered out. He ran through his spiel, flashed Grace's photo, got bemused head shakes and polite rebuttals. Another door closed, nothing out of place or suspicious, another name ticked off. He'd already detailed some uniforms to do this but he knew he wouldn't be totally satisfied unless he did it himself.

He spent the next two hours in a repetition of knocking,

asking, thanking, leaving. The tenants were on their way to late shifts or in the middle of changing a baby's nappy, or doing the laundry, the washing-up, the day's crossword. They scrunched up their faces at the interruption, glanced cursorily at the photo, shook their heads and went back to their lives. He passed through cramped flats smelling of disappointment and loss, through lives lived in small boxes, piled atop each other, work and sleep the only two certainties. No one was interested in why the police were asking about this one girl. Branch had expressly forbidden them to mention that she'd been murdered, knowing how soon this would leak to the press. But with only a photo no one cared, no one thought twice about saying no. There was still a sanctity about murder; people who usually wouldn't say a word to the police offered up all kinds of evidence and rumour. No one cared if the girl next door was a prostitute or drug dealer but if she'd been murdered then they could be next.

He reached the last flat on Grace's floor and pressed the buzzer. It was sticky with something, like most of the buzzers, and he wiped his hand on his trousers, thinking of the coffee and cheeseburger he was going to have when this was finished, diet be damned. He could hear the buzzer ringing inside the flat, competing with the sound of relatives arguing, washing machines spinning, TVs blaring and kids screaming. It didn't surprise him that most of the residents didn't welcome the knock on the door. Bayswater had always been a place for immigrants fleeing religious persecution, revolution and dictatorship. They took the last of their savings and bought a one-bedroom flat, somewhere they could lock the door, not answer the bell. Huguenots in Paddington and Romanovs in Queensway. Now there was a new breed fleeing civil wars and uprisings across Africa and the Middle East. They lived lives of quiet solitude, sequestered in their flats, not really part of the city, occasionally meeting in émigré groups, rehashing old tales, their eyes always fixed on the door. He wondered if their lives were really better here—safer, yes, but cut off from their own history and culture they seemed to wither like plucked flowers.

The door opened slowly, a centimetre at a time, and a middle-aged woman with straggly grey hair peered at him through the crack. 'I'm not buying anything.'

He tried for his best smile. 'That's all right, I'm not selling anything.'

This seemed to throw her; she stood there looking him up and down, clucking to herself and shaking her head.

'If I could take a minute of your time, please?' He showed her his warrant card.

'You here about the noise?' she said, letting the door open a further few inches. Carrigan squeezed himself through. 'I've been to the porter but he's always drinking, doesn't care about us tenants.' She stood so close to Carrigan that he could feel the heat of her breath on his neck.

'I'll make a note to speak to him,' he said, looking around the room. There were photos of the last Shah of Iran on three of the four walls. The same photo, different frames, the glass polished and immaculate. The room was neat and ordered, so different from most of the flats he'd seen. Rugs covered the wooden floor, ornaments hung from the bookshelves and windows, pictures of two boys—running on a beach, practising football, play-fighting with one another—were spread across the white mantelpiece. 'Your sons?' he said, attempting small talk, but when he saw the expression on the woman's face he immediately regretted it.

She looked at the photos as if seeing them anew, then shook her head. 'Once upon a time,' she replied, her English lilting and accented but strangely beautiful. 'They disappeared ten years ago in Tehran.' She stated this as if she was telling him which university they'd gone to, her voice resigned to whatever ten years of not knowing eventually left you with. He thought of his best friend Ben and his two daughters, the constant grief and worry, nights spent up waiting for them to come back home, and he was glad he didn't have children; there was too much danger out in the world and there was too much awareness of that danger.

'I'm sorry,' he said.

The woman shrugged and offered him tea. He accepted, letting her gather herself together. She came back out of the kitchen with a large brass jug and two clear glasses. The tea looked like molten honey as she poured it from the jug, high above the glass, letting the liquid cool on its way down. It tasted both sweet and bitter in his mouth and he felt the caffeine kick in instantly. He took out the photo and passed it to her. 'Do you recognise this girl?'

The woman looked at it, nodding to herself and taking a tiny sip of tea. 'She lives down the corridor, yes. I saw her in the lift many times. What has she done?'

He looked over at the photo of the woman's kids, thought about the last nine doors he'd knocked on. He was tired of playing Branch's game. They'd get nowhere if people thought they were after Grace for drugs or prostitution. 'She was murdered in her flat on Sunday night.'

The woman's head snapped up and she dropped the photo onto the table as if it were infected. She put a hand to her mouth but nothing came out.

'We're trying to find out if anyone saw or heard anything.'

'She was a good girl?'

The question surprised Carrigan. He nodded. 'From what we know, yes, she was.'

The woman picked up the photo again, nodding to herself as she stared into Grace's eyes. 'Her boyfriend was the troublemaker.'

Carrigan felt the tingle at the edge of his fingers, tried to keep his voice steady. 'Why do you say that, Mrs. . . . ?'

'Najafi, Golshan Najafi.' The woman put down the photo. 'Always arguing, those two, you could hear it all the way across here. The boyfriend he liked to shout. The girl not so much.'

'You heard these arguments?' Carrigan moved forward in his seat so quickly he unsettled the tiny glass, sending tea spilling across the table.

She picked up a cloth and started mopping up the spill. 'Not the words, you can't make those out, but the shouting yes, arguing all the time.'

'How can you be sure it was her?'

Mrs. Najafi clucked to herself as if the answer was obvious. 'I stepped outside to tell them to be quiet. I saw this girl and the boyfriend. She always apologised, he just stared at me, those eyes, I felt like I'd been . . .' She looked down at the folds of her dress.

'What did he look like?' Carrigan's fingers were trying to keep up with the information, the squiggles and crossings in his notebook coming fast.

'They all look the same to me. Young. Those eyes, like I said.' Carrigan coughed, wrote something down. 'Black, white . . . ?'

'Black.'

'How young?'

'Maybe in his early twenties, it's hard to tell. He wore a dark suit. Always with the fancy suits, that one. I knew he was wrong, a man who does not know how to behave with a woman.'

Carrigan's clothes were heavy with sweat, the room seemed to be superheated, the windows all sealed with what looked like clingfilm. 'When was the last time you saw him?'

She poured another glass of tea for Carrigan. 'Sunday night. That's why I remembered. When you said that.'

He burned himself taking a long sip of the tea, kept his mouth closed and bit down on the pain. 'Tell me what you heard, Mrs. Najafi.'

'The usual shouting. I just turned the TV louder, then the shouting seemed closer. I opened my door and that man, her boyfriend, was outside the girl's door banging his fists against it. He was shouting her name, making threats. I closed the door before he could see me.'

'Did you hear what kind of threats?'

'He said she was a whore. Called her that several times. He demanded that she open the door.'

'Did she?'

The woman shook her head. 'I would have heard.'

'What time was this?'

She bent down, picked up a TV guide and flicked through the pages. 'About six in the evening. *Come Dine With Me* was on. I remember watching the first half, then the shouting started.'

'How long did it last?'

'He was out there for about ten minutes, then I heard the lift go. He shouted one last thing, this time he was closer to my door so I heard every word. He said *You will pay for tonight.*'

The sun was still out as Carrigan finished the last of his espresso, letting the thick liquid roll around his mouth before swallowing. It was almost perfect, bitter yet sweet, thick and full-bodied, the crema lasting till the last sip. He crunched down on a biscotti, sending crumbs scattering all over his jacket, promising himself the diet would start tomorrow. He wiped his mouth, checked his watch and was about to enter St. Joseph's when he noticed something. Too much coffee? Maybe.

A man was standing on the other side of the road staring at him. Carrigan was certain he'd seen him earlier, outside King's Court. He blinked and when he opened his eyes the man was gone.

The inside of St. Joseph's church was a strange mixture of

smells: incense, sweat and detergent. There were two people kneeling at pews, mouthing silent prayers. The coffee felt good rushing inside him, the last two hours all piling up to that last piece of information. Grace had a boyfriend. They fought often. He was heard banging on her door and making threats the night she was killed.

The priest confirmed George Monroe's alibi. He was a thick-set Polish man, in his late sixties, with a face that seemed to have marked every travail in his life. He sighed and coughed as Carrigan spoke to him, said that Monroe attended Mass almost every night, was one of the few regulars. 'You don't ask where a man has come from when you know where he's going,' he added.

Carrigan thanked him and took a seat. He felt the peace that always settled on him in a church, the deep quiet and vaulted ceilings, the hum of liturgy, the tight concentration of the congregation. He'd never worshipped as a child, his parents doing everything to pretend they were modern-day English progressives and not the newly arrived Irish immigrants they really were. He remembered the arguments, his mother always saying it would be good if he went and then his father, the heavy brogue unaffected by his years abroad, browbeating her with words like 'superstition', 'magic', 'poppycock', explaining that this was why they'd left the old country, to get away from all this and the violence and grief it brought.

He sat in a pew near the back, going over the few leads they had, as people began wandering in for the evening Mass. He saw women and men, kids dragging reluctantly from their arms, workers and schoolboys, a traffic warden and two younger girls in McDonald's outfits.

The service was in Polish that night, the thick-set priest intoning strange conglomerations of consonants and vowels between racking coughs. Everybody but Carrigan had their heads down, kneeling, totally immersed in the moment. He sat back and listened, not understanding a word, enjoying it all the more so because of that, the dark mystery of the liturgy, its meaning only revealed in timbre and resonance. He closed his eyes and waited for something to happen.

9

Carrigan had told her to take the evening off, come back fresh in the morning and go through Grace's belongings then. The last thing Geneva wanted was time off. She didn't want to go back to her flat, to her mother's messages on the answering machine, the empty fridge and stacked boxes crowding the floor. This was the perfect way to avoid her life. She understood this was not going to be like other police work; this wasn't something you could leave at the station, forget for twelve or so hours, then pick up again. This would be everything until it was solved—and if it wasn't—well, she didn't want to think about that.

She stuck her head into the incident room, the flickering fluorescents and glare of computer monitors making her squint. Karlson was on the phone, his face scrunched up in intense concentration as he ordered curries for the constables working through the night. She sidled past Berman, tried to catch his eye, but he was hunched into his wall of monitors, his fingers playing the keyboard with such speed and dexterity he could have been a concert pianist.

'Singh, you free?'

DC Singh was suddenly engrossed in her monitor when a minute ago she'd been chatting with Jennings. She said something about following up certain leads but when she saw the look on Geneva's face she frowned, flicked her hair back, and got up. They walked down the long empty corridor, out of the green gauze and into the sudden sunglare of the main building.

It struck Geneva how peaceful the new extension was compared to the bustle of the main station, public streaming in and out, faces wracked with worry, uniforms crowding around the coffee machine, support officers standing around looking lost. The desk sergeant snorted when Geneva explained what she was here for, mumbled a room number and went back to his copy of the *Sun*.

'They don't like it that we're in the new wing,' Singh said as they surveyed Grace's belongings, smudged and tarried by fingerprint powder, stashed in two brown boxes with a long string of numbers printed on each.

Geneva stared at the young constable, her raven black hair and green eyes making her look a most unlikely candidate for the Met. Singh kept checking her watch and smiling to herself as if she'd just heard a piece of good news but was told to keep it secret. 'You mean they don't like Carrigan.'

DC Singh looked up, thought about it, and nodded. 'Never have, the uniforms. There's something about him just doesn't spell copper to them.'

They picked up the boxes. 'And you?' Geneva said. 'What's your opinion?'

Singh brushed her hair behind her ear. 'He's better than some I've worked with.'

Geneva noted the tact in the statement. 'But . . . '

They were now back in the new wing and Singh's voice sounded unnaturally loud as it echoed through the empty corridor. 'You know those dogs that hang on no matter what? You admire them but at the same time you don't want to get anywhere near them?' She gave Geneva a lopsided smile. 'Frankly, they're all weird in one way or another. What being boss does to you, I guess.'

Singh kept smiling inanely—Geneva couldn't tell if it was because of what she'd said or something else but it was starting to get to her, this constant jollity in the midst of what they were doing.

They entered the incident room, now smelling of curry and milky tea. Geneva took one look, sniffed, and directed Singh to take the material to one of the smaller offices situated round the back.

'You worked with Carrigan a long time?'

Singh put down the box and straightened her blouse. 'Nearly a year now. Why?'

Geneva looked down at the table, avoiding the DC's eyes. 'Just trying to get a sense of what I've come into.' She stared at her hands, noticing the small red marks that had appeared overnight, a sure sign of stress, and wondered if her curiosity was because she really wanted to know or because she had a report due for Branch. She scratched her red patch.

Singh gave her a strange look, part sympathy, part something else—Geneva couldn't tell. 'I'm sure you've heard the stories.'

Geneva had—some anyway, and what Branch had told her, couched in innuendo and knowing looks. 'Enlighten me.'

Singh glanced at her watch. 'You've seen the scar on his arm?'

Geneva nodded, opened the first box and started taking out Grace's belongings, carefully laying them on the table in front of her.

'Got it on 7/7,' Singh replied. 'Apparently he was one of the first officers down on the platforms. He was a DI out of Paddington Green at the time, opposite Edgware Road, where the bomb went off. A colleague of mine was working under him then, said as soon as they heard the bang Carrigan was out of the office, not a word to anyone. Some PCs saw him disappear down into the station but it was all smoke and noise and no one knew what was happening yet.'

Despite herself, Geneva was fascinated. She stared down at Grace's belongings and tried to keep her face neutral and disinterested.

'Disappeared for over four hours,' Singh continued. 'They

thought they'd lost him but, you know, it was so crazy that day, no one knew what the hell we were supposed to do. Anyway, some five hours later, Carrigan comes out of the smoke and rubble, he's covered in soot, bleeding from a large gash in his arm and he's got this small terrier in his hands.'

Geneva's head sprang up. 'He saved a dog?'

Singh nodded, and then they both started laughing, hard and uncontrollably, the stress of the past twenty-four hours easing if only for a moment. 'A Yorkie,' Singh added, gripping her sides, trying not to laugh any harder. 'You can imagine the welcome he got at the station that evening. They called him the Dog Whisperer for about a year. You know what the lads are like.'

Geneva had stopped the pretence of looking through Grace's things, utterly enthralled by this unexpected glimpse into another side of Carrigan. 'Did he explain what he'd been doing?'

Singh had just about managed to stop laughing. 'No. Wouldn't tell the chief what happened but my colleague saw him when he came back from Edgware Road and said there was too much blood on him for it to be just his own or the dog's.' She looked up, shook her head. 'But the weirdest rumour I ever heard about him was that he used to be in some indie band.' She checked her watch again as she placed the last bundle of paper on the desk, a huge grin appearing on her face and then just as quickly disappearing.

'What are you so happy about?' Geneva finally snapped, wishing she could take it back, surprised by the tone of her own voice.

DC Singh looked down, hiding behind the thick curtain of her hair. 'I'm meeting my fiancé for dinner,' she replied hesitantly. 'We're getting married next week. I'm just . . . I'm so excited. I know I shouldn't be with this case and all, but I can't help it.' She flashed her ring, the diamond cut small and fine against its setting. 'You with someone?'

Geneva shook her head, she didn't want to get into that right now, and looked down at the table, the circular stains of coffee cups and food smears, trying not to think about her own flat, the empty rooms and unmade bed, the messages stacking up on her machine. She felt bad for the ungenerous thoughts she'd had about Singh. 'So, what do we call you when you get married?'

'Singh,' the young woman laughed. 'Lucky thing about being a Sikh, I guess, you don't have to change your name.'

Geneva smiled. 'You better go.'

Singh shook her head. 'It'll take you ages to go through this alone. I can text him.'

Geneva quietly placed her hand on Singh's. 'It's fine,' she said. 'You shouldn't let work fuck up your personal life.'

DC Singh thanked her. 'I hate doing this part,' she said as she pulled on her jacket. 'Don't let Grace become real,' she warned. 'It's much easier that way.'

Geneva nodded and watched as Singh, flushed and bright with love and the prospect of a late-evening rendezvous, left the room. Suddenly it was quiet, she was alone again, and the weight of the case slumped back down on her like something physical and there was nothing left to do but sink into these objects, try to trace an outline of Grace from the things she'd left behind.

Preliminary reports from the constables, a photocopy of the pathologist's verdict, an inventory, and next to her feet, two brown boxes containing anything from Grace Okello's flat deemed worthy of a second look. Tomorrow she needed to brief Carrigan on how far she'd got.

Tomorrow she would need answers but tonight she wasn't even sure which questions she was supposed to be asking.

The SOCOs had finished their 'walking' of the room, the slow painstaking centimetre-by-centimetre trawl through fibres, fabrics, spills and invisible stains. Their report was due tomorrow. She would have to wait and see how much of himself the killer had left. What she had in front of her was two days' worth of quotidian police work. Routine calls and enquiries. Hastily written reports at the end of a shift. Most policemen found this material boring, unlikely to give up its secrets, but she knew it was in here somewhere—the thing that elides your eye the first few times catches it like a loose nail the seventh.

She scanned and reread. She made notes in a fresh notebook, drew up timelines and lists of questions. She went through Carrigan's first-on-the-scene report, impressed by his concise use of language, so refreshing after the vague and rambling summaries of the uniforms. She scrutinised the text, forcing it to give up its meanings. This was what her mother had taught her to do. This was her childhood, squeezed into small rooms, always moving from one to the next, evenings next to her mother, scanning dense passages of Modernist poetry.

'You have to learn to read closely,' she remembered her mother saying, and she, maybe twelve or thirteen at the time, leaning forward, pressing her face up against the pages until her mother laughed. That carefree but shadowed laugh that could only have come from eastern Europe. Saying, 'No, dear. Not like that.' Her words both a kindness and a criticism. Evenings when she should have been watching stupid TV shows with her friends. Weekends she should have been out playing. The whole free time of her childhood pressganged into tiny rooms, books with pages coming loose, the print old and degraded, thumbprints of previous readers left like discarded secrets at the edges. 'Read the sentence and then read it again. Interrogate it.' She could still hear her mother's accent, that curious Czech enunciation mixing with thirty years of North London. 'Ask it what it means. Don't go on to the next sentence until you've turned the last one inside out. A page of poetry should take hours to read.'

She picked up a report from DC Berman, who'd gone through the building's CCTV tapes. He'd watched hours of footage, from the day of the murder and two days before. Faces going in, backs going out, the diastolic rhythm of everyday life.

Grace Okello entered her building at 5.24 on Sunday evening. She would be dead less than six hours later. Was there anything in her face as the camera caught its swift entrance that showed she knew? That evinced fear or apprehension or even the excitement of waiting for a boyfriend to come over? Berman hadn't noted. He described what she wore, the time, and anyone who entered five minutes to either side of her. The problem was, they didn't know what they were looking for. No one yet knew what they were hunting. Berman had noted anyone who seemed suspicious, who looked up at the camera on entering or left in a hurry during the timeframe of the murder. He'd printed off a few blurry stills but the closer she looked the more the images disintegrated into discrete dots like one of those French Sunday picnic paintings at the National Gallery. She would have to watch the CCTV footage for herself. The DC had done his job but it was always worth doing it twice.

The statement from the porter was equally thin and blurry. Jennings had noted that he was a long-term drunk, halfway into some savage bender, reeking of whisky and almost incoherent. The porter said Grace seemed a quiet girl, sometimes brought friends round, but there were no complaints and he'd never had to knock on her door and tell her to keep it down. He said most of the tenants were animals and so the ones who kept quiet stuck out. She put the statement to one side, a steadily growing pile of leads she wanted to go through again, and moved on to the list of items found in Grace's flat.

It was sad what constituted a life. Sad that when all else was gone these pathetic remnants should sum up an entire span on this earth. Our belongings tie us to the world but they remain after we're gone, mute witnesses. Things take on significance out of context. She knew this was why Carrigan had blown up the shots of Grace's wounds and pinned them to the wall. Repeat something often enough and sometimes, eventually, a gravel of truth will slip out.

She bent down and unpacked the next box, trying not to think about the boxes in her flat, and removed a stack of papers and books. Carrigan had asked her to take a cursory look at Grace's university stuff, the usual shaking out of pages and scanning for underlinings or torn diary entries hiding beneath the covers. She wasn't sure if he was sidelining her or not. This was a pointless task: the chances of finding anything among Grace's personal belongings were slim. She remembered Branch's comments, that she had a report to hand in to him in two days' time. Her head began to ache.

She unpacked the rest of the boxes. She took out books and photocopied sheets, graphs and maps. She spread them on the table, separated them into groups and started with the books that had been on Grace's bookshelf.

Books about torture and politics. Books about the psychology of pain and military interrogation manuals. A book on Nazi doctors, another on the Pinochet regime, one on SAVAK, the Shah of Iran's secret police force. Several books on Ugandan history, Idi Amin taking precedence. Other books on Equatorial Guinea and Libya, possibly samizdat, printed on cheap material, falling apart, the print fading, the books all buckled as if imitating the flow of water. There were no works of fiction, nothing for entertainment or leisure. There were Amnesty International reports, photocopied hastily and randomly collected in a binder. Graphs whose abstract delineations crazed her vision. She shook the books out, riffled through the pages looking for cryptic notes or hidden messages, but nothing more was revealed. She made a note to request the books for further perusal.

Apart from books and clothes there was little else. She ticked off all the things present on the landlord's inventory, noting nothing missing or cracked or broken. This left her with copies of the *Guardian*, the *Economist,* the *Daily Monitor* and *East Africa Today*. A handbag containing lipstick and powder, an Oyster card, a Ugandan passport, a packet of Silk Cut and a mobile phone. She made a note to requisition the Oyster card, surprised that the DCs had been so sloppy. If it was a registered card she would be able to trace Grace's movements over the last few weeks from this one small piece of plastic.

The mobile phone had been scanned and the address book copied and printed onto a sheet of paper. She stared at the names, some only initials, amazed at how few people were in Grace's list of contacts. Did she really have this few friends or could she remember the important phone numbers in her head? She made a note to find out how long Grace had owned this phone and to see whether any of the call logs could be traced. There was nothing obvious in the names, no 'Mum' or 'Dad', or anything else signifying family. One of the DCs would have to spend a long morning glued to the phone.

She unpacked the last box, the one she'd been dreading. It contained all of Grace's dissertation work. There were hundreds of printouts from the internet. Pages of hastily scrawled notes. Photocopies of journal articles annotated and marked. She scanned through some of these, dense theoretical arguments for the use of violence, dense theoretical arguments against it. One sheaf, almost a hundred pages long, seemed to consist of nothing but names and numbers, the names all African, the numbers seemingly random as if picked from a lottery card. There were pages of graphs, economic analyses, the glyphs and scribbles like some arcane language she couldn't decipher. Over twenty or thirty badly printed pamphlets, Marxist rhetoric in bold caps and exclamation marks. Several were heavily underlined, the name Black-Throated

Wind appearing in gothic type on their covers. There was something about the phrase that made her quickly put the pamphlets to one side. She stared at the image emblazoned on their covers: a heart free of its body, suspended in space, dripping thin red strings of blood.

Underneath was a stack of identical flyers for something called the African Action Committee. She remembered Cummings mentioning that Grace had joined an African society in her first year. Geneva looked down at the flyers, basic Photoshopped headlines and a crossed-through silhouette of a black man carrying a machine gun. She scanned the tiny print, saw that the flyer was for a weekly Thursday night meeting in Hackney and remembered Cummings saying that Grace had stopped going after her first year. Geneva took the flyer and put it to one side. She looked away from the table and out through the green mesh. London was darkening outside her window, she could hear buses and cars shuffling through the streets, the faint hum of a radio playing chart hits. She went back to her task, flicking through internet articles, pages from Wikipedia, the BBC News website, other news feeds, and then she realised.

She looked up from the pages and stared at the objects on her desk, confused.

She picked up the inventory and scanned it again, just in case she'd missed it the first time round. She got on her knees and went through the boxes, unpacking the books and papers, making sure she hadn't overlooked it. She glanced back at the table.

Grace was a student. Grace had printed all these pages out. So why hadn't they found a computer anywhere in Grace's flat?

10

The incident room, 6.30 P.M. Carrigan sat at his desk finishing off a packet of crisps. He rubbed his fingers on his cords and watched as Berman sat hunched over his computer screen, three other screens shielding him from the rest of the office, naked motherboards and strange boxes with wires surrounding his desk. Jennings was wolfing down a Big Mac, the smell instantly making Carrigan feel hungry again. Karlson was on the phone, his face shielded, his voice low, sweet talking some new conquest, no doubt.

Carrigan got up, saw that Geneva was late and Singh was missing, but started anyway. 'How are we doing with forensics?'

Jennings wiped his mouth, and quickly scanned through some notes. 'Still waiting for the DNA and other samples but they managed to get a fingerprint off the glass of milk left in the kitchen. Same fingerprint they found on the plastic ties that were used on Grace.'

Jennings smiled like an eager schoolboy trying to please his favourite teacher. Carrigan could tell he was giving him the good news first. 'But . . . ?'

Jennings hunched his shoulders, his eyes straying from Carrigan's. 'No hit on the PNC. Far as we can tell, the killer doesn't seem to have ever been arrested.'

'I was hoping we'd get something,' Carrigan said. 'Someone like this, it's hard to believe he's kept his nose clean.'

'Maybe he's just better than we are,' Karlson suggested.

'The fact he's not on the database might only mean he's been too clever so far.'

Carrigan looked up from his notes. 'Then why, all of a sudden, does he get so sloppy as to leave not one but two sets of fingerprints behind?'

Karlson's silence didn't make Carrigan feel any better. 'Jennings, fax the prints over to immigration, see if he's on any of their databases.' He thought of the man he'd seen outside King's Court not once, but twice now. 'Karlson, anything at SOAS?'

DS Karlson stopped jotting in his notepad, looked up. 'Not much of interest. I spoke to some of her classmates, got pretty much the same story from all of them.'

'Which was?' Carrigan hated the way Karlson always teased everything out, the secret pleasure he got from it as if it were the only thing that brightened his day.

'Everyone I spoke to agreed that Grace was a model student but none of them really seemed to know her. Studious, polite, but cold was the consensus. I asked about drugs and everyone seemed very surprised we would ask that concerning Grace. I didn't get the sense that anyone was covering up for her.'

'Good,' Carrigan replied. 'DS Miller should be here soon. She interviewed Grace's professor so let's see what she has to say.' He stared down at his notes, then back up at the room. He told them about questioning the tenants on Grace's floor, Golshan Najafi's description of the row Grace had had with her boyfriend on the night of the murder.

He heard low whistles and feet shuffling as the team assimilated this information. 'Did anyone mention anything about Grace having a boyfriend?'

Karlson shook his head. 'I did ask but no one seemed to know her outside of class.'

'Then we need to go back and reinterview them. The boyfriend is our main priority now.'

'Wouldn't you have been better used here than going round doing door-to-doors? It's a job for the uniforms.' There was a faint smile creeping across Karlson's face.

Carrigan snapped his head round. The suit the sergeant was wearing was shiny and looked to have been shrink-fitted to his physique. 'Are you telling me how to run this investigation?'

Karlson smiled thinly. 'No, just wondering if it was the best allocation of resources.'

Carrigan felt his lips tight against his gums, he forced a smile. 'You wondering about how I'm running this case is a waste of resources.'

The door crashed open and Geneva came in balancing a stack of papers and books in her hands. The tension in the room dissipated as everyone looked at her. 'Sorry, I'm late,' she said, dropping the bundle onto her desk, straightening her blouse and taking a seat.

'How did it go with the professor?'

She summed up what Cummings had said, more or less duplicating what Karlson found out from Grace's fellow students. 'Good work,' Carrigan replied, remembering the old newspaper reporter's maxim that every piece of information needed at least two corroborative sources. 'And how did Cummings strike you?'

Geneva checked her notes. 'I think he likes playing the role of the cool hippy professor on campus a bit too much but he was genuinely shocked when I told him she'd been killed. I didn't get any sense that he was hiding anything and his alibi checked out.' She took a deep breath, not sure how to go about this, terrified, here in this new team where everyone was looking at her, every-one immediately judging her, but she'd learned that keeping your mouth shut never endeared you to anyone and besides, there were more important things than her career at stake. 'He talked about her dissertation a bit and I had a look through some of her books and notes.' She paused, taking in the mood around her.

'And?' Carrigan said impatiently.

Well, here goes, she thought, back to being a constable again. 'The SOCOs didn't find a computer at Grace's flat but all her notes, everything, was printed out.'

No one said anything—Karlson was giving her a strange look but DC Berman's head had finally risen from his various screens. 'I think this is something we need to look at,' Geneva continued. 'She was dealing with some pretty serious political stuff in her dissertation. I'd like to follow up on that.'

Carrigan looked at her, still trying to understand what her role was, why Branch had seconded her. 'It doesn't make sense,' he finally replied. 'Why take her computer yet leave all her notes and books behind if it was about her work? They would have taken everything. Besides, the MO's too personal. We wouldn't be seeing such overkill if this was about her work. She probably just left it in her locker at SOAS. We need to concentrate our resources on finding the boyfriend. It's our only viable lead at this point,' he continued. 'He was seen arguing with Grace a few hours before her death; it's much more likely that this is something that got out of hand then some conspiracy against her.'

Geneva stared down at her notes, surprised by Carrigan's rebuke. This was the first time she'd seen him like this and she wondered if it was because of the case or something else—had he worked out why Branch had put her on his team? 'We should at least check whether she had an internet connection. It won't take that much time.'

'Sure.' He shrugged his shoulders as a peace offering but could see she wasn't accepting it, her lips pressing against one another like two thin pieces of wire. 'Jennings, I want you to keep hassling forensics, see if they can get that DNA sample analysed soon. Karlson, go back to the university, talk to her friends again, someone must have seen her with a boyfriend or heard her mention one, you know how students talk.' Karlson frowned and was about to say something but then changed his mind.

'Professor Cummings also mentioned a close friend,' Geneva interrupted. 'Cecilia Odamo, another Ugandan. He said she hadn't showed up to an important meeting she had scheduled with him on Monday morning and no one's seen her at SOAS since.'

'Shit,' Carrigan said, wondering if his words from yesterday were coming back to haunt him, if this really was the start of a series and not a one-off.

Carrigan went back to his desk, the sound of the other detectives on headsets, tapping away at keyboards, scratching down notes, surrounding him. He picked up the phone and got the number for the Ugandan embassy.

He got through on the first ring, a man with a rough-and-tumble accent answering breathlessly. Carrigan explained who he was and gave the man Grace's full name and passport number. 'Anything you can find about her parents, next of kin, would help us tremendously,' he added.

He could hear the young bureaucrat on the other end humming to himself and the distant hammering of fingers on a keyboard. 'Yes,' the man returned to the line. 'We have here . . . uh . . . Okay . . . please wait a minute.'

Carrigan was put on hold. He cradled the receiver to his ear, watched Geneva throwing a pile of notes and papers onto the floor, then sat up when the voice came back on the other end of the line.

Except this time it was a different voice, the man altogether older and with a much better command of English. 'DI Carrigan?'

'Yes?'

'I'm afraid we have nothing in our system concerning Ms. Okello.' The man's tone was smooth and urbane.

'But the person who answered the phone said he'd found . . . '

'Thank you for your enquiry, Mr. Carrigan, but I'm afraid we can't help you.'

The man hung up the phone before Carrigan could ask him any more questions. He stared at the lifeless receiver in his hand, the buzz of work around him. A strange feeling crept up his spine but he told himself it was nothing, just hearing that accent again, that was all.

He slurped the remainder of his drink, his stomach reeling, feet jittering, the memories swirling and sluicing through his brain like wild things unloosed. The thought of going back home filled him with dread, he didn't want to stare at the walls waiting for the day's adrenaline to wear off like some unexpected drug and so instead he called Ben.

They'd gone to university together, gone to Africa together, and now they met once a fortnight, discussed each other's lives and watched old TV shows. They weren't scheduled to meet for another couple of weeks, the yearly trudge down to the Dorset village where David was buried, but Carrigan didn't want to go home tonight, his head still ringing with the day, images of Grace flickering behind his eyes, the phone call to the Ugandan embassy fresh in his mind.

He got off the train at Turnham Green, walked past the fields where the blood-soaked Civil War battle had been fought, past the church where Van Gogh had preached his mad fiery sermons, and crossed the Great West Road. He turned into the narrow cobbled lane and walked through Chiswick Pier. It had been redeveloped during the last decade, erasing the park where he'd kissed his first girlfriend, the pub where he'd puked all over the landlord on his eighteenth birthday, the particular bend of the river he liked to sit by. They'd replaced them with faux-Georgian condos and security gates. Each development had a quaint name, as if it were some isolated Cornish village. Stoney Reach. Potter's Quay. Each condo had gates within gates, numbered fingerpads, scrolling cameras, signs that warned 'PRIVATE: KEEP OUT'. A sense of an encased, preserved Britain—but one which was entirely fake.

Ben's house was the first past the development, the old river residences butting up against the new. Jack unlatched the gate, knowing this was the kind of life he could have had if he'd made the right choices, if things had turned out differently.

He stared down at his shoes, noticing how the leather had torn and wilted from the tips, and pressed the buzzer. He brushed some crumbs from his jacket and beard. Dvořák rang out, faint and sickly sweet. Jack hoped it would be Ben who answered the door but instead it was Ursula.

Jack held his breath and met her eyes; something flickered then died like a match left too long in the wind. History flashed between them in that split-second, twenty-three years reeling down the decades to when he first laid eyes on her in his lecture class, her long black hair cascading down her shoulders, the way she entered a room, the sound of her voice.

They'd quickly become friends, discussing music theory, sharing cold drinks and warm chips. He'd been breathless the first time they spoke. All that term he'd been waiting for the right moment, knowing it was the hardest thing to negotiate from being friends to something more and how easy it was to end up losing both. She came from country-house dinner parties and foggy Sunday-morning hunts, beagles yapping at her ankles, a shotgun nestled in the crook of her arm. He came from Shepherd's Bush. He'd wanted her to meet his friends, not just another poor London Irish kid with dubious cohorts. It was obvious the first moment they locked eyes, her and Ben, and there was nothing Jack could do about it but step back and force his desire down to where it could be kept locked and bolted. And it had worked for a long time. It was only recently that he'd started thinking about Ursula in that way again. He knew it was more to do with nostalgia than lust. For all the span of his marriage to Louise and those dark years after her death he saw Ursula only as Ben's wife. But now something had changed, an imperceptible shift, the revoked past snapping at his heels every time he pressed the buzzer.

'Good to see you, Jack,' she smiled, holding the door open for him, her teeth white and perfect in that soft mysterious mouth of hers. He nodded, saw her eyes drift down to his midriff, the overhanging belly and crumpled clothes, thought he detected a note of pity in her expression and shuffled past her, through the elegant hallway bedecked with hunting scenes and into the river room.

Every time it got him. Every time he was taken aback by the sheer sense of space in the room as it tapered into a wall made entirely out of glass behind which the river glistened like molten metal.

The afternoon sun sliced through and illuminated Ben, crouched in his favourite armchair, a pair of headphones clamped to his head. Jack stopped at the threshold, not quite ready yet. It was a place he knew as well as anywhere and yet he'd never felt comfortable here. These days he preferred small rooms, dark garrets and subdivided office spaces, places where the world was contained without.

Ben jerked up when he saw Jack, catching the headphone cord on the side of the chair, apologising and awkwardly extricating himself from the spaghetti tangle of leads.

'Hey.' Jack took off his jacket and sat in the chair opposite Ben. The fabric settled and moulded itself around him; over the years it had taken on his shape, changed as his body had, accommodating the middle-age spread around his waist, the years of too many coffees heavy with sugar.

'I'm really glad you called.' Ben's smile was the first thing everybody noticed about him. The gleaming white teeth. The way his eyes crinkled. It was the smile that had made him a regular on early evening TV, always in a white suit, his eyes blue as azure. He'd started by making documentaries about civil war and genocide and then a one-off special about the origins of man had led to his own show, *The Risen Beast*, a mix of erudite anthropology and narrative history that had proved wildly popular.

'Sorry if Ursula was a bit snappy,' Ben apologised while pouring the drinks. 'She's pissed off at me. We were supposed to be seeing some friends of hers for an awfully tedious dinner party in bloody Greenwich of all places.' Ben laughed and Jack remembered not just the smile and charm but the laugh too; even in their darkest moments that laugh could be guaranteed to lift them. It was working now and the day began to slough off with the first drink like the rain trickling from the folds of his jacket.

'I can go if it's a bad time.'

Ben shrugged. 'Your phone call saved me, don't you dare leave!'

They both laughed. They settled down into patterns. They settled down into routine. Repetition comforted them in this room that hadn't changed over ten years, belying the fact that they had. They fell into small talk, into catch-up and miscellaneous chatter as old friends do, picking up conversations from last week, last year, a lifetime ago. Jack felt the whisky diminishing the din of the day, the languorous rhythm of their conversation dragging him back into the world.

'So you're off next week?' Jack said. 'Finally got your chance to teach at Berkeley.'

Ben's face gleamed. 'You know how long I've been waiting for this.'

Carrigan smiled. 'Good for you.'

'How's your mum doing?'

Jack rubbed his head, saw real concern in his friend's eyes. 'I was supposed to visit her today but this fucking case . . . last time I visited her she didn't even recognise me. Kept shouting to the nurses that someone had broken into her room.' He didn't need to say more—you reached a certain age and these conversations were always hovering in the air, a kind of heavy weather everyone ignored until it was too late.

'I'm sorry.' Ben set his glass down on the table, uncrossed his legs and leant forward. 'Are you sure you're okay?' His wiry frame seemed to take in all the space around him, gangly arms and legs extruding at impossible angles like some altarpiece Jesus. 'You look beat.'

Jack took a deep breath and gave him a brief summary of the case.

'You telling me you want an easy one?' Ben replied when Jack was finished. 'The husband who stabs his wife and sits there crying at the dinner table with the knife still in his hands when you guys show up type? Come on, Jack, you'd go up the wall if the case didn't have some nasty shit attached to it.'

Carrigan conceded the point. It was always like this, as if Ben knew the things that Jack hid from himself. 'It's not that. It's not the blood, the senselessness, all the official departmental shit that goes with it. It's none of that.' He drained his drink and put it down a little too heavily on the table.

Ben winced. 'What, then?' he asked, his voice a tad uncertain.

Jack picked up the bottle and poured himself a half-glass measure then took a large gulp. The whisky burned going down and it was a good feeling, pain well earned and deserved. 'It's Africa.'

Ben was about to say something but didn't. He took a sip of his drink instead and sat back on the chair. 'The girl,' he finally said. 'The girl you were just telling me about was African, right?'

Jack nodded. 'Ugandan.'

Ben's eyes widened. 'This can't be the first time Uganda's come up in a case?'

Jack shook his head, too many to recount, every one taking him back to that week twenty years ago when he and Ben and David were still young, their eyes blazing with the future they were going to write upon the world. He looked down into the dark swirl of his drink. 'More and more these days.'

'So why's this one upset you so?'

Jack considered this—it was more a feeling, something he hadn't put into words even in his own mind. 'I don't know. Maybe because it's the first Ugandan murder I've dealt with. It's . . . I don't know . . . the brutality of it, the sheer fucking waste.'

'You're just getting older,' Ben smiled, reaching for his glass. 'We both are. It's natural to get like this when you see it day to day.'

Ben was right but he knew it wasn't as simple as that. 'She was writing her dissertation about Kony and the LRA.'

Ben let out a long whistle of air. 'And you think that's connected to her murder?'

'No,' Jack replied emphatically, 'but my new partner thinks it's something we should be looking into.'

Ben's smile softened his sun-creased features. 'Since when do you have a partner?'

'Got foisted on me by upstairs.'

'What's he like?'

Jack thought about Geneva, the way she seemed to be anywhere else but where she was, her wild hair and white earphones. 'Her name's Geneva and she's good, surprisingly. Sharp and perceptive, more so than most of my regulars.' He looked out at the grey sky. 'But I suspect Branch sent her to spy on me.'

Ben laughed, 'You're joking?'

Jack hunched his shoulders. 'He must be desperate if he's sending rookies. Trouble is, I don't know if she's working to some agenda Branch cooked up or not.' He thought of the deep concentration in Geneva's eyes at the morgue, the trenchant questions she'd asked.

'Pretty?'

Jack smiled. 'It's work, Ben,' but the answer was clear across his face. 'Anyway, going back to the case—I'm pretty convinced it's a sex killing,' he continued. 'Raped and tortured her, classic predator stuff. The chances are pretty slim that this has got anything to do with Africa, with her politics or the dissertation she was writing. But the trouble is I don't know what Geneva's motives are, whether Branch is checking up on me, so I can't rule it out either.'

'Of course, Jack Carrigan never rules anything out; local police motto, isn't it?'

Jack managed a smile. 'Only thing is I called the Ugandan embassy earlier, trying to see if they had information about Grace. The first guy I spoke to was friendly and it sounded like he'd found something but then someone else came on the line, spoke better English so he must have been a superior, told me they had nothing and hung up. You'd think they'd be happy to help us.'

Ben set his glass down. 'Don't worry, that's just how they are, as if secrecy was the natural order of things. You should have seen the bureaucracy and crap I've had to put up with when we're filming the show. And, of course, over the phone you can't offer a sweetener.'

Carrigan reached down into his briefcase and pulled out a thick spiral-bound file. Inside was a copy of Grace's dissertation. 'I flicked through it, didn't make any sense to me at all.' He passed it across the table. 'You know this area better than me; I was hoping you'd have a quick look if you had the time. Tell me if there's anything worth chasing up.'

Ben took the file, flicked through it quickly then laid it flat on the table. 'Of course.'

Jack took another sip of his drink. 'You ever think about it?' It came out before he had a chance to stop himself. There was no need for him to explain what he meant by 'it'. This was uncharted territory. This was everything they'd edged around for the last ten years in these weekly get-togethers. This was the unspoken pact that allowed them to meet at all. We don't talk about those days. We don't talk about Africa.

After they came back they didn't speak at all. Not for years until Ben made the first move, calling Jack and inviting him to be his best man. Ben had never known about Jack's infatuation with Ursula. Jack had stood smiling as the happy couple kissed and a few months after that they began meeting for drinks and through ten years of haze and life they managed to talk about everything else but Africa. They slipped into their old routines and rhythms as if no time had passed. Except, Jack thought, however much their relationship seemed to be the same, it wasn't. Africa or Ursula or the intervening years, he couldn't say which, had formed an invisible barrier between them, a thin line which they never crossed.

'I think about it all the time,' Ben said. No rebuke for bringing the subject up, no digression or equivocation. 'But mainly I think about him.' Ben's face drifted to the framed photograph of David sitting prominently at the head of his table.

'I try not to,' Jack replied, avoiding the photo the way he always did. 'But that never works, does it?'

The atmosphere in the room had subtly changed. A silence almost waiting to be filled with words neither of them wanted to hear. A misty look as their memories screened images from long ago: a burning laterite road, the stench of diesel and overheating engine oil, the perfume of palm fronds and cordite, the sound of breaking branches.

'I often wonder where I'd be now if we hadn't taken that trip,' Jack continued, saying aloud for the first time the mantra that ran through his head every day, on the way to the bus, brushing his teeth, staring up at the ceiling when sleep had escaped for another night.

'You'd be a famous pop star and I'd be just another over-worked barrister.' Ben tried to make it into a joke but they both knew it was as far from that as could possibly be.

Jack looked past Ben at a photo of the girls, Susan and Penny. There were photos of them all over the house, as if Ben and Ursula needed constant reminders of what their lives were for—even here in Ben's study the bookcase was entirely given over to glossy shots drenched in sunshine and smiles. He thought of his own flat, the clean white walls, the single framed print—he'd taken all the photos down two years ago. In a corner of the attic there were four photo albums he couldn't bring himself to look at any more, each image of him and Louise now become a lie.

'We made a decision,' Ben finally said. 'What's the point of pretending we didn't? It shaped our lives, yes, but any other lives are inconceivable. If it wasn't that road it would have been another.'

He'd rarely seen Ben this emotional but he knew how the past could come crashing up against the substrate of your consciousness like some unstoppable thing and that once it did, everything was changed. 'You believe our lives are predestined?'

Ben lit a cigar, sucked in the smoke, rolling it around his mouth like a taste of fine wine. 'I always thought you should have been a theologian not a policeman, though I'm sure you'd say they were one and the same.' He held the cigar in front of him, watching the burning end flare in the darkened room. 'But no, I don't believe that. I think we have choices but the more choices we make the less choices we have left. Our lives whittle down their own paths. Would other things have happened if we hadn't taken that trip? Yes. Would they have left us here? Well, that depends if you think personality is more forceful than circumstance. Maybe something else would have driven you to joining the Met, maybe you'd be playing Hammersmith Odeon this weekend. I don't think we can know, I don't think we can even guess. This God of yours that you so long to believe in, I'm not sure even He knows which way our actions will lead us. We are where we are and who we are, none of this is changeable.'

11

Geneva followed Carrigan across the street, through another narrow alley and into a covered market. She watched as he scanned the scene in front of them. She put her hand up against her face to shield the glare. Brightly coloured stalls selling a multitude of phone cards to countries she didn't even know existed. Butcher shops with mysterious cuts hanging in their windows or dangling from hooks under the awning. The red explosion of flesh, white strings of fat, the marbled gloss of meat and halo of flies. The smell was different too, no longer the London she knew but something more exotic, a certain allure in the strange scents and muffled yelling in garbled languages. But Carrigan just shook his head and she followed him back into the high street, the long unremitting row of boarded-up shops and shops that looked boarded up but was in fact just the way they did business.

She checked her watch, hoping he'd get the hint. They were already fifteen minutes late for their meeting with Cecilia Odamo. Geneva had got the girl's phone number from SOAS, called early and arranged an interview.

'Can't you just get coffee here?' She pointed to an old greasy spoon, its windows fogged by steam, the badly scrawled menu almost unreadable.

He snorted as if that were answer enough and before she could voice her concern, tell him this interview was more important than his damn coffee, he was off again and she had little choice but to follow.

She remembered what Superintendent Branch had said. His concerns. The complaints from both inside the Met and outside. She'd never done anything like this before, worked both sides of the fence, and it left her feeling curiously enervated. She thought of her mother, how horrified she'd be, but her mother didn't know what it meant to be a female police officer. The extra hoops and ladders, so hard to find, so easy to fall back down. No, her mother wouldn't understand. But did she? As she followed Carrigan across another winding street she wasn't sure she knew the answer any more.

And then she saw him stop, stand still, his head cocked towards a small, precariously leaning stall. A broad grin spread across his face and it so softened his appearance that all at once she was ready to forgive him for all this stress and wasted time.

'Was it really worth the hassle?' she asked, sipping the hot thick liquid, refusing to admit that it was pretty damn good.

Carrigan seemed to laugh, except he wasn't really laughing. 'This is the best part of my day,' he replied, staring at her as if trying to ascertain something. 'These in-between moments . . . we've forgotten how to enjoy them—we pretend they don't matter when they do.' He took another sip and continued. 'I used to always wait for things to get better, tell myself I'd start enjoying life then, but things never really get better, they only get worse. So all we're left with are moments . . . fragments . . .' He suddenly looked lost, as if searching for something just outside his field of vision. She hadn't expected this nor the sudden passion that animated his face and for a brief moment she saw the man he used to be before all the bodies and blood.

He finished his coffee and pulled out a sheaf of newspapers he'd bought at the station. She watched him scanning the *Standard*, the tabloids, rushing through the pages, his eyes concentrated as a laser guide. 'Nothing yet.' He looked up at her, the relief palpable in his voice.

It had been three days and the press hadn't got hold of the

story. This was the crucial time, after a few days the chances of them finding out were much smaller and by now, with the body cold and stored in a morgue drawer, the story had lost its urgency, there were new things to report, new atrocities committed in the grey city streets, and for once maybe they'd get to work this case as they should and not with every latest edition second guessing their investigation, notifying the killer, panicking the public.

Carrigan took another sip, stirring the sugar carefully, watching it swirl and sink. She couldn't tell if he was thinking about the case or the coffee. She looked down the street at two women her age pushing brightly coloured pushchairs. They looked so happy and sun-struck. She turned back and said something but Carrigan wasn't listening. He was staring intently at a young black man on the other side of the street.

'What is it?' She moved closer to get a better view but the man was already gone, disappearing into a crowd of shoppers.

Carrigan stood there, his gaze fixed as a statue's. 'I saw him outside King's Court. Twice.' His voice was soft and shaded as if worried someone would overhear.

The man had looked normal to her, nothing to set her antennae twitching. 'You sure it's the same person?'

Carrigan stared across the street but there were only families, traffic wardens, bin men. 'I think so,' he replied.

Cecilia Odamo's flat was in a basement off the Dalston Road. Once the area had been alive with rickety stalls, barrow boys and their unintelligible cries. Now it was another wasteland, stuck between two sets of yuppified ground, resistant to all attempts to clean up. But just fifty feet away from the main road it was quiet, almost leafy, as if this side street existed in a completely different zone.

They buzzed the ground-floor flat. They heard shuffling followed by the unlocking of several latches, heavy sliding weight and satisfying clicks. The door opened barely an inch.

'Miss Odamo?'

'I want to see some ID,' was the first thing the girl behind the door said.

They waited as she scrutinised their warrant cards. 'Did you come alone?'

It was a strange question but they both nodded. The girl looked over their shoulder, at the road behind them, then opened the door and let them into the flat. Carrigan took one last look at the street but there was no one there.

They stepped over piles of books and loose papers. They stepped over a tray of cat litter and last week's broadsheets. The flat hemmed them in, its low ceiling forcing Carrigan to stoop as he made his way across to the sofa.

'Tea?' Cecilia asked, her voice shrill and taut like a bad note. 'Or coffee if you want. I've got instant.'

Geneva watched with amusement as Carrigan politely refused.

'I'd love some tea,' she said, knowing the girl needed the act of provision as a buffer against why they were here.

The room took Geneva back fifteen years, a student at East Anglia, first time away from home, her mother calling up every night to make sure she was okay. She stared at the walls but there were no posters of cult films or pop stars or even Che or Marx. Just a single faded sampler depicting Jesus. A black Jesus with flowing dreadlocks and arms that were ready to embrace the whole of humanity no matter what grievous acts they'd committed.

Cecilia came back, two mugs of tea steaming in her hands and, balanced on top, a plate of chocolate HobNobs. She looked older than Grace though there were similarities between the two girls, the braided dreadlocks and ramrod posture, the razor-sharp cheekbones Geneva would have killed for.

'I'm very sorry about Grace,' Carrigan said with unusual warmth. Cecilia shuddered, the mug shaking in her hand. She opened her mouth but nothing came out. She took another sip of tea.

'I just can't believe it,' she finally said, her voice barely audible.

Carrigan leant forward, his arms covering the table. 'You were close?' he asked, his voice soft, his body unwound from its earlier tension. Geneva could see Cecilia starting to relax, to mirror Carrigan's pose, yet the girl kept averting her eyes to the window as if expecting a late-arriving guest.

'I met her at freshers week,' Cecilia continued, her hands smoothing the creases in her jeans, smoothing them even though there weren't any. 'We were sharing one of the doubles in Chavez House. I remember coming in on my first day and there was Grace, sitting cross-legged on the bed. Her suitcases were lying all around and she was just sitting there, smiling. I introduced myself and asked her if she was all right. She said yes, she just wanted to savour the moment; it was the first time she'd been on her own and she wanted to remember it. I started unpacking, took out some of my CDs, we discovered we both liked the same bands—that was it—we were friends from that moment on.' Cecilia sighed and took a sip of tea. Geneva could see her spool back to those days, simpler times, Grace still there, the world ahead exciting and unexplored.

'Did you ever meet her parents? Any family?'

Cecilia shook her head. 'They were back home in Uganda. Never really spoke about them much but I don't think they got on.'

'Why do you say that?' Geneva asked.

'Every time I mentioned them she cut me off. Nothing dramatic but she said enough to make me realise she didn't want to talk about her past. She just smiled in this strange way she had when she didn't want to talk about something and say, *That was me then but this is me now.*'

'And you were still good friends recently?'

Cecilia nodded, opened her mouth then shut it again, her eyes briefly flicking to the front window.

'But you saw each other less and less?' Geneva watched the girl's reaction closely. She flashed back to what Cummings had said about Grace changing over the last year.

Cecilia picked up a HobNob and nibbled at the edges, her teeth white and very small. 'You know how it is, work gets more and more important. There's always a deadline.'

'But it wasn't just that, was it?' Geneva prompted.

'Grace changed.' Cecilia bit off a chunk of biscuit. She chewed slowly and with what seemed like great concentration. 'She got really involved in her studies; I wasn't lying. She was always working somewhere, either in the library or in local archives, but it became something more than just work to her. Like a mission or something.'

Geneva gently put down her tea. 'When did you first notice this change?'

'Over the Christmas holidays. I'd call her up, say look there's sunshine, let's go to Battersea Park or the river and she'd say no, she was busy, couldn't spare the time. I only saw her a few times over the whole break. She'd changed in other ways too. She'd been so carefree and light and now there was this terrible heaviness to her. She began to lecture me on politics and human rights. I grew up with that stuff. My father teaches at the university in Kampala; I'd come to London to get away from all that. She would read something and then get all worked up about it. Obsessed. She'd tell me all these horrible, horrible things . . .' Cecilia shook her head, her hands furrowing her jeans, pulling and straightening the seams, her eyes darting between the two detectives and the curtained window.

'How much do you pay for this flat?' Carrigan's question took Geneva by surprise, almost as much as it did Cecilia.

'A hundred pounds a week.' She looked embarrassed, as if she'd been exposed as the victim of some scam.

'Tough being a student. Especially in London, I imagine.'
Cecilia nodded.

'How do you think Grace could afford to pay twice that for a flat in Queensway?' Carrigan asked.

'Really?' Cecilia looked genuinely surprised. 'She always had money. Not a huge amount but more than most students. In the first year she'd often take me to dinner. I felt guilty but she laughed it off, said it wasn't her money anyway. I got the impression she received a sum from her family every month.'

Carrigan wrote something down. He'd already checked Grace's bank account and there had been no sign of any regular deposits.

'Do you know anything about this?' Geneva took out the flyer for the African Action Committee which she'd found among Grace's things, and laid it flat on the coffee table. Cecilia glanced at it, not even long enough to read the headline, and looked back up at them.

'Gabriel,' was all she said.

Carrigan looked at Geneva, then back down at the table. 'Who's Gabriel?'

Cecilia bit into a biscuit; crumbs rained down on her jeans and she began picking them up one by one. 'Gabriel Otto. I guess he was as close to a boyfriend as Grace had. She met him at the end of her first year. I think she'd been impressed by something he wrote in the college paper but . . .' She stopped.

Geneva could tell that Cecilia was unsure about betraying Grace's confidence. She leant forward. 'Go on.'

'I just . . . I never trusted him. He pretends to be African but he was born and grew up here. I think he does the whole political thing to get girls but Grace seemed to like him.'

'Do you know where Gabriel lives?' Geneva asked.

The girl shook her head. 'I only ever saw him at college and those African Action Committee meetings.'

Geneva watched Carrigan scribbling in his notebook, his

fingers clenched white against the pencil's stem. She knew what he was thinking—the boyfriend, the argument the night of the murder. 'Did Grace own a laptop?' she asked.

Cecilia nodded. 'Of course.'

'It wasn't in her flat.'

The girl looked surprised, then upset. 'She was always so careful with it, always checking she hadn't left it someplace.'

'There was nowhere else she might have stashed it?'

'No, she wouldn't even leave it in her locker, she was so afraid it would get stolen.'

'You haven't been to classes this week,' Carrigan noted neutrally, but they both caught a flicker in Cecilia's face before she answered.

'I've not been feeling well,' she replied at the same moment that Carrigan's mobile rang, causing Cecilia to almost jump out of her seat, spilling what was left of her tea, apologising as she went down on her knees to clear it up.

Geneva watched, perplexed. Cecilia was definitely grieving for her friend but she also seemed terrified of something. Geneva could almost smell the fear coming off her. Was she scared of them, two white police, or of something else? She was about to ask her when Carrigan snapped his phone shut so hard it cracked like a whip in the airless room. He held it tightly in his fist until his knuckles turned white. 'We need to go. Right now.'

She followed him into the street and watched as he stopped just short of Cecilia's gate, turned and started kicking the nearby dustbin, shouting and swearing as people walked by oblivious, not wanting to get into trouble, not wanting to know, just wanting to get safely home where the news of Grace's murder had just exploded into thirty million living rooms.

12

The clip ran for two minutes and twenty-three seconds. It was obvious both from the extent of her injuries and the jumpy transitions that the footage had been edited down from a master copy. The clip seemed to have been filmed on a high-quality mobile, possibly an iPhone. The camera framed Grace's face and nothing else. The killer had remarkably steady hands. The lens held a tight close-up, the ends of Grace's hair and chin nudging the edges of the screen. She wore a gag of blue checked cloth. Her lips were pushed back and looked as if they'd been peeled to reveal the skeleton grin of her gums. Every time something happened to her off-screen her face jumped and buckled, the eyes bulging as if trying to escape the confinement of their sockets. That you couldn't see the things done to her, that you could only hear it off-camera, the heavy breathing, the laughter, the slash of knife against flesh—made it worse and even though everyone sitting in that room knew what had happened they couldn't stop their imaginations from gliding away, seeing things even more grotesque than what they knew to be so.

Grace still had a lot of life left in her, that was clear from the violence of her struggle. She hadn't hit that point yet when you realise you're not getting out of this, when you see something in the killer's smile, or the way he looks at you, and you know, know for sure, that the real and only reason you are here, tied to a bed—bleeding and wounded and screaming in pain—is so that someone can watch you die.

For two minutes and twenty-three seconds Grace writhed against her restraints, her face draining of blood, glistening in the camera-glare. Then came the moment everyone watched the clip on repeat for. The moment everyone told their friends about when they forwarded the link.

Three fingers appeared on screen. They were visible for maybe two seconds but that was all the time needed to remove the gag. Grace lurched forward, her face shaking with muscular spasms, the breath spilling out of her as if she were vomiting air. Branch turned the volume all the way up and Carrigan and Geneva could suddenly hear the heavy breathing in 87 King's Court, the sound of a fire engine outside, the opening and closing of windows in the courtyard, people coming home from dinner and taking off their clothes, running baths and greeting their spouses. Then all they heard was Grace—a massive intake of breath, her eyes focused on the camera, her lips parted, her voice weak and parched.

'Daddy!'

Just that one word, then a cut, her face appearing at a slight angle to the previous frame and, as she opened her mouth, for a split-second you could catch her life—who she was, the things she'd done—and then it was gone and she uttered her last words.

'Help me, Daddy. Please help me.'

The clip ended abruptly, leaving a window asking you if you'd like to watch it again or see similar items.

'Jesus Christ!' Carrigan's voice was dry and raspy, choked by the thought that this clip was being watched by hundreds, maybe thousands of people, not only here, but across the entire world.

'We got a call from YouTube,' Branch said, his face red and veined like someone about to experience a massive stroke. 'They yanked the video after receiving several complaints. Christ, it had been on the site for nearly three hours by then. They thought it was a fake but they called us just in case.'

Geneva blinked, trying to rid herself of the dread images she'd witnessed. 'Why us? How did they even know this happened in London?'

It was a good question, Carrigan realised, wondering why he hadn't thought of it.

Branch hung his head, his thick fingers covering his skull. 'The video's labelled *Murder in Queensway*.' He looked up at them, his eyes turning black and opaque.

'We knew this would eventually leak out,' Geneva offered, trying to soften her voice against what she'd seen, against the flood of fire snickering up her synapses and rushing through her blood.

'You knew someone taped the killing and would post it on YouTube?' Branch shot up, the chair tumbling from under him. 'You're obviously a better detective than I ever was, DS Miller—since my career is pretty much crucified because of this video, maybe you want to step in and take my place?'

'She didn't mean that,' Carrigan interrupted, his voice as firm and unyielding as his stare. 'Forget the fucking politics for a minute and you'll see it's better this way. The video will help us. We're not seeing anything now but that's because we're looking in the wrong place.'

Branch moved forward so that he was less than two inches from Carrigan's face. Geneva saw his hands curled into fists, held rigidly at his sides. 'Where in Christ's name *are* you looking?'

Carrigan didn't blink. 'Her boyfriend was seen arguing with her the night of the murder,' he said slowly. 'We're concentrating everything on finding him.'

Geneva started to say something then stopped, her eyes darting down to the desk.

Branch turned towards her. 'Spit it out, Miller, for God's sake, if you have anything else to add.'

'I think we should be looking at what she was working on,

her dissertation; see if she offended anyone, wrote something that made her enemies.' Her gaze remained fixed on the desk, unable to meet the super's glare.

Branch stood up and walked towards the window. He stared at the grey sky then turned back. 'A waste of time, Miller. Find the boyfriend. We're not that desperate we have to chase up long shots yet.' He looked down, seemed to be thinking about something. 'At least I hope to Christ we're not.'

The mood wasn't any better in the incident room, the assembled detectives silently hunched over the small computer monitor, the light flickering on their faces as they watched Grace die.

Carrigan waited until they were finished, seeing his own thoughts wheeling like dark crows in their eyes; the anger, frustration and fury of the last few days exploding in 'Fuck!' and 'Christ!' and other, more imaginative, epithets. He wanted to give them some good news, a promise that this case wouldn't end up unsolved, a silent rebuke filed away in a dark cabinet somewhere, but his eyes could not hide the truth.

'From here on, everyone's watching us.' His voice was measured, calm and controlled, but inside he felt himself shaking. 'It's already made the TV news. The press will be all over this by tonight, the tabloids will go wild with it tomorrow.' He didn't need to explain to them the nature of a case conducted in the public eye, the way it warped procedure, geared up pressure, turned the death of a young girl from tragedy into politics. 'Branch is apoplectic, as you can well imagine.' Some laughs and nods of complicity from his men; even Karlson, he noticed, was quieter and less bullish than usual. 'And that means he's had the ACC screaming down the phone to him all afternoon. Which means we've now got targets painted on our backs. But, having said that, we have to continue as before, pretend none of this matters.' He took a deep breath, knowing that such a thing would be impossible. 'We've got to look at this video as a break in the case, we've now got something to work on. Berman . . .'

DC Berman raised his head from the computer screen, his eyes blinking hard like some nocturnal desert habitant. 'Already on it, sir,' he replied. 'I'm running the clip through an enhancement program. We should be able to improve the image quality once that's done, maybe see something we can't see now.' He spoke in a strange, lilting rhythm, the words breaking off now and then into mumbles and stutters. Carrigan watched him nervously fingering some kind of prayer shawl he wore under his uniform as he returned to his keyboard.

'Karlson, I need you to talk to Scotland Yard, see if they have any kind of skin or finger database. The killer showed us his fingers. We must be able to learn something from that.'

'From a three-second flash?' Karlson was sitting backwards on the chair, slouching into the frame and running a finger through his elegantly manicured stubble. 'I doubt it. All they can tell us is that he's black, and that's bleeding obvious.'

Carrigan turned his head sharply. 'Do it. I'm not asking for your opinion.' He took a deep breath. 'We know from the clip that the killer is an IC_3 male but that's it—ask them if there's anything about the shade of his skin, anything we can use to narrow this down.'

Karlson grumbled and noisily slurped his tea as Carrigan continued. 'Also, can we find out what type of phone was used to film it?'

Berman looked up. 'Shouldn't be a problem once we figure out the resolution and coding parameters, though I can't see how much help it'll be; bound to be a common one.'

'Everything we know about this man will help us find him. Everything. We all know what he did to Grace, what he's capable of, the rush he must have experienced during the killing.

Uploading the clip is probably his way of trying to replicate it but soon that won't be enough, he'll want more. They always do. Do we even have a clue where he uploaded it?'

Berman fingered his prayer shawl. 'I'm onto it.'

Carrigan smiled—it was time for some good news. 'We now have a lead on the boyfriend courtesy of Grace's best friend, Cecilia Odamo. His name is Gabriel Otto. According to Cecilia he runs a group called the African Action Committee. There's an AAC meeting in Hackney tomorrow night, which me and DS Miller will be attending.' He stopped, noticed the dark hooded glare that Karlson gave Geneva, ignored it and continued. 'Jennings and Singh, I want you to go back to SOAS, find out what you can about this group and about our friend Gabriel.' He looked around the room. 'This is what we have to deal with now. It's not the way any of us would have liked it but it's the way it is. Let's use the video to help us catch him. Uploading it was his first mistake.'

13

Asmall upstairs room of the Queen's Arms just off Mare Street. Carrigan and Geneva paid their two pounds entrance fee and climbed the narrow stairs to the weekly meeting of the African Action Committee.

They were greeted by a room so packed it felt as if the floor was moving. People sitting on chairs, on the floor in between the chairs, cramped into corners and up against walls like Mannerist effigies. The heavy smell of sweat, beer and impatience hung like weather in the room. Other smells too, fainter but more unusual—roots and herbs and strange green drinks swigged from unlabelled bottles.

But it was the screaming and shouting that gave them pause, made them feel as if they'd stepped into an alien world. A wailing chorus of remarks, insults and exultations. Some in English, others in languages unknown to them, others still in hybrids where English words poked between Swahili and local dialects, their owners shifting from one to another as if some were better suited for particular forms of expression. Carrigan could see Geneva fidgeting and tight-lipped and knew he should feel the same way too, here among people who'd lost so much to policemen in other countries, their eyes locking on the two white intruders, seeing in them past injustices and fresh indignities. But he was enjoying it, the noise and chaos and heat. The utter strangeness of it, here in the heart of London.

A young man stood by a chipped wooden lectern. Behind him was draped a large red flag with a crossed-through clenched fist on a white target at its centre. The man's eyes popped and rolled as he addressed the crowd. It was obvious he was loving every moment of it. The catcalls and insults, the exhortations, hollers and electric sting of the room. With each cry from the crowd his voice rose and glided across the massed heads, alternately enraged and calm, his hands reaching out as if promising salvation or something better.

'And I say it again, brothers, we are not brothers, we are not them and we are not the others. We are our own people.' A cheer rose from the packed huddle. The temperature was soaring, an electric fan spinning elliptically but to no effect in the corner of the room. 'They, these people who call themselves our brothers, they are the ones killing our sons, raping our mothers, destroying our villages. All in the name of brotherhood. Of progress. Of God.'

Another loud cheer crested by a stream of booing and insults. The young man smiled and continued, his voice seemingly feeding off the crowd, filling with urgency. 'Yes, as Jesus declared, each man must atone in his own heart for that which he is not and each man's heart is a darkness that no other man can hope to penetrate.' He took a pause, more for effect than to catch his breath, then continued. 'We will give them the chance to atone but if they do not take it then we must be ready. We must learn from them, these killers, these godless men who try to impose God in our hearts through the sword. If they will not repent we must use their own ways against them.'

Another cheer, more booing. Carrigan felt the atmosphere in the room suddenly shift, a subtle variation in the air like at a football game when trouble is about to kick off.

'We must make our land a graveyard for all intruders. There is no other way. This is the way of God and the way of man.' Booing. Screaming. Insults. Jeers. 'We must take the Lord to Kony as he has taken it to us. No more . . .' Gabriel Otto stepped back, watching with delight as the crowd erupted. 'No more blood. No more villages burned to the ground. No more of our children recruited for his war.' Booing and cheering filled the packed room until it was hard to distinguish one from the other. Two men, both dressed in ill-fitting grey suits, started fighting near the front, punches were thrown, glasses crashed to the floor, blood streaked the wall. Carrigan saw Geneva's eyes flicker with fright, wondering what they'd got themselves into.

It had now been twenty-four hours since they'd seen the YouTube video. Twenty-four hours of flashed images, scrolling film, echoed screams. Twenty-four hours of newspaper headlines and breathless news reports. By the time they'd seen the video, it was being watched all over the world. Branch explained that although YouTube yanked the clip, a host of mirror sites were already streaming it, an exponential splash of horror bouncing across the web from one site to the next. Atrocity sites. Sites where you could watch the flicker of your sickest nightmares. Carrigan had spent an hour going through these sites earlier that morning, entering a realm that fed on and relished what the normal world abhorred. He'd thought he'd seen the worst in his years as a detective, but he now realised he'd seen nowhere near the worst; with each click of the mouse there were darker worlds and blacker provinces yet. It had started with photos of car crashes, DIY accidents and impaled bodies on park fences. From there it was both inevitable and logical that smuggled photos of torture and executions in South American prisons should appear, that people filmed their friends overdosing rather than trying to help them.

The morning's newspapers had all carried Grace's face, frozen mid-frame, splashed across their front pages, the headlines each trying to trump one another: WEREWOLF OF LONDON STRIKES, THE IPHONE KILLER, and the one Carrigan liked the best, THE VALENTINE SLAYER. People's faces on the Tube were rapt with a deeper concentration than usual as they scanned the latest edition of the *Standard*, the steady pulse of their lives hiccuping for just one moment and then returning to normal. Phone calls had come in like artillery barrage; impossible sightings and hoaxes, fake confessions and religious ravings.

Carrigan could feel the case starting to slip away from them. There was so much they didn't yet know. So many moments lost to them. The only thing they knew for sure was that the man standing on stage, Gabriel Otto, head of the African Action Committee, was probably the last person to see Grace Okello alive.

Carrigan had obtained a copy of Gabriel's photo from SOAS and shown it to Mrs. Najafi in King's Court. She had confirmed that Gabriel was the man who'd been shouting and cursing outside Grace's door the night she was killed.

Carrigan stared at Gabriel. His hair was cut tight against the skull, his eyes unnaturally bright as if a fire smouldered silently beneath them. He wore a neatly tailored brown suit. He was short and wiry yet gave the impression of someone bigger, something in the way he moved, a feral sort of calm and poise. Could this be Grace's killer? Was it possible to look someone in the eyes and see the residue of their history illuminated there?

'Next time they come for our children—we will be ready.' Gabriel's voice had soared above the maelstrom, effortlessly enunciating each syllable, the sibilants crackling against the microphone like lightning strikes. 'Not just Kony and his men but Museveni too.' A loud cheer rippled across the room. Several men stood up and shouted in Swahili, their arms outstretched, making shapes in the air as if too incensed for language. 'Yes, our president who helps us with our milk and babies. Our president who hires mercenaries and sends them into the northern jungles to hunt for Kony. Who tells them, *Anything you come across on the way is yours*. And where are we in all this? Where do we fit in between one madman armed with the ten commandments and a machete and another armed with UN resolutions and IMF funding? It is time to take action. We must arm each and every villager. The old man who does nothing but stare at the river. The young girl who only wants to meet her boyfriend in the bush. This is the true gospel, brothers and sisters, the gospel of blood and retribution. This is how we will earn our place in heaven.'

Gabriel bowed theatrically as the room exploded into clapping, booing, the smack of fist against flesh, a rushed and cramped pandemonium that brought a huge smile to the young man's face.

Carrigan watched as a group of men immediately surrounded Gabriel. Black-suited, his bodyguards or disciples, it was hard to tell which. People got up from their seats still arguing with their neighbours, trading insults in both word and gesture, gathering their things, making their way out into the frozen London night. Some tried to shake Gabriel's hand or say something to him but the bodyguards kept him inviolable. He spoke to his congregation through the curtain of bodies like John-Paul II in his Popemobile.

Carrigan and Geneva waited until the crowd thinned out. They scanned the room, watching the people, all of them averting their gaze except for one man, standing against a side wall, a big rangy brute with bloodshot eyes, cropped black hair and white beard. Every time Carrigan looked, the man was staring directly at him, unabashed and with a smile on his face. It wasn't the man he'd seen outside King's Court and near Cecilia's flat, he was certain, but there was something vaguely familiar about him, a feeling that made the back of Carrigan's neck itch.

He crossed the hall, Geneva at his side as every face turned to watch them, immediately making them for what they were: white and police. As they approached Gabriel, the bodyguards seemed to contract like a curtain being pulled shut. Carrigan flashed his warrant card but the bodyguard in front of him didn't even glance at it. He stood, arms crossed, his head round and shiny as a bowling ball, a look of surly indifference learned from the bouncer's rulebook, plastered across his face.

'We'd like to talk to Mr. Otto,' Carrigan said, his voice flat, brooking no argument, but the bodyguards didn't budge until Gabriel himself tapped the two in front of him lightly on the shoulder.

'You don't like what I'm preaching?' he said to Carrigan, ignoring Geneva, his accent pure North London sass and glare.

'I couldn't care less about that,' Carrigan replied. 'This is about Grace.'

He caught the slight squint in Gabriel's face and the one-word command that sent the bodyguards back into formation, impenetrable as a concrete wall. He saw Gabriel disappear through the stage door, flanked by two massive acolytes. He pushed against the curtain of bodyguards, calling after Gabriel, but it was like trying to walk through a brick wall. He began to reach for his truncheon when he felt two hands, cold and hard as steel, clamp themselves around his arms and then, before he could take another breath, his feet were off the ground. The bouncer lifted him until they were eye level.

'Mr. Otto does not want to see you,' he said, his breath dank and rotten like something found under a rock. Carrigan tried to twist out of the bouncer's embrace but it felt like his arms were trapped in a vice.

'Get your hands off him, now!'

The bodyguards looked at Geneva and laughed. Carrigan stared at the bouncer's eyes and twenty years peeled back like a curtain as he felt the blood filling his mouth again, the stench of the cell, the broken teeth scattered across the floor. The bouncer's voice snapped him back to the present.

'Please, go home, this is no place for you. This is our affair, our history, our future. None of this is your business.'

'A girl has been murdered. That's our business.' Geneva stood to the right of Carrigan, fingers cradling her can of pepper spray, trying to slow her heart so that her voice wouldn't tremble and falter.

The bodyguard put Carrigan down and examined Geneva as if she were a strange dish he was surprised to find on his plate. His voice, when he spoke, was surprisingly gentle. 'Our girls are being murdered every day back home. Kony's troops come and rape them until they die. Then the government comes and those that have survived are accused of collaboration. This happens every day, for every week and every month of every year, and here you come and tell us a girl has been murdered and you're all concerned and you want to talk to Mr. Otto. Well, one girl is nothing. You do not live every day with death. You do not know how death becomes your life, how it loses its power when you rub shoulders with it every moment of your existence.'

Carrigan couldn't help thinking he'd just summed up what it was like to be a murder detective while Geneva looked stymied by the bodyguard's eloquence and reasoning. Carrigan could see her weighing options, her hand fidgeting her belt. There was no way past the bodyguards. Gabriel was probably long gone via a back door, vanished into the London night. All Branch needed now was a race riot, accusations of racial insensitivity. He looked at Geneva and with relief saw that she'd come to the same conclusion.

'Every murder. Every single body we take seriously here,' he said. 'Maybe if you did that over there things wouldn't have got so out of hand.'

The bodyguard's fist came so fast he had no chance to duck or flinch. The blow landed square on his jaw and suddenly the world was black and silver.

'Tell Gabriel I'll be waiting for him,' Carrigan said through a mouth filled with blood and pain. He rubbed his jaw and nodded to Geneva. They turned and walked slowly through the now empty hall, waiting for the lunge of a knife, another fist, but there was nothing, and when they entered the chill evening air it felt as if they'd been trapped inside that room for ever.

14

Carrigan stared up at the grey tower blocks stacked against the dismal sky. Winter was finally here; frost on the ground crunching under their feet, a chill in the air which required gloves and face protection. He took a sip of watery coffee then spat it back out, watching it melt the frost surrounding his feet. He stared back up at the towering estate, counting floors, wondering if Gabriel Otto was at this moment staring back at him from one of the high blacked-out windows, watching the team stamp their feet as they waited for tactical to arrive.

It hadn't been Carrigan's idea. Branch had called him in this morning, all pained smiles and polite chit-chat, but he'd got to the point quickly enough. He'd heard about the AAC meeting, the bodyguards, the rebuff, and was sending a team to arrest Gabriel. How had Branch found out? Carrigan took out a pack of Tic-Tacs and swallowed several. It wasn't something he wanted to consider right now.

He waited as the tactical support team arrived and kitted up out of the back of a police van like gladiators preparing for some dark spectacle. He stood in the cold wet wind watching the spitting rain carouse off the pocked concrete buildings, the early-morning straggle of workers hunched into themselves, eyes red and bleary, setting out into another day, knowing that at the end of it they'll return here, to the grey gloom and cramped rooms of this dying estate.

They split into three teams. One for the stairwell, another for the lift, one outside to catch any runners. They talked and chatted for as long as possible, putting off the moment, but Carrigan could see they were all fired up and waiting to go. He remembered days when he'd arrived at work in the same state, couldn't wait to knock heads, break doors, chase leads, but those days now existed only in memory.

'We ready?' The TAC-team commander's voice cut through the drizzle and mist. Carrigan knew him but couldn't remember where from, the years and cases running into one.

The smell of piss and vomit surrounded them as they split between stairwell and lift. That the lift even worked was a miracle in itself. Nothing had been done to make these common spaces the least bit attractive. There were only old chicken cartons reeking of oil and fat, broken vials cracking under their feet, graffiti so impenetrable it could have been conceptual art.

The door splintered with one swing of the ram. Carrigan went first, into a narrow humid hallway, books and magazines stacked up on either side of the floor, the smell of old laundry heavy in the air. He could hear the stuttered footsteps of his men behind him, see the fogging of the windows against their breath, heard shuffling and swearing in the room off to his right. He signalled the sergeant and together they took the door.

Gabriel Otto was sitting upright in bed, bare-chested and sweat-slicked, smoking a joint. His eyes turned hard and shiny as marbles when he recognised Carrigan. The bed began to move, the sheets rippling and snagging, slowly revealing a foot, an ankle, the pale white skin of a girl, her legs blue-veined and alabaster.

She raised her head, rubbed the sleep out of her eyes with a clenched fist and registered Carrigan and his men, blinking and staring at them as if they were alien creatures, things that weren't meant to be seen when awake. Gabriel took another toke and laid the spliff in an ashtray beside the bed.

'Put your clothes on, we're going to the station.' Carrigan

tried not to look at the girl, her sleep-rumpled body slowly unfurling into the morning.

'What's going on, Gabriel?' she said, her voice wispy and accented in the stuffy room. Gabriel ignored her, reached for the joint, about to take another drag, when Carrigan slapped it out of his hands.

'You better get dressed.' Carrigan smiled as he picked up a pair of trousers hanging off the back of a chair and handed them to Gabriel.

'You're making a big mistake,' the young man replied, struggling into his trousers.

Carrigan threw him a shirt. 'Get some new lines, Gabriel. Heard that one countless times.' He looked away, disgusted. The girl grabbed Gabriel's hand and asked him when he'd be back, her eyes milky and unfocused, still lost in dream-melt. She pulled him down and whispered something in his ear. Gabriel turned towards her, a smile lighting up his eyes, then struck her cleanly across the face.

The sound cut through the room, through the bustle of policemen searching the flat, the buzz of the elevator and the garbled talk of neighbours gathering outside the door. The girl's face blushed red, Gabriel's handprint visible on her left cheek.

Carrigan leant forward and took Gabriel's arm, twisting it behind his back and snapping on the cuffs. He used his body as a weight to pin Gabriel to the wall, breathing heavily, feeling as if his heart was about to explode. Gabriel made some kind of clicking sound with his teeth and Carrigan brought his foot down hard on the young man's instep, feeling a small measure of satisfaction as he let out a long agonised moan.

15

Ex-boyfriends can be a pain but they certainly have their uses, Geneva thought, stubbing out her cigarette. She watched the people walk by, their day unclouded by death, and though she envied them this, she knew her life could be no other way. Mothers with prams, postmen and Polish builders, a young black man talking into a mobile phone across the street from her. She looked back, sure that he'd averted his eyes the moment she looked at him, and she remembered Carrigan's reaction outside Cecilia's flat. She looked up but the man had gone, and she shook her head, knowing she was imagining things, putting it down to her nervousness at meeting Lee again after all these years. She smoked two more cigarettes outside his house, turning up the volume on her iPod until it was so loud she couldn't bear it. When she stubbed out the third cigarette she knew there was no more time to prevaricate or wander round these old familiar streets. She was here because a girl was lying dead in a West London morgue. She was here because no one else thought that Grace's thesis had anything to do with her murder.

She knew Carrigan didn't think much of her theory. He still saw it as a sex murder, lust and compulsion not politics the motivator. She didn't think he trusted her. Branch's involvement had pretty much guaranteed that. Yet it was strange how every time Africa came up Carrigan's face pursed and his lips turned white. Was this something she needed to put into her report to Branch? She crushed the cigarette under her shoe until the tobacco and paper disintegrated. She thought of her mother's constant tirades against collaborators and cowards, the usual dinnertime refrain over a couple of bottles of wine. Her mother would never forgive her. Would she be able to forgive herself, she wondered as she walked past the swinging gate and up to the front door. Are there acts you commit which cannot be forgiven—even by yourself?

The doorbell chimed a melody of something trite and heard on too many adverts. She made an effort to stand straight, stop her hands from fidgeting, her voice from cracking.

Ten years since she'd last seen Lee. Ten years and different lifetimes. But here she was. He was surprised but not that surprised when she'd called late last night. Lee could never really be surprised, she remembered, not when you believe the world is as unpredictable and chaotic as he did. Or maybe he'd changed. She wasn't the same woman she'd been when they first met at East Anglia. She wasn't the same woman she'd been when they moved back to London, set up in a flat off the Kilburn High Road, her walking the uniformed beat, day in, day out, in wind and rain and snow, and him packing his leather bag, furiously writing notes through the night, calling sources, off to another war zone to write his pieces on misery and suffering and pain.

But he knew Africa, she reminded herself, fighting the urge to light another cigarette, and, last night, going through the notes she'd made at the African Action Committee meeting, going through Grace's folders full of references and citations, she realised how hopelessly lost she was in all this. To understand Grace's death she needed to understand the context of her life.

'Oh my God, Geneva,' Lee said, opening the door, his face still a young man's, breaking into a smile she remembered so well, a plump pink baby cradled in his arms.

'Lee,' she replied, and for a moment neither said a thing, standing frozen on either side of the door.

'Come in, sorry,' he apologised. The baby began crying. Lee stroked his forehead and turned back into the corridor. Geneva followed him, trying to corral all the feelings welling up inside her, Lee settled down in North London, a baby in his hands, another woman, another life. This was work she told herself, only work.

Lee led her into the main drawing room then excused himself, taking the baby upstairs. She was glad for this momentary respite. She settled down into the worn brown sofa and put her earphones away. She was dying for a smoke but there were no ashtrays anywhere nor the smell of extinguished cigarettes. She remembered their first flat, the noise and damp and constant pall of smoke. Her smoking. Him puffing away non-stop as he worked another deadline through the night. The thought made her stomach twist and she felt suddenly dizzy. She wondered whether this was a good idea. Whether she should have just contacted someone at the university for the information, but before she could rush out of the house Lee came in with two steaming mugs of coffee and a smile that took her back to younger years.

'Oh, Geneva,' he said again, gently setting down the coffee. His hand brushed her shoulder and she felt a tremor in her bones but that was all. Too many years had gone by for them to kiss or hug or even shake hands.

He sat opposite her on a leather chair that was falling to pieces. It was falling to pieces fifteen years ago and she suddenly had a memorysnap of the two of them making love on it some evening in the mid-nineties and the insistent smell of leather and coffee was almost too much.

'Still a cop, then?' His voice sounded different, lower, drained of excitement and mystery.

She nodded. 'Still a journalist?'

Lee's eyes clouded. 'Yes and no. Lifestyle journalism they call it.' His voice took on a harder sheen, his eyes looked anywhere but at hers. 'I write about IKEA houses and Belgravia dinner parties.' He laughed and Geneva did too, though both knew there was nothing funny about it. 'Believe me, society dinners can get every bit as brutal and savage as civil wars.' And this time it was the genuine Lee laugh, the one that got him out of trouble too many times to count; the one that got him Geneva all those years ago.

She stared up at the framed photos on the wall. 'You're happy with the choices you made?'

Lee looked away, across the hall, then back at Geneva. 'What kind of question is that, Genny?'

The use of her nickname startled her, she hadn't heard it spoken in so many years. 'I'm sorry.'

'And you,' he said, 'what about your choices? Did you make the right ones?'

'I'm happy being a cop.'

'I meant Oliver.'

It was like a blow you expect and all the more painful for it. It was all the years collapsing into each other. That day on the platform at King's Cross, saying goodbye. Lee crying. Her crying. Oliver waiting for her in his house up in the north. The end of childhood and the beginning of something else.

'I didn't leave you for him. Didn't marry him because of you.'

'I know, Genny, I'm not talking about that. Your mother told me what happened. The undercover work. Oliver and the other woman. I'm sorry, I don't want to bring all this up, I just want to know you're okay.'

She reached out her hand, met his halfway across the table. Their palms fell into each other like it hadn't been ten years. 'I'm okay now.'

'And you're happy?'

She gently pulled her hand away. 'Now you're the one asking stupid questions.' And for a moment the years faded and disappeared and she was sitting here with the man she loved and this was their life ten years on, in a quiet suburb, in a nice house, a baby upstairs, a life fulfilled. But when the baby started crying and Lee got up, she suddenly remembered who she was again.

Suddenly the room felt intolerable. Suddenly she felt light-headed and sick. The dark, the smell of baby things, the look on Lee's face as he came back in. This was all a mistake, she realised, one big fucking mistake. You can never go back.

'You said you wanted to pick my brain about Africa?'

'It's . . . it's a case I'm working on.' She was relieved for the change in topic, reached down and pulled the notes from her bag.

'The dead girl on YouTube?'

Geneva nodded. Everyone, it seemed, now knew Grace as the dead girl on YouTube. 'I remember you spent a lot of time in the Congo, Uganda, Sudan.'

Lee nodded. She could see a part of him slip away to God knew what horrors and frights in jungles and deserts, but it was a look of sad remembrance, not relief or happiness.

'I'm having trouble with the background on this case. Grace was involved in East African politics. She was writing a thesis on insurgency in post-colonial Africa. She was from Uganda. I was at this meeting yesterday and I didn't under-stand half of what they were saying. It was all acronyms, NRA, LRA, SPLA. I remembered you used to cover the region,' she continued, hoping Lee didn't catch the stumble in her voice. 'What can you tell me about Ugandan politics? Especially rad-ical stuff.'

'Radical?' Lee laughed. 'It's all pretty radical compared to what we call politics here. Where do you want me to start?'

He told her of the missionaries spreading through Uganda in the 1870s, the first whites to expand into the land. The for-mation of the Uganda protectorate in 1894 under the aegis of the British East Africa Company. The long bitter years of colonialism then the shock of the new world order. The Obote coup in the 1960s. Counter-couped in 1971 by Idi Amin, the years of torture, repression and economic collapse. Then the Tanzanian invasion in 1979, the deposing of the paranoid Amin and the return of Obote. Obote's deposing by another general and his subsequent removal six months later in the bush war by Museveni's National Resistance Army.

'Museveni's seen by the West as some kind of paragon. In African terms at least. But he's not that much better than those who came before. A virtual one-party state. Torture and intimidation. Your basic African politics.'

'What about Joseph Kony? They kept talking about taking arms against the government and against Kony.'

Lee leant back and laughed. 'Kony's a true character. Something only Africa could have produced. And within that, something only Uganda could have come up with. There's something about that country which drives people to extreme religious outpourings. It's like Jerusalem except without any historical antecedents. Cults and religious groups have always flourished there. Kony's only the last in a long line of self-appointed mystics and leaders. In the end though, there's no heaven on earth, no peace and goodwill, there's only severed ears, abducted children and mass rape.'

'My victim was looking at the use of torture as policy. How does that link with all this?' She felt better talking about these far-flung worlds as if after all these years apart they could only talk through a barrier, like inmates in a prison.

'Everyone uses torture and terror. It's a way of life out there. But no one wants to admit to it. It's all being done behind closed doors, in cells and dungeons far away in the jungle. This is no longer the time of Idi Amin where the secret police's torture cells were located on Kampala's main street, the windows always left open so that women on their way to market, kids coming back from school, could hear the screams twenty-four hours a day. It's all hidden now. There's too much at stake. Massive loans from the IMF, development grants, foreign aid—all that money disappears when allegations of torture and human rights abuses come up. They're learning to play the game, to hide what the West doesn't want to see and cash their cheques. The IMF and aid agencies, they don't really care, out of sight and all that, they just don't want to hear the screams while they're partying. So, yes, anyone who was going to expose any of this, especially government torture, well you can imagine . . .'

She could see the faraway look in his eyes, the hunger for action and danger. It was what had attracted her to him in the first place but what happened when you could no longer achieve those goals? What happened to your life when you voluntarily gave in?

'Now Kony and the Lord's Resistance Army are a whole different thing.'

'We're still talking Uganda, right?'

Lee nodded. He got up and walked over to his laptop. Unplugged the power cord and brought it back to the table. 'Northern Uganda. Kony's Lord's Resistance Army's been operating there since 1987. If you want to understand Uganda you need to understand Kony.'

They sat side by side on the sofa. Lee was close but not touching. 'It begins with Alice Auma, a native Acholi from northern Uganda, a Catholic convert who worked as a medium. One day she's contacted by the Holy Spirit who tells her it is her God-given duty to overthrow the Ugandan government, the government that since Museveni took over has been persecuting her people, the Acholi. She starts the Holy Spirit Movement. She's well respected and her powers are venerated. Many join. It's a strange army, led by this woman, part saint-mystic, part holy warrior. They suffer terrible defeats at the hands of the Ugandan army. They bless stones so that they'll turn into grenades when the enemy soldiers walk over them. They rub anointed oil on their bodies to protect themselves from bullets. They march in cross formation singing hymns. This is a popular uprising turned into holy war. The government clamps down hard and Alice is exiled, the movement splits into many splinter groups—among those is one led by Joseph Kony who says he is a cousin to Alice and that he too has received a message from the Holy Spirit.

'He forms the Lord's Resistance Army in 1987, a band of Christian guerrillas who want to implement a theocratic state based on the ten commandments. Many join. Kony is charismatic and charming. What's more, under his leadership they start winning decisive battles against the Ugandan army. They had up to three thousand soldiers at one point, some say even more.'

'Villagers?'

'No, the villagers were sitting on the fence. They feared the LRA and they feared the government troops. Kony's speciality was abduction. Ninety per cent of his soldiers were child abductees. They abduct boys and teach them to fight. They make them rape and kill, often their own families, to bond them to the LRA. Then they give them a gun and send them out to battle. The government soldiers have families back home; they're doing it for the money in a country where unemployment is disastrously high. The child soldiers kill because that is all they know. The villages are in between. Kony's men come and take food and abduct their children, then the government troops accuse them of helping the LRA and burn down their huts, ship them off to a refugee camp for their safety. They also do their fair share of raping, looting and killing. There's nearly two million people still living in filthy refugee camps since 1996 when the government forcibly evicted them. These poor bastards are caught between. No one cares. It's not Rwanda or Bosnia. It's too complex, there's no good guys and no way to see a resolution. It's one of those wars that goes on for so long that the reason no longer becomes its meaning, only the cycle of retribution and blood. It's the closest we humans have come to creating a perpetual-motion machine.'

She thought back to Gabriel's impassioned speech the previous night. The call to arms. She could understand his position, her mother would even donate time and money, but Geneva couldn't see how more guns could help. She looked up at Lee and there he was, the twenty-two-year-old boy she met at university again, his face younger, his eyes bright. She blinked away the thoughts swirling through her head and took out Grace's notes and essay plans. 'There's a lot of references to something called the Black-Throated Wind. I think Grace was concentrating on that from the look of things. Do you know anything about them?'

Lee's face became tight, his lips almost disappearing. He looked away. 'It's not a them, it's a him.'

Geneva felt her skin tingling at the word 'him'. 'Who is he?'

'His name is Lawrence Ngomo but he called himself the Black-Throated Wind. He had many other names too.' Lee shook his head. 'I met him once . . . Shit, Genny, you still smoke?'

She nodded, took out her pack of Lucky Strikes. 'You allowed to smoke in the house?'

Lee shook his head. 'No. Haven't touched one of these for seven years.' He took two cigarettes out of the pack and put them both in his mouth, lighting them simultaneously before passing one to her. It was a gesture she remembered well and something in her chest felt like it was popping. Her hands shook as she took the cigarette. 'Shouldn't we go outside?'

Lee stood up and opened the window. 'Fuck it, I haven't done this in too long.'

He sat back down next to her. 'Ngomo's a piece of work,' he continued, coughing, taking deep drags on the cigarette.

'He's belligerent, violent, paranoid, and holds grudges for ever. He wouldn't answer any of my questions when I interviewed him. When I asked him why he agreed to do the interview he told me he fancied killing a white man today but that he'd changed his mind.'

Geneva smiled. 'Nice. Who is he?'

'He was one of Kony's lieutenants. Then he split off, set up his own splinter faction. Called himself the Black-Throated Wind. There's a lot of rumours and not much fact. People saw him as some kind of religious saviour. They say he modelled himself on Savonarola, the medieval Florentine monk who created the bonfire of the vanities. Ngomo didn't burn luxuries, though, he burned villages—he believed that the land was cursed by blood and that only through fire, by clearing the land and starting again, could peace come.'

'He had followers for this?' She was always amazed at how people fell so willingly for anyone who promised a return to some mythic former age.

'Many. You have to realise that someone like Ngomo makes the world very simple and a lot of people are drawn to that. They believed him a saint, something more than human, sent down from heaven to purge the land. Many people claim to have seen him walking across the surface of Lake Albert. They say he recreated the Eastern Wall of the Jerusalem temple in the bush, stone by stone; that he translated the Bible into Luganda, changing a word here, a word there, until its meaning had changed too.' Lee took a deep breath, crushed out his cigarette. 'There's substantial evidence he was involved in the murder of those aid workers back in 1990, you remember that?'

She shook her head.

'Four British girls on their gap year, trying to do something meaningful rather than just getting drunk and sunburned, working for one of the food-aid NGOs. One was the daughter of a backbench MP, one was a doctor's daughter . . . good girls from good families. When they didn't turn up at their base in Gulu, a massive search entailed but it was fruitless. A few weeks later a video began turning up in West African markets and backroom shops. The video showed the girls praying, then cut to a shot of them dead on the ground. There were always rumours that an unedited version existed but it was never found. There was a lot of noise in the British press at the time, a speech in parliament, but the Ugandan government insisted that the girls' killers were themselves dead, the result of army gains in the north.'

She scribbled it all down feeling something in her blood fizz and jump. 'What happened to Ngomo?'

'He disappeared around seven years ago. Some of those closest to him said he'd had a revelation in the bush, saw God, renounced the sword; others say his body is rotting in the long grass, shot by an eight-year-old near the town of Baringo.'

'What do you think?'

Lee's face creased into a grin she knew well. 'I think he's a lot closer than that.'

She looked across the room and their eyes met. 'Lee?'

He stared down at his shoes, 'I think he got out when he could. There was an international warrant for his arrest that was rescinded seven years ago; they've never done that before. I think he gave up names and positions in return for immunity.'

'You think he's living *here*?'

Lee got up, went upstairs, came back down with an old dusty file. He flicked through it then stopped and pulled out a yellowed copy of the *Daily Mail* from two years ago. He sat down and opened the paper, turning to the centre spread. WAR CRIMINALS LIVING LARGE IN LONDON, the headline ran, eight grainy black-and-white photos underneath. Lee's finger hovered over the second from last, an old man with grey hair and a black moustache, the name Lawrence Ngomo in 10-point type under it. 'I think he made a deal, got some kind of immunity and residence here,' he stopped and looked at her, something flickering behind his eyes. 'It makes you wonder though, what he could have given them that was worse than the killing of the aid workers.'

The interview room was cold and damp. It hung in their nostrils and crept through their clothes as they sat across from Gabriel Otto, watching him strip a packet of cigarettes to fine cardboard streamers.

'What are you going to make out of that?' Carrigan leant forward, his breath heavy with coffee and fatigue, the exertion of the arrest having taken its toll. 'A key to get out of this room?'

Gabriel continued stripping the pack, ignoring the two detectives, his eyes focused intently on the object in his hands.

'You missed one,' Geneva said and Gabriel looked up, his lips slowly peeling into a smile.

'You could be halfway pretty if you tried.'

Geneva felt Carrigan tense, a slight shift in the room's pressure. She looked at him, shook her head and turned back to the suspect.

'Why did you kill her, Gabriel?' Her voice was cold and uninflected. 'Or should I call you Derek?' She stared into his eyes, forcing herself not to smile.

His head snapped up, a look of pure malevolence in his eyes. 'No one calls me that.'

Geneva pulled a sheet of paper from her file, slid it across the desk. 'Your parents did, at least according to your birth certificate.'

Gabriel dropped the shredded cigarette pack and stared directly at Geneva. She could feel the skin on her arms contract, a tiny burst of panic deep down in her gut.

Gabriel put his hands on the table, his fingers skinny as pencils. 'What the fuck do you want?'

Geneva leant forward and pushed a stray hair neatly behind her ear. 'When did you last see Grace?'

'Don't remember,' he replied, his voice steady and even. 'Maybe the day before she was killed, maybe the week before . . . who keeps track?'

'How about on the night of her murder?' Geneva kept her hands on the table, noticing Gabriel staring at her fingers, admiring her nails. 'We have witnesses who saw you, who heard you arguing with Grace the night she was killed. Those court-yards carry sound. You were Sunday night's entertainment, the building's very own reality show. Then she threw you out. You banged on her door and shouted and threatened to kill her.'

'Wouldn't be a relationship if you didn't threaten to kill the little woman every now and then.' He glanced at Carrigan.

'Except this time you went ahead and did it.'

Gabriel sighed theatrically, his eyes roving Geneva's neckline. 'You've got nothing,' he said, his voice like a kid who didn't get the birthday present he'd been expecting. 'How do I know that? Because I did nothing apart from argue with her and bang on her door a few times.'

'So you admit you were there that night,' Carrigan said.

Geneva tapped out a cigarette and offered Gabriel one. 'Just as long as you don't destroy my pack.' She lit it for him, his hand cupping hers before she could pull away.

'I told you. I didn't kill her.'

'You need to convince us of that. Everything says you did it. The witnesses, the forensics, the video footage.'

Gabriel slammed his hand flat on the table. 'When I left she was still alive. Alive enough to fucking shout and call me a collaborator.'

Geneva's eyes flicked up. 'Collaborator? What did she mean by that? Who did she think you were working for?'

They both caught the momentary look of panic in Gabriel's expression. 'Okay, okay, fuck it,' he finally said, looking down at the table. 'If I tell you what happened then you'll let me go, right?'

Geneva nodded.

'We were supposed to be going out that night but at the last minute she called to say she couldn't make it.'

'Seems you're not short of company,' Carrigan interrupted, liking Gabriel less and less. 'Why didn't you take one of your other girlfriends?'

'It wasn't like that,' Gabriel replied. 'White girls are good for sex,' looking directly at Geneva. 'A bit of fun here and there. Grace was different. She was from home.'

'You mean Harlesden?' Geneva flashed her teeth.

'What's that got to do with it?' Gabriel snapped.

'Why do you call Uganda home, Derek, when you were born and raised in North London?' Carrigan was impressed by her change of tone, hard and sharp one moment, the next sounding like a kindly schoolteacher, the type you'd spill all your secrets to.

'My father is Ugandan,' he replied. 'Your country brought him here to work, he never had a choice. Africa will always be home to black-skinned people, makes no difference where you ship us to.'

Geneva didn't want to hear his brand of fashionable rebellion; she was sure it went down well with the home-county kids at SOAS but both she and Carrigan had seen enough not to be moved by rhetoric and imprecation. 'Tell me about Sunday night, Derek.'

'Don't call me that again.'

Geneva smiled. 'I promise.'

Gabriel seemed to take this at face value. 'There was a Ugandan band playing at the Empire that Grace wanted to see but it was sold out. I'd managed to get a couple of tickets.

Then she calls me up that afternoon, says she can't make it. Just like that. I said, *What the fuck?* She told me she was meeting someone and then she hung up on me.'

'So you went over to King's Court to talk to her?'

Gabriel nodded. 'She was seeing someone else, I was sure of it. Why else break such a date?' Carrigan could think of a multitude of reasons but kept his mouth shut; Gabriel's bitterness towards Grace was serving them well. 'She let me into the flat. She was all dressed up. She'd never dressed like that for me.'

'Dressed how?' Geneva stubbed out her cigarette, her eyes never leaving Gabriel's.

'She was wearing traditional clothes, her mother's. It's a sign of respect back home. I asked her who was she seeing tonight, who was so fucking important? She refused to tell me, asked me to leave.'

'So you got mad at her, well that's understandable,' Carrigan muttered conspiratorially.

'Of course I got mad. I paid a lot for those tickets, even booked a restaurant for afterwards.'

'Lucky girl didn't know what she was missing,' Carrigan replied.

'I said to her, tell me who you're meeting, all dressed up like that,' Gabriel continued, oblivious now to the detectives, his mind reliving the evening's slight. 'She just stood there shaking her head, saying, *You don't understand.* I told her I understood fine. She said, *You never understand.* And then she started laying into me about the AAC, saying I was only doing it to get girls, that I had no heart, that it didn't matter to me what was going on in Uganda. I told her I wasn't leaving. I wanted to see who her new man was. She told me it wasn't a boyfriend. She said it was work. I laughed. This is not an original excuse. This is half past six on a Sunday evening. She said she was meeting an important source, someone who knew stuff they shouldn't. She said the man only agreed to meet at her flat. She said this would bring it all together. I didn't believe her. I called her a liar and a whore. She pushed me out of the room. She slammed the door and said she never wanted to see me again. I banged on her door and told her exactly what kind of girl she was.'

'And then?'

'And then I went home. I called Greta, this girl I sometimes hang with, and we went to the show. She didn't get it but we had a nice time and I went back to her place. That's all. I never saw Grace again until I switched on the news.'

Gabriel crushed his cigarette in the ashtray. The room was cloudy with smoke and Carrigan felt that old hunger rising up inside him as he thought about what Gabriel had said. 'Try this for a minute,' he suggested. 'Imagine you're the policeman and I'm the one feeding you this bullshit story. Would you believe me?'

Gabriel shrugged, his shoulders angular and spiky, tiny knots of bone.

'You weren't particularly upset when we saw you at the AAC meeting.'

'Don't give a fuck for her any more. She used me. She fucking used me and then when she had someone better she let me go. You think I'm going to cry over something like that?'

'What do you mean she used you? You sound like a girl,' Carrigan said.

'Not like that, man. She used me for my connections. For her fucking thesis. She cosied up to me, came to all the meetings, hooked up with a lot of émigrés from back home. She was always looking for information, always working out who could help her and who couldn't.' Gabriel's smile was strange and unsettling. He leant back in the chair. 'At first I really thought she had another boyfriend, then I realised no, she was right when she said she didn't care about that. It was this source that mattered to her more.'

'And she didn't tell you anything more about this man she was supposed to meet, this "source"?'

'Nah. And if she did, by that point I wasn't listening. All I know is she seemed excited, and Grace only ever got excited when it was about her work. It was like some fucking mission for her.'

Geneva opened the green file lying on the table, thinking back to how Cecilia had used almost the same words to describe Grace. She took a grainy photograph from the file, looked at it for a few seconds, then slid it towards Gabriel.

Gabriel sprang back and almost toppled from his chair, as if the photograph were a snake thrown across the table.

'So, you do recognise him?' Geneva said, watching Gabriel's face drop for the first time that afternoon.

Carrigan briefly glimpsed an image of a black man with a small moustache and receding hairline. They hadn't talked about this before starting the interview. He wondered who the man was as he watched Gabriel looking everywhere but the photo. Geneva was biting the inside of her lip, trying to keep her face blank, but there was no disguising the glee in her eyes.

'Of course I recognise him,' Gabriel said, still avoiding the photograph. 'Find me anyone from Uganda who doesn't recognise the Black-Throated Wind.'

Carrigan looked at the photo, seeing a grainy image of a man who could have been any of a thousand men. Where had she got it from? Was this Branch's idea or had she found it in the box of Grace's work notes? Was she still pursuing her thesis theory despite his objections and all the evidence to the contrary?

'Tell me about him.' Geneva placed her hands on the table, fingers slowly spreading like a fan. Gabriel scraped his chair forward. He took a deep breath, turned over the photo so that only the gleaming white back reflected into the room. 'The Bible says thou shalt not *murder*, not, as is commonly thought, thou shalt not *kill*. You understand the difference?'

'I understand that everyone has a different understanding of the difference,' Carrigan replied. Geneva looked at him, a smile of mild surprise perched on the left side of her mouth.

'Well Ngomo certainly understood,' Gabriel continued. 'The Black-Throated Wind.' He said the name with a chilly reverence, a name only to be whispered in shadowed rooms and subterranean spaces. 'You know why the Bible speaks to us Africans? Why we believe in it as a literal thing?' He didn't give them a chance to answer, in full oratory mode now, his fists clenching the table. 'The Bible speaks to us because we live in a biblical world, a world of flood, famine and plague. The Bible is never metaphor for us, it is always a literal telling, the flesh and blood of God. You need to understand this if you want to understand Uganda. If war is your god then the battlefield becomes your church, the blood and bullets your sacraments. A man like Ngomo who has no ideology, no politics, whose world isn't filled with complications and mitigations— for a man like that, it is easy to succeed. With only one road ahead, you make many miles.'

'Do you think that Grace's source may have been Ngomo? Do you think it's possible Ngomo set up a meeting and killed her?' Geneva turned the photo over, General Ngomo somehow looking more sinister now, his face peppered with stray ash from the table.

Gabriel laughed as if he'd just heard the world's funniest joke. He shook his head. 'You cops are so stupid.' He took Geneva's empty cigarette pack and began stripping it. 'I've told you everything I can about that night; now either release me or charge me and let me see a lawyer.'

There was a collision on the south side of the Great West Road, almost directly opposite his flat. A still-steaming snarl of metal and glass spread across two lanes. The rain had turned from drizzle to downpour. Red and blue lights cut through the mist and haze like lighthouse beacons. Carrigan locked his car, briefly considered crossing over to the accident site where two constables were stretching crime-scene tape while medics crouched on the ground, their arms in frenzied movement, their faces intently clenched. But there was no need for him there. They were doing what they could. The traffic was filtered through the left lane and already there was a chorus of horns, a symphony of different timbres and tones clashing against the bullet spray siren of the approaching ambulance.

He could see the vehicle involved, a family SUV, the tyres shredded, thin black tendrils hanging from the undercarriage. A dark smear of blood on the asphalt was already washing away in the rain. Slivers of glass sparkled and shone in the paramedics' searchlights like tiny stars against the deep black ripple of tarmac. There was blood on the inside of the windshield. In the back seat there were children's toys scattered and upside down, handbags and summer hats. He tried not to stare but there's no way you can look away. He could see it in the cars that were passing at a crawl, their occupants' eyes all turned towards the scene trying to glimpse something while hoping not to. They'd drive a little slower tonight, he knew, hold their wives' and husbands' hands after dinner, have trouble falling asleep hearing their child in the cot next to the bed breathing a little too heavily. But tomorrow they'd be driving again as they always did, convinced of their immortality. He didn't begrudge them their curiosity; in the deepest nights he knew this was part of the reason he'd become a policeman. He turned, shaking the images from his eyes, and that's when he saw the car.

It was the fact that they weren't looking at the accident which made him notice them. Parked on the other side of the flyover, the two occupants shrouded in darkness. From where they were sitting they had a clear view of his front door. He tried to think of other reasons for them being there, then crossed the road and headed towards his flat.

He'd bought it for the view. That was the joke he told everyone who came here. Except it wasn't a joke. The three-bedroom terraced house sat alongside the Great West Road overlooking the Hogarth roundabout and M4 flyover. His living-room window looked out onto the grey stretch of the approach ramp as it spiralled high into the drizzled sky. The traffic never stopped. The city never stopped. He liked nothing better than to sit in the evenings and stare out at the snake of cars hitting the ramp at sunset, the majority heading for the airport, for queues and flights, sunshine and wonder. It had been twenty years since he'd been abroad but he loved looking at their faces, rapt in streetlight fix, staring exultantly at the black road ahead and the sky above as if they'd already forgotten who they were.

He picked up his mail and entered the flat. He sensed a difference as soon as he stepped into the living room. He stopped and looked, sniffed. Nothing he could point a finger to, a subtle disturbance of air, a vague unfamiliar smell. He felt the sweat rolling down his back as he checked the front room and bedroom but everything seemed in place. He stared through the window out into the night but the car that had been parked there was gone, a pale scar where it had sealed the asphalt from the rain. He checked the other rooms and then made himself a drink. It was only when he was sitting in his chair that he saw it.

A small brown envelope lying underneath the phone. He put his glass down slowly, careful not to make a sound. He walked over, pulled out a pair of latex gloves from his jacket pocket, snapped them on and picked up the envelope.

There was no name written on the front and it hadn't been sealed. He felt his fingers tremble as he took out the photographs and stared at them. A picture of him standing outside Ben's house a few days ago. Another of him greeting Ursula at the door. He glanced to the left, thinking he'd heard something, but it was just the boards settling. There was another photo of him saying goodbye to Ben by his front door. Then a new set. Susan and Penny, Ben and Ursula's daughters, on their way to school, standing around the playground, waiting to be picked up outside the gates. Carrigan took a deep breath, flicked through the photos again and carefully placed them back in the envelope.

He poured himself a long drink of whisky and sat down in front of Louise. He touched her photo, feeling a slight electric charge leap across his fingers, and told her about his day, the weather and the lunch he'd had—omitting the three Dime bars—and then he told her like he always did how much he loved her, how the days dragged interminably without her. Finally, he kissed his fingertips and pressed them against the cold glass. He took a deep breath, feeling her in every crevice and fold of his heart, then made himself a microwave meal which he binned half-eaten, the taste bitter and lingering. He checked the flat again, room by room, until he was satisfied there was nothing else amiss, and then he moved the armchair so that it was facing the door. He sat there until morning, waiting and watching.

17

Mﾠore paperwork. Geneva loved it. Most other cops dreaded the moment they had to sit behind a desk and go through pages and pages of seemingly point-less information. They would rather be out on the street, chas-ing the case, but Geneva knew the case lay in these pages and not out in the greater city beyond.

The music screamed loud, too loud, on her earphones, drowning out the drone of the cranes outside. The light glowed green and sickly no matter how many fluorescents and table lamps were switched on. The pages began to merge, words and dates no longer differentiated among the mass of notes, ticks, coffee stains, ash and heat. She kept rubbing oint-ment on her fingers: the stress of the last few days making her skin break out in rashes, red patches and migrating itches.

Grace had begun her thesis with the intention of covering ten or so rebel movements from different African countries. It was a compare-and-contrast exercise. Charles Taylor. Joseph Kony. Robert Mugabe. The names were familiar and not, sound-grabs caught in passing from TV sets and stray conver-sations. She read long detailed descriptions of factional dis-sent, bush tactics, demographic fixing. She flicked and faded, faded and flicked, Coke keeping her wired, too far to sneak out for cigarettes.

She was going through Grace's recent notes when she noticed that something had changed in her approach. She flicked back, scanned and skimmed the previous term's work, noted that the change had occurred around last January.

She leant back and thought about this. She shuffled songs until she found one that suited her. She tried to recall what both the professor and Cecilia had said. She thumbed through her notebook, seeing the scrawled reminders of the two inter-views, desperately hoping she'd written it down.

Miles Cummings had mentioned that Grace's appearance and performance had begun to change when she came back from the Christmas holidays. Geneva took a long drink of Coke and flicked to her notes for Cecilia. There it was again: the Christmas holidays.

Grace had gone off to the Christmas holidays the same Grace she had always been, yet when she came back every-thing was different. Not only that, but the scope of her thesis began to change radically. From looking at ten different rebel groups, Grace had focused on just one: a small splinter faction of the Lord's Resistance Army led by General Lawrence Ngomo, aka the Black-Throated Wind.

Geneva swivelled back on the chair, blood pounding through her fingers. She held her breath, released slowly. She had to double-check, verify, find out more before she could be sure, before she could go to Carrigan with this. She'd seen his reaction when she'd pulled out Ngomo's photo in the inter-view room, his face falling as if they'd been friends and she'd betrayed him in some small but essential way.

The door opened and Geneva jumped, gathering herself together as she saw DS Karlson come in, two mugs of tea in his hand. 'Sorry, I'm late, was chasing something up,' he said by way of apology, handing her a mug and taking a seat next to her. She pulled down the sleeves on her shirt to hide the red patches and began explaining what she'd just discovered.

'You sure the dates match?' Karlson was wearing one of his expensive suits, she could see the fine tailoring and raised stitching, the shoes polished until they resembled something made of onyx. She wondered how long he spent on grooming every morning—much longer than her, she was sure.

'Both mention the Christmas holidays. Something happened to her during the break—it's not just what people said but also the scope of her dissertation. There's all these references to finding the "tapes"—she never fully explains this.'

Karlson smiled one of those smiles; she couldn't tell if it was directed at her or for his own benefit. 'I take it, then, that you don't buy Carrigan's sex-predator theory?'

She looked up from her notes, trying to read Karlson's face, but it was inscrutable, the eyes hooded and bright. 'The more I find out about Grace the less I like that idea,' she replied, grateful for the opportunity to sound out her theories. She told him about Lee's assertion that Ngomo was living in London. 'You should have seen Gabriel's face when I passed him the photo.'

Karlson ran his fingers through the stubble on his head, the sound crisp and sharp in the still room. 'So Grace was researching this General Ngomo and somehow he finds out about it; he's been here several years, presumably living under the radar, and suddenly all this is going to disappear because of some student writing her thesis.' Karlson looked up, thought about it, but she suspected he was thinking about something else. 'Makes sense . . . more so than Carrigan's theory that this is just about sex.' He took out an unusually shiny apple and began eating it. 'I don't understand why he shut you down so quickly.'

Geneva felt her skin itch, resisted the maddening impulse to scratch. 'You know him better than I do.'

Karlson laughed, almost choking on a piece of apple, coughing and righting himself. 'Doesn't like to be contradicted, our Jack,' he replied. 'We've all learned to keep our mouths shut.'

She thought about the report she had to write for Branch, due on Monday. 'Not the first time, then?'

Karlson turned to her, his voice dropping low. 'Not by a

long shot.' He smiled, moving his chair closer. 'Why would he be so reluctant to follow all possible leads?'

'I was asking myself the same thing,' she replied, then caught something in Karlson's look. 'You're not going to tell Branch, are you?' She was suddenly aware that she might have said too much. She caught herself scratching her wrist, stopped.

Karlson shook his head. 'I think we're better off giving Carrigan enough rope, eh?'

'You don't like him much, do you?'

Karlson shrugged. 'He used to be a good copper is what I heard, but he's got sloppy these last few years. Makes our job that much harder. You remember the leaked government report on police profiling?'

Geneva nodded, it had done more damage to the Met than any hectoring *Independent* editorial or police cock-up.

'It was Carrigan who left the file in a coffee shop.'

She recalled the ensuing scandal, the helpful member of the public who found the document and passed it on to a journalist. She could picture the whole scene in her head, Carrigan taking the last sip of his coffee, his mind elsewhere. 'What did they do to him?'

'Moved him to a different station but this was after his wife . . . they were feeling more generous than they ought to have been, a slap on the wrist, nothing more.'

The mention of Carrigan's wife piqued her interest. She continued going through Grace's notes, flicking through sheet after sheet, trying to hide her expression from Karlson. 'I noticed he wears a wedding ring—what's up with that?'

Karlson ran his fingers through his lapels, straightening them and flicking off imaginary lint. 'Never took it off,' he replied cryptically.

'Divorced?' She thought of Oliver's voice on her answering machine, the years she wished could be erased from the ledger of her life.

Karlson shook his head, his teeth glinting as he grinned. 'Nah, killed herself, didn't she? Can't blame her, though, probably couldn't stand Carrigan any longer, took the easy way out.'

Geneva stared at the page in front of her but the words had become fuzzy. She wanted to turn and punch the smiling sergeant in the face. Her stomach dropped abruptly as she realised that while she thought she'd been grilling Karlson about Carrigan, it had actually been the other way round. What had she said? Would this come back to haunt her later? Of course it would, she told herself, everything you say is only stored away until the day it can be used to hurt you. She smiled thinly and chewed the end of her pencil, wondering what she'd just got herself into then, so that she wouldn't think about that, she began thinking about what could possibly have happened to Grace over the Christmas holidays.

She focused back on the pages in front of her, Grace's elegant handwriting filling her vision while Karlson started on another apple. More than ever she felt the answers would be found somewhere in here.

Grace's notes from this year were focused exclusively on General Ngomo. There was a brief summary of his life previous to joining Kony, a short précis worthy of *Who's Who*.

Lawrence Ngomo was born in the Kitum district of northern Uganda sometime in the 1950s. Kitum was part of Acholiland, the ancestral home of the Acholi people. He grew up in the brave and terrifying new world of decolonisation. There were rumours he began a course at university, later to be pushed out during the crackdown on the Acholi people instigated by a president unsure of their loyalty and troubled by their strange ways, their beliefs in spirit mediums and dark angels. The next time Ngomo appeared it was as a senior member of Kony's LRA, rampaging through the north-east of the country. There was no indication of what happened in between. It was up to her to connect the dots. One day Ngomo is a student, the next he's a lieutenant in a rebel army. She knew no life was as simple as that, no trajectory so deliberate as when traced out in print.

She imagined a young man setting out one morning like every morning before, making his way to classes, books in hand, some lunch packed in a small sack, another day of lectures and essay preparations, just another day. Then he's turned away from the main gates or, even worse, called out of the classroom to attend the principal's office. There's the tense and confusing meeting with the head of the university who apologises profusely and then throws his hands up in the air as if saying, *What the government asks, I can but do.* The awkward moments when Ngomo is sitting there, the words tumbling through him, then the realisation that it's over. There won't be that walk tomorrow, there won't be those books under his arm, no more packed lunches, no more essays. Does he argue? Does he shout? Does he try to persuade the principal that he has no politics?

Then comes the blank time. The passage between diligent student and rebel commander. It was easy to trace a line where there was none. It was easy to say that his expulsion from university on the grounds of tribal origin put him on this road which ended with a green uniform and a crouching serenity in the bush, a path that would lead to the days of the Black-Throated Wind.

'Oh my God.' Geneva's head snapped up.

Karlson put his apple down and leant over. She could smell the heady scent of his aftershave as she ran her finger down the page of scrawled transcripts. 'Grace interviewed an ex-child soldier a few months ago; she quotes him in full—listen to this: *General Ngomo liked to get close. He liked to participate when he could. He enjoyed looking into a man's eyes and telling him that he was sorry for what he was about to do but souls needed saving and it wasn't his to question the role that God had made him for. Then, while the soldiers held the captive down, Ngomo cut him open and extracted his heart. I saw this myself several times. He had a medium-sized leather bag with him at all times, into which he placed the heart. They say he kept the heart of every man he killed—that deep in the jungle he'd built some kind of temple and in the deepest room of that temple was a pit filled with thousands of dry and desiccated hearts. He called it his storeroom for the Rapture.'*

Karlson let out a deep plume of air, taking the transcript from her, rereading it, his eyes widening with every word, but Geneva was oblivious. She was on hands and knees, unpacking Grace's boxes until she found what she was looking for. It was under all the other books and papers, a slim pamphlet hued in dark red lines. She pulled it out and stared at the cover. The Black-Throated Wind appeared across the top. Below that, the graphic that had so disturbed her when she'd first seen it: a severed human heart suspended in space, dripping streamers of bright-red blood.

18

He'd started to hate coming into the incident room, the pictures of Grace staring at him from the walls, the unspoken disappointment in her face magnifying day by day until he couldn't bear to look at them any more. The rain was assailing the glass now that some of the gauze had been removed and he could hear the short sharp tattoo as each drop exploded against the window. He checked the daily incident logs, spoke to the HOLMES team and was back at the desk filling in some paperwork when he saw two men enter Branch's office, both black, both wearing suits. He tried to concentrate on the evidence form in front of him but the sound of argument and raised voices coming from the super's office kept distracting him.

He began filling in the action sheets for the week then turned to his computer and saw that he'd received an email from Derbyshire CID. A young boy had gone missing two days previously. Carrigan had a request out for such information. In this new world of computerised policing it was no longer a matter of random phone calls and crossed fingers. He read the boy's description, saw that it fitted with the rest. Private school, fifteen years old, a classical music geek with a good family and better prospects. Until he hadn't returned from school. Carrigan saved the email, he had too much too think about with Grace and maybe, he hoped, the boy would turn up, nothing but a flash of teenage rebellion gone as quickly as it had flared.

Ten minutes later the team began shuffling in for the evening briefing.

'Anything?' He could hear the sharpness in his tone, the brittle edge that the last few days had worked into his voice. He saw the constables looking down at their tables, the cups of tea in their hand, avoiding the walls, avoiding him.

'You're not going to like this,' Jennings's voice sounded thin and parched, 'but we compared the video footage against the photos we took of Gabriel's hands.' Jennings stopped and stared down at his notebook.

'And . . . '

'Gabriel's definitely not the man on the video clip,' Jennings replied apologetically.

Carrigan rubbed his beard, noticing the bristles had grown longer. 'We're sure about this?'

'Gabriel's skin colour is a lot lighter than the man on the video's; also he doesn't bite his nails, the man in the clip does. He may have done something to darken his skin but there's no way he could have faked that. We also compared Gabriel's fingerprints and they don't match those found at the crime scene.'

Carrigan put his head in his hands, rubbed the sore spot blossoming on his temple. It only confirmed what he'd already known. They hadn't had enough evidence connecting Gabriel to the actual crime scene and had had to release him without charge a few hours earlier. Branch had been furious, calling Carrigan into his office, shouting and cursing before Jack had even had a chance to sit down. Carrigan explained that if they charged Gabriel with so little evidence it could seriously derail the chances of getting a conviction if he was indeed the killer. But Branch wasn't interested in that. Branch wanted an arrest, a press conference, newspaper headlines and no more phone calls from the assistant commissioner.

Carrigan turned to Berman. 'Any luck with the video clip?'

Berman looked up from his screen and hunched his shoulders. 'The clip was definitely filmed on an iPhone. The software used to edit the footage is easily available for free on the web. I'd say by looking at the editing that we're not dealing with a professional but at the same time this isn't the easiest software to operate so we're not talking about a beginner either.'

Carrigan looked out of the window at the green sky, thinking how the planning and preparation of the video clip was so at odds with the frenzied and brutal way the killing itself had been effected.

'Also . . .' Berman continued, 'all the scenes from the clip are from quite late on in Grace's ordeal. It's possible he only started filming it near the end.'

Carrigan nodded, thinking this over. 'Which makes you wonder did he plan this all along or did something happen while he was torturing Grace that caused him to take out his phone and film it? Are we any closer to finding out where he uploaded it?'

'An internet cafe on Queensway, Wednesday afternoon. It's one of those fly-by-night places; went down there this morning but they don't have cameras and no one could remember anyone acting suspicious that day.'

Carrigan hadn't held out much hope but it had been necessary to check—problem was every time a lead came back dead he could see the disappointment slump his men's faces as they realised it would only get harder from now on.

'Sir?'

Carrigan turned to see DC Singh tapping her fingers impatiently on the table.

'Maybe we need to look at this in reverse.'

'Explain.'

Singh's fingers stopped their metronomic drumbeat. 'We're assuming he killed Grace and made the video as a souvenir, but what if it's the other way round?' She paused, watching the others take this in. 'What if the video is the point? What if he killed Grace expressly so that he could video it?'

Carrigan hadn't expected this from the usually demure DC. 'You're talking about a snuff film?'

'It's worth a look, right?' Singh replied.

Carrigan scratched his beard. 'It's a good point, but I don't think it's going to help us find this man. If it is something to do with snuff films then our best lead is still going to be focusing on the physical evidence. The "why" won't tell us where he is.' He hadn't wanted to knock Singh down, was pleased at her initiative, but delving into alternative theories wasn't going to help anyone now. The super had made that abundantly clear earlier in their meeting. Branch had seemed to know a lot about the details of the investigation, details Carrigan hadn't supplied in his report. He looked around the room, hearing muffled shouts coming from Branch's office. 'Anyone know where DS Miller is?'

'Pursuing a lead,' Karlson smiled, teeth perfect as a dentist's poster.

Carrigan stared at his sergeant, knowing something had shifted in the dynamics of the team, something subtle yet fundamental. A week ago he would have said he didn't care, that the job had lost whatever promise it had once held out to him, but now, enmeshed in this case, unsure of his team's loyalties, he found with surprise that things had changed. 'I didn't see anything noted in the action book.'

Karlson shrugged. 'That's probably 'cause she thought you'd shut her theory down if she told you about it.'

'"Her theory" . . . is that what it is?' Carrigan replied, annoyed at himself for rising to Karlson's bait yet helpless to ignore it.

'She thought you weren't taking her seriously enough.'

'Any problem I might have with DS Miller is none of your business. It makes me wonder if you really want to solve this case, Sergeant?'

Karlson glared up from his mug. 'Perhaps you should be asking yourself the same question.'

Silence filled the room. Carrigan stared at Karlson, not sure where to take this or how far. Then Berman broke the silence. 'Just spoke to someone at London Transport. Miller asked me to trace Grace's movements through her Oyster card,' he explained.

'Yes?' Carrigan said impatiently.

'There was nothing unusual expect that she made regular trips, at least once a week, to Willesden Green.'

'Willesden Green?' Carrigan racked his brain trying to think of a connection. What was there for Grace in Willesden? Neither Cecilia nor Gabriel lived anywhere near there nor anyone else connected to the case. 'Good work. Get some uniforms to show the photos, see if anyone remembers her. We should look at the possibility that she had a secret boyfriend there and . . .' he paused, watching the uniforms scribbling notes, faces clenched in tight concentration, '. . . and find out where Professor Cummings lives.'

He felt relieved to leave the incident room but when he passed Branch's office things only got worse.

'Carrigan. A moment please.' The super's face was red and spotted, his glasses smudged, his tie askew. Carrigan had little choice but to follow him in.

The two men in dark blue suits he'd glimpsed earlier were standing in Branch's office. Both looked hot and impatient. They watched Carrigan carefully as he entered and took a seat.

'Just the person I wanted to see.' Branch smiled genially; Carrigan knew from experience that this was a bad sign. 'This is DI Carrigan,' Branch explained. 'He's leading the investigation.' He turned back to Carrigan and shrugged. 'The Ugandan embassy is very interested in our progress. I told them that we're close to finding out who did this. I wasn't wrong, was I?'

Carrigan stared at the men. Was there something in their gathered shape, standing side by side, that reminded him of the two men in the car outside his flat last night? Or was he suddenly noticing African faces the way he had on coming back twenty years ago? 'A couple of days should wrap it up,' he replied through gritted teeth.

'Good. Good. We know how expert the British police is in these matters,' the bureaucrat in charge said, shaking Carrigan's hand, his grip firm and unyielding. 'So, Inspector, I'm sure you have your suspects and your theories?'

'We have several,' Carrigan replied. 'But it looks like a sex killing, someone who knew her or was at least familiar with her.'

The bureaucrat nodded slowly as if processing this information. 'Then why, Inspector, if that is indeed so, are you looking into ancient history?'

Carrigan shot Branch a look. 'I don't know what you're talking about.'

The Ugandan shook his head. 'We know that your partner, the female detective . . .'

'DS Miller,' Branch filled in immediately.

'Yes, Miller,' the Ugandan said, still gripping Jack's hand tightly. 'We know that's she's looking into things no one wants to look into. Things that have nothing to do with this case.'

'Ancient history,' Carrigan said, the Ugandan missing the sarcasm in his tone.

'That is so,' the man replied, 'and no one is interested in history. I know you will find out who did this to one of our citizens and I thank you.' His hand finally unclenched from Carrigan's, Jack having to rub the feeling back into his flesh. 'These monsters who take a woman and do to her what they please, there is only one punishment for them.'

Carrigan marched out of the office not looking back and he was almost out of the station when his phone rang. He checked the display but it was only telling him he had two messages. He pressed a button and Ben's voice, thin and strained, crackled through his headset. 'I need to see you. Penny's gone, Jack. Someone took her from football practice at school.'

He never got round to listening to the second message.

Carrigan drove through the darkening city oblivious to the swirling world around him, the sound of Ben's voice ringing in his head. He tried not to think about it, there was nothing he could do until he got there, and he ran through the last hour again, still unsure of its implications. The Ugandans had known a lot about the investigation. He remembered the phone call to the embassy, the junior diplomat who'd been about to tell him something then stopped. What had he seen?

He crossed the Great West Road and watched with envy the cars streaming through the twilight like illuminated candy. The spiralling lights announced themselves before he'd turned the corner and instantly something in his blood perked and simmered. Every time he heard a siren he wondered what new evil had occurred; they were never neutral lights flashing mysteriously in the night—always blood, bodies and broken lives. But he wasn't prepared for the sight that greeted him as he turned into Ben's street and saw the parked cars, lights flashing, the SOCO van, the sense of hurried concentration on the uniformed men's faces.

He flashed his warrant card and rushed past them. Ben's door was swinging open, the stained-glass panel with its retinue of gold bedecked angels dazzling in the late sinking sun. He found Ben talking to a Chiswick CID inspector in the main room, his tone flat and unruffled, his eyes quickly acknowledging Jack.

'Thanks for arriving so quickly.' They came together in a semi-hug, Carrigan smelling the whisky on Ben's breath and below that a sour tang of sweat. He looked to his right and saw Ursula holding Penny in her arms, the little girl crying and shaking as a Family Liaison Officer tried calming mother and daughter down.

'When did she come back?'

'Someone dropped her off at the end of the street a few minutes ago,' Ben replied, his hands still shaking, his eyes continually looking in Penny's direction as if to assure himself she was still there.

'Is she all right?'

Ben stared across the room at his daughter. 'I think so. I'm not sure. I don't know, Jack, Jesus look at her.'

The girl was crying, shielding herself from the group of policemen gathered around her. A sergeant was trying to ask her some questions. Ben grabbed Jack's arm. 'Let's go upstairs.'

Ben led him into the study, the smell of cigars and whisky heavy and dolorous. They sat down and Jack poured them both drinks. 'Did she see who took her?'

Ben stared out the window. 'No, not really. He picked her up from the school, said we'd sent him, somehow convinced the coach.' Ben looked down at his hands and shook his head. 'She got into the car with him, Jesus Christ!'

Jack passed him the drink, watched as Ben downed it in one. 'He just drove her around for a few hours then dropped her off. She said . . . she said he was African. What did he want from her, Jack? What the fuck did he do to my daughter?'

'I don't know,' Jack admitted. 'I don't understand it myself. I'm sure the inspector downstairs will find out.' He could see that Ben was barely hearing him, his eyes bright with fear and worry. 'You didn't by any chance get a look at the material I gave you, Grace Okello's thesis?'

Ben nodded slowly, his feet tapping the floor, the adrenaline rush of a near miss coursing through his veins. 'I saw the YouTube clip. Jesus. The things they did to her.' He looked up from his glass, sympathy draining the years from his face. 'This is your life, isn't it? Murder, distraught parents who think they're never going to see their kids again. I never really thought about it before, the shit you have to go through every day.'

Jack sat back down and cradled his glass. 'Was there anything in the thesis? Anything that might have got her killed?'

Ben slid forward on the chair, propping his thin elbows on the table. 'This Okello woman was looking into things that no one wants exhumed, not the government and not the bad guys. But, to go back to your question, I don't think it's very likely. The thesis hadn't yet been published, most of it's in the form of notes, there's no accountable chain of evidence for her conclusions. You really think that someone killed her because of it?'

Carrigan stared into his best friend's eyes knowing he couldn't put it off any longer. 'I think the Ugandan embassy may be involved in some way. I keep thinking we're getting closer and then I realise we're only seeing a small fraction of the whole,' he continued, not sure how to break the news. 'And whenever I get a sense that I'm being followed during a case, I get hinky, I start wondering about things . . .'

'Someone's following you?' He heard the concern in Ben's voice that the missing years hadn't managed to revoke, remembered their shared oaths of loyalty to each other, David's smile when they all agreed never to forget those days.

He told him about the envelope in his flat, the pictures of him and Ben, the pictures of the girls. He watched Ben's eyes hood and turn dark as he assimilated the information. He watched Ben slowly pour himself a large measure of whisky.

'Photos of my girls?' Ben said, trying to stop his bottom lip from twitching.

Carrigan nodded, knowing he could never understand the fear and panic of a parent, that he'd always be the one giving the news rather than receiving it. 'I think he's been following me since the first morning,' he added, looking down at the floor. 'He saw me come here the night I gave you the thesis. He took the photos then.'

Something in Ben's expression changed as if a switch had been flicked. 'Are you saying you led this man here?' His voice had taken on an inflexible authority that Jack had previously only heard him use on hapless students. 'Fuck, is this the man who took Penny? Is this what you're talking about?'

Carrigan thought of Cecilia and Gabriel, Geneva alone out on the streets. 'Maybe,' he admitted.

'Jesus fucking Christ!' Ben suddenly exploded, fear blushing his face a deep scarlet. 'You put my family in danger?'

Carrigan saw the whole scenario click itself into place in Ben's head, the sudden thickening of life into something more than missed engagements and petty arguments. Ben reached across the table and gripped Jack's wrist. His face was white, the muscles jumping below the skin. 'What the fuck does this man want with my family?'

Carrigan shrugged and Ben tightened his grip. 'Jack, fucking tell me.'

'I don't know, I really don't, Ben,' he answered, seeing his friend's face drain and collapse. It was easy to forget the everyday fear that cops had to become inured to. Easy to forget not everyone lived their lives like that. 'It could be he's trying to scare me off the case.'

He watched Ben's face fall. Full marks for putting the victim at ease, Carrigan sourly thought. 'You keep the shotgun here or at your parents' house in Dorset?'

Ben's eyes widened then squinted down to two small blue stones. 'Here,' he said, so quietly that Carrigan almost missed it.

'As a policeman they'd sack me for telling you this, but as a friend . . . I'd advise you to keep it handy until all this is over.'

Ben hung his head, clenched his fists and ground his feet into the floor. 'This is because you gave me the fucking dead girl's thesis? That's what this is all about?' He got up without waiting for an answer, strode over to his desk and started throwing papers and pamphlets onto the floor until he found what he was looking for. He walked back over to Jack and threw the copy of Grace's thesis into his lap. 'Fucking keep it,' he snarled. 'Don't get me involved again.'

Carrigan walked along the river for half an hour, not noticing the people strolling past, the sunset, or the boats slowly moving up the silty water. He got to the bridge where his childhood friend had leapt from, his body lost in the current, and went into a newsagent where he bought ten Camels and a lighter. He stood by the river and smoked his first cigarette in a year, coughing and choking on the acrid smoke, and then he flung the rest of the pack into the grey water. He watched as it was pulled and pushed by the current. When his phone beeped he felt an unexpected rush of excitement, hoping it was Geneva, but it was only a reminder that he still had one unchecked message.

'I need to see you.'

He recognised Cecilia's voice immediately, except that the panic and fear had drowned out everything but the words themselves. 'I didn't tell you everything when you interviewed me. I'm so sorry.'

19

The storms came more often now. Raging, bruised thunderheads approaching from east of the city and breaking upon its streets as people scuttled home on the Tube or flagged down a bus, its windows steamed with condensation and finger-smear.

Carrigan stood under a low bridge of the Regent's Park Canal, suspended ten feet below the city streets, trying to get out of the worst of the rain. He felt like a bit-part character in a bad late-night film, the one who always gets killed a third of the way through. Joggers ran past him, their faces staring into the distance, oblivious of all around them, their sneakered feet beating out a rhythm on the concrete embankment. The pleasure boats and guided taxis were mostly gone for the day, the residents of the numerous houseboats all battened down and behind closed shades. Ducks sailed by, gleaming like wooden toys; leaves twisted and fluttered and gathered at his feet.

Some days the Regent's Park Canal could look like Amsterdam. Some days Venice, if you squinted hard enough. But today it looked like something from another century, a world of coal-laden tugboats slowly inching their way up the water, bedraggled mules pulling them along; a ghost of London past shimmering out of the drizzle and then just as quickly dissolving. Carrigan thought of the lost and hidden rivers of the capital, the Effra Brook, the Fleet, the Tyburn, the Neckinger, and the Walbrook, this other city humming beneath his feet; stand still long enough and you could hear it through the soles of your shoes.

He watched the rain sluice across the grey-green canal water and checked his watch for the third time in ten minutes. She was almost an hour late.

He started at every noise, every crackle of foliage or hum of rail. The scream of macaws and other exotic birds from the nearby zoo made him feel uneasy with unbidden memories. He was checking his watch again when he saw a figure approach from the other end of the tunnel.

She stopped halfway, a dark shrouded thing suspended in the middle distance. He stood still, didn't make any sudden moves. He watched her head turn one way then another as if she'd heard some unexpected noise behind her. She looked back one last time, then continued walking.

They stood there for a moment, under the dark shadow of the railway bridge, both unsure what to do as a lone canal boat glided silently across the water. Cecilia ducked behind a stanchion as it went past.

'I'm glad you called me,' Carrigan said.

Cecilia looked like a bad photocopy of the girl they'd interviewed only a few days ago, the spark and flare drained out of her. She glanced to either side of him, then down at the floor. 'He's been following me all this time. I had to leave the flat, stay over at a friend's after I saw . . . I saw the video.' Her eyes darted like trapped things, her voice trembling in the cold air. Carrigan stepped closer and gently took her by the arm. 'It's okay now, I'm here.'

She nodded and for a moment Carrigan saw something else beneath the granite grimace and hunted eyes, a young girl who'd found herself locked in the attitude and bearing of a person she never thought she'd be.

'What happened, Cecilia?'

She was staring up at the cross-hatched girder-work on the

underside of the bridge as if the metal and brass were a language only she could decipher. A train rumbled overhead, causing her to flinch. 'I'm sorry. Maybe this was a bad idea. If he sees me. If he followed me . . .'

'Who? Gabriel? Gabriel Otto?'

Something crossed Cecilia's face and then it was gone like sunlight hitting water. She managed a small dry chuckle. 'Gabriel's an idiot.'

'He struck me as somewhat more than that when we interviewed him.'

Cecilia looked momentarily confused. 'You arrested Gabriel for . . . ?' She couldn't say it, didn't want the words to come out of her mouth and seal this thing in truth.

'We're looking into it.' A noise in the bushes caused them both to turn, fall into silence, but it was nothing, just squirrels or the wind upsetting the litter. 'Why did you laugh when I mentioned Gabriel?'

Cecilia stared at the bushes. 'Gabriel's a fool. Just a spoiled kid playing grown-up games. He's not capable of such a thing.'

'How can you be so certain?'

'People who spend all their time talking about violence and struggle are normally the last to take up arms.'

He wasn't sure how good a defence that would be in court but something about it rang true.

'Grace never took him seriously.'

'And that didn't upset him?'

For the first time, Cecilia laughed unguardedly. It sounded like another girl, one who was carefree and content, whose life had never hiccuped, never grown thick with death. 'Gabriel just goes on to the next one. He doesn't care.'

Carrigan flashed back to the pale-skinned woman wrapped up in Gabriel's sheets, the dead-eyed look on the young man's face. 'Grace told Gabriel she was seeing a source; he said she seemed very excited about it.'

'Shit. Shit.' It was the first time he'd heard her swear. 'I told her not to meet him,' she finally said, 'I knew he was wrong from the minute I laid eyes on him.'

Carrigan took a deep breath to steady himself. The canal water tilted and the screaming of jungle birds carried like the cries of abandoned infants. 'Who are you talking about, Cecilia?'

She looked across the water. 'I saw him outside my flat after you two had left that day. Just standing there, staring at me.' Carrigan clutched her arm, felt the blood and tension simmering inside. 'Why didn't you tell us any of this before?' He tried to smooth the frustration out of his voice but he could tell from the girl's face that it wasn't working.

'I was scared,' she replied. 'I thought if I didn't speak of him he wouldn't come back. I'd just heard about Grace, I was so confused that day.'

'But it was because of him you missed your meeting with Professor Cummings and haven't gone back to SOAS?'

Cecilia nodded.

'How did Grace meet this man?'

'As I told you before, Grace had become obsessed by her work, spending day and night in the library reading every book there was on East African history and politics, but what she really wanted was first-hand accounts. She used Gabriel to make contact with several émigrés. But she didn't find anyone who knew what she needed or who was willing to talk. She started posting messages asking for information on this Ugandan chat forum we use to catch up with what's going on back home.'

Carrigan could feel the creeping cold against his skin, the biting canal wind whipping through the trees, the sense of time speeding up like on a fairground ride. 'What kind of messages?'

'She wanted to get in touch with ex-child soldiers from Ngomo's army.'

He breathed deep, stared at the water. A dog barked somewhere in the distance. 'Did anyone get back to her?'

'She had a lot of replies but mainly she deleted them, saying it was the wrong part of the country, or the wrong years, but there was one reply a few weeks ago that got her excited. I remember because we were both sitting in the library when she received it. She turned to me and said, *This one's dates match.* She kept rereading the email, saying how she'd finally made a breakthrough. I tried to warn her, tell her that she didn't know who had sent this, what their reasons were, but she just called me paranoid. She wrote back and said she was very interested in meeting him. I told her I'd accompany her but she didn't want me to. We had our first real argument over that. She said this was a very sensitive thing, that if I turned up it might spook her one and only chance at finding out the truth. At least I persuaded her to make the first meeting at the university cafeteria.'

'It sounds like she was after a particular bit of information. Do you know what it was?'

'No. She never spoke about her thesis, even to me. It was her little secret, she used to say.'

Carrigan stood absolutely still, the rain soaking through his coat and plastering his shirt to his skin. He'd so quickly dismissed Geneva's theory about a connection between Grace's work and her murder. He couldn't tell if it was because the evidence hadn't pointed to that conclusion or because he'd suspected that Branch had fed her the story to discredit him.

'I followed her,' Cecilia continued, her voice drawn and tired. 'I'd waited until she left class that morning and I could tell from her mood, her expression, that she was going to meet this source.'

Carrigan suddenly leant forward, startling Cecilia. 'Did you say *source*? Was that the word Grace used?'

'She called him her source. I thought she was being overly dramatic, like this was Watergate or something.'

'Did the man turn up?'

'Right on time. He approached her table, Grace got up, they shook hands, exchanged greetings and then both sat down. I couldn't hear what they were saying, there was some kind of birthday party going on, loud music, but they were talking heatedly, friendly but fast. It seemed like they were getting on well.'

Carrigan felt his heart beat in his chest, the slow fade and pulse of his own life. 'What did this man look like?'

'Acholi. Under twenty definitely, maybe only seventeen or eighteen. The moment I saw him I knew he was wrong. There was something about him. Those eyes. Everyone from my country has seen that stare before. There was nothing there. Like a ghost. He had short dreads and wore an orange T-shirt and torn jeans. I sat there hoping, wishing, that Grace would sense something too and I'd see her get up, say thank you, and walk off into the rest of her life.'

'But she kept talking to him?'

'For half an hour at least. Then, at the end, something strange happened.' Cecilia looked around at the empty towpath. 'This man, he reached his hand out across the table and Grace took it. She held his hand in hers and that's when . . .' She looked away, snared by some sound. '. . . That was when he saw me. He held Grace's hand and stared directly into my eyes and it was like he was judging me right there and then and he'd found me wanting but that wasn't the worst thing . . .' Carrigan saw Cecilia shudder as she stared down at her feet, 'The worst thing was when he smiled . . . his teeth . . . they were sharp, pointed . . . like . . . like the teeth of a vampire.'

20

The bar was dark and dingy, the way bars were in his memory, but this was just the doldrums of a Sunday afternoon. There was only one occupied table, four male students, drunk already, their voices rising with each sip of their beers. Carrigan walked over to the bar and stood there for a couple of minutes as the barman resolutely ignored him, chatting on a mobile phone and stacking bottled ales.

Carrigan was glad for the pause, it gave him time to think, to clear his head which was still reeling from Cecilia's revelation. The music screamed with wailing guitars, the smell of old beer and chips hung in the dull air. He remembered another student bar, very much like this one, the three of them sitting around a table like conspirators, degrees in pockets, planning their trip to Africa. He felt a sharp pain rattle through his chest. He missed David so much and all these years of pretending he didn't, of trying to carve out a new life for himself, made the pain all that much more acute now.

'What can I get you?' The barman looked at Carrigan with barely concealed antipathy. He was tall and wore long blond dreadlocks slung across his shoulder like a lion's mane. His T-shirt declared capitalism is dead and his face was decorated with hoops and piercings, tattooed bar codes and silver rings.

Carrigan pulled out his warrant card, watching the barman's eyes turn narrow and guarded when he saw what it was. The music got louder, Carrigan sure the barman had just raised the volume. His ears began to ring, a high-pitched whine that was a constant reminder of Africa. 'Can you turn it down, please?'

The barman looked up from his chores. 'Listen, old man,' his accent pure Notting Hill, public schools and Sunday-afternoon cricket matches. 'If it's too loud for you, you can always leave.'

Carrigan bit his lip, turned and walked over to the jukebox. The drunks stared up from their pints as he took the cable and wrenched the plug out of the wall with one quick snap of his wrist. The music died mid-song. The students shot him dirty looks but, drunk as they were, even they could see the tightness in his features, the thinness of his lips, and decided that, actually, no music was fine by them.

Carrigan reached the bar and placed both his arms across the wooden surface. 'What's your name?'

'Flash.'

'That's what you use to clean the toilet with. What's your real name?'

Flash looked left and right then whispered 'Tarquin' so quietly Carrigan barely caught it.

'Hmm,' Carrigan snorted, 'I think I prefer Flash. There was a birthday party here two weeks ago, Friday the seventeenth. I need to get in touch with whoever was organising it.'

The barman tossed back his mane of hair and looked down at the scratched surface of the bar. 'Can't remember,' he replied, turning his back to Carrigan and started stacking bottles again. Carrigan laid Grace's photo flat on the bar. 'How about her? She was here that Friday. I don't suppose you remember serving her?'

Flash turned back and glared at Carrigan. He picked something out of his teeth with a long curved fingernail. Carrigan could smell the man now, unwashed clothes, stale smoke and something else, far less pleasant, underneath. 'What? You expect I'm some fucking memory man?' Flash replied. 'You know how many people come here on a Friday night?'

'But a big birthday party, lots of tips, you'd remember that surely?' Carrigan could feel the moment slipping, he'd come here flushed with hope that Cecilia's statement would be the break they'd been waiting, praying, for but now he realised he'd been as foolish as his most callow constable.

'I do my job, serve up the drinks, anything else—not my concern.' Flash turned back to the refrigerators and continued stacking.

'Come here,' Carrigan said, his voice thick with authority. Flash slowly turned and shuffled up to the bar. Carrigan reached forward and grabbed the young man by one of his long dreadlocks. He immediately regretted it, the hank of hair greasy and sticky in his grip, revulsion crawling up his throat, but he held on. 'You know cops have this extra sense thing,' he said, twisting the young man's hair, 'like a sixth sense. Like how I can see your future by just looking into your eyes.'

Flash struggled against Carrigan's grip but there was nothing he could do. 'Yeah?'

'Yeah,' Carrigan replied. 'And guess what? I see you with short hair, a suit and a BlackBerry in your hand. A nice blonde wife from Hampshire and a flat in Limehouse close to your office in the city.'

Something in Flash's eyes recoiled as if he'd inadvertently caught a glimpse of his true self in a passing mirror.

'Serving people, that's what you do, isn't it? Must be hard these days,' Carrigan continued, changing the subject, 'what, with girls looking much older than they actually are. Would be easy to make a simple mistake, serve someone under-age, get yourself into a lot of trouble.' He let go of Flash's hair and wiped his hand on his trousers, registering the barman's eyes, the way they widened then shut down. 'Now you wouldn't want me sending in uniforms on a regular basis, making ID checks, would you? Might drive some of your customers away, having the police in here all the time.'

Flash's face blanched; he tried to hide it but it was no good. 'What do you want?' he said under his breath.

Carrigan pointed up at the CCTV camera. 'How long do you keep the security tapes before you recycle them?'

The barman smiled. 'Wiped every week,' he replied with great satisfaction. Carrigan held his jaw rigid, tried not to let the disappointment show.

'But you do remember the birthday party, right?'

The barman shrugged. 'What, someone snuck a fag? You're here to solve the mystery of the missing Marlboro?'

'No,' Carrigan calmly replied pointing to the photo of Grace. 'This girl was murdered last week and we believe she met her killer here.'

The barman stopped what he was doing, stared at Carrigan as if suspecting this was some kind of joke, then picked up the photo and studied it. 'I know the day you're talking about but I wasn't lying when I said I couldn't remember her.'

Carrigan nodded. 'You don't happen to know the name of the person whose birthday it was?'

Flash put the photo back down, actually thought about this for a second or two. ''Fraid not. Some girl, that's all I know.'

'Shit!' Carrigan slammed his fist down against the bar, making Flash jump as if he'd been on the receiving end of an electric shock. Carrigan looked down at the photo of Grace, silently mouthing an apology, and started to gather up his things.

'But you should check Facebook,' Flash said.

Carrigan looked up. 'What?'

'Facebook. You know what that is, old man?' He smiled, revealing teeth yellow as corn husks.

Carrigan nodded though he'd never actually been on the site himself and had no real idea what its purpose was.

'They posted all the photos there. Sent us a link. There'll be the name of the lucky girl at the top of the page.'

But it wasn't her name that Carrigan was interested in any more as he waited for the surly barman to copy the address off his laptop.

He rushed into the incident room, his jacket all rumpled, hair messed up by the wind and rain.

'Sir?' DC Singh raised her head from her desk, flicked back her hair. 'I was just wondering . . .'

'Not now,' Carrigan cut her off, marched past Berman and Jennings and entered his office. He'd left the window open and one quarter of the room was covered in rainwater. He put his coffee down on the table, the smell making him feel human again. He could see the others staring through the glass partition, wondering what was up, but he ignored them, booted up his computer and sat there feet tapping, his fingers unable to sit still as he waited. He took a sip of the coffee, restraining himself, wanting to make it last, and thought about David again, the student bar bringing back sour memories, and then when his browser was ready he typed in the Facebook link that Flash had given him.

He thought it would be simple. He thought it would be easy. He thought all he needed to do was type in the address and he'd find what he was looking for.

But first he had to sign up. There was a box on the right-hand side of the screen asking for his personal details. He typed slowly: name, username, password, confirm password . . . then clicked. The screen refreshed but it was the same screen. He stared at it, frustrated, not sure what he'd done wrong. His password was highlighted in red, he must have typed it differently the second time. He corrected the mistake and pressed enter.

Nothing. The screen refreshed and told him there was something wrong with his fields. He shook his head, ground his feet into the floor and re-entered all the information from scratch. This time the site accepted his registration but just as the new page was loading the browser crashed.

He refreshed it and entered his details for the fourth time. Watched as a new page unscrolled in front of him. There were so many options, so many boxes to fill, and what the hell was a 'profile' anyway? He tried entering the address he'd been given but the site kept demanding he create a profile first. He started filling out the form, ran out of time, the page refreshed, and he lost all the data he'd inputted.

'Shit!' He punched the keyboard in frustration, catching the end of his coffee cup and sending it flying across the desk, covering the computer in thick sweet liquid. He cursed, reached into his drawers for some tissues and tried to soak up the worst of the mess but it seemed to just make it spread faster and there was now an acrid burning smell coming from his hard drive. He got up, brushed the coffee off his trousers and stuck his head through the door. 'Berman!' he shouted, watching as the constables snapped their heads up then quickly back down when they registered his expression.

Berman got onto the site in less than a minute. Carrigan stood behind him, taking deep breaths, telling himself this was probably nothing, another dead-end, no reason to get too excited.

'You know how Facebook works?' Berman looked up from the screen.

'Don't know and don't care,' Carrigan replied. 'Just see if they've posted photos of the birthday party.'

Berman nodded, his left hand shooting down and worrying the ends of his prayer shawl. His other hand skimmed across the keyboard, clicking furiously. 'Two hundred and forty-four of them.'

'Jesus!' Carrigan shook his head.

'Digital cameras,' Berman replied. 'People just snap away, doesn't matter what they're snapping.'

A bit like mobile phones and Twitter, Carrigan thought, people talking just for the sake of talking, yet it was this very randomness he was pinning his hopes on. He watched as Berman clicked and a new window opened, a prompt asking whether they wanted to see the pictures individually or as a slideshow.

'One by one—and slowly,' Carrigan said, pulling up a chair and taking a seat next to Berman.

Berman clicked photo after photo. The birthday girl was blonde and lovely. Carrigan felt something in him ache—she reminded him of Louise the first time they'd met, across an interview table, her beauty untarnished by the clients she represented, her voice the only thing he could hear that day.

Most of the photos were blurry, indistinct, people smeared in bouts of movement or shot in such close-up all he could see was bad skin and gleaming teeth. They looked so young these students, so unencumbered by life.

Berman quickly flicked through a set taken at the birthday table, endless bottles of wine and half-filled glasses surrounding the group. 'Faster,' Carrigan ordered, tapping his foot, impatient, wondering whether this was all another crazy waste of time when he suddenly grabbed Berman's arm and said, 'Stop.'

There she was. Grace. Sitting at a table, a huge smile on her face, caught in the margins of the photo. Carrigan felt his heart speed up, saw that Berman was now staring at the screen with a new concentration. They both looked at the shadowed form of the man's back. The man sitting opposite Grace. Her killer.

The party had started to break up and the photographer was now moving around the room. Berman flicked through the next sequence but there was nothing but smiles, misty eyes and raised toasts. Then he stopped, staring at the screen, holding his breath. Carrigan pushed his chair forward and leant across Berman. 'Oh my God.'

They were staring at a photo of the birthday girl. She was standing to the right of the frame, holding a bottle of champagne and the waist of a young man. But it wasn't that which drew the two detectives' eyes, it was the background.

They could see the back of Grace's head, her luxurious bounty of hair, one hand raised in the middle of some unknowable gesture. Across from her sat a young black male, his face illuminated by the camera flash.

'Can we get this any bigger?'

Berman clicked some keys and the picture opened up in a new browser window. He clicked and panned until the man's face was at the centre of the photo.

Carrigan blinked twice as he finally stared into the killer's face. He looked so young, terribly young, that at first Carrigan felt a slight disappointment, but there was something about his eyes, the more you looked at them the more they seemed to be looking at you.

As he stared at the image of Grace's killer he saw the eyes which had stared back at him that first day outside King's Court.

PART TWO

Back Then . . .

Time began to move in strange currents, simultaneously speeding up and slowing down as Jack opened the car door and saw the soldiers' guns shaking in their drunken hands, the flare of birds tearing the night sky above them.

They'd been told about these sudden roadblocks—hushed voices in their Kampala hotel relating stories of miraculous escapes, ugly situations diffused with a timely joke. He hoped this was all it was, another all-purpose story to reel out at future dinner parties.

'Passports!' The lieutenant was younger than them but the oldest of his group. He looked barely past puberty. He gestured with his rifle and watched as Ben and David got out of the car and took their place next to Jack in the clearing. The other soldiers stood by the roadblock passing a bottle of murky liquid among themselves and laughing, their voices echoing through the jungle night.

'It'll be okay,' Ben whispered as he handed his passport to the lieutenant.

Jack saw David mumbling to himself, his head hanging down and the small blue book fluttering in his hands as if it were some rare butterfly longing for the sky.

The lieutenant flicked through their passports, pressing his face close to the pages as if this would divine the truth of these items. When he got to Ben's and saw the folded money, he paused, and Jack held his breath, watching the lieutenant's eyes look up and find Ben.

'You must think we are animals,' he said, his voice surprisingly soft and melodic.

Before Ben could reply the lieutenant turned to his men and barked an order and suddenly they were inside the car, going through their stuff, throwing things out onto the dark muddy track.

'We were trying to get to Murchison Falls,' Jack explained, the moment contracting and pulsing, a strange feeling, like slipping out of time, his head rattling with possible outcomes, every click and cough magnified.

The lieutenant smiled revealing a mouth totally barren of teeth, pink as a baby's fist. 'This is restricted territory,' he replied curtly, his eyes scanning the interior of the car like a pair of searchlights.

'But the guide book said the park was open.'

The lieutenant looked at Jack. 'How can a book know the truth of the world?' He seemed genuinely perplexed. Jack was about to reply when one of the soldiers handed the lieutenant something he'd found in the car. He took it, nodded and looked it over. Jack felt his heart skip as he recognised his own notebook.

'What's this?' The lieutenant waved it around as if it were too hot to hold.

'It's my notebook, I write songs in it.' Jack's voice quivered and he felt Ben's hand light reassuringly on the back of his arm.

The lieutenant flicked through the pages of melodies and themes, bass clefs and crotchets. He shook his head then looked back up at them. 'If that is so then why is it written in code?'

The truck crashed against the dirt road, sending dust and small stones into their faces and hair. They were handcuffed to a pole at the back of the truck's open bed. They were facing away from each other, keeping their eyes closed against the wind and grit.

The truck lurched and span and Jack couldn't hold it in any longer, puking over his own clothes, the fear and nausea drowning his lungs. He hung his head and concentrated on the rusty flaked bed of the truck but all he could hear was a strange breathless burble of words and then he realised it was David, his voice cracked and faltering, the Lord's Prayer coming out of his mouth and just as quickly disappearing in the wind and jungle screams.

'Stop fucking praying,' Jack snapped. 'You're freaking me out.'

'What's going to happen?' The panic in David's voice made Jack wish he hadn't interrupted. 'What are they going to do to us?'

'Nothing,' Ben said firmly. 'It's just a stupid misunderstanding.' He had to raise his voice to be heard above the truck's motor. 'They'll take us to their commander who's bound to be slightly more intelligent and they'll realise they made a mistake.'

'What if they don't? What if—'

'Shut up, Jack,' Ben screamed. 'Now's not the time.'

Jack turned his head and faced the road, seeing the jungle fly by in their wake, the smear of colours, green and black and blue, like something painted by a lunatic.

The room was small and hot and stank of sweat and shit. A one-eyed soldier was sitting behind an old wooden desk going through their papers, passports, toiletries, tickets. He stroked a thin goatee which hung like moss from his chin as he consulted the documents with all the seriousness of a small-town bureaucrat. His eye-patch was made of red leather, scuffed and faded like an old cricket ball. He held out the notebook. 'Whose is this?' His voice was flat and grainy as if he were wrestling the very words in his mouth.

'It's mine,' Ben replied before Jack had a chance to answer.

'He's lying.' Jack stepped towards the desk. 'It's mine. It's got my name on it.' He turned and glared at Ben—he wasn't David, didn't need Ben to protect and shield him from the vagaries of the world.

The soldier flicked through the book then put it to one side. 'You are a spy.'

Jack didn't know what to say—for a moment he didn't even understand and then he did. 'We're tourists,' he protested.

Eye-patch shook his head and wiped sweat from his brow. He held the notebook up, pointing at one of the scrawled pages. 'This is not English. This is code. Only spies use code.'

Jack understood how quickly things had changed. 'It's musical notation,' he replied and tried to explain what the symbols stood for then grasped that the soldier had probably never even seen a piano before let alone written music. It was infuriating, trying to explain something so obvious and realising that what you took for granted was not really so.

Eye-patch considered this, looking back down at the notebook, flicking through its damp pages, then putting the notebook up against one ear, his face clenched in mock concentration. 'Music? This is not music.'

Jack watched as Ben and David were quickly surrounded. He could feel the air literally stop in his throat, something he'd always thought only a metaphor, and he had to will himself to take another breath. The soldiers took Ben and David, leading them through the door into a corridor shrouded in darkness. David looked back at the last moment and Jack saw tears running down his face.

'Where are you taking them?' Jack screamed, finally letting the rage, frustration and weariness explode through him. Being reasonable hadn't helped, maybe outrage would.

'This is a war,' the soldier stated flatly. 'In war spies must be killed.'

'It's *my* notebook.' He felt a thin red thread of panic uncoil in his stomach like some long-sleeping sea monster finally woken. 'Let them go, it's nothing to do with them. You can keep me till we get this sorted out but please let them go. I told you we're not spies, it's . . . it's just fucking ridiculous.'

Eye-patch shook his head sadly as if admonishing a favourite nephew. 'And if you were spies . . . would you not likewise say that you were not?' He paused looking down at Jack. 'You are an intelligent man, yes?'

Jack nodded.

'Then you must see my problem. How can I tell the true man from the false?'

21

At least this time she wasn't made to wait. Branch opened the door and ushered her into his office. The room smelled hot and close, cigar smoke and stale male sweat as if a group of rugby players had only just vacated it. Geneva took shallow breaths through her mouth and sat down.

She'd been dreading this ever since her first meeting with Branch, a week ago. It seemed like much longer but that was the thing about murder investigations—they existed on their own timeframe and it was all too easy to lose track of the world.

Branch was going through a bunch of papers, nodding and shaking his head, aligning them and straightening the edges. She could see her own typed report fluttering in his thick fingers, his eyes going back and forth across the sentences she'd had so much difficulty putting together.

'So, how are you liking your promotion?' Branch looked up but he seemed preoccupied, his eyes constantly glancing towards his row of phones.

Geneva shuffled on the chair and tried to work out what he wanted from her, what role she should be playing. She knew his innocent question was anything but.

'It's good to be back on a major case,' she replied.

Branch nodded, stared down at the line of mobiles on his table. 'Of course it is.' He pressed a button on one of the phones. 'I've read your report,' he said, his eyes fixed on the blinking light of the handset. 'A bit thin—I was hoping for something more from you, Miller.'

Geneva stared down at her shoes, rubbed the red patch on her wrist. 'I didn't feel the need to repeat anything that was already in the daily incident log.'

Branch eyes flicked up. 'That's not what I meant.'

'I can only report what I've observed.'

'Of course, of course, but you know very well that's not why I gave you this secondment.' Branch put the report down, all one page of it, picked up another piece of paper and read it briefly. It was handwritten. She thought she could see her name on it. 'Tell me about Carrigan.'

It was the question she'd dreaded, the only reason, she knew, that he'd asked her in here for this meeting. She opened her mouth then closed it, looked up at the photos of blood-soaked boxers. 'You asked me to report what I'd seen and that's what I've done, sir. You didn't ask me to write a psycho-logical profile.'

Branch stared at her silently, trying to work out whether she was being sarcastic. She could hear the clock behind him ticking off the seconds. She thought about the briefing she was missing and how the next few minutes could affect the rest of her career. 'He hasn't done anything wrong that I've observed,' she added.

'And you're certain he's following all possible lines of inves-tigation?'

The way he glared at her made her think of the handwritten report she'd seen on his desk, the use of that particular phrase a reminder of an earlier conversation she'd had. She wanted to lie to Branch, an unexpected loyalty to Carrigan rising in her, but when she looked up Branch was slowly shaking his head. 'Just tell me, Miller. Don't think I don't know anyway.'

'I'm . . . I'm not sure that he is . . . pursuing all avenues.' She felt deflated once the words were out, the sound of them like a shrill cry in her ears. 'I don't think he trusts my input. He thinks I'm working for you and that everything I come up with is some ruse to trap him.'

Branch looked up. 'And why on earth would he think that?'

Geneva let it drop. 'It's undermining my attempts to investigate this case properly.'

Branch squeezed a thin smile through his lips, dropped his reports and nodded. 'Go on, explain what you mean, Sergeant.' He emphasised the last word, his eyes crinkling behind his glasses.

There was no way back now, she had to tell him. She hoped Carrigan would understand.

She explained about her research into Grace's thesis, the missing laptop, the way Grace had come back from the Christmas holidays changed and how her thesis manifested this change by narrowing its focus to General Ngomo. She told him how the ripped-out heart was the general's signature back in Uganda and how certain she was of these connections. 'There's too much now for it to be just coincidence.' She looked at the clock, felt her confidence returning as Branch listened without interruption. 'I think General Ngomo found out that Grace was investigating him and his past deeds and decided she was better off dead.'

She sat back in the chair and took a deep breath. She didn't know if what she'd just done could be counted as a betrayal of her DI—Carrigan would definitely see it as such—but she'd always believed that the case was more important than any one person's feelings.

Branch put a hand up to his head, running his fingers through greying tufts of hair. She could see him digesting the information, his eyes narrowing as facts and theories clicked. He looked up finally, gave her a pleasant smile. 'Nonsense. Absolute nonsense.'

Geneva wasn't sure she'd heard him right and leant forward, about to speak, to defend her theory, when Branch cut her off.

'I know you're young and inexperienced but believe me you'll find over time that nearly all murders have simple basic solutions. We'd never even get our clearance rate over ten per cent if murder was this baroque conspiracy you think it to be.'

She'd thought this was what he'd wanted—ammo against Carrigan—but she realised that once again she'd read the situation wrong.

'This is a sex murder plain and simple and that's how we're going to work it. I didn't put you on this team to conduct your own investigations and if you don't like it then you can go back to being a constable again any time you want.'

She rubbed her wrist, the itch maddening, like a burning hole in her arm. 'Carrigan put you up to this, didn't he?' she said before she could lose her nerve.

Branch blinked twice, looking genuinely confused. 'Carrigan? I haven't spoken to him at all. This is about facts, DS Miller, and how you read them. I believe you need to go back and look at this again, not waste time on far-fetched speculation.' He sighed, picked something up then put it back down. 'And besides we now have a photo ID of our suspect and I can tell you that he's a lot younger than your general.'

She didn't know what to say to that. She stared at Branch waiting for further disclosure but he was sitting back in his chair, arms crossed, a smile of smug satisfaction on his face. Geneva managed to nod, keeping her face frozen, not wanting him to read her true expression.

'Sir, just one more thing . . .' glad she'd saved it for last. 'Yesterday I got in touch with the morgue to ask if I could view Grace's body again.' She watched the change in Branch's face, the way he'd begun chewing the insides of his cheeks, the drumming of his fingers on the white paper.

'And why on earth would you want to do that?'

Geneva smiled for the first time that morning. 'I needed to

double-check something about the bite wounds, but the funny thing is . . . ' She let it hang there for a moment, enjoying Branch's discomfort. '. . . Myra Bentley told me that they no longer have the body, that it had been claimed, but when I asked her to check the records she said no one had signed it out.'

Branch leant forward, puffed out his cheeks. He looked down at his desk and crossed his arms. 'That's correct, Miller, the body has indeed been claimed.'

'By whom? Her parents?'

Branch shook his head. 'I'm sorry but I'm not at liberty to tell you that.'

'I'm supposed to be working this investigation, why can't you tell me?'

Branch began kneading his fingers, the flesh white and agitated. He leant forward and continued in a whisper. 'I really wish I could but this isn't my decision.'

'So I should talk to the chief superintendent?' She watched his reaction carefully, saw him rising to the bait as she'd known he would.

'I'm afraid that won't do much good. Believe me, last thing I wanted was for the body to be released so early but this goes way above the chief, above the ACC and commissioner.'

'But if it was her family we need to get in touch with them.' If this went higher than the commissioner then it must be governmental, Home Office—the ramifications span through her brain so that she almost didn't catch Branch's last words.

'They'll bollock me to kingdom come for saying this but,' he looked down at his row of phones, 'fuck them. What I can tell you for certain is that it definitely wasn't her family who claimed the body.' He took a deep breath and picked up an unlit cigar. 'To be frank with you, Miller, I'm not sure what's going on here and it's all way above my pay grade so the sooner we're shot of this case the better. We can only come out covered in shit the longer this goes on.'

Branch was about to say something else when the door to his office burst open and Carrigan marched in, hair slicked across his face, red-cheeked and breathing heavily.

22

Branch exploded from the table, the huge mass of him rising out of his seat, sending papers and pencils, old reports and a half-filled mug of tea flying onto the carpet. 'What the hell do you think you're doing barging in here like that?' he screamed, his face turning beet red.

Carrigan was about to reply, then felt a shift in air currents, a slight shuffle of feet, and turned to see Geneva sitting in the visitor's chair. He glared at her for a few seconds until she could no longer hold his gaze.

'What's she doing here?' He stared at Branch, trying to work out what had transpired in the room before he'd come in.

Branch sat back down, straightened his shirt and took a long sip of water. His face returned to its normal ruddy complexion. 'Sit down, Carrigan,' he said wearily, as if talking to an old and recalcitrant dog. 'I was just about to page you, as it happens.'

Carrigan took a seat next to Geneva, avoiding her gaze. 'I can't believe you set up a press conference without consulting me.'

Branch rubbed his palms together, wiped sweat off his brow with an old folded handkerchief. 'Last time I looked I was your superior officer. Perhaps you should reacquaint yourself with the chain of command.'

'I had to learn about this press conference from DS Karlson, for Christ's sake. How do you think that makes me look in front of my team?'

The super smiled and gathered up some loose papers. 'Since, thanks to your persistence and hard work, we now have a photo of our suspect, I believe it's time to take this public.'

Carrigan stared at the empty space behind Branch, the towers of glass gleaming in the distance. 'We don't need a press conference,' he said, keeping his voice steady. 'It'll only make things worse.'

'I don't see how things could get any worse,' Branch replied.

'It's a waste of our time,' Carrigan said. 'We'll be swamped for days with pointless phone calls. Jilted lovers or angry business partners wanting to get revenge, everyone who thinks black people all look the same.' He looked back to see Geneva staring blankly at the wall, her muscles taut and her lips white as candles. 'But forget that for a moment. We have a press conference and if we flash this suspect's photo we lose our one advantage. He doesn't know we know who he is yet—what do you think will happen once he sees his own face on TV?'

'He'll panic, he'll make mistakes, he'll show up on our radar,' Branch replied bluntly while taking out a stack of clean white paper from his drawer.

'Not this one,' Carrigan said. 'He's not some amateur that fucked up and is slowly unravelling. Everything we know about him says he'll go further under—he's illegal, he knows bolt holes and hiding places we wouldn't have the first clue about. You put that picture on TV and I guarantee we'll never find him.' Carrigan leant back in the chair, out of breath and exhausted, just wanting to leave.

Branch began writing something down on a sheet of paper. 'Are you telling me, Inspector Carrigan, that you're not willing to pursue all lines of investigation?' Jack looked at the super then back at Geneva, who was still silently sitting in her chair. What had she told him?

'I'm pursuing the most credible leads,' he finally replied, 'the same as I've always done.'

'We've got to look like we're doing something, for God's sake,' Branch said.

'We *are* doing something. We're following viable leads.'

Branch shook his head sadly. 'I said *look* like we're doing something. I'm sure you're aware of the difference. This is no longer just about you, Carrigan. I'm getting fucking pressure you wouldn't believe because this fucking video happened to have been filmed on our patch.' Branch looked down, concentrating on his papers, scribbling furiously. 'Do you have anything to say, Miller?'

Carrigan turned his head, caught Geneva trying to avoid his eyes. 'I . . . I agree with Carrigan,' she replied hesitantly, her voice barely above a whisper. 'I think it'll drive our suspect under.' She finally looked at Carrigan but there was nothing he could read in her expression and he didn't bother acknowledging her.

Branch took off his glasses. The sound of the rain punctuated the silence in the room, each drop like the heartbeat of the world. 'Well, it's already set up for tomorrow morning, nothing I can do about it now.'

'There was never was anything you could about it, was there?' Carrigan pushed his chair back and stood up. 'Who's pressuring you? The Ugandans?' He glared at Branch but the super was staring through the window. 'Why the fuck are they so interested in our case?'

'I wish it was just that, Carrigan,' Branch replied. 'Believe me, this is something I have as little control over as you do.' Branch coughed into his hand. 'I'll see you at the press conference.'

'I'm not doing it.' Carrigan's voice was stronger than he'd intended. 'I'm meeting a DI in Peckham tomorrow, following a real lead. I'm not going to fuck that up for a stupid piece of theatre to please your bosses.'

Branch was smiling now, a thin serpentine smirk that stopped

Carrigan in his tracks. 'Which is exactly why I've asked Detective Miller to stand in for you.' Branch finished writing something and evened the pages out, tapping them squarely on the table.

Carrigan stared at Geneva but she looked just as surprised as he was, her eyes blinking fast. He shook his head and left the room without saying another word.

23

Carrigan read the grease-splattered menu though he knew every item on it by heart. He'd been coming to this small Chinese restaurant for as many years as he could remember, though Louise had never liked it, preferring one of the trendier establishments up the road. But he liked the dinginess, the steamed-up windows, the waiter who was always popping down the road to the local casino between orders, the tourists put off by the dangling strings of bright orange and yellow intestines hanging in the window, and the cough-wracked cook presiding over the soup by the entrance.

He nodded over his favourite waiter, a skinny pock-marked twenty-year-old with pale eyes and ferocious weed breath, and ordered a plate of Ho Fun dry, won ton soup and chilli dumplings.

His food arrived and he started feeling better, the familiar wallpaper and unsmiling faces making him feel at home, the closest he ever got anyway.

And then he saw her coming in, holding something in her hands, talking to the waiter, his long bony arm pointing towards Carrigan's table.

She was the last person he wanted to see right now so why did he feel a sudden quickening as he saw her approach, unconsciously rubbing his beard free of crumbs and finally noticing what it was she was holding in her hands.

'I thought you might need one.' Geneva placed the small

coffee cup in front of him. 'A triple,' she added, 'from that place you like.'

He was about to lay into her, his face tightening, and then he smelled the coffee and all those feelings were quickly washed away.

Geneva sat down slowly, still unable to meet his eyes, doing everything she could, sorting through her things, playing with her drink, staring at the unfamiliar, chaotic restaurant. 'Jennings told me you'd be here.'

'Good coffee,' he replied, taking a sip, feeling the caffeine kick through his system. 'Now tell me what you told Branch.'

She lay her hands flat, curling up her fingers at the stickiness of the table mat, surprised by his sudden brusqueness but knowing she deserved it. 'I'm so sorry,' she said, flustered, squeezed into a corner table, the heat and smell making her dizzy. 'I didn't know Branch was going to spring that on you, I swear. I didn't tell him anything that would compromise the investigation.' She paused, trying to gauge his reaction but his face was buried in the menu. 'Or that would compromise you.'

He looked up, thinking about this, and waved her qualms away with his hand. 'No need to apologise.' He knew he'd been too snappy with her, that she'd been played like he had and that there was nothing to gain by making an enemy out of her. 'I should have realised he'd have something like this planned.'

She took a sip of coffee, wiped her top lip. 'He's asked me to do the press conference but I told him no.'

Carrigan was impressed by the steel in her voice, the cold gleam of her gaze. 'You should do it,' he replied. 'Don't let my problems with Branch get in the way of your career.'

She was surprised by his words, searching for hidden meanings or slights, but there were none she could see. 'If you don't want me to . . .'

'Nonsense. It'll be good for you to experience what one of those circuses is like. Nothing to be gained by going against

Branch.' He paused, looking up at the fuzzy TV. 'Not for you, anyway.'

'You really think the press conference is a bad idea?'

Carrigan put the menu down. 'It's not a great one.' He called over the waiter with a practised flick of the wrist. 'But Branch is half right, I just don't like anyone telling me how to run my investigation. Especially as it's my head on the line and not Branch's if this fucks up.'

'I don't think I realised what I was getting myself into.' A shade of doubt crossed her face then just as quickly disappeared.

'I don't think any of us do, ever,' he replied but it seemed to her he was thinking about other things when he said it, his eyes staring up towards the yellow ceiling. 'You hungry?'

She nodded—the stress of the day, the smells around her— horrified at the thought that perhaps he could hear her stomach rumbling.

Carrigan slid over the menu but as far as she could see it was written in Cantonese with no English explanations or useful diagrams. He told her about finding the suspect's photo on Facebook as he jabbed his finger at different entries, saying 'try this' or 'I think you'll love this' until it all began to spin and flicker and she asked him to order. She watched as he told the waiter what he wanted, the man making quick slashing marks on his white pad. She thought about what had gone on in Branch's office and what she'd found out before that. She knew it was probably the last thing Carrigan wanted to hear.

'I know you've dismissed this, I know all that . . . but I'm convinced that Ngomo is part of this case.' She told him what she'd found out about the general. 'It can't be coincidence,' she explained. 'Grace is writing a thesis about his crimes and then we find her murdered with her heart cut out, the same signature Ngomo was notorious for back in Uganda.' She sat back, watching the food, watching Carrigan, expecting him to explode and dismiss her theories with another of those practised brushes of his hand, but instead his whole body seemed to fall into focus. He pushed his plate aside and laid his arms squarely on the table.

'This is your theory, right, not Branch's?'

She nodded, unfolding one of the napkins which seemed made out of cheap toilet paper; she dreaded to think what they stocked the toilets with. 'You've seen what Branch thought of my ideas.'

Carrigan scratched his beard and took another sip of coffee. 'It still doesn't make any sense,' he said. 'Grace is writing a thesis that in all likelihood only two people will ever read. Do you know how improbable it is that Ngomo somehow stumbled on it?'

'I don't think he stumbled on it, I think Gabriel told him.'

Carrigan looked up. 'It's still barely a set of coincidences, circumstantial at best.'

'You going to give me the nearly-all-murders-are-simple-and-basic spiel?'

He noticed she was smiling. 'No,' he replied. 'I assume you're aware of that. But we have a photo of our suspect, what more do you want?'

'An explanation as to how someone like that could get Grace's body released from the morgue.'

Carrigan stopped what he was doing and put down his cup. She told him how the body had been claimed and how Branch had assured her it had not been family. 'If Grace's source is everything we think he is,' she continued, 'then there's no way he could have done all this alone. He must be working with someone, someone who has access.'

'We shouldn't rush to a conclusion just because it appears to make sense of things,' Carrigan replied, but she could see a subtle shift in his expression as if he were trying to convince himself of something he knew to be false. He'd filled his mouth with noodles before she could ask him to elaborate, at the same time using his other hand to point out to her a small dish with three round dumplings on it. He swallowed his mouthful and used one of the napkins to clean the grease from his beard. 'The man we have in the photo killed Grace, I'm sure of that. I don't think there's any doubt. But I agree that there's too many loose ends to this case, things that just don't make sense.'

She tried picking up the dumpling with her chopsticks, failed miserably and, humiliatingly, had to ask for a fork. 'Such as?'

Carrigan poured them both some dark tea. 'Why are the Ugandan embassy involved in this case? Why are they pressuring Branch? That's for starters . . . it's the inconsistencies I'm more worried about—the killer savagely rapes and tortures this girl yet calmly films it, then edits the clip and uploads it onto the internet. Not the behaviour of a compulsive sex killer at all. The computer missing and yet all of Grace's notes untouched. The ungagging—I'm always coming back to that— why does he do it, why put himself at risk like that?' Carrigan noisily slurped some soup, put something that looked like a baked dog paw in his mouth. 'I don't think this has anything to do with her thesis,' he said, 'but I agree that there's more to this than we first thought.' He told her about the photos left in his flat, Penny's surprise ride home. 'I'm being followed and whoever's doing it is using me to clean up. What scares me is that he's not even trying to hide it.'

'But if it's more than one man then we've got to be talking about something in her work,' Geneva objected. 'Something not only Ngomo but the Ugandan government are desperate to suppress.'

Carrigan took a long drink of tea and picked at a dumpling, shaking his head. 'Crazy to think that writing can get you killed.'

He'd meant it ironically, but he saw that Geneva had taken him seriously, a shadow darkening her face almost immediately.

'Writing is a dangerous business,' she replied.

He speared another dumpling. 'Who said that?'

'It's what my mother always used to tell me,' she said, finally working up enough courage to go for the entrées. 'She nearly got killed for her writing.' She enjoyed the look of momentary surprise on Carrigan's face—she'd been wondering if someone as undemonstrative as him was even capable of such an emotion. 'My mother is Katrina Valenta. You wouldn't have heard of her but back in Czechoslovakia she was the most popular female poet of the sixties. She was friends with Havel and Dubček and a lot of the young writers and revolutionaries of the time. She wrote these long epic poems about freedom and mountains, about eastern Europe and Lenin's beard. She spent two years in a Soviet-controlled prison for dissidents in the Czech woods. She was freed just before '68, the Prague Spring. She quickly got back into the fray and was there at the barricades, throwing rocks at the Soviet tanks. But it wasn't for this she had to leave the country in the middle of the night, it was for a short ten-line poem she wrote depicting Stalin as a child abuser and Czechoslovakia as his victim. They issued a warrant for her arrest. Friends of hers helped her get across to Austria. She eventually made it to London where a lot of Czech dissidents lived.' Geneva crunched down on the meat, recoiling at the sound of snapping tendons in her mouth and continued. 'It's not too different from the African diaspora. London has always been a safe place to write, argue and agitate. She continued writing poems but she was never the same after that. The poems were never the same. Her critics loved the new work, the poems about walking through Highgate cemetery and sitting by Marx's grave, the sonnets about crossing Europe in cars and buses—but she never thought they were worth anything. She once said to me that the only poems that count are the ones that can get you killed.'

It was the most he'd heard her talk about her own life and when he saw the sadness and droop of her eyes he understood why. 'Growing up must have been a lot of fun.'

She stared at him and, for a split-second, all the days they'd worked this case were rendered mute, then she smiled, a thin grudging smile, and shrugged as if to say growing up is never fun.

He thought about David, the look in his eyes that day when he saw the man being beaten by the soldiers in Masindi. Their refusal to take a stand, to risk their lives for something they believed in. 'She must have been delighted when you joined the Met.'

'She almost disowned me,' she laughed, though Carrigan could tell there were things lurking behind that laugh that weren't so funny, nights of arguments and slammed doors and words you wish you hadn't said. 'For a dissident like her, for someone who was always on the run from the police, it was as if I'd gone and joined a cult or become a heroin addict—much worse, actually.' Something crossed Geneva's face and her voice stumbled. 'We all have to learn to live with things. She's learned, but that doesn't stop her sending me neatly clipped job ads from the *Guardian* at every opportunity.' She put down her fork and looked up at Carrigan. 'All I wanted to do was prove to my mum that the police were the good guys.'

Carrigan stared at his plate, something suddenly gone out of him like a popped balloon. 'I think I wanted to prove to myself the same thing,' he replied, thinking about that road again and the look on David's face as he was being led away.

'It must have been nice to have always known what you were going to do, though; you can't imagine the shit I went through before I decided.'

His laugh caught her off-guard, there was so little mirth in it. 'It was the last thing I had in mind. I was a singer once, played some instruments. I made an album.'

'You're kidding. What happened?' She remembered DC Singh's comment about the wildest rumour she'd ever heard about Jack Carrigan.

A look of regret poured into his face, making him almost unrecognisable. 'Life happened. The way it always does. I used to do that and now I do this.' He wiped his mouth, ran his fingers through his beard and finished his tea. 'I'm meeting DI Spencer in Peckham tomorrow. He's supposed to be an expert, or the closest the Met have got to one, on the African diaspora.' He looked up at Geneva, saw her eyes flash blue. 'I think we're getting close now,' he said, his face softening for the briefest of moments.

She could feel the sense of excitement and resolution coming off him. 'You want me to come with you?'

He shook his head, called over the waiter. 'We need to find out more about Grace herself. I want you to go back to SOAS. I want to know why she visited Willesden Green so often—did she have a boyfriend or family there? Someone's bound to know. And I'm uneasy about how little information the university seems to have on her. Talk to the registrar, lean on them if you need to—but there must be more official documentation. She was under eighteen when she started her course, there's got to be a signed consent form somewhere, application papers, qualification records, references.'

She nodded, secretly pleased that she would have a chance to go back to SOAS. She watched Carrigan wave her away when she tried to pay, she saw a couple of hapless tourists trying to decipher the menu, being shouted at in Cantonese by one of the waiters, and decided she liked this place. 'This was nice.'

Carrigan looked up and smiled.

24

It was like another country dropped down in the middle of London. A different city existing independently and yet congruent to the larger metropolis. Rye Lane, Peckham, on a Tuesday afternoon. Carrigan had lived in London for over forty years and yet he'd never been here. It was one of the things he loved about the city, the way you could turn a corner and fall into another world. But this morning he had no time to savour this nor the way the sun seemed a different shade here, reflecting off the bright multicoloured awnings like something from a lower latitude.

He'd seen him again.

Carrigan had come out of the train station half an hour early for his meeting with DI Spencer. He bought some bad coffee and was staring into the window of a shop advertising African DVDs when he noticed him in the reflection, the man who'd been eyeballing him at the AAC meeting. He turned round but the man was gone. He scanned the pavement but the faces all blurred. He thought back to the two Ugandan diplomats in Branch's office, the men in the car outside his flat, Grace's missing body. He checked his watch, saw that he had enough time, and started walking down the street at a relaxed pace, not looking back. He turned into a small alley at the end of which he saw the elongated shadows of garages darkly delineated under a railway arch.

As he'd expected, behind him he could hear footsteps, a single pair, steady and resolute, getting louder. He felt the blood-buzz rush through his head as he walked down the alley then quickly turned into a sheltered niche reeking of oil and spilled petrol, flattening himself up against the wall.

He waited, holding his breath. When his pursuer passed, Carrigan leapt out, grabbed the man's arm and twisted it up against his back. He slammed his own bodyweight against the man, causing him to crash against the wall.

He was pulling out his handcuffs when the man spoke.

'Second pocket, right.'

Carrigan held the man's arm up against his back and pulled to tighten the pressure. The man just grunted and tried to ease the strain on his arm.

A couple of school kids watched as Carrigan reached in and extracted a thin wallet from the man's pocket. He flipped it open with his teeth and was surprised to see the face of the man he was holding against the wall staring back at him from a police warrant card.

'How about my arm?'

Carrigan let go, gave DI Spencer back his warrant card and apologised. He explained about the man he'd seen following him.

'It's 'cause I'm black, right?' Spencer eyeballed him, his face rigid as rock. Carrigan averted his gaze.

And then Spencer couldn't hold it in any longer and burst out laughing. 'Just fucking with you,' he said, big saggy pouches under his eyes as if they held a reservoir of tears he'd been unable to cry. 'Damn, it was worth it to see your reaction.' He shook his hand vigorously, letting the blood flow back into circulation.

'You were at the AAC meeting.' They stood opposite each other in the small dank alley. Carrigan felt that peculiar after-effect of adrenaline, the enervation and relief coursing through him.

DI Spencer straightened his fleece, lit up a cigarette. 'I'm looking into them, part of a case we're working on. When I saw you and your partner I thought you were going to fuck every-thing up for us. I wanted to know why you were interested in the AAC, so imagine my surprise when I get this call yesterday from a DI out west who wants to meet and then when I get here I see you.'

Spencer explained that his team, based in Hackney, were looking into the AAC. 'Reports of troublemaking, sending threatening letters, that sort of thing. But what really interests us is how did this Gabriel Otto get his funding. He's just a stu-dent but this is a well-organised and well-financed group.' Spencer finished his B&H and ground it under his size-fifteen shoe.

'Well, I'm glad you agreed to meet me,' Carrigan said.

Spencer laughed, a deep and resonant sound that Jack could feel in his chest. 'Couldn't let you come out here all by yourself, they'd eat you alive.' He pointed to two skinny kids standing lookout on a corner. 'You don't exactly blend in.'

All around him Carrigan could hear the whirling maelstrom of voices, the hard and soft staccato of Swahili, the languid tones of Luganda, the eerie musicality of Arabic, a mix of accents and intonations that felt as strange and otherworldly as the smells of spices and herbs saturating the damp air. There was a density and concentration of shops and people found nowhere else in the city, every available surface crammed with a bustle of colour and language.

Yet there was also something desperate about this place and he felt an overwhelming pity for everything—the shops with nothing anyone wanted to buy, the immigrant owners' hopes faded like the once-bright signs adorning their storefronts.

'We headed anywhere in particular?'

Spencer stopped, lit another cigarette. 'There's a house round the back of the high street, a lot of ex-child soldiers doss down there.'

'Child soldiers?'

'I've worked up a basic profile on your guy from the info you faxed me yesterday.' Spencer pulled a sheaf of folded papers out of his jacket.

'Thanks.' Carrigan took them, placed them in his own pocket. 'Give me a quick rundown.'

'Well, I didn't have too much to go on,' Spencer replied, 'but from the information you gave me I think your informant is right: the man you're looking for is an Acholi from northern Uganda.' Spencer paused. 'Which is bad news in the scheme of things. Not sure this morning's press conference would have helped.'

Carrigan mumbled something Spencer didn't catch.

'Saw your girl on telly. Looked good but the whole thing might have scared off your suspect.'

Carrigan flashed back to the press conference, the killer's face flickering across millions of TV screens. He'd watched it in a small cafe while eating breakfast. Geneva had looked composed and radiant under the flash-pop of camera lights. She stood behind the big Met logo, Branch and the ACC flanking her, but her eyes were centred on the camera and her voice was steady and calm. She was assured and convincing—Carrigan could tell she'd go far if only she would allow herself to. 'Wasn't my decision,' Carrigan replied, giving Spencer one of those looks that said everything in the curl of an eyebrow.

'Yeah,' Spencer replied, 'never is, is it? Always the people furthest from a case think they know best how to investigate it. Anyway, in all likelihood, this man you're after is an ex-child soldier, or ghost soldier as they're known. From looking over the post-mortem report I don't think there's any doubt; the level of violence certainly fits. This is a growing problem we're having to deal with. Look,' Spencer pointed through the steamed and grease-rimmed windows of a closed-down greasy spoon. Inside, a huddle of men, skinny as spiders, sat crouched around a large table. Their skin shone under the light, their eyes bloodshot, all of them chewing with serene concentration then spitting out strings of thick green juice. Carrigan remembered the bitter taste of Khat that first day in Kampala, the white rush that came after the juices sank into your gums and then the instant need for more.

'They're kidnapped from their homes when they're very young. They're forced to either watch or more often participate in the killing of their own family, then they're shackled and marched to one of Kony's camps up in the north, taught to fight, beaten and bullied until there's nothing left in them but hate. The girls are taken for use as sex slaves. Your man will not stop, will not listen to reason or compromise, you have to realise this. They come from war and just because they're in London now doesn't mean anything changes. War is all they know. They're brutalised at such a young age that this is what they've become.'

Carrigan shook his head as he stared at the cafe's interior, the lost vacancy in these men's eyes.

'Those scars,' Spencer pointed to the photo of Grace's source, the asymmetrical lines carved into the man's face, 'they're typical of people who've been fighting in the bush. It's the teeth I'm more worried about.'

'The teeth?'

'Some African tribes still use teeth filing as an initiation rite but not in this part of Uganda. We've heard stories. An elite group of child soldiers, Ngomo's shock troops, survivors of countless bush skirmishes, their teeth filed to resemble the name they chose for themselves—the Wolves. If your man's an ex-Wolf then you've got a big problem.'

Spencer led him to a gutted house standing on a corner two streets down from the market. A recent fire had painted its facade black and sooty, making it resemble some old Gothic greystone from the nineteenth century. The windows were missing and in their place grey Sitex screens had been mounted by the council to prevent squatters. But there was smoke and noise coming from inside, a sense of movement and life.

'You sure about this?' Carrigan asked as they climbed the stairs and Spencer prised open the door.

'The ones in here are too fucked up to do anything.'

But this didn't reassure Carrigan in the slightest as he ducked under the splayed door and into a dark unlit hallway reeking of sweat, ammonia and the bright acrid tang of burning crack.

They entered the main room. The smell and stench of bodies, of toilets that no longer worked, of drug sweat and fear and sex and hopelessness, made Carrigan gag. He'd smelled it once before and his life had never been the same since. On the floor, wherever they looked, prone bodies, thin and delicate as Giacometti sculptures, lay on flattened-out cardboard boxes.

'Give me the photo,' Spencer said and Carrigan didn't argue. He knew he was totally out of his element. This was his city but this was not his city, not here. He tried to breathe slowly through his mouth, to be invisible, a white man in this room of misery and surrender. He watched as Spencer bent down and gently talked to the few who were still awake or lucid enough to even note his presence. Carrigan wondered about their homes, their villages, the mornings waking up under the glaring African sky, the endless plains and hunting grounds and now they were here, poor, bedraggled, and lost in a civilisation that didn't understand them and didn't want to. So, like spiders they found the dark corners, the out-of-the-way places, the waiting rooms where their hours leaked out slowly until there was no difference between death and life.

Spencer approached him, grabbing his arm, bringing him back to the present. 'I got something.' He led Carrigan to an empty corner. 'A few of them definitely recognised him,' he said, handing back the photo of Grace's source. 'They looked scared shitless when they saw it. One told me that your suspect used to hang out at the Drillmaker's.'

'What's that?'

'A nasty pub across from here. Not the kind of place you'd go for a quiet drink.'

Carrigan smiled. 'What are we waiting for?'

The Drillmaker's Arms was once an old-fashioned London pub. That was apparent from the sign hanging loosely at the front but nothing inside resembled any pub Carrigan had seen since the mid-seventies. The heavy plush sofas were ripped and worn and of a colour not easily identifiable. The pall of cigarette smoke hung over the tables though it'd been a while since the smoking ban came into force. There was a raised stage to the left of the bar, and on it, under a splash of gaudy lights, a middle-aged bleached blonde was slowly taking off her clothes.

A group of young African men sat around the stage, staring into bottles of Primus, pulling on long white-tipped cigarettes and watching the floorshow. Carrigan felt a sharp pang of sadness, this whole scene, the stripper that no one in his right mind would want to see stripped, the dark and gloomy bar, the measure of cigarettes and spark of bottles being opened in the musty air.

The woman took off her bra to reveal scars and stretch marks. The crowd cheered listlessly like it was something they'd been instructed to do. It was only two in the afternoon, a bright glaring October day, but in here it could've been the middle of the night. The stripper smiled and tripped, falling over her own discarded clothes. No one looked up from their beers.

Carrigan found a seat as Spencer went round trying to get some sort of reaction from the customers, shoving the photo under their eyes, standing in front of the stripper, blocking their view. Carrigan felt the mood change in the bar like a sailor could feel the tiniest splash of rain in a cloudless sky. Men were shuffling in their seats, some looking nervously behind them, others shaking their heads and raising their voices. They all shared a certain expression despite their differences, a surly nonchalance bubbling at the surface, a wariness like that of predatory birds.

Carrigan moved next to Spencer, waiting for the first flare of fist or knife, but everything was muted here, the rage and violence distilled into stares and shrugs and monosyllabic rebuttals. The stripper continued her act but no one was really watching or they were only watching in the way you look at something but don't see it.

'What kind of black are you?' One of the young men challenged Spencer.

Spencer leant down into the youth's face. 'The kind you'll never be.'

It happened so fast Carrigan was caught completely unprepared. Suddenly, Spencer was surrounded. Fists flying and the silver flash of something worse. Carrigan stepped into the swirling mass of bodies, pulling out his baton, hearing the click of its extension as he slammed it into one man's forearm.

The crack of bone splintered cleanly and the man fell to the floor sobbing and massaging his useless arm. Carrigan turned and hit another assailant in the face but the man barely reacted, just smiled and jumped on top of Carrigan. Their bodies crashed to the floor. Carrigan felt the man's breath on his face, twisted, and shot his knee into the man's crotch. The African's eyes bulged but he didn't relax his grip on Jack's neck. Carrigan saw black skies explode in white star showers, then heard a sharp tattoo of cracks.

Blood from his attacker's head began streaming down onto his own face. He pulled away to see Spencer standing with a truncheon in his hands, wide smile plastered on his face.

Spencer pulled him up. The room tilted and span. Carrigan

grabbed a table to steady himself, saw the men bloodied and bruised slowly taking their seats, Spencer leaning over them like their own shadows unloosed. He was taking out his handcuffs and notebook.

'Assaulting a police officer's something we take very seriously around here.' Spencer's voice boomed across the afternoon pub but there was no reaction on the men's faces. They stared at each other, at their useless hands, the mess surrounding them. 'But assaulting *two* policemen . . .'

'You gonna put us in jail?' one of the men sneered, massaging his jaw, blood and spit curling at the edge of his lips. 'We've been there before.'

Carrigan sat down next to Spencer, felt the heat of the table, the amassed looks and imperceptible nods and tells. He took the photo of Grace's source out of his pocket. 'We have a fast-track programme for you.' His voice was unrattled, calm and modular despite the pain he was feeling in his ribs and skull. 'Prisons being overcrowded here and you not being legal residents and all.' Carrigan watched their faces as he let the words hang in the smoky air. 'So, for something like this, as serious as this, we just fill out a form and pass it on to your embassy.' He scanned their eyes, saw tiny flickers at the mention of the word embassy. 'Which means, practically speaking, forty-eight hours from now you'll be on a plane back to your beloved homeland. What they do to you there, it's up to them.'

He leant back in the chair, watched their eyes fall on the photograph, silent looks exchanged across the long table. 'A nice surprise for your families, I should think, having you back for Christmas.'

Someone reached for the photo. One of the younger men, scars like ripples across his cheeks, long skinny fingers caressing the edges of the paper. 'You only want this man?'

Carrigan nodded.

Silence. No one looking at each other. The man who'd taken

the photo sent it spinning back across the table. 'Haven't seen him for a few weeks. He used to hang around with Solomon Onega.' The man looked to his friends but they avoided his gaze.

'And where can we find Onega?' Carrigan kept his voice soft and low.

'The Church of the Blood of the Redemption,' the man mumbled. 'He works there most days.' He looked up at Carrigan. 'What about us?'

Carrigan put the photo back in his pocket, snapped his truncheon back onto his belt. 'Lucky you,' he said, pointing to the stripper who was still gyrating on the stage. 'You get to keep watching Marilyn over there to your heart's content.'

25

Geneva waited as the SOAS registrar continued some private conversation on the phone. She stared at the sterile room, the cold white lights, the framed photographs of old alumni, feeling unreasonably tetchy. She'd made the appointment after her meal with Carrigan last night but this morning it seemed the registrar had more important things to do. Finally, tired of waiting, the case going on without her somewhere in Peckham, Hackney, Streatham, she walked up to his desk, loudly slamming her Coke can down on the table, watching his eyes follow the liquid as it splashed onto the wood.

'Yes?' His voice sounded weary and tired but when he looked up and noticed her something in his expression softened and he coughed, apologised, put down the phone and smiled. 'What can I help you with?'

She flashed her warrant card, noticing his surprise, the way he looked from the card back up to her face as if convinced of some deception.

'I need to see your records for Grace Okello, East African History, third year.'

The man's eyes lingered on her chest before he nodded and turned to an old computer, his fingers hovering hesitantly over the keyboard. Geneva stood there and waited. She wanted to be out in the streets following their new lead yet Carrigan had expressly told her to come here today. She felt that after last night something had changed between them and she'd woken this morning feeling better than she had in a long time.

'That's strange.' The registrar swivelled his seat, his eyes hovering over her breasts as if drawn there by gravity. 'Are you sure she was a registered student?'

Geneva looked blankly at the man, mid-forties, balding, his life sequestered behind a computer screen, having to watch young boys and girls blossom into their lives in front of him year after year, and she suddenly felt sorry for him, a snap twinge she quickly had to bury. 'Of course she was,' she replied a little too sharply. 'Can you please check again?'

The registrar nodded, turned back to his computer, shaking his head. 'We don't seem to have any records for a Grace Okello.' He turned back to Geneva, his face a mess of confusion. 'I'm sorry, the system's normally airtight.' He saw Geneva's expression and blushed. 'But I can check the basement. Even if somehow it got deleted from the server the original documents will be stored there.'

Geneva flashed him her best smile. 'I'd be extremely grateful.'

The man shuffled off, taking one last look at her breasts, promising he'd be back within five minutes. Geneva sat back down in the chair trying to understand what this could mean— had someone expunged Grace's records or was it only a technical glitch? She was jolted out of her thoughts by the vibration of her phone. She picked it up, hoping it was Carrigan, but the voice on the other end was the last person she'd expected.

'Hello, Geneva.'

Her hand tightened against the phone. She swallowed but her mouth was desert dry. 'Oliver.'

'Been trying to get hold of you,' her soon-to-be ex-husband replied. The voice that had once sent her body into shuddering delight now made her feel like something was crawling up her arm. 'Wanted to have a chat, no lawyers, none of that, just you and me like old times.'

She stared at the dirty wooden floor, the tips of her shoes.

'That's not going to happen, Oliver. You know that.' She heard him breathing on the other end of the phone, a silent measured pulse that made her want to scream. 'What did you want?'

'Saw you on the telly this morning. You looked good. It's nice to know you're doing well.'

'Oliver, the only thing I want from you is to tell me you've signed the papers.'

'That's what I was calling about. We need to talk,' he answered, his voice now steely, 'about the house.'

'What's there to talk about?' She saw people in the office looking at her, realised she'd been raising her voice. 'The lawyers agreed, a fifty-fifty split. *You* agreed.'

'I've changed my mind,' Oliver replied. 'My lawyer looked at it and reckons that because I paid the deposit, your contributions only amount to rent and the house is legally mine.'

Suddenly the room was spinning, her eyes watering, the registrar coughing and trying to get her attention. She was about to say something to Oliver but there was nothing she could say. She snapped the phone shut and went up to the desk.

'No mobiles in here.' The registrar was pointing to a sign behind her.

'Police business,' she replied curtly. 'Did you find anything?'

The man shrugged. 'This is certainly most unusual. You're absolutely sure she was a student here?' Geneva nodded. 'Well, I went through the files and it seems there's not one piece of paper relating to a Ms. Grace Okello.'

'None at all?' Geneva stared at him, not having expected this. 'How could that happen?'

The registrar shook his head. 'If it was just the computer it could be a glitch, but the computer and paper files? I'm going to have to go to the dean with this, it's highly irregular.'

Damn right, Geneva thought as she made her way to the library. Why would anyone want Grace's records to disappear?

She thought about the man in the photo, Grace's source—there was no way someone like that could have got access and removed both the electronic and paper files, it was too professional, too sophisticated a job. Which made her think about Carrigan's speculations last night, the strange suited men she'd seen in Branch's office at the weekend, the name Ngomo echoing through every nook and cranny of this investigation.

She needed to know more about General Ngomo if she was to understand this case. Carrigan was beginning to see her side of the story. The involvement of the Ugandan embassy, Branch's adamant denials, the missing records from the university—it all pointed to something more complex than a random sex murder and she knew she needed to immerse herself in whatever she could find out about this man as a hunter must study his prey.

The books, monographs and archived periodicals arrived. The librarian passed them to her, his glasses so thick she could see her reflection twice in them. He made no comment, just handed over the material, torture and guerrilla warfare no different to him than worker relations in pre-industrial Britain or the taxonomy of tropical butterflies. She thanked him and carried her precious bundle to a table, this weight in her hands, holding so many lives and deaths.

The silence enveloped her. The smell of wood and old pages fluttering in the air-conditioned room comforted her in a way she found surprising. She'd spent her life trying to get away from books and now here she was, her mother's daughter despite herself. She thought it funny, but not really, how we always become the very thing we spend our lives running away from.

She arranged the material chronologically. She piled up a collection of monographs on the conflict in northern Uganda. There were reams of Amnesty International reports, taxonomies of death, an accountant's version of the apocalypse. She should have felt disheartened but this was the part she liked most about murder-work, the way each death, each investigation, opened up a world entire and infinite.

After an hour her eyes became more practised and she could glance down a page and ascertain almost immediately whether there was mention of Ngomo. She made notes in her small spiral notebook. She read testimonies of torture survivors, the cruel imagination of men making her heart shrivel. She scanned demographic surveys, PhDs dense and packed with statistical data. Kony appeared in every monograph, every dissertation, like the archetypal enemy, a four-letter cipher for the blood and horror of the interior.

She kept searching until she found a list of current warrants the Ugandan government had issued against rebels and soldiers.

The main charge against Ngomo was for the murder of the aid workers—the video that had been passed from hand to hand, TV station to TV station, as everyone watched four young girls crash against the end of their lives. There was a lesson there: you could kill as many Africans as you wanted but kill a white woman and your name hits the top of the list. It seemed this was the big mistake Ngomo made. The increased pressure from the West led to further government incursions, further massacres, Ngomo retreating deeper into the tribal heartlands, beginning his own campaign known as 'The Days of Blood'.

The aid workers hadn't been found until five years ago, their bodies excavated by accident while another organisation was building irrigation systems in the north. There was a side column about hapless tourists ending up in the clutches of Kony's men. Kony's LRA had taken over half of northern Uganda. Guide books hadn't been updated. She squinted at blurry photos of gaunt white men and women being led dazed onto planes at Entebbe, the lucky ones, the ones that had made it out of the bush. She was about to go on to the next sheaf of reports when something caught her eye like a thing glimpsed from a passing car.

She borrowed a magnifier from the librarian and hunched over one of the photos. If she looked too close all she saw were dots, a pointillist abstract, but from a distance all she could see was a grey blur. Yet one of the faces . . . there was something about it. Two white men boarding a plane, thin, bearded and ravaged. The caption said they were freed by government soldiers. She looked again, put aside the magnifying glass and brought the paper up to her face. There was something familiar about the man on the right, his pose, the way his shoulders tumbled from his neck.

She looked behind her. The librarian and students were busy, heads down in their books, no one watching her. She looked up but didn't spot any CCTV cameras. She looked around again, then took a deep breath and carefully ripped out the photo, the sound of the paper tearing louder than she would have thought possible, her palms sweating as she stared up and scanned the room before pocketing the scrap of newspaper, feeling her heart like a crazed bird hammering at the cage of her ribs.

She continued going through the material, trying to not let her imagination get carried away. In a newspaper article from 2004 she read about Ngomo's disappearance. The Ugandan government must have been sure of his death; the warrant against him was rescinded that year. There were sightings of him in Zurich and Paris. Rumours of political asylum in the UK, the same story Lee had heard. She wondered how such a man could slip through so many nets but it happened all the time. Look at Karadžić, all those years practising alternative healing, his beard and face grown long, riding the Belgrade transport system, unnoticed, unknown. Did he feel a withering as he rode those anonymous buses? This man who'd commanded armies and battalions, who'd overseen camps of such bewildering brutality? Did he sit on the bus and see his life shrunk to nothing? Perhaps he even wanted to be caught, his face back in the headlines, his crimes once again news. It made her think of Milton—was it better to be a slave in heaven or to rule in hell?

She was going through the last pile of articles when she happened to look up at the exact moment that Gabriel Otto was entering the library. His gaze immediately caught hers, recognition flashing through his face, and then he swiftly turned, knocking one student almost to the ground, and disappeared back into the main hall.

Geneva looked down at her notes, looked back up at the entrance, and decided to follow him.

26

Carrigan and Spencer headed back out into the rain and wind. Darkness had settled on the market while they'd been inside the pub and now it seemed as if the road were a theatre and a whole new troupe of actors had come in to replace the day shift. Gone were the traders and old ladies with their tartan shopping trolleys. Gone the housewives and art students, families and schoolgirls. In their place young men stood on corners strutting and pounding their stuff. People walked faster, their heads bowed, avoided all contact and huddled into the relative safety of buses or pubs looking like civilians caught out by an unexpected curfew.

'Surprised me to hear this guy you're looking for hangs out at the church,' Spencer said as they crossed the high street, ducking into a narrow leaf-strewn alley and heading towards the grey stone building, its spire like a black finger pointing at the sky. 'It's one of the few places we have no trouble with.'

'With a name like the Church of the Blood of the Redemption?' Carrigan's shoulder and back burned with pain and his breath was short and laboured.

Spencer laughed. 'More of a social mission than church these days. They emphasise the redemption part over the blood.' They passed by back gardens strewn with old furniture, discarded toys and broken bicycles. 'The priest in charge has more or less converted it to a home for ex-child soldiers. A rehab unit. The socials come in every day and help with counselling.'

The door to the church was opened by the priest himself.

Father Piper looked as if he'd just been woken from a ten-day nightmare. The old man's eyes seemed desiccated, squinched into the hollows of his eye sockets. His beard was white and ran down one side of his face in a strange zigzag, the canyon of an old scar shining pink in the bulblight. Though he was skinny and short Carrigan could see the fibrous muscles running up and down his arms like someone who'd worked their whole life in the fields.

'We'd like to talk to Solomon Onega,' Spencer said.

The priest didn't look as if he'd heard, turning and silently walking back into the emptiness of the church. 'I hope he hasn't been in trouble,' he finally said, stopping to right a hymn book that had fallen from the pew. 'He's one of our few regulars.'

'Just helping us with our enquiries,' Spencer blandly replied.

They walked past the nave and vestry, the hanging garments like ghosts of former masses, the smell of incense and wood filling Carrigan's nostrils with memory and longing. Father Piper explained how so few people had come to church over the last ten years, either moving away from the old Catholic rite towards louder and more ecstatic forms of worship or abandoning church altogether for the altar of the glowing TV set, the panoply of saints and sinners on daytime chat shows. 'But more and more I see these children. These children like no children should be,' the priest continued, the words coming faster now. 'They come here to this country and everything they have learned comes with them. War owns their souls. They join gangs and teach English kids lessons learned on different shores. The elders, the people from the tribe who would traditionally take care of these lost kids—they don't want to go near them. They remember the night-time raids, the blood and suffering, the laughter of small children.'

They went through another door and down some stairs into

a musty, badly lit basement. It took Carrigan a few seconds to make shapes out of the gloom, see a group of boys sitting on the floor, listening to an older man talking in Luganda, a blackboard behind him with pictures of chickens and rabbits pinned to it.

Piper explained that he had to get back to his chores and left them in the basement. Carrigan watched as Solomon Onega pointed to the diagrams on the blackboard, making rabbit noises or dog barks when he lighted on the relevant animal. The kids stared at him as if hypnotised. There was none of the fidgeting or playing up endemic in classrooms these days. Solomon leant down and pulled a handful of stuffed animals out of a large brown box. He held each one up, said something, then handed it out. Some of the boys took the toys warily, as if not yet sure of their intention, while others held them tightly against their faces and began crying. There were Snoopys, stuffed dogs of all varieties, Miffy rabbits, beavers and bears and others whose shapes seemed a melting of several species into one.

When he was finished Solomon walked straight up to them. They introduced themselves and then Carrigan flashed the photo of Grace's source. Solomon took it from him and smoothed it out.

'I knew one day police would come asking me about him.'

They were sitting in the church kitchen. Massive pots of stew simmered on a four-ring hob watched over by two portly women who couldn't stop laughing. A radio played airy calypso songs. Solomon Onega sat opposite them on the only table, a scarred and chipped Formica construct wobbling precariously under the weight of their elbows.

'His name is Bayanga,' he said, still holding the photograph.

Solomon was small and wiry but gave the impression of someone whose body had been packed into too tight a skin.

Muscles and tendons rippled the surface of his neck and arms as if trying to fashion a way out. His voice was soft and serene but the signs were there for them to see, the thin scar where his stubble had never grown back, the one eyelid slightly drooped, the way he awkwardly positioned himself on the chair. 'It is the name he chose for himself when he went to war.'

Carrigan wrote it down, trying to keep his hand from shaking. Bayanga.

He said the name silently to himself. It was a fitting name for this ghost he'd been chasing through the London streets all week. 'You know him from back home?'

Solomon shook his head. 'From here. He was the first person I talked to when I arrived.' Something in his eyes seemed to drift back to previous days, a sudden vacancy registering there.

'You said you knew we'd eventually come asking about him.' He'd thought Solomon would be even harder to reach than the men back at the pub but he seemed genuinely happy to talk to them.

'Men like Bayanga, the police always eventually come round, doesn't matter what country.' Solomon took a long sip from a can of Coke, wiped his lips. 'When you first arrive in London you always have one phone number you picked up somewhere on your way to England. Every community has its numbers, its places of sanctuary.

'When I got here it was cold, grey, a thin sky you couldn't even see. I phoned the number, the man on the other end asked me some questions then gave me directions to the house.' He laughed but Carrigan could hear a sadness in it as if Solomon couldn't believe he'd been that person only a year ago.

'It smelled like a prison. I'd been in enough to know. The smell of human fear and dreams, intermingled with sweat and alcohol. Over a hundred men crowded into a small three-storey house in North London. Everyone called it the Village but it was an ironic name for it was as far from the feeling of a village, a community, as you could get and still be under one roof. You never knew how many people lived there, everyone was in and out, some working nights, coming in tired and bitter in the morning, others setting off as dawn broke, heading for the first trains, jobs sweeping and mopping up before the white workers got there.

'I was shown to a room on the second floor. There were several men lying on sheets of cardboard. It was hard to tell how many, they lay stacked, arms and legs intertwined, pressed against the corners where there was more heat. Bayanga was the only one who acknowledged my entrance. He held out his hand and welcomed me. He pointed to a filthy piece of cardboard, oil-smeared and ripped at the edges, which lay in one corner of the room. *That's my bed*, he said, *but you can use it while I am at work*. I was so tired that first morning, so overwhelmed by this city that seemed so strange, I just thanked him, moved over to the corner and fell asleep.'

Spencer leant across the table. 'Who else lived in the Village?'

'Men like me. Like Bayanga. Many with missing fingers, limps, the constant dream of blood.' Solomon abruptly looked up and seemed to be scanning their faces for something. 'You think we're so different from you? But the line that divides us is very thin. Let your policemen go on strike. Let your CCTV cameras malfunction. How long do you think it would take for London to turn into Nairobi or Lagos?' He sat back and watched the two detectives. 'The measure of a man is what he does when no one's looking, when the only law is the one in his own heart. You people always talk about wanting to know yourselves but if we could truly read our own hearts we would run away in abject horror at what we had seen.'

Solomon finished his Coke and wiped his lips, then lit a cigarette. 'So yes, every night there were fights. I'd wake and see two men in the centre of the room arguing, the flash of a knife and then that smell would fill the air and take me back to Africa—the smell of fresh blood—there's nothing like it in the world. At first it makes you sick, really sick, then you don't notice it for a time until one day you realise just how much you miss it.

'But I never saw Bayanga get involved in these fights and arguments. He would just sit cross-legged in the corner of the room with a smile on his face like this was arranged purely for his entertainment. I had met many men like him back home and I hoped that here I wouldn't have to meet any more.'

'But you became his friend?' Carrigan asked.

'He became mine, which is not the same,' Solomon replied. 'I was new, didn't understand the city, didn't know how the trains ran, how the streets unfolded. I imagine it would be like if you were suddenly to find yourself in the bush. All your points of reference, everything you know, would be gone. You would be in a world so utterly alien and hostile and yet you would see the natives going about their lives and their lives would strike you as strange and abhorrent and yet they survived in this environment and you would know that you must become a little more like them if you too were to survive.'

'Did Bayanga use drugs?'

Solomon shook his head. 'No, he didn't even drink alcohol. All I ever saw him drink was milk.'

Carrigan looked at Spencer. 'What did he do for money?'

'Money?' Solomon coughed on the cigarette smoke. 'We had no money. We ate food that people threw away. One of the men who lived in the house collected food from outside restaurants, from those black plastic bags they leave on the street. Bayanga showed me this and said what kind of people can they be, to throw all this good food away? He was always laughing at English people. He saw a city laid low by welter and waste. By money, bad dreams and secular arrogance. He saw emptiness and hunger in all the white faces, a hunger for something they would never have. He would quote the Bible as he showed me well-dressed men drunk and drooling, passed out on pavements outside pubs. He said we had arrived in the fallen world and that we had to be careful.'

'You said you thought Bayanga was helping you but you realised differently. What happened?' Behind them Carrigan could hear the sounds of kids playing, high voices shrieking with pleasure and astonishment, the contented barking of a dog.

'One day, I came back from the street and saw him sitting alone in the room. I took out my bottle of wine and sat next to him. I could tell something was different. He seemed brighter, more excited, not as bitter as he often was and he started telling me about how when he had the money he would move from this hell-hole and into one of those nice houses we always passed on our way to the Village. How he would buy himself a suit and a car and ladies to go with it. I'd never known Bayanga to resort to these common fantasies and so I asked him how he would get this money. He laughed and said it was almost a done deal. He told me that he'd been walking in the city and had bumped into someone he knew from back home. The man called him a week later and offered him a proposition. He said that perhaps there was a job for me too in this.'

Carrigan rubbed his chin, the sound like an angry insect trapped inside a clenched fist. 'He said he met someone from back home? From Uganda?'

'That's what he told me. I asked him what kind of work, wondering if it was drugs. He said the kind of work we used to do back home and smiled. In that smile I knew that things had changed for him as much as I knew that I would never be part of it. The kind of "work" we used to do back home was how we always talked about fighting, killing, the work of war.'

Carrigan felt the blood coursing through his veins, the sensate feel of his own body. '*He* said it was killing work?'

'He didn't need to say it like that. It was obvious what he meant.'

Carrigan felt the scratch of his pen against paper as he

wrote it all down, trying not to leap to conclusions, not to see that one name glowing insistent in front of him, Geneva's voice ringing in his ears with *I told you so.*

'You never saw this man?' Carrigan asked.

Solomon shook his head. 'I'm not sure I even fully believed him until he came home that day with the phone.'

'Phone?' Carrigan looked up from his pad. 'When was this?'

'A couple of weeks ago. He came in, it was morning and he was smiling and couldn't wait to show me his new phone. It was one of those big ones with a screen and internet.'

'An iPhone?' Carrigan interrupted.

'I don't know,' Solomon admitted. 'He also gave me twenty pounds from a large roll he had in his pocket. This was the first time I'd ever seen him with more than loose change. He told me everything was going to plan, said he still had room for me if I wanted to join him. I thanked him and said no. I told him I was working here, had met the priest, that this was the work I wanted to do.'

Carrigan noted it down, his handwriting speeding up as he tried to preserve all this new information. 'When did you last see him?'

'A couple of days after that. He gave me his corner. Said he was moving to a better place. Said I could have joined him if I had been more of a man but that was not the man I wanted to be.' Solomon shook his head, pointed to the darkness of his makeshift classroom. 'We all have to make our decisions, Inspector, that's the easy bit. The hard part is we have to live with them. I learned this in Uganda. I was lucky enough to have a second chance, to make another choice, but Bayanga would always make the same choice no matter what. The work of killing, some men are forced into it but others, it finds them like a long-lost brother.'

27

It was easy to get lost among the crowds, easy to merge into the flow so that even when Gabriel looked behind him he didn't see her, only a tight compacted group of chattering students. Geneva followed him through dusty corridors, past classrooms emptying out, and into the student bar. She watched as Gabriel bought a can of Fanta, talked to a girl he knew then, just as he was making his way past her, Geneva grabbed the sleeve of his jacket. 'Thought it was you.'

Gabriel looked wildly around, his hands buried deep in his pockets. 'What do you want?'

She pointed to a small dark alcove to the left of the bar. Gabriel looked behind him once then followed her to a black table, its surface sticky with spilled drinks.

'Lucky for me, huh?' she said as he opened his Fanta. 'Had a few questions for you, save you a trip to the station.' His eyes flared for a moment then dimmed back into their sockets. 'Don't worry, Gabriel, anyone sees you with me they'll think you're just chatting up another white girl.'

His fingers danced around the edge of the can but the fear didn't leave his eyes. 'I have a lecture to get to.'

'Glad you're such a conscientious student,' she smiled, 'and, as you're so eager to get back to class, I'm sure you'll answer my questions quickly.'

Gabriel looked around him but there was only a blur of people drinking, shouting into each other's ears over the din of music, the clatter of empty glasses.

'I had nothing to do with Grace's death.'

'Wasn't what I was going to ask you.' She laid her hands flat on the table, remembering how Gabriel had stared at them during the interview. 'Instead, why don't you tell me about General Ngomo?'

He didn't say anything, kept his head down, his fingers circling the top of the can so fast he cut himself, a thin whistle of air escaping his lips and a single drop of blood flowering on his thumb.

'I know you recognised him.'

'So? He's a famous figure back home, everyone recognises him.' His voice had reverted to its earlier petulance and Geneva knew she was halfway there.

'I'm sure they do. But I think you know what I'm talking about.' She stared at Gabriel, saw him trying to feign nonchalance, but his muscles twitched and jumped as if an electric current was being run through them.

'We know all about him,' she continued. 'We know who he is and what he did to Grace.'

Gabriel's head snapped up, his eyes showing a certain amusement. 'You have no idea.'

'Oh, I think we do. And I don't think it'll be too long before we find him.'

Gabriel tried looking everywhere but across the table. Geneva could feel the tension in his bearing, the way he was struggling to hold himself together. 'Think about that, Gabriel,' she continued, trying not to enjoy this too much. 'We know Ngomo killed Grace because she was writing an exposé of his deeds. He ripped out her heart—that's his signature after all, isn't it? My boss, he's not sure who told Ngomo what Grace was writing about, how he found out, but I think, you and me, we both know the answer to that.'

Gabriel's eyes blinked rapidly, his skin turning grey. 'Bullshit.' He stood up so fast the can went flying across the table. Geneva watched as he glared at her, shook his head, and headed off back into the main building.

She should have gone home. She should be unpacking boxes, calling her mother, her divorce lawyer, studying the case file. But instead she found herself following Gabriel through the twisting corridors of the university, wondering why he seemed so much more scared today than when he'd been under arrest for murder.

He didn't look back once. He walked straight past the lecture theatres and empty classrooms and out into the drizzled daylight. Geneva huddled next to a group of students by the stairs, camouflaged among the bright Puffas and woolly hats, and watched Gabriel heading down Great Russell Street. She was about to turn back and go home when she saw him take out his mobile phone, start punching in a number then stop, look around and put the phone back in his pocket. He crossed the street and entered a public phone box.

She watched him from the other side of the road, protected from view by the bus shelter and huddle of people waiting in the rain. He lit a cigarette as he waited for his call to be answered. His face looked grim and solemn when he spoke. She couldn't hear what he was saying but there was no need; his body language was as expressive as someone signing to the deaf. Gabriel shook one hand in the air, then banged the phone back down into the cradle. It bounced off and crashed against the glass as he exited the booth and headed for the Tube.

She crossed the road and followed him into the station. Every hair on her arms stood up as she saw him take the lift to the platform. She leapt down the stairs three at a time, glad she wasn't wearing her heels.

She reached the platform just in time to see him slip into one of the far carriages of a waiting train. A good-looking young businessman held the door open for her and she thanked him as she got on, her heart booming in her ears.

They changed trains at Bond Street. The scrum of rush-hour passengers hid her as she followed him through the tunnels.

He took the Jubilee Line, northbound, getting off at Willesden Green. She stared at the station sign, remembering Grace's Oyster card.

She followed him past a small parade of shops and watched as Gabriel turned down a long tree-lined street, power-walking past two old men and their straggly nicotine-stained dogs.

She crossed to the other side of the street, breathing heavily, and crouched behind a parked car. Gabriel stopped and opened the gate to a small semi-detached house. He looked behind him once then headed for the door. He leaned on the buzzer until the door opened and a man greeted him from the darkened interior.

There was no small talk. They evidently knew each other, the man stepping aside to let Gabriel through, and it was then, in a flicker of light, as Gabriel entered the house, that she saw the occupant clearly, his balding skull gleaming under the bare bulb light, his moustache thin and groomed and his eyes, those same eyes she knew so well from the photos and books she'd spent all week immersed in.

She quickly ducked down feeling a sick rush of adrenaline as General Lawrence Ngomo looked up and down the street then, apparently satisfied, turned and shut the door.

28

Carrigan had waited ten minutes to see whether Geneva would show up for the afternoon briefing he'd called and then started. 'I'm handing you a one-page profile of our suspect put together by DI Spencer of the Trident Unit.' He heard groans and whistles as the constables passed around the photocopies. 'I know, profiles don't catch anyone and all that . . . nevertheless it's important we know who we're dealing with, the kind of person this Bayanga is. He's not our normal scum—believe me, this is a lot worse.' Carrigan wiped the sweat from his brow and continued. 'We know that Bayanga met someone from back home who offered him work. A week before Grace is killed he suddenly turns up with a new smartphone and a roll of money.' He paused. 'I know how seductive this chain of events is but we have to be extremely careful here—we still don't know motive and we can't rule out coincidence but, having said that, it does look like this is the man who killed Grace and it looks as though someone paid him in advance to do it.'

He watched their faces as the realisation sunk in—this wasn't just a sex murder any more but something far more professional and they all understood how much harder this would now make their jobs. 'DC Berman?'

Berman looked around the room, his eyes narrowing as if the daylight was too much for him. 'I traced the site on which Grace and Bayanga corresponded.' He shuffled on his seat, fingers worrying the end of his shirt. 'The company that runs the forum, after a bit of persuasion, let us look at their data. I managed to find the email address Bayanga used.' Berman paused, watching the detectives' faces all fixed on him, Carrigan blinking rapidly. 'He only sent one other email from this account. It was addressed to *My dear comrade, Lawrence* and it said, *I have the thing I promised to give to you. It is time for us to meet.*'

'When was it sent?' Carrigan asked.

'Yesterday morning.'

Carrigan closed his eyes for a second, rubbed his temples then turned to DC Singh.

Singh said they'd had no luck in tracing Bayanga. They'd shown the photo around likely areas but had no response. Carrigan had hoped someone would have seen him—there was something about Bayanga, something about his eyes that made you notice him.

The door opened and Geneva came in, her face red and flushed, hair all over the place, one earphone dangling across her left shoulder. She walked up to Carrigan, whispered in his ear, telling him about following Gabriel to Ngomo's house. No one else could hear what she said but everyone noticed Carrigan's face light up, his eyes widening as he turned to them. 'I'll let DS Miller explain,' he said and took his seat.

Geneva recounted how she'd spotted Gabriel running away from her, questioned him then, not satisfied with his answers, decided to follow him. She told them who answered the door.

'Sir, I'm still not sure I understand how all this links up to Grace.' Jennings's upper lip quivered as he talked, his eyes downcast and dark.

'I think DS Miller can explain better than I can.' Carrigan turned towards her.

She resisted the urge to scratch her wrist and cleared her throat. 'Grace was writing her thesis about General Lawrence Ngomo. A thesis which basically amounted to an exposé of his many war crimes. She was particularly interested in the 1990 murder of four British aid workers. I believe Ngomo got wind of this, realised it would upset the new life he'd created for himself in London, and hired or asked Bayanga, one of his former soldiers, to kill Grace and get rid of the evidence. I think that Bayanga has Grace's computer.'

'I know we've been through this before, but if he took her computer then why didn't he take all her notes too?' Karlson asked.

'I don't think he was interested in her thesis,' Geneva replied, having readied herself for this. 'I think there was something else on the computer far more damaging to Ngomo than anything Grace had written.' She looked up and saw that she'd snared Carrigan's attention. 'I believe Grace had managed to get hold of uncut footage of the aid workers' murder and it was stored on her hard drive. I think that's what Bayanga meant in the email: *I have the thing I promised to give you.*' She stopped, suddenly aware of every face turned towards hers and stared down at her papers.

Carrigan tried to sense if there was any of the I-told-you-so in her tone but he couldn't discern anything but her excitement at this new lead. He looked at the team, his decision made. 'I'm going to go for a warrant on Ngomo's house. We have enough evidence linking him with Bayanga to persuade the judge. Karlson—we need to bring Gabriel in for further questioning. He's involved in this somehow. I'm putting a surveillance car outside Ngomo's house tonight, make sure he doesn't suddenly decide now's a good time for a holiday. Tomorrow, five sharp, assuming we get the warrant, we take him down.'

He sat in the car and watched the river sway and shimmer against the sun's dying rays as he ate a cereal bar, crumbs and raisins raining down on his beard and jacket. He read Geneva's précis on Ngomo, the things she'd found out at SOAS, impressed by the sharpness of her logic, her persistence in the face of his own obstinacy.

He left the car on a double yellow line and walked up through the verdant garden, the crumbly stairs, his finger lighting gently on the buzzer. He brushed the crumbs off his jacket, watched them fall to the floor, squirrel food, and waited for Ben to come shambling down from his study.

Ursula opened the door. If she was surprised to see him, she didn't show it.

'Hi.'

She nodded back but her eyes were now staring at some point behind Carrigan. He turned to see what she was looking at but there was only the river, the mossy banks of Barnes on the other side, a single ketch slicing through the waves.

'I suppose you'd better come in.' She turned away, letting the door swing open.

He followed her into the silent hallway feeling encroached upon by the dusty hunting scenes lining the wall, the sense of a house abandoned to fear and darkness.

'Ben around?' he asked, sitting down in the living room, trying to keep his eyes off Ursula's lest some snapcharge of memory derail his composure.

'I thought you knew.' Her voice sounded different he noticed, the way she crossed her arms as if defending herself from an unseen attack.

'Knew what?' He tried to remember their last conversation but all he could recall was the look on Ben's face when he realised what they were dealing with and how quickly that look had turned into one of a man betrayed.

Ursula walked over to the cabinet and poured them both a drink. 'He flew out to Berkeley last night; his classes start tomorrow.' She put the glass down clumsily, avoiding his eyes, turning quickly and retreating to the safety of her armchair. 'You look disappointed.'

He shuffled in the seat and looked at the photos on the mantelpiece. 'I was hoping he'd help me with something.'

Ursula's face narrowed, the lips pulling in against each other, her skin whiter than ever. 'I'm surprised at your audacity, I really am.' She took a sip of scotch, her hand trembling the glass. 'After what you've done to us.'

He wasn't surprised at her attitude, knew the girls were the most important things in her life and that anyone endangering them was immediately and without question her sworn enemy.

'I'm sorry.' He realised how useless the apology sounded the moment it left his mouth. He was good at dealing with grieving families, distraught spouses, but in front of people he knew he could never do it, never achieve the necessary mix of compassion and dissemblance. 'He left you alone?'

She shifted in the chair, her legs emerging from under the folds of her skirt. 'Is that an accusation?'

'No,' he replied. 'I'm just surprised, that's all.'

'Because you would have never done such a thing, hey?' She crossed her legs and he tried not to look. 'He had to go, Jack, you know that. It's his job. If there's one thing I'm sure you understand it's the importance of doing your job.'

He looked down at his shoes, cheap and scuffed, bought for efficiency rather than style. 'The girls?'

He caught it briefly before she turned away. 'They're staying with my sister until this thing . . .'

'It's okay to be scared,' he said.

She leant forward, propping elbows on knees, her hair covering her face, and for a second she looked decades younger and all the years and bodies were erased leaving only the two of them sitting in some student cafe away from the harsh blur of textbooks and blackboards.

'Will this man come back?'

She said it so quickly he almost missed it. He tried to bridge the distance between them, knowing it was impossible, that the roads they'd taken had led them further apart than either would have thought possible. 'No,' he lied, 'I don't think so. We're getting closer to him now. I don't think he'll take any stupid risks again.'

'You don't think?' Her words, laced in sarcasm, made her mouth seem ugly. He hadn't realised she'd been so afraid. 'Who is he?' She stared out the window at the grey sky and wheeling somersault of birds.

He told her what he could, Bayanga's name, Spencer's profile, some of what Solomon had told them.

'I've seen someone outside the house,' she said, her blood-red nails tapping against the table. 'A couple of times now, just standing there, looking up at the windows.'

'Was he—?'

Ursula nodded. 'Yes he was black.' Disappointment in her face and a brief flash of something else, panic or dread he didn't know. He showed her Bayanga's photo and saw her eyes darken as she slowly nodded.

They sat there in silence for the next five minutes, each taking small sips of their drinks, nothing left to say to each other, the years finally drawing them irrevocably apart. He promised to look in on her, gave her his mobile number, told her to call him anytime she needed, then exited the house into a bright blush of sunlight feeling as if he'd escaped the confines of some terrible prison. He took one last look, remembering how he'd thought it was the perfect house, the perfect life, shook his head and headed to his car.

He sat there for an hour, parked out of sight from the house. He'd put Ben and Ursula into this situation, he'd let his life leak into theirs and they'd been unprepared for the rupture it would cause, the constant fear and doubt, the double-checked locks and fumbled alarm settings.

What if Bayanga did come back, found only Ursula alone in

the big house? Carrigan crunched his eyes shut, tried to erase the thought, but it was no good.

It didn't take him long to decide. He dialled the station and was put through to the surveillance car outside Ngomo's house. They reported nothing, no movement, no visitors. He held the phone in his hand and thought about it again, then spoke before he could change his mind.

'I need you somewhere else.'

29

Ngomo's house was in one of a series of terraces backing onto the railway embankment and each time a train thundered past, the windows shook in their frames as if convulsed by an inner weather.

'That's it.' Geneva's voice floated through the rain and traffic din as Carrigan stared at the properties, wondering if the residents had got used to the regular shake and rumble of the passing trains or whether they bit down, ground their teeth and locked their jaws every time it came. But most of all he was thinking about Ngomo. From lord of the bush to this. From enormous skies and unfenced miles to this small three-bedroom house, the railway tracks his new sky, the identical houses across the street his vista.

Behind them, the constables were getting ready out of sight, finishing their teas, stubbing out cigarettes. He'd driven over to the judge's after the surveillance car had arrived at Ursula's house the previous night. The warrant sat in his pocket as he stared at the curtained windows, the trashed front garden, the broken roof tiles shimmering in the harsh sunlight.

No one answered the buzzer. Carrigan let his finger rest on it, hearing the muted echo fade into silence.

One of the uniforms walked up the drive, a ram firmly in his hands. He gave Carrigan a smile as he lifted the device and thrust it through the door, splintering it open.

Carrigan pushed the door ajar, stepped inside, stood still. He felt nothing, no sense of someone being in the house, that coiled tension in the air he always dreaded. He turned and motioned to Geneva, told the uniforms to stay outside, monitor front and back exits.

He cautiously entered the hallway. A small table held a phone and a leather address book. There were no decorations on the walls, just a rack with two coats and an old-fashioned trilby. Two doors led into the front and back rooms. A staircase rose steeply in front of him. He stood looking at the doors, then the stairs, wondering which to try first. He could hear Geneva breathing behind him, short, urgent swallows. He was reaching for the living-room door when the house started to shake.

A booming detonation exploded above them like a thousand footsteps dancing on a wooden floor. He felt the door knob tremble in his hand, the floorboards shuddering beneath his feet, and then it was over, at least until the next tube train thundered past.

He wiped his hand on his shirt, wishing he'd brought some water, something to get rid of the horrible taste in his mouth, then reached for the door. He could sense Geneva's impatience like something trying to burst out of her skin. He let the door swing open, waited, heard nothing, and entered the room.

He blinked but he knew it wouldn't change what lay before him.

'What? What is it?'

He watched her come in, her gaze immediately directed towards the recliner chair in the middle of the room. Her eyes widening, then something worse—the very same thing drowning his stomach like acid, the knowledge that they'd got here too late or that they'd got it all wrong.

General Ngomo was sitting in his brown recliner. He was facing the TV and wearing a bathrobe but he wasn't watching anything. His eyes stared out of their sockets, his hands were bound to the armrests by makeshift ties and his feet were pocked and bloody, but it was his neck that Carrigan and Geneva couldn't keep their eyes off.

It looked like his neck was pregnant, or like a python that had dislocated its jaw in order to swallow a much larger prey. The skin around the swelling was purpling, yellow and brown flecks circling it like tiny planets. Ngomo's neck veins stood out in stark relief like a renaissance sculpture's, his mouth half open not in a scream but in a last reach for unattainable air.

Carrigan turned and saw Geneva staring up at the ceiling. 'Did you hear something?'

She met his eyes. 'I don't know, maybe.'

'Call the SOCOs, report the body, don't let the uniforms fuck-up the crime scene. I'll go check.'

She started to object but he'd turned and was already up the stairs. She looked at Ngomo, wanting to tear his eyes out, those stupid staring eyes, for being dead, for not being able to tell them what happened, why he killed Grace. And then she stopped herself. Tried to focus on the scene, what was there, physical evidence, and not think about what this spelled for the case.

The stairs creaked under Carrigan like loose-lipped neighbours. He stopped and waited for the next train to scrape and scream across the rails and he took them two at a time, making it to the top at same instant as the noise faded into the distance.

He stopped and waited but, as downstairs, there was no movement. Ngomo had been dead for over an hour, the coagulated blood along his wrists and mouth attesting to this, but judging from his body temperature he hadn't been dead for that much longer, which meant Bayanga could still be in the house. The sensible move would have been to flee straight after the murder but, as they were quickly realising, nothing about Bayanga was within the definition of sensible.

There were three doors leading from the landing. Two bed-rooms and a bathroom. The carpet was worn and revealed a cross-hatched underlay that looked like diseased skin in the pale light.

The first bedroom was empty. The sheets were still rumpled and crevassed from a night's worth of bad dreams. The win-dows were fogged with small beads of condensation, each mir-roring the room entire. Carrigan took a deep breath of the stale air, the smell of old men and restless nights the same the world over, and tried the bathroom.

It was a narrow room, only three feet wide, with a browned ceramic bowl at the end. Toilet rolls lay scattered and unfurled on the cistern lid. The room was clean but there was no allowance of comfort to it, no rug or splash of colour nor even a toilet seat. The floor was bare wood boards, unvarnished and unsanded, the only window too high to reach.

He heard Geneva talking on the radio downstairs as he crossed the empty landing towards the second bedroom. He expected to find it as stripped and utilitarian as the other rooms but he was wrong.

The room didn't look as though it belonged to this house, not to the austere monkish ambience of the other rooms but to some other place, a place that would be called home, where you'd return from your day to the smile of your wife, the small hands of your children.

Carrigan closed the door behind him. The rain whispered on the ledges as he turned on the light, a piercing 100-watt bouncing off the collection of framed photographs and certifi-cates, the glass gleaming opaque, resisting intrusion. At first he could see only his own reflection and then, as he stepped closer, he saw the face in each of the photos, the name on the certificates, and hung his head.

Geneva heard the sirens as they approached, the frenetic

stutter of their piercing whine cutting through the rain and inner beat of her bloodflow. She called up to see if Carrigan was all right but his answer sounded muted as if he were somewhere else, his voice only a shaky transmission. She was about to climb the stairs when she saw him, ashen, coming down the hall, shaking his head.

The sirens whooped to a stop before she could ask him anything. The heavy clop of massed footsteps sounded outside. The interior of the house was suddenly bathed in swirling blue neon, Carrigan's face flashing at the top of the stairs. 'Quick.'

She looked behind her, saw the cars and men gathering outside and set off up the stairs. The SOCOs entered the house as Carrigan showed her into the second bedroom. They heard the unmistakable bellow of Branch's voice reverberating through the floor and then a train came rushing through and blotted everything out.

Everything but the room.

She stood there and stared and didn't say anything. He let her take it in, remembering his own sense of dislocation and shock when he'd understood what this meant. He watched the same realisation rip through her body, the muscles in her shoulders and back tensing, drawing her into herself, her head turning, not knowing where to look or quite what she was looking at.

'What the Jesus fucking hell is going on here?'

Carrigan turned to see Branch, red-faced, tie askew, spittle flying from his lips. 'What the fuck is that down there?'

'That was General Lawrence Ngomo.' He watched Branch take this in, his eyes shrinking into small dark pools. 'The man we suspected was behind the murder of Grace Okello.'

'Is he fucking suspected of his own murder too?' Branch pushed past Carrigan and entered the room. He stopped and surveyed the photos on the wall. 'Jesus Christ, it just gets better.' He looked at Carrigan, then at Geneva, as if he wasn't sure which one was more to blame. 'So tell me this hasn't just got a million times more screwed up then it already was?'

Geneva began to say something but Branch interrupted. 'That was a rhetorical question, Miller. Any idiot can see that you've got another dead bloody African and what the fuck is that in his throat? Don't tell me he choked trying to swallow his fucking dinner.' Branch snapped his head towards Carrigan. 'Are you fucking listening?'

But Carrigan was lost in the wall of photos, in how wrong they'd been, how totally and utterly wrong and how stupid they were for not having seen it, especially when the video clip had made it so clear. He cursed himself for not having listened hard enough.

'What is it with you two?' Branch looked from Carrigan to Geneva and back. 'And what the fuck is up with all this?' He gestured around the room. 'Some sort of stalker's shrine?'

Carrigan sensed that neither he nor Geneva wanted to put it into words. Once spoken there would be no room for anything else. He turned to Branch. 'We thought Ngomo had hired Bayanga to kill Grace but we were wrong.' He pointed to the photos and graduation degrees, the honours and swimming trophies, the encased preservation of this museum room.

'Ngomo wasn't Grace's killer. He was her father.'

PART THREE
Back Then . . .

He hadn't thought it would be possible to feel this cold in Africa but once again he was wrong. His body shook against the hard edges of the chair, his teeth loudly snapping against one another, the muscles in his legs convulsing to some hidden beat. This was the way fear played itself out, a sudden physical reaction, that bitter taste in your mouth, the palpable presence of your own heart. In the end even your body betrayed you.

There was nothing restraining him to the chair. Every shudder rocked him against the cracked metal and threatened to throw him onto the floor. His feet were bare and he could feel small wet things crawl across his toes, the cement hard and unyielding beneath him. He wasn't sure how long he'd been in the room.

Eye-patch watched him as if he were a part of the landscape; there was no expression on his face, no reaction to Jack's muscle spasms or pleas for water. He could have been a wax dummy and in the mean splintered light the young soldier almost looked like one, the skin drooped and folded as if one side of his face had been exposed to tremendous heat.

The room was small, without air, but Jack felt the cold like something physical attacking his bones. Eye-patch sat behind a gnarled wooden table, his feet up, a badly rolled cigarette jumping between his fingers, a poster behind him revealing a cruel glint of blue sky.

'You look like a man who wants to help his friends.' Eye-patch leant forward, placing arms long and sinewy as sticks of liquorice on the scarred wooden surface of the table. His fingers had once been broken then set wrongly. The nails on his left hand had stopped growing, fallen away, leaving half-moon slivers of pink and red at the edges of his cuticles.

'Where are they?' Jack was surprised by the sound of his own voice, the fear and apprehension underlying each word.

Eye-patch nodded. 'They are not very far from here,' he told him, his voice slow and measured as if searching for each word and its definition one at a time. 'But what will happen to them is in your hands.'

The sentence hung in the air like the rancid smoke of the soldier's cigarette. Jack swivelled his head, fighting the instant explosion of nausea in his stomach, but there was nothing but the room, the soldier and him.

'You want some water, a cigarette?' He smiled revealing a set of crooked teeth, splayed and misaligned as if not meant for that particular mouth. Jack nodded and watched as Eye-patch went over to a small sink, the tap constantly dripping, and filled a glass with brown water. He handed it to him, his fingers touching Jack's skin, making him recoil and nearly drop the glass. He drank it down in one go. It tasted strange; metallic and bitter.

'Good,' Eye-patch said. 'A man needs water like he needs the truth.'

Jack wasn't sure what he meant but he nodded anyway hoping for a refill.

'Without one a man becomes an enemy of his own body,' Eye-patch solemnly continued. 'Without the other he becomes an enemy of his own soul.' He took the glass, got up, turning his back on Jack and headed for the sink.

Jack frantically looked around. The only door was to the right of the table. He could see through the half-inch gap the dark outlines of two teenagers standing guard. There were no windows or other doors. He thought about escape—but only for a second. Even if he were fast enough to creep up on Eye-patch what would he do then? Try to bargain Eye-patch's life for Ben's and David's? He ground his bare feet into the floor, felt the sharp sting of the concrete, the soft crush of an insect below his left heel.

'Now,' Eye-patch said, returning to the table and handing Jack the glass, 'it is time for you to decide if you want to help your friends or not.'

Jack gulped at the water as he considered the few options available to him.

'You are good friends, no?'

He put down the empty glass and nodded.

'It is important, you know. Most men go through life and they have friends but they are not friends, not real friends. You do not know if friends are really friends until you have something to lose.'

Jack was trying to keep up with the soldier's logic, but like everything else in the last few days it made as much sense as a rabbit speaking Chinese.

'This . . .' Eye-patch pointed to his missing eye, '. . . is how you measure friends.' He carefully licked the end of a new cigarette shut and placed it between his lips. 'I too had good friends but when they had to choose between my eye and their comfort, it became very clear just how good these friends were.' He pulled the cigarette out of his mouth, puckered his lips and spat out a thin string of tobacco. 'But it is better a man learns this sooner rather than later, don't you agree?'

Jack wasn't sure what he was agreeing to but he nodded anyway.

'You have been friends for a long time?'

Jack realised that if he pretended this was an ordinary conversation, the kind you have on planes and boats, waiting for a bus or in empty cafes, then the fear and chill which had consumed his body might start to fade. 'Ben and David know each other from childhood. They grew up together. I met them three years ago when we started university.'

Something in Eye-patch's expression changed. He took the cigarette out of his mouth, placed it carefully over the edge of the table and nodded. 'I too once thought I would go to university.' His voice seemed different now, softer, more resigned.

'What stopped you?' Jack asked, knowing immediately it was the wrong thing to say.

'When there is a war there is only one kind of studying that needs to be done. There is no use for history or geography. These will not help you in the bush.'

'I'm sorry,' Jack replied quietly, suddenly aware of how different their lives were, how choice figured so little for most of the world, so he was surprised by Eye-patch's laughter, a full throaty amusement lodged deep in the soldier's throat.

'Do not be. Sometimes you find the world and sometimes the world finds you. I was lucky. I didn't know who I was and I might never have found that person if war hadn't intervened.' He put the cigarette back into his mouth, puffing until thick plumes of smoke flowered from its tip. 'Perhaps you too were on the wrong road and now you have the chance to find the right one. Perhaps it was God who brought you here, or fate . . . if you prefer.'

'I don't believe in God or fate,' Jack replied, trying not to think about the gazelle crossing the Jango Road.

'Then I feel sorry for you,' Eye-patch said mournfully. 'You come from a place where you celebrate your advances, the progress your race has made, but look at you, you are empty and in need of something you cannot even name. Yes,' he nodded sagely, 'perhaps you have truly come here for a reason.'

'We were trying to get to Murchison Falls. We took the wrong road.' Jack felt the cold snuggle up against him once more, the chill in his lungs every time he took a breath.

Eye-patch ground the dead cigarette under his boot and

reached for a stained brown folder lying to his right. He began flicking through the pages, humming to himself. Next to the folder Jack could see his own notebook lying like an accusatory witness.

'No, I think you took the right road, the road you were always meant to take.' Eye-patch put the folder down and stared up at Jack. 'What would you have done if none of this had happened, if you'd boarded your flight back to London?'

Jack wasn't sure what he meant, but he knew that the longer they talked the longer it would be until the other things, the things that weren't talking. 'We'd just graduated; we were going to find jobs.' He stared down at his bare feet. London seemed like something from another lifetime.

'What kind of work were you going to do?'

He wasn't sure if Eye-patch was genuinely interested or whether this was all just a part of his interrogation technique. 'I told you, I'm a musician.'

'And your friends?'

'Ben's going to be a lawyer and David's entering the seminary in September.'

'It seems you have your whole lives planned out in front of you.'

Jack was about to say something but this time managed to keep his mouth shut.

'Then why,' Eye-patch turned and picked up the notebook, 'with all this future ahead of you would you involve yourself in spying against Uganda?' His tone hadn't changed, nor had his facial expression, but the words came out like hard shards of glass.

'I wasn't spying,' Jack protested. 'I write songs in there.'

Eye-patch flicked through the pages again. 'Yet you felt the need to write in code?'

Eye-patch's calm tone of voice was exasperating him, it would almost have been better if he'd been shouting. 'It's not code, it's musical notation.' He tried to think how to demonstrate this, the steady progression of notes and staves, bass clefs and crotchets, but looking at the walls of this abandoned schoolroom he knew that Eye-patch had never seen sheet music before. 'Look,' Jack said, leaning forward, gesturing for the notebook. Eye-patch slid it across the table. Jack picked it up, flicked it open, staring at the jumble of his own script. It was hard enough for him to decipher it. He laid the notebook flat on the table, placed his finger at the start of a bar of music and hummed as he traced the notes lifting and falling. 'It's musical notation, for a song. I write songs.' He hummed the melody he'd written three days previously in Kampala. Eyepatch showed no expression but let Jack finish the song.

'I see,' he said when Jack had passed the notebook back, 'but you too must see my problem.' He leant back in the chair and folded his arms across his chest. 'As I said before, if this were true you would be saying it,but if you were a spy and this was code you would be saying the same thing. You see my problem now? How can I tell when the liar and the honest man say the same thing?'

'I'm not lying,' Jack shouted.

'Prove it.'

'What?'

'Sing. Sing for me your songs then I will decide if you are a singer like you claim.'

Jack closed his eyes and dry-swallowed. His heart felt like something alien to his body, too large and too fast, a thing made for a much larger receptacle. His voice cracked on the first note, the words shearing away into silence and coughing. He tried again, focusing on the blue sky of the poster behind Eye-patch, wondering what the rest of the picture held.

He sang quietly in his chair, the first side of his soon-to-be-released album, then the second. Eye-patch remained silent and still, occasionally nodding his head, which Jack took to mean he was starting to believe him. He ran out of songs and began to sing other people's songs, songs he'd practised in his bedroom, songs he'd listened to late at night, his ear pressed tight against the radio.

'Very good,' Eye-patch interrupted after a couple of hours, passing Jack a glass of brown water. When he moved forward, Jack caught a glimpse of the poster behind him and it was as if a door had been opened, letting in a fan of fresh air. Eye-patch sat back, repositioning himself so that Jack could now see the whole poster. The blue canopy was only a small part of the image, the rest was covered by a gleaming white mountain ascending towards the sky. He focused on the clean white planes of the mountain as he continued singing, making up songs, doggerel, ad jingles, whatever came to mind.

Every time he stopped, Eye-patch barked a single command—*'Sing!'*—and he began again. Occasionally he was given water as the room filled with cigarette smoke and night. He sang through the dark and into the day, light leaking through the cracks in the schoolroom walls, singing beyond tiredness and fatigue, his voice a small cracked thing and each time he stopped there it was again: *'Sing!'*

He concentrated on the poster of the mountain and thought about Ben and David. He wondered where they were right now; they could have been two doors down and neither would know; they could be dead; they could be free. The thoughts paralysed him, brought the cold rushing back in, and he focused on the mountain. If he squinted hard enough he could see two or three tiny blue dots halfway up the face. He imagined himself one of these, a climber on his second day in, slowly making his way up from base camp, and as the songs fell out of him, songs he didn't remember he remembered, songs he swore he'd never sing again, he saw the blue dots making their ascent and he did his best to follow their careful progress.

'Enough!'

He'd been singing all day and most of the night. Every time he opened his mouth, his lips pulled away from each other taking layers of dry skin, his throat so desiccated he could no longer swallow without an immense act of will. He stopped in the middle of a Will Oldham song he barely remembered. He stared down at his feet and watched the roaches scuttling across the concrete.

Eye-patch pulled something out of the top drawer of the desk and laid it on the table. 'You now have to make a choice,' he said. 'You have to decide whether you want to help your friends.'

'Of course I do,' Jack croaked.

'Then tell me who you are spying for, sign this paper and I promise all will be well for them.'

'I'm not . . .' and then he stopped, knowing there was no point any more. He understood that there was only one way to save Ben and David and that all options had narrowed down to this.

'I was spying for England.' He thought it would be harder to say but the words came out as if he were reciting his name.

A long smile cracked Eye-patch's face open, revealing the buckled teeth and wet pinkness of his tongue. 'Good. That is good,' he laughed, 'but we already know you are spying for England, this is not news. You want to help your friends, you will tell me what this book says, what you have already sent back home to your employers.'

Jack stared at the poster but he could no longer see the blue dots. Had they achieved the summit? Were they now on the other side making the dangerous descent? 'You promise my friends won't be hurt if I tell you?'

It had been his decision which road to take, his idea of going to Africa in the first place. If it wasn't for him Ben and David would never have been in this situation. The logic was inescapable.

He gave Eye-patch details and information, motives and reasons, map coordinates and targets. He didn't know what would happen when the soldiers discovered he'd been making it all up but he never got the chance to find out.

The door crashed open, sending searing sunlight into the room, making Jack's eyes squint and water with tears. Two soldiers entered, agitated, both talking at once to Eye-patch, both running their words together, their eyes flicking wildly. Eye-patch listened, nodding his head, then pulled out a thick wooden stick from his belt and smashed the younger soldier over the head with it. The boy collapsed to the floor and Eye-patch leant over him, coiled and ready to strike again, then put the stick back in his belt. He left the room, the upright soldier helping his comrade up, blood pouring from his head filling the air with a hot salty tang. A few minutes later Eye-patch came back, his face tight and contorted as if his skin had been shrink-wrapped to his bones.

'Get up!' he shouted at Jack, the genial tone of earlier now gone entirely. Jack tried to do as he was told but fell to the floor. He hit the concrete full in the face and saw two of his teeth skitter out from under him. Before he could move the soldiers were lifting him and dragging him out of the room.

The sun was worse than the cold floor, exploding like a poisonous flower in his head. He wanted to wilt, fall back down, let the earth cover him, but the soldiers kept frog-marching him past the barracks, the schoolyard, the playing grounds, and finally back out into the bush, the camp a misty haze in the distance. They dropped his body to the ground and disappeared. He waited for several hours for the bullet, but no bullet came. He waited for men to come out of the reeds with machetes and smiles on their faces, but no men came. He waited for some animal to smell his fear and blood and come stalking out of the bush, but no animal came. He waited for Eye-patch to return, tell him that he was sorry but there was only one punishment for spies, but he would never see Eye-patch again.

He lay face down listening to the reeds part as the footsteps of the soldiers drew nearer,but it wasn't death that was coming.

They dropped him next to Jack, dust rising in the air as the soldiers left the clearing and headed back towards the camp. Jack turned to see Ben's torn and bloodied face, a huge purple swelling under his right eye. He felt for Ben's breath but there was none. He looked around the small clearing but there was no one there and he began to scream. The hours and minutes inside that small room burst out of him like some well dug deep into his soul and then he heard something move and he stopped.

He turned quickly, expecting more soldiers, but instead he saw Ben shuffling and moaning on the floor next to him.

For a moment they looked at each other like strangers caught face-to-face in a lift, and then they began to laugh, hugging each other in the thick wet grass. But just as suddenly as the laughter had started it was gone.

'Where is he?'

Ben looked away, shook his head. Jack grabbed him with all the strength he could muster, the buried rage of the last two days burning through his fingers.

Ben pulled free, his hand shielding his face. He turned and vomited onto the ground, a deep tumultuous wrenching that continued long after there was nothing left to expel.

'We need to go back and get him.' Jack looked around the clearing, saw the spire of smoke from the camp a few hundred feet away. He started to get up, a swooping dizziness exploding behind his eyes.

Ben grabbed his leg, his fingers gripping tightly. 'No,' he whispered. 'He's gone, Jack.'

'Then we need to find him.' Jack tried pulling away but Ben's grip was surprisingly strong.

'You don't understand.' Ben let go of Jack's leg and turned away, unable to face him. 'David's dead.'

30

Photographs.

Black-and-white, colour, sepia-tinted. Sun blanched, faded, and creased from too much folding.

Photography as the persistence of memory and metonym of a life.

A face, a body, a pair of hands in close-up. Some so clear it was as if the person depicted therein was actually in the room while others were so faded it was impossible to tell what they represented, as if the paper itself had forgotten the image bestowed upon it.

A whole arc of history from black-and-white schoolyard Polaroids to digitals so sharp they looked as if they couldn't possibly be real. Photographs laid out side by side on the table in front of them. Every photo different but with one constant.

Grace.

They were in the incident room, eighteen hours after the discovery of General Ngomo's body, still sorting out his treasure chest of memories and eating Chinese takeaway from silver boxes. Ngomo's flat had been searched but they hadn't found Grace's computer or any other evidence linking Ngomo to the crime scene. All of Ngomo's personal possessions had fit into two cardboard boxes which now lay at their feet. Geneva was sorting through the photos as Carrigan stared at the cross-hatched scars on the table, rubbing his head, feeling the past invade him like some foreign entity. The memory of seeing Ben again in that wet jungle clearing was still so fresh after all these years, the joy followed by the bitter realisation.

He unsnapped two paracetamol from the foil and dry-swallowed them, then went back to the layout of photographs, picking one up, examining it then replacing it in its rightful place, a chronology of Grace from birth to death. He looped some noodles onto his chopsticks, feeling Geneva's silence behind him, the hard warm shadow of her presence.

She hadn't said much since he'd told her the story on the way over from Ngomo's. It was a story he thought he'd never tell again, but once the initial words came out everything else seemed to follow as if a plug had been pulled and the words were water rushing down a drain.

'You're eating too fast.' She looked up from her box of noodles. 'You'll get stomach ache.'

Carrigan nodded but didn't slow down. 'You don't seem surprised,' he said, remembering how when he'd told her the story of what had happened to him in Africa it was as if he were confirming something she'd already known.

Geneva sipped her Coke and stared down at the kaleidoscope of images, trying to make sense of it all: Grace staring back at her from her high-school graduation, Grace about to board an aeroplane, Grace in a white dress holding a bottle of beer somewhere in the jungle. She'd only just begun taking in what they'd seen in Ngomo's upstairs room when Carrigan had finally told her what had happened in Africa.

'That stuff in Uganda, why didn't you mention it before?' She tried not to sound accusatory but there was no other way to say it, and besides she felt, if not a little betrayed, then something close; they were supposed to be partners on this case.

He turned so quickly that he sent some of the photos flying to the floor. She was about to pick them up but then stopped.

'It had nothing to do with the case.'

'How can you know that?' Her voice sounded brittle, like metal scraping against metal.

'I just know.'

She saw his face stretched long and thin, the sleepless nights and early-morning calls and wondered what he'd been like before Africa.

'Explains that twitch every time Uganda came up.'

He put the last photo in its place. 'You noticed?'

'Hard not to, though I'm sure everyone would just put it down to too much coffee.' She picked up a photo of Grace with an older woman, both elegantly dressed, standing in front of a white church with an impossibly tall spire. 'Did you ever find out what happened to David?'

It was suddenly there again, the darkness in his eyes, the sense of a locked room inside his head. He looked down at the table as if the answers were inscribed on its knotty surface. 'The embassy tried locating the body after we arrived in Kampala but it was a war zone up in the north; no one wanted to go there to search for one corpse. We buried him in an empty grave in his father's church. There's not even a coffin, only a damn stone.'

Geneva caught the bitterness in his voice and pushed aside the noodle box, reaching inside her pocket. She took out the newspaper clipping she'd found at the library and silently handed it to him.

He wiped his hands on his jacket and took it from her. He smoothed out the folds and stared at the badly reproduced black-and-white photo. At first there was nothing and she watched as he brought the clipping closer, squinted, and then, all of a sudden she saw it in his eyes.

'That's me?' he said, pointing to the left-hand side of the photo.

Geneva nodded. 'I think so.'

'Where did you find this?' He tried to make out the two

dark body-shaped smears with their arms round each other at the centre of the print.

'Press took it when you left Uganda.'

He turned towards her. 'Did Branch ask you to do this? To investigate me?' He dropped the clipping onto the table.

'No, of course not,' she replied, though that was exactly what Branch had asked her to do—how to explain that she'd fudged her reports in Carrigan's favour? 'I stumbled on it while looking into Ngomo at SOAS.'

Something crossed his face. 'But we weren't in one of Ngomo's camps, we were in an army camp.' He picked up the photo and looked at it again. She could see the sudden concern darkening his expression.

'They get it wrong a lot of the time,' she offered, realising that something had changed between them and that what she'd thought would be a peace offering had turned out to be anything but.

'You should have been looking into Ngomo, not wasting your time on me.'

'I wasn't—' Geneva began as the door opened and DC Jennings walked in then stopped, sensing he'd disturbed something.

'What is it?' Carrigan snapped.

Jennings looked down at the floor, unprepared for Carrigan's tone, the icy silence between the two detectives. 'I . . . I've just come back from—'

'Where's everyone else?' Carrigan wiped some Chinese food off his shirt and stared at the young DC.

Jennings started to say something then changed his mind. 'DC Singh's out at SOAS trying to track down Bayanga. Berman's getting a fix on where Bayanga sent his emails from. Um . . . I'm not sure where Karlson is, said he was following a lead.'

Carrigan nodded. 'And what about Gabriel?'

Jennings stared down at his shoes. 'He hasn't been to lectures today, hasn't been seen at SOAS at all and he missed his weekly AAC meeting.'

'Shit.' Carrigan looked up at the whiteboard. Gabriel had been either the last or the last but one person to see Ngomo alive.

'He's gone, sir,' Jennings continued. 'I tried his flat, no one there, his phone's been disconnected and the mobile's just going through to a dead tone.'

Was it possible that Bayanga and Gabriel were working together? Carrigan rested his head in his palm—nearly two weeks into this case and there was still so much they didn't know. He thought about the surveillance car he'd reassigned to Ursula's house—would they have seen Ngomo's killer if he'd left them to do their job? How long before Branch found out?

'We've got to keep trying,' Carrigan muttered pointlessly, then saw that Jennings was still there, shuffling nervously as if trying to dance without moving his feet. 'What is it?'

'Umm . . . sir . . . I was trying to tell you when I came in.' He stopped, looked for confirmation to go on, took the silence as such. 'I've just talked to the SOCOs. They're almost done in the general's flat. They found some letters hidden under the carpet in the top room.'

Carrigan frowned. 'Why didn't you tell us this before?'

'I tried, sir.' Jennings was looking paler and paler.

'Well?' Carrigan had retrieved the photo of himself and now held it in his hands as if it were some obscure talisman, his fingertips daubed black by the printer's ink.

'There were seven letters, sir. They found them under a loose bit of carpet next to Ngomo's desk. They're going over them right now, said they'll be done in a couple of hours and have them delivered to you.'

Carrigan checked his watch, he wanted to go over to the SOCO lab immediately and see why the letters were the only thing Ngomo had bothered to hide but he was due to meet Myra Bentley for the results of the post-mortem on Ngomo. 'Did you at least get a chance to look at them?'

Jennings nodded. 'Only a brief glimpse, you know what the SOCOs are like—but enough to see that each letter started with *Dear Daddy*,' he paused as Geneva and Carrigan took this in, both of them looking down at the photos chronicling the moments of Grace's life, 'and each was signed, *Your loving daughter.*'

31

Carrigan stared at the shrivelled lump of meat on the table. Spotlights bathed it in harsh white glare but couldn't hide the labyrinthine passageways and dappled folds of the dark-hued tissue.

They'd had to cut open Ngomo's neck to remove it.

He bent down but there was no smell to it, the thing already worn and dry as antique leather. He tried to imagine it once beating, a small red muscle sustaining life, and a sharp pain flared behind his eyes. He stepped back, felt the iron grip of Myra Bentley's fingers on his arm.

'Too much last night, huh?'

He could swear she was enjoying this. He steadied himself on the table and nodded, it was easier than trying to explain the real reason. He popped two more painkillers, the bitter residue coating his tongue, the taste of Chinese food still lingering in his mouth. He couldn't wait to get out of here, back to the incident room, wondering if the letters had arrived from forensics yet, what new secrets they would reveal.

'I do love you, Jack Carrigan,' the pathologist smirked, taking a long flat spatula made of shiny steel from her instrument table. 'Never fail to surprise me.' She used the spatula to prod and poke at the heart. 'Can't wait to tell my colleagues about this.'

Carrigan waited for her to expand but she was hunched over the table like a human comma. He stared down at the heart—it looked like something you would find in a field, a fire-blackened root vegetable of some sort.

'It's what killed him, in case you're wondering.' She put the scalpel to one side. 'Stuffed deep down his throat, crushing the windpipe. Someone held it down until the job was done.' She pointed to two shallow indentations on the surface of the heart. Carrigan leant forward and saw the distinctive ridges belonging to a set of fingerprints.

'Forty years I've been doing this and I've never seen a person choked to death on someone else's heart.'

'I'm glad you're entertained.'

Bentley continued prodding, making the organ emit small popping sounds. 'Made my day, this has.'

Carrigan looked down, saw the floor spinning away from him and blinked. All he could smell was the sharp bite of disinfectant and underneath that something sweeter and far more sickly.

'It's definitely Grace Okello's heart,' the pathologist continued, her voice as affectless as if she were reading out train times. 'Not that we have that many stray hearts, but we did check.'

'This was her father.' Carrigan was glad to see—if only for the slightest of intervals—the look of professional curiosity wipe itself from Bentley's face.

'A poetic sense of humour, your guy.'

Carrigan looked at the old woman. 'Too poetic.'

'Amazing, isn't it?' Bentley continued, interrupting his thoughts. She was still using the blunt end of the spatula to prod the heart. 'To get it down Ngomo's throat it was pummelled and squashed totally out of shape and yet look,' another prod, the black muscle collapsed then went back to normal as if nothing had happened, 'even dried out as it is, it retains its shape.' She finished her inspection and turned towards Carrigan. 'The resilience of human tissue is really a thing to behold, don't you think?'

It wasn't the first time he'd noticed how she spoke about

the human body as if it were some deity, enthralling in its absolute mystery. He stared down at the organ and thought how small it was, he'd never thought a heart would be that small. That feeling crept into his belly again, uneasy and memory-soaked, but he told himself it was only too much coffee, too many pills, too many days in a row.

'Oh, and I thought I probably should mention it,' the pathologist continued, 'not that it has any bearing on the case, or none that I can see anyway . . .'

'Please.' He just wanted to get out of there, out of the harsh bright lights, the gleaming metal furniture, the humming of the dead behind their freezer doors.

'Ngomo had cancer.' Bentley coughed into her handkerchief. 'Pancreatic, pretty far gone, probably knew he had it too. Only a few months left. It would have been very painful . . .' She stopped for a moment as if to contemplate the gravity of this. 'Though, I dare say, this was probably worse.'

32

He came in soaked as a dog, his hair matted and wild, shirt stuck to his skin, his jacket droopy and water-logged. She smelled the coffee before she saw him. Turned and there he was, wet with hooded eyes, two small cups of espresso in his hands.

Geneva looked up from the table where she'd been separating and arranging the letters. 'Managed to hold your lunch down this time?'

Carrigan smiled and put the coffee down next to her, unwrapped a massive Florentine encrusted with pistachios and broke it in half. 'Get your blood sugar up,' he said, passing it to her.

She took it, bit in and let the wonderful taste submerge her senses as Carrigan told her what the pathologist had found. The biscuit suddenly tasted flat in her mouth, bitter and dull. 'It's as if he had it planned all along,' she said, using a napkin to wipe the crumbs and coffee stains off her lips.

But Carrigan didn't answer—he was looking down at the table, the neat row of letters flattened and laid out side by side, the same handwriting, cursive and stylish, adorning each envelope. 'The SOCOs find anything?'

She finished the Florentine and rubbed her hands on her jeans. 'Only Ngomo's fingerprints. Everything else was too smudged.'

He took one of the letters and held it up. The paper smelled of chemicals and dripped a white powder like dandruff. He sniffed the envelope, luxuriating in the sharp odour of the fingerprint reagent, wondering how long the SOCOs had spent with these letters, white hooded figures in a silent room poring over yellowing vellum with their powders and brushes as if divining some ancient mystery; modern-day alchemists transmuting invisibility into identification. 'You've read them?'

Geneva nodded. 'Sorry, I wasn't sure how long you'd take.'

'Glad you did, save us some time.' He took a last sip of his espresso and binned the cup. 'So, anything we can use?'

Geneva looked down at the letters spread in front of her. 'You want the long or short version?'

'How about medium?' Carrigan smiled.

'I've put them in chronological order. The first one's from eighteen months ago and the most recent from two weeks back.'

The envelopes were almost identical: white, rimmed with a border of blue flowers, their stamps peeling from repeated handling. The paper inside was thick and watermarked but otherwise showed no peculiarities. It had been folded and refolded so many times that creases ran like scars through each third of the letter.

'The earliest one sounds like it's the first time she's written to him since Ngomo left her and her mother seven years ago.' Her voice had thickened from the coffee and Carrigan sat back in the chair, listening as Geneva recounted Grace's attempts to reconnect with a father who she'd thought was lost to her.

'In the first letter, Grace tells Ngomo that she's studying in London. She talks about how she spent her teenage years trying to understand who he was. The father she remembered or this man whose name people only ever mentioned in whispers. It feels quite cold and formal, as if she's writing to an old teacher or something.'

Geneva put the letter carefully back in its envelope and Carrigan finished writing his notes. The sound of the pipes mumbling in the walls, the hiss and steam of the motorway outside, their own breathing in the small room. The silence filled with images of Grace lying on her death bed, the bite marks, the hair matted with blood, the last words of the video, Grace's final words—*Help me, Daddy. Please help me*—now exploding like a depth charge in their heads.

Geneva picked up the next three letters. 'She writes a lot about being in London.' She looked up at Carrigan and began reading: '*There is a coldness to this city that is like death. I feel it in the huddle of crowds on the Underground, in the faces of the people serving in shops, in this dark block of flats that feels like a thousand coffins buried in the earth. I do not think I will ever grow to like it here. They tell me, how can you say this when your country is full of poverty and violence and chaos, but I do not see anything to replace it here but brightly-lit shops full of things I would never need. Where is the colour and light of Uganda? The long nights of autumn?*

'*I am practising getting my accent right. Our vowels and consonants are like the land we lived on; harsh and staccato, full of sudden stops and empty spaces. When I open my mouth I can see their eyes shade, the whole history of Africa coming back to them in the lilt of a sentence, something they would rather forget. So now I am learning to speak like someone who belongs here and I have noticed how it changes the very things I say, not just the way I say them. Maybe this is what happens to all immigrants— what they love to call assimilation—but I feel as if I am stranded at some point I will never be again, my past and homeland only a memory to me now and this country still so distant.*

'*But I am becoming too broody, that's what this weather does to you, you sit inside all the time and stare at the world from your window as if it were something other from you, and you will always be the figure behind glass trying but never fully understanding the events that take place without. I think windows are what separates them from us. I think when they invented windows they began to shut out the world, to enclose themselves, and that is how these Europeans lost track of the world and became only interested in themselves. I blame the window! Okay, Daddy, I' rambling now and I really began this letter to say something else but somehow I kept pushing it back.'*

Geneva stopped, took a sip of her coffee. 'She wants to meet him, settle the past. The fourth letter, dated just after Christmas, talks about their first meeting. She remarks on how good he looks. A lunch they enjoyed in town.' Geneva paused, dying for a cigarette. 'From her account, the first meeting was tense but by the next letter she talks about Ngomo's interest in her thesis, her unexpected delight that he supports what she's doing. This is where it gets interesting.' She slid one of the letters towards Carrigan. 'We thought it was Gabriel who got Grace involved in the AAC but it was the other way round.'

'Grace set up the AAC?' He fingered the letter, wondering how many times Ngomo had read it, all those nights alone in that house, the train thundering past every few minutes like a hard jolt of memory.

'She and Ngomo talk a lot about direct action, setting up a group that would address the problems in Uganda. She tells Ngomo about Gabriel and how he would be the perfect front-man for this group. Ngomo agrees and promises he'll send money for the cause. Something happens here, just after the Christmas break.' Geneva picked up another envelope. 'In those first letters Grace is very cool and withdrawn, but after they've met a few times she accepts Ngomo's justifications wholeheartedly, no longer questioning him—listen to this:

'You told me that I was doing a good thing, not just for our country but for you too, and then when I looked surprised you told me how much the past weighs on you, how the stories of who you are have become the truth. I know you did bad things, you told me yourself some of these. But that is who you are. This I accept. And that is who we are too. Ugandans. We have to live in a world that is so different from the one of my fellow students that they cannot understand it as we cannot understand the lives of ants. Our country has been ripped apart from every side and I

believe you when you said joining Kony was the only way to protect your family and your people.

'She goes from questioning his actions to being an apologist for them.' Geneva explained. 'There's one letter where she talks almost exclusively about the aid workers' murder:

'*I thank you for your honesty. That means more to me than the deeds you have done. I believe you when you say you had nothing to do with the death of the aid workers in your camp and that you can prove this. I look forward very much to our next meeting and the documents you promised to hand over. I think you thought at first that this project of mine will separate us forever but, Father, it has only brought us closer together here in this grey city and I will always be your daughter, the past cannot change that—*'

The door to the incident room crashed open, ripping them both away from the spell of Grace's words, the sound of massed footsteps and heavy breathing suddenly filling the small dark room.

Branch was holding the door open for the two Ugandan diplomats who'd been in his office a couple of days ago. The older diplomat caught Carrigan's eye and smiled.

'What the fuck's this?' Carrigan bolted up from the chair.

Branch raised his hand as if to shoo a pesky child. Carrigan saw the calluses and bruises on his skin, the florid complexion of his face, the way Branch's eyes couldn't meet his. 'This is Mr. Ondutu and Mr. Akimbi from the Ugandan embassy.' Branch looked down at the table where the letters lay spread out. 'I'm really sorry about this,' he said, his voice stumbling.

'Sorry for what?'

Branch shrugged. 'They have permission to take all material found in the house in Willesden Green.'

'What?' Carrigan exploded. 'This is bullshit.' He placed his body between the table and the men. 'This is our case and important evidence in a murder. No fucking way are you going to confiscate it.'

Branch put his hand softly on Carrigan's shoulder. 'There's nothing I can do, Jack; this is higher than me. I'm afraid you'll have to hand over those letters.'

Carrigan knocked Branch's hand off. The super was sweating heavily though the room was cold.

'Please take your hands off those,' the older Ugandan commanded Geneva, who was busily trying to fold and sequester the letters. 'They are no longer your property.' He made a move past Branch but Carrigan stopped him, laying an arm across the man's chest.

'These are the property of the Met and they're staying that way.' He could feel the man's muscles jumping under his touch, the cold steely eyes regarding him.

They stood there like that for several seconds, the electricity in the room jumping from face to face as each decided what they were prepared to do and what they weren't. Carrigan glanced down at Geneva, saw her shake her head, then looked back up as the other Ugandan flanked him and reached across the table. He knew there was no way he could keep them both away with force just as he knew that he would try as hard as he could to do exactly that.

He never got the chance. The stand-off continued, Branch trying to explain to Carrigan the seriousness of the situation, chain of command, protocol. Carrigan turned abruptly and grabbed the letters off the desk, held them tightly in his fist, waiting for what was to come next.

But it wasn't a fist or rush or scrum for the letters but a man in a perfectly tailored pinstripe suit who walked into the room as if he'd been waiting in the wings, watching this play out, finally aware that he had to intercede like a referee in a boxing match gone too far.

'I think it would be better for all of us if you handed over those letters.' The man's accent was sharp, his eyes cold and blue.

'This is John Marqueson,' Branch explained, trying to defuse the situation. 'He's come from the Foreign Office. I'm afraid he has all the paperwork, Carrigan. There's no choice.'

Carrigan stared at Marqueson. The man looked calm and collected, as if he were reading the Sunday paper on a park bench somewhere. 'I'm sorry, Detective, but this case is about a lot more than a dead student.' Marqueson checked his nails, smiled without revealing any teeth. 'Of course, that's not something you would have knowledge about, so please, take my word, we don't want this to turn into something else.' He watched Carrigan. 'I'm sure that once the embassy have satisfied themselves, you will get all the material back.'

Carrigan looked towards Branch but the super was looking away. Geneva sat quietly in her chair. The letters fluttered in his hand. He could smell the rancid breath of the Ugandan in front of him, see Marqueson's gold cufflinks flashing in the fluorescent light.

'Fuck it.' Carrigan unclenched his fist and let the papers fall to the floor. 'Take them,' he snarled. 'Keep protecting Ngomo.' Carrigan kicked the letters across the floor. He could see Branch reddening like a man about to burst. 'What the fuck did Ngomo give you for your loyalty?'

'I'm afraid I don't know who you're talking about,' Marqueson replied.

'Of course not.' Carrigan picked up his jacket and tucked it under his arm as one of the Ugandans bent down and started collecting the letters, the other taking the pile of photographs. Carrigan eye-fucked Marqueson, shook his head and walked out of the incident room. Geneva got up and was about to follow him.

'Miller!'

She stopped, swivelled round to see Branch facing her.

'My office. Now!'

33

Branch barely glanced at his secretary as he threw open the door and slumped down in his chair. Geneva sat down and watched him randomly flick through a pile of boxing magazines, his face tight and his eyes so small they were almost invisible, just pouches of baggy skin humped and swollen as if he'd been punched.

'What just happened?' She tried to keep her voice steady.

Branch put down his magazines and cleared his throat. 'Believe me,' he replied wearily, 'there was nothing I could do.'

'That was our case. Those letters could have led us to Bayanga.' She kept her hands at her side, the itch growing steadily worse with each passing second.

Branch nodded. 'I'm sure someone of your competence would have made copies.'

Geneva looked down at her feet, annoyed that Branch had read her so easily. 'That's not the point.'

'Who do you think I am?' Branch raised his hands in protestation. 'I sit in this office with my secretary outside, I shout at you and Carrigan, I decide which cases we're going to prioritise,' he carefully took off his glasses and wiped the lenses with a paper napkin, 'but that's it. I'm not the fucking chief constable, I take my orders just like you do.' He put his glasses back on and his face softened. 'You think I'm happy that someone else is interfering in our case? Some foreign government who should have no jurisdiction here? It makes me fucking mad but there's nothing I can do, not when the Foreign Office calls and makes it clear I have very little choice in the matter.' Branch hung his head and she could see the spreading whiteness of his bald patch, his fingers constantly worrying the few strands of hair left. 'It stinks, I know, but you better get used to this kind of bullshit if you're going to stay in the job, if you want to spend your career doing more than knocking on doors.' He reached for a cigar lying dormant in the ashtray, rolled it between his fingers. 'Anyway, that's not why you're here, is it?' He looked at her sharply but Geneva was still staring down at the floor. 'You said you wanted to see me about something important?'

She'd been tearing herself up over it these last few hours. Running the facts and protocols through her head, each time coming up short. What would her mother think of this act of betrayal, what would happen when Carrigan found out? She'd known since the moment he told her the story of his African ordeal, known but kept making excuses for him, reasons why he'd kept it from her—but she no longer felt she had a choice. She had to inform the commanding officer of Carrigan's possible conflict of interest, the history that turned his face into a mask every time Africa was mentioned. It had been the worst few hours of her professional life but in the end the case was more important than sparing Carrigan's feelings or betraying his trust.

'I don't know how to put this . . .' she began, but her voice faltered and cracked as Branch scrutinised her, a look of amusement lodged on his face.

When she was finished there was an unexpected sense of relief as if a weight had been lifted, the words buzzing in her head these last few hours like maddened bees. She sat back in the chair and watched as Branch stared darkly down at the table, his hands cradling his head as if it were suddenly too heavy for his neck to support.

'We know all about Carrigan.' He put the cigar down and, using his nail, carved a sliver of ash off the tip.

She thought she'd heard him wrong, her brain somehow making faulty connections. 'You already knew?'

Branch's laughter caught her off guard. 'You really thought we wouldn't know about something like this?'

'You knew?' she repeated, all other words stripped from her.

Branch nodded. 'We've known for years. Christ, Miller, don't you think I wish I could use this to crucify Carrigan, get him off the case?'

She wondered if this conversation would get back to Carrigan, had no doubt that Branch would use it one day as he saw fit.

'Concentrate on the investigation, Miller. Tell me what we have.'

She cleared her head, rubbed the itchy patch on her wrist. 'We believe that Gabriel Otto may have been the last person to see Ngomo alive—we're out there looking for him.'

'This is the same Gabriel you released two days ago?' Branch replied.

She nodded. 'Neither Carrigan nor myself believe that Gabriel killed Grace or Ngomo.'

Branch looked up at the wall, the blood-spattered faces gleaming behind glass. 'But if you'd kept him in custody you'd know for sure? No—don't answer that. So now you have to find him again, wasting valuable time and resources. What about Bayanga?'

'We got a positive ID on him from a neighbour of Ngomo's. The old woman was weeding her front garden and saw Bayanga ring Ngomo's doorbell. Bayanga said something and Ngomo let him in. The neighbour's evidence ties in with the time of death Myra Bentley gave us. I think we can say pretty certainly that Bayanga killed both General Ngomo and Grace Okello.'

Branch sighed heavily, shook his head. 'But you have no actual evidence, and you're no nearer finding him, I assume?'

Geneva shrugged. She flashed back to the sight of the Ugandans leaving the incident room with Ngomo's belongings. Was it possible that Bayanga was proving so hard to find because someone was hiding him?

Branch snorted. 'As far as I can see it's been over a week and Carrigan's got nowhere on this case.'

'That's not true,' Geneva retorted, surprised to find herself defending Carrigan the way she'd always defended one parent to the other following the divorce. 'We have a name and a photo of our main suspect and we have fingerprints from both the Grace scene and Ngomo's flat that will tie him unequivocally to the murders when we find him.'

'And another dead body—you forgot to mention that.' Branch coughed into his hand. 'You have four more days to bring this case to a close, it's out of my hands after that.'

She felt the air leave her lungs, her skin itching madly. 'What do you mean?'

Branch looked down at his desk, picked up a file, put it down, picked up another. 'Marqueson, the man from the Foreign Office—he's going to be taking over the investigation then.'

The words struck her like pellets of hail. 'It's our case, how can they justify taking it over?' She snapped her head up, met Branch's eyes. 'Have you asked yourself who they're trying to protect?'

Branch slammed his fist down on the table. 'Enough, Miller. I don't want to hear this kind of shit. I'm disappointed in you. This isn't some big conspiracy, this is a cluster-fuck pure and simple, a mess that the government have decided to clean up. Nothing I can do about it.'

'That's not fair, sir.'

Branch stood up, his stomach popping and rolling within the constraints of his shirt. 'Fair? What the fuck's fair? You think anything in this world is fair? Jesus, I didn't think you were such an idealist. This is the way it is.'

'How long have you known that the Ugandan embassy have an interest in the case?'

Branch's face reddened, the veins pulsing at the surface as his eyes narrowed. 'You should be careful with your accusations, Miller. Do you know that I can probably kiss my career fucking goodbye because I spent all morning arguing your case to that Marqueson prick? No you didn't, did you? Smarmy fucker wanted to take the investigation over immediately. I had to fucking plead and beg and get nasty with him so you and Carrigan could have a few more days.'

She avoided his eyes, cursing herself for letting emotion take over like that. It was just what the men above her wanted to hear, what they expected from a woman, 'I'm sorr—'

'I don't want your fucking thank yous or contrition, just get me Bayanga or Gabriel or anyone we can arrest by Monday so that I don't look like a fucking fool, so they don't send me to Whitby or Lancaster or some other shithole for the rest of my career.'

34

The car was cold and damp, the battery too weak for him to sit with the heater on. He'd parked in the same spot, half a block down from Ben's house, for two nights in a row. Nights of watching Ursula through a window, her body heavy with sorrow, her eyes hidden from him behind layers of glass and rain.

After the fiasco of the rerouted surveillance car, going to Branch and asking for another would only have resulted in a very unpleasant conversation, and so he'd decided to do it himself, realising unexpectedly how much he began to crave these moments away from the case, alone in a car in the dark watching a woman pull the curtains on her day, the lights of the house going off one by one, the rain turning the street into a river of jewels.

He looked at the photo in his hands, the one Geneva had given him, the fuzzy likenesses and strange dislocation of seeing yourself from another person's perspective, and thought of the man he was back then and the man he was now. He remembered the first time he'd seen Ursula, the pale blue scarf she wore in class, the sound of her voice and ruffle of her jumper against his neck. Would he have led her to this house—this life with kids and garden and the river right outside the front door?

He was thinking about that, thinking about the roads taken and the ones not, when he saw the splash of knuckles against his window, the harsh urgency of the knocking pulling him abruptly back into the night. He turned his neck to see who it was, felt a sharp crackle of electricity fizzle through his shoulders and rolled down the window. He didn't even recognise her at first, she looked like some drowned thing, hair matted all across her face, shivering and soaked. He reached for the passenger door, took one last look at Ursula's window and let Geneva in.

The smell instantly wrenched him from his gloom. Geneva held two cups of coffee. 'Thanks for inviting me in,' she said, handing him the drink, crawling into the seat, the smell of coffee, rain and perfume suddenly flooding Carrigan's senses.

'How did you know I'd be here?' He pulled the lid off the cup and took a long sip, burning his tongue but not caring.

'Supposed to be a detective, remember?' She widened her eyes and stirred her coffee. 'You weren't at the office, you weren't at home, I knew you wouldn't be in a pub. Didn't leave many options.'

Carrigan wasn't sure whether to be annoyed or glad for the company. He watched the house through the rain but there was no movement or light coming from inside. He knew Ursula would be up soon—two nights he'd been watching and she hadn't managed to sleep through one of them. She'd wake, stare out the window at the dark then turn and head down to the kitchen. The light would go on and he imagined her pouring a strong drink, looking at the pictures of her life and wondering about the same things he was: fate and luck and how you end up as someone unrecognisable to yourself.

'And, besides, I knew you wouldn't leave a lady in distress alone.' Geneva pointed to the house. Her fingernails had been cut and painted black and he wondered if she'd been on the way to somewhere, whether she had a boyfriend or family or friends, someone to take her away from everything they'd been through these last few days.

'You and Ursula,' she added.

He stared down into his cup. 'Ben's my best friend; I'm just watching out for his wife.'

'Yeah, right,' Geneva laughed. 'A woman can tell these things, you know.'

He stared back up at the silent house and said nothing, there was no point in explaining. 'You haven't told me what you're doing here.'

She shuffled in her seat as if to draw herself in. 'I went to see Branch,' she said, her voice whispery and hesitant. 'I told him about your connection to Africa.'

'You should have told me first,' Carrigan replied, his voice strangely muted. 'I thought we'd established some kind of trust between us.' He shook his head and looked out the window, knowing he was letting his emotions get the better of him. 'Forget it, you did the right thing and that's what matters.' He looked to see how she was taking this but her face was gaunt and drooped. 'What's wrong?'

She sipped her coffee, noticing the crisps littering the car, chocolate wrappers and crumbs stuck between the ridges of the seat fabric. 'Branch gave us a deadline. Four days.'

Carrigan stared out at the failing light. 'I have a feeling it won't take that long,' he replied. He took a sip of coffee. 'You were right about why Grace's heart was taken, the connection to Ngomo, that was good work. I'm sorry I didn't pay attention earlier.'

She shook her head vigorously. 'But after all that it wasn't Ngomo. I was so sure he killed Grace because she was going to expose him.'

'The heart led us to Ngomo.' It was good she'd come, good that she was here in the car on this wet dark night with him. 'You were right about it being his signature only we understood it wrong.' He turned away from the darkened windows of Ben's house. 'Suppose the signature was the same because someone wanted revenge on Ngomo? What better method than to kill his own daughter in that way? It certainly would have sent out the right message, one Ngomo couldn't have ignored.'

She felt the heat of his words as they crossed the small space between them. 'You really think this is about revenge?'

Carrigan nodded. 'Yes and no. Revenge, but the heart was also used as a lure.'

'To trap Ngomo?' She could see where he was going with this, the disparate and contradictory threads of the case that had so perplexed them finally coming together.

'Yes. Killing Grace was only the first part. Remember Bayanga's email? *I have the thing I promised to give you*?'

Geneva nodded, silently agreeing. 'But why bother with the YouTube clip?'

'Because he wanted Ngomo to watch his own daughter die and to know that all over the world people were doing the very same thing.'

She picked at her dress. 'Explains why Bayanga took off the gag at the end.' She looked out at the drenched lanes, the hunched figures of commuters battling the wind and water. She had to agree it made sense of everything which until now had seemed contradictory—yet hadn't Carrigan himself warned her about the seductions of narrative? 'You still believe someone hired Bayanga to do it, that he wasn't working alone?'

'I can't see Bayanga as the type to think that far ahead, to come up with something this complex. One the one hand Bayanga's profile and the nature of the killings suggest that we're dealing with a disorganised and chaotic killer, but the filming, uploading, luring Ngomo—this is the work of a killer who's highly organised and controlled. The two impulses are contradictory.

'Solomon Onega said that Bayanga bumped into someone from back home. I think whoever he bumped into knew Ngomo was living in London, someone with an old grudge to settle.'

Geneva scratched her nails against the fabric of her dress and sighed. 'Leaves us with pretty much the whole of Uganda as suspects.'

Carrigan looked away, his eyes unfocused, a strange turbulence brewing behind them. 'This is where I think Gabriel comes into this. I think he's the key.'

Geneva balanced her coffee on the dash. 'Singh and Karlson were at his flat but almost everything's been cleared out; neighbour said she saw him leaving with a big rucksack on his back.' She didn't want to contemplate the possibility that her first murder would remain unsolved. She'd wanted answers, explanations, a story to make sense of everything—it was one of the reasons she'd hated uniform work and joined CID.

'What's your take on Gabriel?' Carrigan crushed his espresso cup and flung it to the floor.

She thought about it for a moment. 'I knew a lot of people like him back at university, my mum's friends too. They focus so hard on one thing, one cause, that it distorts the rest of the world for them.' She flicked something off her dress. 'Gets them a lot of girls, though . . . it's almost always the reason they're doing it.'

Suddenly Carrigan sat bolt upright, his whole body shaking into focus as he slammed his fist against the steering wheel.

Geneva's eyes shot wide open. 'What is it? What did I say?'

Carrigan turned to her and smiled. 'I know where Gabriel's hiding.'

Back in the incident room Singh and Berman were working late shifts, their eyes sunk deep into sockets from too much screen time, the smell of pot noodles and microwaved lasagne hanging heavy in the air.

'When we arrested Gabriel, did anyone take down the girlfriend's name?' Carrigan had barely got his breath back after having insisted on using the stairs when the lift was taking too long.

Singh opened her desk drawer and flicked through her notebook as Carrigan tapped his feet against the floor.

'Greta Nykvist,' she said, her eyebrows wrinkling with relief.

Berman was punching keys before Carrigan could give him the order. 'What's this about?' Geneva asked.

Carrigan turned to her. 'Gabriel had a girl at his place when we arrested him. He also mentioned he took the same girl to the concert the night Grace was killed and that he stays with her sometimes. How has he disappeared? How the fuck have we not found him yet? He's not Bayanga, he doesn't know all the bolt-holes and underground termini. Like you said in the car, his type are in it for the girls . . . where else is he going to hide?'

35

They arrived as dawn broke, the light leaking meanly into the concrete plaza. The Biko estate stood grey and hazy in the early-morning mist, its top floors obscured by low cloud and intermittent rain. There'd been nowhere to get breakfast on the drive over and Carrigan felt stretched at the edges, hungover from too little sleep and too many pills, his stomach burning and his brain reeling with theory and supposition.

They parked under a grey overhang of concrete, silently got out of the car, checked their equipment and radioed in their position. Singh and Berman had wanted to come as back-up but Carrigan had quickly vetoed the idea—the last thing he wanted was another blazing blue-light entrance freaking Gabriel and making him run. And if they were wrong—if Gabriel wasn't here at all—then Branch would punish him for wasting resources, use this failure as another reason to pass the case over to the Foreign Office. Carrigan didn't know how much longer he'd be in the job,but he was determined to finish this case regardless of the consequences and it surprised him, this new-found energy and sense of mission—he thought he'd lost it permanently a couple of years ago, that this was what happened when you'd been in the job too long. He couldn't tell if it was the shadow of Africa, the deviousness of Bayanga, or having a partner like Geneva, but on this cold and grey morning he felt like a rookie on his first big case.

Geneva put on her vest, mace, belt and gloves. 'How are we

doing this?' She stared up at the looming tower, tried to count floors, isolate the sixteenth where Greta Nykvist lived, but the building disappeared in a smear of cloud ten floors up.

Carrigan shut the car door. 'We're just going to ask him to come in for a friendly chat and not mention Ngomo at all,' he replied as she followed him through the path and up to the entrance. He pressed several buzzers, said 'Parcel for you', and listened for the sound of the release catch.

They waited for the lift, silent, each eyeing the doorways either side of them, the dark maw of stairs rising to their left. The lift was surprisingly quick, the numbers flashing by so fast that they were unprepared when it came to a shuddering halt, the door sliding open and depositing them in Greta's hallway.

There were three flats to either side of them, an overflowing rubbish bin and a fire escape. Geneva took a deep breath and knocked on Greta's door.

She jumped back as it swung open under her fist, the lock unlatched. She looked at Carrigan, saw the same concern darkening his features as he moved in front of her, pulling out his baton, and using the tip of his shoe to hold the door open. 'Stay here, call back-up.' He turned to her, his face white and stretched.

'You're not going in there alone.'

Carrigan thought about it for a moment, realised there was no point arguing.

They could both smell it as soon as they walked into the flat. Burning toast, stale smoke, and something else underneath it all—fresh and coppery. Carrigan signalled Geneva to follow him as he stepped into the hallway. He could feel every pore on his skin puckering, sweat sliding down the back of his neck, the sound of his own heartbeat, as he slowly opened the door to the living room.

He stepped inside ready to find anything but there was only a TV, a DVD player, posters of French cult films and a large collection of fashion magazines splayed across the floor. 'Clear.' He turned and Geneva followed him down the corridor to the bedroom. He inched the door open and took one step inside.

From the way his body froze, tension marking out every muscle on his neck, Geneva could tell he'd found them.

'Christ!' He stared at the two bloodied corpses piled up against each other in the corner of the room. The smell made him gag, swallow, wipe his brow. He heard Geneva behind him, the sharp intake of breath as she saw the bodies— slumped, scarred and lifeless.

'Oh my God.'

They didn't move any closer, not wanting to disturb the crime scene—there was no doubt that Gabriel and Greta were dead and that they'd died with the utmost suffering. Wounds covered their naked bodies, the same bite marks Carrigan knew from the autopsy photos and other, more fiendish embellishments. Gabriel's left eye was missing, his ears loosely hanging by shredded strings of cartilage. The smell of recently burned flesh sat in Carrigan's throat as he turned and walked out of the room.

They checked the bathroom, hall cupboard and kitchen. Then they checked the living room again. 'All clear,' Carrigan confirmed as they met in the hallway. 'Call forensics too,' he told her. 'Tell them we need them here as soon as possible.'

Geneva took out her mobile and started dialling as Carrigan stepped back into the kitchen.

He stood staring at the meagre utensils and charred cooking pots wondering how long Gabriel and Greta had been dead. He could still smell the hot metal of their blood, the perfume of scorched flesh, but there was something else underneath it. Something fresher, familiar.

He looked down at the kitchen table, a meal left half-eaten on the plate, a glass of milk, the burned-out ends of several cigarettes nestling in an ashtray. Then he bent down, picked up the plate and brought it close to his face.

His heart began hammering. He put one finger on the surface of the cheese and felt it give, residual heat warming his skin. He looked at the ashtray, the glass of milk, and panic flooded him. He scanned the kitchen but there was nowhere for Bayanga to hide. He called out Geneva's name but there was no answer.

Bayanga had been in this kitchen making himself breakfast a scant few minutes before they'd arrived. How had they missed him? There were only two ways in and out of the block—the lift and the stairs—had Bayanga been running down the stairs, making his escape at the very moment that they were in the lift going up?

Geneva ended the call and placed the phone back in her pocket. The SOCOs would be here in ten minutes, Berman and Singh in five. She took a deep breath, gagging for a cigarette, something to take away the awful smell residing in her nostrils, and stood in the hallway wondering what Carrigan was up to, trying to shake her mind of the images she'd seen, the two slumped bodies and the things that had been done to them. Something kept niggling at her—she couldn't quite place it, running a mental checklist of everything they'd seen since entering the flat, the living room, bedroom, hallway, kitchen, bathroom . . .

What was it about the bathroom?

She opened the door and stepped into the tiled white interior once more. She looked around but there was very little to see, the long tub with the shower curtain fully drawn, the old toilet, a chipped and dirty sink, towels hanging on a rack, a small cabinet with a broken mirror, a pile of well-thumbed *Vogues*—and then she looked back.

Behind the towel rack she could see a door. It looked like

an airing cupboard. Big enough for someone to hide in? She couldn't tell from where she was. She walked over to the towel rack and held her breath as she slowly unhooked it from the latch.

She heard something from the other side of the door and jumped back, almost tripping over a rolled-up bath mat. A slight clunk like someone fidgeting followed by what she could swear was hissing coming from behind the door. She closed her fingers round the cold metal handle and stopped. There was only one way to do this.

She stepped back, took another deep breath, and opened the door in one swift motion. She let out a sound that was somewhere between a scream and a laugh when she saw the boiler rattling and hissing away. She closed the door, replaced the towel rack, and was about to leave when she stopped, turned and stared at the bathtub.

The shower curtain was marbled white and she could see the far end of the tub through it, fuzzy and indistinct. She took a couple of steps forward and scrunched her eyes. There was a dark patch at the bottom of the tub, she could see it clearly now and, as she was watching, it began to move.

She blinked at the exact same time as it uncoiled and rose up. She tried to reach her mace but she never got the chance.

Carrigan stepped out of the kitchen, turned in the narrow hallway and stopped.

He saw Geneva first, her face emerging from the bathroom, and he smiled but she wasn't smiling back. He noticed the hand covering her mouth and then the man behind her and all the blood drained from his head.

Bayanga had pulled a curved blade out of his jacket and was pushing it up against Geneva's throat. His other hand was making its way through her uniform. Carrigan saw Bayanga move his hand and suddenly Geneva crumpled, her face turning white, gasping and choking in pain. Bayanga laughed and pulled her upright, placing the knife back against her throat.

Carrigan felt a white burst of panic and pushed it firmly down. He stared at the man they'd been hunting these past two weeks.

Bayanga was small and wiry, short black dreads framing his skull, a baggy yellow T-shirt and a pair of worn board shorts revealing skinny scar-crossed legs ending in a pair of outdated hi-tops. He was almost a disappointment.

'Let her go.' Carrigan could feel the impotence of his words as soon as they were out. He didn't need Bayanga's subsequent laugh to realise his position.

'I don't think so.' Bayanga smiled again and this time Carrigan saw the two sharpened fangs at the front of his mouth. He pressed his left hand against Geneva's liver, probing with his fingers, and she exploded in a fit of vomiting. 'I can do things that will cause her pain for the rest of her life,' Bayanga said, his voice thin and wheezy. 'I can make her wish for death, so bad will her suffering be. This isn't what you want, I know. It is what I want but what I want more is to leave here. Let me do that and I promise I will only hurt her as much as I need to.'

Carrigan stared at Bayanga, wondering how long until Berman and Singh got here. He saw nothing but a bright hard fury in Bayanga's eyes. 'Okay,' he said, taking a step back into the kitchen, 'you win—just leave her and go.'

Bayanga smiled, his teeth gleaming in the bulblight. 'You know what will happen to her the moment you try anything?' He pressed the edge of the blade against Geneva's throat, a small red droplet flowering on her skin.

Carrigan retreated another couple of steps as Bayanga slowly inched his way up the hallway. There was nothing Jack could do as they passed, Bayanga turning so that now he was walking backwards out of the flat, using Geneva as a shield. Carrigan watched the two of them shuffle through the front door like unlikely partners in some exotic tango. He saw Bayanga take his left arm away from Geneva's liver and press the lift's call button, his other hand still firmly holding the knife.

They faced each other across the open doorway as the lift arrived. 'Close your door,' Bayanga said, walking backwards into the lift. 'If you open it and I'm still here then I will kill her.'

Carrigan wondered why he couldn't hear Berman and Singh's siren as he watched Bayanga press the button. He closed the front door and stood staring at the coat rack, counting silently.

At ten, he opened the door, ready to rush Bayanga, but the lift doors were closed and he could hear it making its descent. He staggered out of the flat, flung open the fire door and began running down the stairs.

How fast had the lift been? He couldn't remember but it was sixteen floors and if he didn't fall he might be able to beat it.

He took the stairs two, three at a time. He gripped the banister, jumped and ran. The pain screamed in his shoulders and back, his lungs searing like they'd been set on fire.

Three floors down.

He listened for the lift, wondering where it was, realising that Bayanga might have tricked him, gone up instead of down.

He slipped on the tenth floor, almost crashing down a whole flight, managing to right himself at the last moment, using the momentum of the fall to leap down even quicker.

He cornered the third floor, was rushing down the second when he heard the unmistakable hydraulic groan of the lift doors opening. Despite the pain in his lungs, the urge to crumple and puke, he leapt the last few stairs and landed winded on the ground floor just in time to see Bayanga coming out of the lift, Geneva still tightly in his grip, the curved knife at her throat.

Bayanga stopped just short of the front door and saw Carrigan. He moved his right arm slightly, down and across, almost too fast for Carrigan to catch, and when he pulled the blade out of Geneva's thigh it was shiny and slicked red.

Geneva looked down at her leg, her eyes widening, and then Bayanga let go of her and she collapsed hard onto the cement, her head banging against the floor.

Bayanga wiped the knife on his jeans and looked at Carrigan. 'You have a choice—her or me.' He laughed then turned and ran out the door.

Carrigan looked down at the floor, Geneva passed out, the blood slowly pooling around her, and knew he had no choice. He saw Bayanga disappear over a rise, silhouetted against the early-morning light. He leant down, took off his tie, and used it as a tourniquet. He cursed loudly as he tightened it around Geneva's thigh, feeling the blood spurt on his hands and hearing her moan.

He held Geneva as she began coming to, her body shaking in violent convulsions which he tried to contain in his arms, the blood turning his tie black. He took her hands in his and, as the screaming sirens came to a halt, he felt her small fingers entwine in his and press once, gently.

36

By the time Berman and Singh had arrived with back-up, Bayanga was nowhere to be seen. They'd spread out and executed a grid search of the area around the tower block but they found nothing. Bayanga could have got on a bus, or had a car waiting, and been out of the area by the time anyone had even started looking for him.

Carrigan had held Geneva, staunching the bleeding in her thigh, pressing his palm into hers, letting her know he was there watching over her, until the paramedics came. She'd been admitted to hospital, stitched up, given a fistful of painkillers and released the same evening. He'd waited for her outside the steps of the hospital and when she'd appeared, surprised but happy to see him, he'd driven her back to her flat, refused her offer of a drink and watched as she closed the door firmly behind her. He sat in the car outside her house, yet another darkened vigil, and when morning broke he silently eased it out of its spot and into another day.

He unwrapped another piece of chocolate, put it in his mouth and let it slowly melt. The rain had stopped for a while, leaving the road slicked with a wet membrane reflecting the passing lights of cars. It was his favourite time in the city—when everything looked mysterious and bright, the red and green traffic lights smeared on the wet road like long neon streamers, the huddled forms of people racing through the blurred streets. He finished the chocolate and took a long slurp from his Thermos. His eyes itched and his head roared. He swallowed two more pills with the last of the coffee and tried stretching his legs.

He'd spent the last four nights hunched in the car, watching the house, seeing Ursula's silhouette leak and flitter across different rooms like a dancer who's forgotten their steps. The car was parked up the road, giving him free view of the garden, the back windows and side wall. Every time anyone approached the house, walked past the gate or crossed the road, his heart ratcheted up, but they always passed by, headed towards someone else's front garden. He eyes kept drifting back to the piece of paper in his hand, the clipping Geneva had given him, trying to see himself in the stricken expression of the young man climbing onto an aeroplane, one arm draped across his best friend's shoulders. It looked nothing like him and however hard he stared at the photo he couldn't persuade himself of its truth.

He flicked the windscreen wipers, watched the smearing of raindrops and waited for Geneva to show. She'd turned up again the previous night, knocking on his car window, sitting beside him, the heat coming off her in waves. Sometimes they'd talked and sometimes they'd just sat in silence watching the rain. She'd been offered a few days' leave but had refused, downplaying her injuries, though Carrigan noticed how she kept holding the place where Bayanga had touched her, grimacing in pain every time she had to turn or stand.

His stomach soured at the thought of how close they'd been and how Bayanga had so easily read him, knowing Carrigan would stop and help Geneva before anything else.

Bayanga had turned into a ghost. One of an unseen army living their lives under the radar, a shadow London of hospital cleaners, dishwashers and street sweepers. A city he passed every day yet never noticed. Invisible because they wanted to be, invisible because we preferred them to be so. Perhaps the city was always like this—two parallel realms that rarely touched—the murder being a random intersection, an abutment of worlds.

He woke suddenly, crumpled and numb, his heart beating fast in his chest. How long had he been asleep? The night was still dry and silent and the clock on the dashboard said it was only just past one in the morning. He caught his face in the rear-view mirror, saw the lines and wrinkles highlighted by the overhead bulb, the roll of fat under his chin, the dead past swimming in his eyes, and then he heard the crash of breaking glass. He shook his head free of the memories and looked up at the house. He saw Ursula cross one of the upstairs hallways then stop dead in her tracks. At that exact moment a light went on downstairs.

37

He was out of the car immediately, coat snagging, his feet numb from lack of movement. He glanced up at the house as he ran. He could see the door swinging open, the stained glass smashed and jagged in its frame.

The silence inside was overwhelming. Not normal silence which was never really silence but something else, a constriction of the air, as if all the oxygen had been leached out of the building. He stood there for a moment willing his breath to slow and quieten, then took a few tentative steps and nudged the living-room door open with his shoe. It was empty, the kitchen too. He passed by the fireplace, still smouldering, then turned back and picked up a long brass poker from its tray. It felt both cold and hot in his hand as he gripped it tight, getting used to the weight, and then he headed for the stairs.

He was halfway up when Ursula screamed. A terrifying out-of-control yelp exploding from her lungs. There was no time to react. The ensuing gun blast filled the silence, leaving his ears ringing. The next thing he heard was a thud, like an exhalation of breath, from somewhere upstairs—the dead weight of Ursula's body hitting the floor.

He took the stairs two at a time willing his mind to block out the images that were flooding it: Ursula supine on the floor . . . Ursula with her head missing, a halo of blood curdled around her neck . . . Ursula turning to him in a darkened lecture theatre . . . He concentrated on putting one foot in front of the other, never having noticed there were so many steps before, and made the landing winded, almost unable to stand.

A thin tendril of smoke curved up from the door to Ben's bedroom. The smell, sharp and rich, filled Carrigan's nostrils as he approached. He kicked open the door, swinging himself into the room, poker raised in his right arm, ready for anything but what he saw.

It took him a second to readjust, to focus, and then fear took over as he stared into the black rings of the shotgun's barrels.

'Don't!' he shouted, dropping the poker, standing rigid in the doorway. 'It's me.'

Ursula was standing at the far end of the room pointing the shotgun at him, using her left arm as a crook. Her eyes didn't even register his entrance.

'Ursula, put it down.' He glanced at Bayanga's body sprawled out across the Persian rug. The young man was still twitching, a series of involuntary jerks and burbles as he gasped for air.

Ursula's eyes met his and for a moment he thought she was going to pull the trigger and then he saw a flicker of recognition pass across her face and her eyes rolled back into focus. Bayanga twitched once more and took a cracked breath which he never exhaled.

'It's okay.' Carrigan didn't dare move, the scene frozen, only two ways it could go from here.

Ursula looked down at the body on the floor, then back up at Carrigan. Her arms suddenly gave way and she dropped the gun. Her hands began to shake now they weren't holding anything, a slight ripple that turned into a rumbling torrent as her body caught up to the scene in front of her. Carrigan walked over and took her hands in his, surprised by how cold they felt. He put his arms around her. 'I'm here now.'

Ursula didn't answer, her eyes fixed on Bayanga. 'I . . .'

Her voice faltered and cracked. 'I . . . I thought he was going to kill me.'

Carrigan held her tight. 'There was nothing else you could have done,' he whispered. 'It's over.'

He stood next to her as she sat down in Ben's armchair, shaking so much it seemed as if she would break apart in front of him. 'It was you or him, he wouldn't have hesitated.' His voice sounded foreign to him here in this room of memories, the nights and conversations he'd shared with Ben, the history they skirted around, the dark lure of the beckoning past. 'He's already killed at least four we know of.'

He watched to see if she was taking this in but she seemed cocooned in a world of her own, slowly withdrawing from the room around her. She sat on her hands, her eyes staring at a blank spot of wall. He picked up the gun, the metal still warm, and placed it to one side, away from the spreading pool of blood which outlined Bayanga.

He knelt down and checked the Ugandan's pulse but it was only a way to stretch the moment, put off what he was dreading. His skin was still warm and Carrigan thought if he pressed his finger deep enough he'd be able to feel the echo of the young man's heartbeat, a last communication into the world. But there was nothing except a deep sense of disappointment flooding his stomach. This was the man they'd been chasing, the man who raped and killed Grace, who'd hurt Geneva, the man who held all the answers to this case and here he was, mute and silent for eternity. There would be no clink of handcuffs, no face-to-face in a hot interview room, no confession, nor explanation of why and how. Just this dead body, a large red hole gaping where his stomach should be.

He checked Bayanga's pockets but there was nothing except a knife and a wallet. The knife was small and curved and he recognised it, the wallet held £240 in crumpled notes and a photo of Geneva. The latter made Carrigan's blood go cold. He stood back up and looked at the sluggish river wind its way out of view. 'We'll get this all sorted out,' he promised Ursula, sitting down next to her and taking her hand.

She looked up, caught his eye and started shaking, hard shuddering jolts that looked as if electricity was pouring through her body. 'I wasn't going to let him take me too.' She was staring down at the floor, trying to wipe blood, something sticky, off the bottom of her slippers. 'What's going to happen to me, Jack?'

'I'm afraid we're going to have to arrest you formally and take you in but I'll be there with you all the way.'

She cried a little more and then she took a handkerchief from the table next to her and wiped her face, and coughed, and stared out the window at the grey river as they waited for Geneva and the others to arrive.

Carrigan explained the situation to Geneva as quickly as he could. He watched silently as two uniforms led Ursula out. She stopped once, picked up a photo of the girls and held it tightly in her hand as they took her outside. He'd promised he'd meet her back at the station once he'd secured the crime scene.

His headache pulsed ferociously as he watched the patrol car leaving with Ursula. He saw her look back at the house once and then he turned away.

As he waited for the SOCOs to arrive, he crossed the room, trying to press the pain away from his temples, the sense of hidden things rising to the surface. He avoided the body, saw the blood staining one of Ben's rugs, vaguely remembered a story of how Ben had bought it in Pakistan, how it had been woven by hand, was supposed to represent something about God. He blinked the thought away, looked around the room trying to determine if there was anything amiss but it was impossible. This room he knew so well looked like a foreign battlefield, everything sheathed in smoke and dust.

He eyes drifted to the mantelpiece, the photos deep with memory and contentment. He picked up a few, his fingertips tingling: Ben on his first field trip back to Africa, Ben in Khartoum and Addis Ababa, Ben, Ursula, and the kids sitting over Christmas lunch, uncles and grandparents, photos of the girls at school pantomimes and sports days, the happy family on holiday in Zermatt, Vail and Acapulco.

He took out the smudged news clipping from his pocket, smoothed out the edges and looked at the murky shadows of the two of them boarding the plane at Entebbe. The paper felt like it was burning his hands. He carefully folded it back up and placed it in his pocket.

Next to the mantelpiece were two photo albums with red leather covers. He picked one up, sat down in the armchair and began flicking through it. The book was heavier than he expected, all the weight of years and memories pinned like butterflies against the black pages.

He followed Ben's rise to stardom and fame, the clothes getting more expensive with each year, the haircuts sharper, the smile more confident and assured. He saw photos of Ben at Oxford, Ben giving a lecture at some symposium in France. There was a photo of Ben and Ursula taken on the night of their wedding, Ursula as he remembered her, her smile so genuine it looked as if it could cure cancer.

His breath caught in his throat when he recognised the picture of the three of them. A memory bright and present as a toothache blossomed in his head; the moment the photo had been taken—Ben, David and him standing on the mound at the front of the Great Hall, degrees in hand, the whole of their lives in front of them. He looked deeply into Ben's eyes, David's, his own, but could see no presentiment of how their lives would shudder and crack on that African road only two weeks later.

He flicked through photos of a young Ben smiling in the

equatorial sunshine on his first field trip. Ben standing in front of a new excavation, his helpers all around him. Ben wading in one of the great lakes, a stork caught mid-flight above his head. Ben at a refugee camp, his arms around his assistants, Ben talking to the bishop of Gulu, Ben standing . . .

. . . He flicked back and stopped, looking at the photo in the right-hand corner of the previous page, convinced it was a trick of the light.

Ben was standing on a dirt road next to a group of colleagues. They had their arms draped around each other. Carrigan carefully lifted the clear plastic and peeled off the photo.

He stared out of the window, towards the river, trying to clear his head, and then he looked down at what he held in his hands, realising how badly they'd misinterpreted Solomon Onega's words.

W here the fuck is he?'

Branch was red as an apple, leaning forward, both arms planted squarely on the desk. He ripped his glasses off, snagging them, wincing and cursing under his breath.

'Carrigan?' Geneva replied, trying to stall, think of what to say even though she'd been going over it in her head these last few hours.

'No, Lord Lucan. Who the fuck do you think I'm talking about?'

'I don't know where he is, sir.'

Branch sighed. 'I'll choose to believe that for now.' He picked up one of the mobiles on his desk and pressed something, his face scrunched in concentration, cursed and picked up another phone.

She watched as he clumsily began texting, his large fingers splayed across the keypad, his suit ruffled as if he'd slept in it several nights.

It had been two days since she'd seen Carrigan. Two days since anyone had heard from him. He hadn't turned up at the station after Ursula's arrest nor was he at his flat. Geneva had tried his mobile, leaving several messages, but as yet there had been no reply.

Branch read something off one of his phones, smiling to himself. He looked up at Geneva as if she'd only just stepped into his office. 'Good work, Miller, I'm very impressed.'

She didn't know what to say, hadn't been expecting this at all. 'What for, sir?'

Branch put his hands together in front of him, pursed his lips. 'For bringing this case to a satisfactory conclusion, of course.'

She leant forward in the chair, feeling its rough bristles chafe against her tights. 'It's Carrigan you should be thanking. If he hadn't been there when Bayanga—'

'Nonsense, Miller,' Branch interrupted. 'All very well to give credit to your superiors but I think both you and I know that Carrigan should have cracked this one much sooner.' Branch pulled out a sheet of paper from a yellow file folder and studied it. 'Anyway, it's over for him.'

'Sir?'

Branch sighed. 'He's gone missing, for God's sake. No one's seen him since Ursula's arrest. He's finished.'

She could tell that he was happy Carrigan had given him the opportunity he was looking for to shut down the case. 'But if Carrigan hadn't worked out that—'

'People have noticed you, Miller,' Branch interrupted her again, his voice serious and grave. 'What you've done to bring this case to its conclusion, the risks you took in the line of duty. Your reinstatement to detective sergeant is permanent, effective immediately. You should start thinking about where you want to go next.'

Geneva sat back in the chair, taking a deep breath. The pain came again, sharp and sudden, making her reach for her side. She bit her lip and counted to three, waiting for the spasms to subside. 'I'd like to stay on Detective Inspector Carrigan's team, sir.'

Branch tapped his fingers on the table, a slow and steady rhythm. 'I'm not sure that's really what you want. I'm not sure DI Carrigan will still be here once the review board's had its say.'

'Well, if he is,' she felt a pulse throbbing behind her left eye, 'that's where I want to be.'

'You should think carefully about this, Miller. Think what being associated with someone like Carrigan could do to your career. As I mentioned, people have taken notice of your work; even that prick from the Foreign Office told me to congratulate you.'

She felt it in the tone of his voice, the glare of words that weren't being said. 'The case hasn't been resolved yet. Not to my satisfaction.'

Branch took off his glasses, breathed on them then put them back on. 'That's exactly the kind of thing I'd expect from Carrigan.'

Despite the insult, Geneva felt strangely proud.

'We have the killer, that's what matters.' Branch looked up, his glasses smeared and whorled with fingerprints. 'You're not in any doubt that Bayanga killed Grace, Ngomo, and the others?'

'No.'

'Well, then.' Branch smiled.

She crushed her shoe against the side of the table, thought carefully about her next few words. 'Bayanga was working for someone, we're certain of that. He was hired to kill Grace and until we find out who paid him, the case is still open. We need to interview the Ugandan diplomats who took our evidence, we need to find out more.'

'Christ, Miller, can't you just take your win and go home and relax?' He passed over a stack of newspapers lying on his desk. She could see Bayanga's photo plastered above the fold, the headlines WEREWOLF OF LONDON GUNNED DOWN and VALENTINE SLAYER SLAIN in bold type.

'Is this Marqueson's work?' Geneva pushed the papers back across the table. 'Did he dictate that to the press word for word?'

Branch opened his mouth then closed it. He looked at Geneva sadly and shook his head. 'We all have a job to do, Miller, and we all do that job to the best of our abilities. You think I'm happy with this? I was supposed to be going on a fucking holiday yesterday. First one in three years. My wife didn't take it well and I don't fucking blame her. So, you see my situation? I've got a choice between giving upstairs a neatly wrapped case and taking my holiday or I can present them with a dubious conspiracy theory from a detective who's gone AWOL, a conspiracy involving the Ugandan embassy and our own Foreign Office. Which do you think I'm going to choose?'

She left the office feeling sick, rushing down the stairs and into the rain-soaked night. She lit a cigarette, picked up her phone and dialled the number.

The man on the other end sounded polite and helpful. 'Who can I direct your call to?'

She said a name, was told to wait, smoked two more cigarettes listening to a synthesised version of Mahler's fourth.

Marqueson's voice, cold and clinical, cut through the phone static and sounded as if he were standing right there next to her. 'Detective Miller, how pleasant. I've been wanting to say how grateful we—'

'You owe me a favour,' she interrupted, cigarette clamped between her teeth.

Marqueson didn't reply but she could hear him breathing on the other end of the line. 'I'm afraid I'm not at liberty to divulge any information about the Okello case.'

'This has nothing to do with the case.'

'Okay . . .' Marqueson replied tentatively.

'I need a list of British nationals reported dead or missing for the year 1990.'

Marqueson was silent, then finally he said, 'I can do that.'

Geneva smiled through the rain. 'And there's one other thing . . .'

39

He sat on the train and watched the rain obliterate the western outskirts of the city. Children nagged their parents, men whispered into mobile phones, computer games bleeped and, above it all, the relentless hammering of the rain against the windows smearing the outside world into inchoate shapes as if only these few remaining travellers had been left unwarped by the weather.

Carrigan flipped the lid off his coffee, stared at the watered-down muck, more beige than black, and pushed it to one side. He looked out as the train scrolled through the western suburbs, the factories and warehouses giving way to endless cities of cars stacked in multi-level parks, reservoirs, shopping malls and gasworks poking through the grey clouds like the battlements of some ancient fortress. It got worse as they headed west. Both his headache and the rain.

He'd sat and waited the days out after Ursula's arrest. His flat seemed smaller and somehow the belonging of someone else, a shadow self he felt no connection with and instead he'd checked into a nearby Travelodge, comforted by the anonymity of his new surroundings.

He couldn't go back to the station, not until he knew for sure.

He'd sat in that tiny rented room, the TV turned low, and thought about the last few days. He went over it again and again, each time coming up short. He wondered whether he was now seeing connections where there was only coincidence.

He ran through every assumption they'd made, every trail they'd discounted, but in the end he knew there was only one way to find out. So he waited and sat, counting down the days until Saturday.

And now here he was, speeding across the waterlogged rim of the country, the Channel a small grey smear to his left, the uplands wet and hooded in the mist like the bowed heads of supplicant monks.

A man argued with his wife, shouting into the small black box of his phone, exasperated, complaining about having to go out again, buy food, do something for the kids. The hassle of normal life buoyed Carrigan with its remoteness to his own, as if the world was divided into those who dealt with death and those for whom it was only the unspeakable shadow in the corner of their lives, the late visitor you'd forgotten was coming.

He almost missed the stop, the tangle of his thoughts and grey swales of rain all but obscuring the small village station.

As he stepped into the storm, the wind and rain lashed up from the Channel shadowing the small houses and twisting streets of the village. He took the back way, avoiding the parade of shops, sludging through two feet of water which had turned the narrow cobbled lanes into torrents.

He climbed the long hill leaving the winking lights and pub signs swaying in the wind far behind him and crested the rise, stopping to stare at the dark murk of water ahead. Somewhere over the fog and rain lay France and the rest of the world but here it seemed the earth stopped at this rocky promontory and that there was no other world beyond, only the illusion of one.

The gate was locked and it took him a couple of attempts before he managed to tumble the cylinders on the padlock and line up the numbers. The soft click, almost hidden by the rain, made his stomach drop as it always did.

The cemetery had turned into a sea of mud and he trudged

ankle deep past old Victorian crypts with their stained nymphs and elegant angels, pointless efforts at pretending those inside had not been wiped from the ledger of the world. The last hill took him a long time to climb, his breath short and pained, the rain smacking across his face, the ground soft and welcoming as if hungry for further souls.

He got to the top and stood for a moment disorientated, getting his breath back, wondering how, after all these years, he'd lost the way. He wiped the rain from his brow and read the inscription on the stone. David's name and dates of birth and death glistened in the rain but the grave itself was empty.

He looked wildly to the left and right and saw the earth disinterred and stacked up beside the grave, the long wet hole by his feet holding nothing but the rain.

He noticed the dark shadows cast by the chapel ahead of him, remembered cold greetings in that bare place, hands shaken slowly, the tears of family and friends, and then, years later, only the emptiness, the way it always seemed colder inside than out, the silences that stretched beyond language.

The path was slippery with leaves, the rain coming down harder, his shoes squelching against the flagstones. The door to the chapel was open as he'd known it would be. He took one step inside and saw the gun.

40

I knew you'd make it,' Ben said, the gun in his right hand, mud and rain streaking his face and clothes. 'You were always predictable, if nothing else.'

When he'd watched Ursula being escorted out of her house, Carrigan had realised that even though he didn't know where Ben was, he was pretty certain where he would be. They'd been coming here for twenty years to mark the anniversary of David's death, the last remaining mourners now that his family was gone. He thought back to the scene on the hill, the dark rain-filled hole, and he could barely get the words out. 'What happened to his grave? What have you done?'

Ben shrugged. 'You're the detective—I'm sure you can work that out for yourself.' He sounded strangely calm as he took a step back. 'Take a seat, Jack.' He gestured with the gun towards the front of the chapel.

Jack crossed the nave, staring up at the black wooden ribs vaulting the ceiling, the murky drama of a stained-glass tableau rattling in its frame, and headed towards the altar, Ben always just far enough behind him so that he couldn't make a play for the gun. 'Is this really necessary?'

Ben laughed, a throaty rumble echoing through the empty stone chapel. 'I think you know it is.'

Jack sat down in the front row of pews, the wood hard and dry against his back, and stared at the dangling crucifix as Ben took a seat one row behind him. A stained-glass window depicting the Stations of the Cross shook and convulsed with each gust of wind. The figures seemed to move and reconfigure themselves, a pulsing tapestry of light and suffering. He felt the water seeping through his shoes, the soft curl of his toes against the concrete floor, the cold kiss of the barrel against his skin.

'Your mobile, please.' Ben reached out and Jack saw the soil and dirt compacted under his nails, mud streaking his fore-arms as if he'd only that moment been birthed from the wet earth. He handed Ben the phone then reached into his jacket pocket, stopping when he felt the gun press against his skull.

'It's just a photo.' He slowly pulled it out, unfolded it and turned it face down. He'd been staring at it for the last four days trying to find a way it could mean anything else, but it was always the same: Ben with his arm around a much younger Bayanga, both of them smiling in the sizzling African sun.

He passed the photo back and, as Ben took it, swivelled sideways, trying to turn, but his legs slid out from under and he felt Ben's fist grab the collar of his raincoat and then the pain, sharp and electric, the gunmetal stinging against his right temple and the rush of the ground beneath him.

'Don't try that again, Jack. I'm going to have to hit you much harder next time and it would be a shame if you were out cold.'

Carrigan sat with his hands on his knees, getting his breath back. The chapel reeled and span and he closed his eyes. 'How the fuck do you know Bayanga?'

Ben's laugh brought unwelcome memory flashes, forgotten moments fading into lost years.

'The only reason I know him is because of you,' he replied, 'because of one simple choice you made.'

The instinct to turn round was sharp and insistent so he concentrated on the crucifix, the bewilderment on Jesus' face, the twisted limbs and dark black nails emerging like flowers from the wounded flesh. 'What are you talking about?'

'The Jango Road.' Ben's voice was suddenly loud against

Jack's ear. 'That fucking road. Why did you do it? Why did you take that bloody fork?'

The day flared bright and orange across Carrigan's vision, the heat and dusty hours scrabbling along the corrugated track, the gazelle flashing across the night . . .

'Did you hear me, Jack?'

. . . Ben telling him to make a decision, any decision, David yawning in the back seat, the smell of spilled cola heavy and thick as burned rubber. 'None of us knew, Ben.'

'But it was your choice. Just like Africa was your choice.'

'You can't be serious?' Twenty years he'd been a detective and he'd never suspected Ben felt like this.

'It was your notebook they found. You killed David when you took that road. And you walked away from it, as always, walked out of there with barely a scratch. You never once thought about what we went through; you never even asked.'

He knew Ben was right, knew he'd been avoiding it like he avoided the pictures of David and the wedding photos, brittle with dust, stored away in his attic. 'I just wanted to forget everything.' The words tasted raw in his mouth. 'I never wanted to think about it again.'

'Convenient, Jack. Every time I tried to bring it up you'd put on that sour-old-man face of yours and I'd know the evening was over if I continued. You thought we could just leave it behind us, chalk it up as some youthful adventure gone wrong? But the world doesn't work like that. A thing such as this has consequences. You can spend your whole life ignoring it but one day you turn your head and realise it's been right there behind you all this time.'

The sound of Jack's mobile punctured the silence. Ben had placed it in one of the Bible stands and it jumped and vibrated against the wood like a trapped insect. Ben caught him looking at it. 'It won't help,' he said. 'No one's coming just like no one came for us that day.'

'What happened in the camp? Tell me what the fuck they did to you.'

'It's not what *they* did.' Ben pulled a quarter-bottle of whisky from his jacket and unscrewed the cap. He took a long drink and wiped his mouth with his sleeve. 'It's what *we* did.'

41

W e saw you sitting in that small room as they led us away. Your head was hanging down and you looked like you'd already given up.'

They should have been doing this face to face. They should have been doing this back at Ben's house over drinks and cigars. The urge to turn round burned through Carrigan like liquid fire but he could feel the sharp poke of the gun's barrel against his back and the way it kept shaking as Ben's voice stumbled and faltered on the words, so he closed his eyes and listened to the chapel buzz and rattle with rain as Ben continued.

'They stripped us of our clothes and marched us to a cell. Thirty men in a space the size of someone's bedroom. Two metal poles stretched across the middle of the room, anchored into each wall. The prisoners were chained by their feet to this pole, their wrists in handcuffs criss-crossed over each other so that if one man moved the whole line would. The guards found a spot for us and manacled us to the pole.

'I lay there in the dark, my wrists and ankles already screaming with pain, not able to move, fighting off the claustrophobia, the panic, the desire to just thrash around and moan. You've never been on the other end of a pair of handcuffs, have you? Well, there's something about it that instantly reduces your body to this pulsing mass of pain.

'I held my breath, trying to stop myself from shaking, and listened to David mumbling the Lord's Prayer over and over. I lay awake all night thinking of what they were going to do to us in the morning.

'But the next day was exactly the same except that it was light and there was no way you could pretend you were any-where but there. Some of the other prisoners spoke in whis-pers among themselves but most had given up and just lay still, eyes wide, staring at the ceiling.

'That second night the guards came and unshackled David. They lifted him up, I heard him gasp as his legs finally straight-ened, and then they marched him off. A couple of hours later they brought him back, reattached the leg and arm cuffs, and left.

'The following morning he seemed quieter and I noticed a few new bruises around his neck. I tried talking to him but he complained that he was sleepy and turned away. I spoke to the man chained next to me but it only made things worse. He'd lost track of time, of how long he'd been in the camp, why he'd been arrested, even who he was; he said everyone had been here a long time and that once the Black-Throated Wind started blowing it never stopped.

'You strip a man of clothes, you take away the light, you put him on a bare floor with other men, and there's very little left. That's something I learned in Africa. We're not irreducible like the philosophers and priests say. We're more like snow; we flourish in the right conditions but we melt so easily.

'On the second day they came for us. They took us to a large room—it had been a classroom, you could still see the posters on the wall, small graffiti from tiny hands, the smell of chalk. But all the tables and chairs were gone. The blackboard hung on one wall, faint smears of writing on it, English sen-tences like *How do I get to . . .* I remember how surreal it all seemed. And what a relief to be unshackled, standing, together.

'Then they brought the girls in. When I saw them hope

spread through me even though I should have known better. I thought they were freeing all Westerners but when I looked over I saw David shaking his head.

'The soldier in charge lined the girls up against the opposite wall. I tried to make eye contact with the women, send them some kind of unspoken reassurance, but when I saw their faces I had to look away.

'The soldiers were drinking. The oldest must have been fourteen. There were empty bottles of Primus littering the floor. They were smoking weed and snorting something too. Their eyes were red and full of glee. The girls were bleeding. Their faces wrecked and bruised, their clothes dirty and torn.

'The soldiers proceeded to get drunker and rowdier. They ripped the girls' clothes off. They stood there laughing and joking among themselves, one had a video camera, this old chunky model, and was filming everything.

'Suddenly it got quiet. The soldier in charge pointed to David. Two other soldiers surrounded him. I saw his eyes and I could tell everything of the David I knew was gone—his certainty, faith and strength. All that was left was fear.

'They marched him to the other end of the room. They stood him in front of the terrified girls, some kneeling now, praying hard and fast. They showed him a pistol, then pointed it at the women. The commander asked *Which one you like?* and when David didn't answer they started punching him in the head. He fell and they kicked him until he got to his feet again. The commander asked the same question and David pointed to the girl at the end. His hand was shaking and dripping blood. The commander gave him the pistol. *Shoot her!* he screamed. David closed his eyes and they hit him with the rifle butt again. *You shoot the girl, you and your friends go free*, the commander urged. The room was filled with crying, moaning, praying and laughter. *Shoot her and you are free*, he kept repeating.

'I could see where this was going. I could see what David

was about to do and what they would do to him in return. *I'l do it. I'l kill her*, I screamed at the soldiers. I looked at David. He turned to me, smiled and shook his head.

'The gunshot surprised the soldiers almost as much as it did me. David looked down at what he'd done, then calmly turned the gun on himself, placed the barrel in his mouth, and squeezed the trigger. A pale mist erupted out the back of his head and his body crashed to the floor.'

'Jesus Christ!' Jack heard the words coming from his mouth but they felt untethered, like radio signals from another room. He stared at the floor, trying to stop it from spinning. 'Why the fuck didn't you tell me before?'

His phone began ringing again, short, sharp trills of sound bouncing off the roof and smashing against the walls. Ben waited until it switched to voicemail. 'You think you would have benefited from that knowledge, Jack? I know how you see David. It was my duty as your friend not to burden you with it. You haven't had to spend the last twenty years carrying this around. I protected you and did David's memory justice. We wouldn't have even been able to put up the gravestone if anyone had known it was suicide. And the newspaper head-lines—I couldn't do that to his family.'

Jack shook his head. 'You should have told me.'

'Yeah, and we should have gone to India . . . '

He tried to imagine what it had been like in that school room, the choices Ben and David had been forced to make, but it was impossible, and he knew that, ultimately, every man's life was always his own. 'What happened after David died?'

Ben passed him the almost empty bottle. 'The soldiers all began laughing and high-fiving each other, the one with the camera came in close, kneeling down, making sure he got David's face in frame. The other soldiers stood over his body, offering each other drinks as the room filled with the smell of David's life emptying out.

'The commander turned, asked me if I still wanted to kill. I shook my head, told him *It doesn't matter now*. He just laughed and talked with one of the soldiers, then came back over. *You want to save your other friend?*

'I looked up at him and, God help me, I nodded.

'He grabbed me and took me past David's body. I had some vague notion that I would turn the gun on them but when I got there soldiers surrounded me and I knew I would be dead before I even tried.

'They started screaming at me, poking me with their rifles, their voices getting louder and wilder. Then they gave me the gun.

'I turned to the woman at the far left. She was on her knees, praying and rocking. She looked up at me and nodded. Then she smiled. I closed my eyes and pulled the trigger.'

42

Jack flashed back to the room again—Eye-patch, the poster of the mountain, the piece of paper he was about to sign. All these years he'd thought he was the one who'd made the sacrifice, that it had been his actions which had freed them.

'David was gone. I had to save you. You were all I had left.' Ben's voice quivered and cracked, the rain hissed and spat against the roof, the windows rattled and clanged in their frames. 'You think it was easy? You think it still is? Every fucking night I think about them. Every time I look at Susan and Penny, I see those poor girls' eyes staring back at me.

'When we got back I watched the news reports. I read about their families, their hopes and fears, the dreams coaxed nightly in their chests. They became real to me when they'd been only ghosts in that room. And then the footage was leaked. You can't imagine how it felt, waiting any moment to see David's face or my face splashed across a million TV screens—then the years of dread, fearing that one day it would show up, the past would come out of some dark hole and consume the present.

'I did what I could to make up for that day. I went back to university, stopped wanting to be a lawyer and studied the region, its history and politics. I wanted to understand what had happened to us and I discovered very quickly that it was happening to everyone in Acholiland. I began travelling back there, collecting information, rumours, lists of the dead. I did what I could but I knew it would never be enough.'

Carrigan looked at his shoes, the mud and cracked leather. 'It's hard to see how your perfect life went so wrong.'

'Everything goes wrong in the end, Jack, you know that. All our perfect lives unravel at some point. The world would be a very different place if things went to plan. That stupid, fucking Grace.' Ben let out a long stream of air, coughed into his hand, the gun shaking in his grip. 'I was helping the country come to terms with itself. My book, the TV show—people were finally waking up to what was going on in Uganda then Grace Okello comes along and ruins it all.'

'How did you even find out about her?' Carrigan wondered whether they'd missed a vital clue. A link between Ben and Grace that could have prevented the bloodletting of the last few days.

'I stumbled upon the abstract for her thesis. I have to keep up with what's happening in the field and it's normally the same old stuff, so it was a surprise, a bad one, when I saw Grace stating she would uncover the real killers of the aid workers. I immediately requested any articles she'd written from the British Library. The next day I had copies of three pieces she'd submitted in the last year.

'All of them were about Ngomo and the Black-Throated Wind. I quickly read through the first two and realised that Grace was getting her information from somewhere other than books. I knew all the literature about the region but her articles contained facts and details I'd never seen before.

'She had a source, someone close to the ground during the early nineties. It was the only explanation. I remembered the video camera that day, the soldier taking home movies—and I knew something had to be done.

'It was easy for me to get her address from SOAS and, my God, when I saw where she lived, whose patch it was, I knew everything that happened was meant to have happened and that none of us ever had a choice once you took that road.

'Bayanga was one of my field assistants during those research trips back to Uganda. He'd been a child soldier, kidnapped by Ngomo when he was very young and rescued a few years later by a group of Dominicans. We'd got back in touch a couple of years ago when he first emigrated here and he was the one I called when I finished reading Grace's articles. I told him she had a source and that this source must have been a high-ranking lieutenant in Ngomo's army. That was enough for Bayanga, given his history with Ngomo. He was never meant to kill her.' Ben was using the gun to stress and punctuate every word. 'It was the source I was after, cut that off and you solve the problem.'

'You should have seen Grace,' Carrigan said. 'You should have seen what he did to her.'

'Believe me, Jack, I never wanted that. I guess when he found out who it was the temptation was too great for him. But filming it—filming it was a stroke of genius. The poetic justice of Ngomo seeing his daughter die the way the parents of those aid workers had, knowing that the whole world was watching . . .'

The door to the chapel crashed open, the sound like a thunder-crack rippling across the nave. Jack turned round but it was only the wind, leaves spiralling through the empty church. The gun pressed up against his skull. 'You think I won't shoot you. I know it's what you're counting on but think how far I would go to protect my family.'

'You've achieved just the opposite,' Carrigan replied, his mouth dry and bitter.

Ben laughed. 'Really? Ursula called yesterday to say she's been released without charge and you've just brought the one piece of evidence that can link me to Bayanga. I should thank you, really—I'd forgotten it even existed.' He took the photo and held it in front of him, from his other pocket he produced a lighter. Jack turned and saw the photo catch and blaze. He watched it crumple and blacken in Ben's hand, then fall to the floor. 'This is about protecting my family, that's all it ever was—you need to understand that. I couldn't protect David but I will not fail my daughters. I made my decision, now it's your turn.'

The smell of burning chemicals filled Jack's nostrils as Ben continued. 'Think about it, Jack—let Bayanga take the fall and we go back to our normal lives. Sit and drink and talk about old times every couple of weeks.'

'And what about Grace?'

'She was just a fucking PR woman for her war-criminal father; she's just as guilty as he was.'

'That wasn't your decision to make.'

Ben pushed the barrel deeper into the back of Jack's skull. 'Why is justice so important to you? You seem to care more about the law than you do about your friends.'

Jack turned quickly, his eyes meeting Ben's. 'Why do you think?' he replied, barely able to keep his voice steady. 'You were there that day. You know why it's so fucking important.'

Ben shook his head. 'I'm giving you a choice, that's more than I ever had. Leave it alone, Bayanga's dead, there's nothing left to gain by taking this further. Everything can go back to normal.'

Carrigan thought about evenings spent with Ben, the river rushing by outside, the invisible presence of Ursula always somewhere behind the door, and then he shook the thoughts away and flashed back to that day in Masindi, the soldiers beating the man by the side of the road, the expression on David's face.

'No.'

'No?' Ben said. 'What do you mean *no*? You can make this go away, you can finish what you started.'

'It'll never be finished. There'll always be a tape floating around somewhere, another witness who suddenly remembers.'

For a moment it seemed as if he'd got through to him and

then Ben finished the rest of the bottle, span the gun round in his hand and, in one clean strike, smashed it against the side of Jack's head.

Carrigan fell to his knees, his head swimming, nausea engulfing him, fingers pressed against the cold wet floor.

Ben got up and slowly approached him. He stood still over Carrigan for a moment and then he pointed the pistol at the back of Jack's head and clicked off the safety. 'I'll give you a few seconds to pray, if that's what you need to do.'

Jack opened his mouth but the words wouldn't come. He searched frantically for them but his vision swam with images of Louise, her hair fluttering in the wind, arms outstretched, Geneva out on the London streets, his mother strapped to a bed, white walls and white corridors reaching for ever. 'Just get it over with.'

And then, as he stared down at the mud-caked floor and waited for the bullet, the words began to come to him, a rushing torrent of half-remembered prayers and childhood hymns, too many words for his head to contain, and when it felt like he couldn't hold them in any longer he opened his mouth and they came cascading out, an avalanche of words, and then he heard one voice rising above the maelstrom, one single voice— her voice—cutting cleanly through the rain and babble in his head.

'Put the gun down and step away. Do it now!'

Jack looked up and saw Ben's face frozen in the harsh glare of the spotlight. Ben was saying something but all Carrigan could hear was the roaring of his own heart.

They sat on a mourner's bench outside the chapel. Geneva passed Carrigan a blanket and helped drape it around him.

'How did you know I'd be here?' He stared at her wet hair, the way it curled around her ears, noticing for the first time how her forehead creased when she smiled.

Geneva moved closer to him, at the same time watching the two local constables reading Ben his rights. 'I managed to find out David's full name, remembered you'd said he was buried in his father's churchyard. A quick bit of research and here I am.'

'And here you are,' Carrigan repeated, staring out at the deluged land in front of him. He tried to explain to her what had happened in Ngomo's camp, Ben's story, but it seemed she had one more surprise in store for him.

'I know,' she answered softly. 'Marqueson told me.'

Jack stared at her, not quite sure he'd heard right. 'Marqueson?'

'How do you think Ngomo managed to get asylum?' She leant forward and brushed some dirt off his cheek. 'The Foreign Office have known for years what happened to the three of you. Ngomo told them everything and they gave him asylum to keep him quiet, so that the story would never leak out. They were protecting your reputation . . . and their own, obviously.'

Carrigan wrapped himself in the blanket, his teeth chattering. 'Thank you . . . I . . .'

She put a finger to his lips and shook her head. 'Enough for now. Get some rest.'

He sat and watched as she got up and conferred with the constables. Then he placed the wet blanket on the ground beside him, turned, and headed for the promontory. He walked slowly, the mud and rain making the world appear drab and drained, and then he stopped, distrustful of his own senses. He blinked the rain from his eyes, trying to comprehend the scene in front of him, but it was almost a thing beyond comprehension.

A river ran where previously there had been only a footpath. He saw the new channel carved by the deluge, the thick brown water hurtling towards the sea, and then he noticed the voyagers journeying on this stream—a flotilla of dead flowers, soft toys, and birthday cards whose messages the rain had obliterated. He stood there for a long time entranced by this spectacle, the rain's strange cargo uprooted from their grave-side vigils and borne upon the flashing water, a silent army of remembrance rushing irresistibly towards the darkness.

Acknowledgements

Lesley Thorne, whose constant faith and unerring instincts guided this book towards what it should be.

Sally Riley, Leah Middleton, and everyone at Aitken Alexander.

Angus Cargill for his belief in me and his skill in seeing what was needed and what wasn't.

The wonderful team of Alex Holroyd, Katherine Armstrong, Miles Poynton, and everyone at Faber & Faber.

Trevor Horwood for driving me crazy with his superlative copy-editing.

Robert Clough for suggesting the idea for the title in the most unlikely of circumstances.

Francis Phillips for generously lending me her pseudonym.

Nick Stone, Damian Thompson, Milo Yiannopoulos, Matt Thorne, Richard Thomas, John Williams, Willy Vlautin, Andrew Benbow, Luke Coppen and the team at the *Catholic Herald*, Lee Child, Dreda Say Mitchell, Portia (now means now!), Ali Karim, Mike Stotter, Mike Ripley, Richard Reynolds, Paul Dunn, Melanie Rickey, Jim Butler, Helen and Kerry, James Sallis, George Miller, and Will Oldham for telling me his Burundi story.

My parents.

And last, but certainly not least, the readers who've kept with me all these years . . . thank you.

ABOUT THE AUTHOR

Stav Sherez is the author of *The Devil's Playground*, shortlisted by the Crime Writers Association, and *The Black Monastery*. He spent five years as a music journalist, mainly for the cult music magazine *Comes with a Smile*. He has also written for the *Daily Telegraph*. He lives in London.